THE JAPANESE LOVER

RANI MANICKA

HODDER

First published in Great Britain in 2010 by Hodder & Stoughton
An Hachette UK company

First published in paperback in 2010

7

A CIP catalogue record for this title is available from the British Library

ISBN 978 1444 70032 9 (B format)
ISBN 978 1444 70033 6 (A format)

Typeset in Plantin Light by Hewer Text UK Ltd, Edinburgh
Printed and bound by Clays Ltd, St Ives plc

Hodder & Stoughton policy is to use papers that are natural,
renewable and recyclable products and made from wood grown in
sustainable forests. The logging and manufacturing processes are expected
to conform to the environmental regulations of the country of origin.

Hodder & Stoughton Ltd
338 Euston Road
London NW1 3BH

www.hodder.co.uk

For my father
and
all Malaysian Indians, wherever they may be

Point of fact.
Batu Tujuh does not exist in Malaysia or anywhere else.

The Old Woman and the Writer

Kuala Lumpur, 2008

Inside the big house all was dark, save the storeroom, where bluish-white light from a streetlamp shone in through a high, uncurtained window. Huddled under a thin blanket on her bench-bed Marimuthu Mami stared at the square of light on the cement floor. Dawn. And she had not slept a wink.

Yesterday, she had stood behind the net curtains in the living room and watched the girl park her car outside the gates. Well, she was not exactly a girl, but she wore denim and to Marimuthu Mami, who was ninety-two years of age, anyone in denim had to be young. The wind – it was the monsoon season – blew the girl's flimsy umbrella inside out and she had run up the paved driveway in the rain. She was propping the ruined umbrella against the wall of the porch when Marimuthu Mami arrived at the door.

Normally, the old lady was not allowed to open the grille gates, for the city had become overrun with illegal Indonesian immigrants who robbed and stole even in broad daylight. However, flash floods had delayed her daughter, and she had phoned through and given Marimuthu Mami permission to open the gates.

The girl occupied the edge of a rattan armchair. It then transpired that she was a writer who wanted her host's life story.

Marimuthu Mami blinked. Hers!

The author construed this to be unwillingness. 'I'll pay, of course,' she put in quickly, mentioning a fair sum. But when the silence looked like it would prevail, she added that she knew Marimuthu Mami had led the sheltered life of traditional wife and mother, and that there would be neither sordid secrets nor lurid exposés. She leaned forward. 'What I'm really after is stuff about the Japanese occupation of Malaya. You know, what it was like for you and your friends. I won't even use your name if you don't want me to,' she promised. 'In fact, I'll disguise you so well that no one will recognise you.'

Marimuthu Mami stared at the girl.

'Or perhaps you could just talk about the community in general? It's only for collaboration purposes,' she insisted, but she was becoming unsure of her mission.

Still, Marimuthu Mami did not speak. She couldn't. Lurking in the folds of her sari were her tightly clenched hands. Speak about the *past*, here, in her daughter's home? After she had finally mastered the art of forgetting things. Now she even had to keep a book to know if she had taken her medication. Sometimes she wandered into the kitchen with the intention of eating only to have her daughter kindly remind her, 'But you have just eaten.' Ah yes, of course.

And recently, she awakened completely lost, unable even to recollect who or where she was. The first time it happened she had cried out with fear, bringing both her daughter and son-in-law to her side.

The sight of them brought back the knowledge that she lived with them here in their house. 'Yes, yes, of course,' she assured their concerned faces. 'I now remember you both.' But they took her to the doctor. Everything was all right with the old woman, he told them. However, he recommended crosswords to improve her memory.

So her son-in-law gave her the *New Straits Times* opened to the crossword page and told her that no one need grow old at all. Ancient *rishis* had left the observation that human beings age only because they see others grow old. She sat docile – she had watched him grow old.

'Try to remember,' he encouraged. 'The past might be more difficult, so just start with what you did yesterday.'

If only he knew. About the past, how deeply rooted it was in her chest, how mighty its trunk and branches. How shocked he would be to know that she remembered all of it, every precious detail. They thought the past was dead because she never talked about it, not even when there was that whole commotion about Japanese war crimes on TV.

The girl leaned further forward, earnest, pleading. 'I don't mean for you to gossip about the other *mamis* or anything.'

Mamis? And just like that, there they were. All of them. Resurrected, the women who arrived under black umbrellas to while away those long, hot afternoons so long ago.

The girl opened her handbag and took out a packet. 'You don't have to give me an answer now, but if you do decide to help you will need these,' she said, and placed the tapes on the coffee table. Smiling, she stood and turned to leave. Then she seemed to hesitate. When she turned back to face Marimuthu Mami, she was no longer the haplessly perching girl, pretending to be on the lookout for unimportant scraps of information. This woman had seen treasure and she wanted it.

'At least talk about the big cobra.'

Marimuthu Mami found she had to look away from the greed shining in her guest's eyes. She said goodbye, locked the grille gates, and sat down in the slowly darkening room to wait for her daughter's return.

The phone rang. Her daughter's voice was anxious. 'Did the woman come? Has she gone? Have you locked up? You sound strange. Are you all right?' Marimuthu Mami assured her that everything was fine and resumed her seat. When her daughter eventually arrived home, she would surely scold, 'You're not sitting in the dark again, are you?' But perhaps, today, just today, she would pity her poor old mother and touch her arm lightly, momentarily. Her daughter didn't like to touch or be touched.

The morning air was cold and Marimuthu Mami shivered. Her wish now was not to rake up the past, but to *die* peacefully, without troubling anyone. She stretched, slowly, carefully. Joint by joint, for they were stiffest first thing in the morning. She sat up and manoeuvred her feet so they did not touch the ground, but slipped neatly into a pair of rubber slippers. The cold breath of the earth was not good for anyone, let alone aged bones. The streetlamp went off. Through the window the banana leaves were flat shapes against the lightening sky, waving gently at her. She had planted those trees herself.

Upstairs, she could hear her son-in-law already about his business. It was time she too was up. She began the first of her shuffling steps of the day, then stopped. Her poor old bones . . . and she began to wish for her bed, perhaps with a freshly prepared hot-water bottle and another blanket from the cupboard under the stairs. But even that seemed too much trouble. She lay back down, and even before she had pulled the blanket over herself she began to dream.

She had put her Japanese umbrella into a plastic bag and boldly, without permission, was opening the front door and going out. Outside her daughter's house ran not a street and houses opposite but a vast field, and there, to her amazement, were thousands of women of all shapes, sizes and colours. And each carried a Japanese umbrella! It had never occurred to her that there could be so many, or that they would be so proud of their umbrellas. Some were even twirling theirs flirtatiously like geishas. And suddenly she too, was no longer ashamed of hers. For the first time ever she unfurled it in public. Let all see its beautiful cherry-blossom design.

And she thought it had been a good life; she would do it all again. Why should she deny any of it? How surprised the young journalist would be to know that she had not always lived like a mouse in a storeroom. That once she had been the mistress of a many-windowed house, the glass, hundreds of them, flashing, like the facets of a precious jewel. And she remembered again the men who had loved her, and touched her mouth; wrinkled, so wrinkled. 'Love, oh, love!' But, she had forgotten nothing.

And the memories came flooding in.

A Snake in the House of Marriage

Vathiry, North Ceylon, 1916

It was a small space, half of which had been temporarily curtained off with a thin blanket. On one side two men sat cross-legged and smoked in silence. The old priest was well fed, but the other was skin and bone, which was surprising considering he'd hardly done a day's work in his life. He preferred to sit at a nearby roadside stall drinking tea with the other layabouts of the village while his wife toiled their plot.

Neatly laid out on the mud floor in front of the head priest was an imported pocket watch in a felt box, a well-thumbed almanac, and a brown exercise book. Once or twice the woman behind the curtain called out to her God, 'Muruga, Muruga.' The priest turned his head towards the muffled sound, but the man beside him took no notice. These were women's concerns, and anyway, the woman was an old hand at this. Already she had given birth to five sons, and one or two – he had forgotten now which ones – had even fallen out of her onto the land as she moved upon it.

'It's almost over,' crooned the midwife, and reaching for the lime on the wooden block, set it on the beaten mud floor with a slight push. It rolled from under the blanket towards the men, to tell them that the baby's head was out. Immediately both men turned to the priest's beautiful watch. Opening his exercise book at a blank page, the priest noted down the exact time 4.35 p.m. In the business of casting horoscopes, a mistake four minutes either way could render the entire reading useless. Consulting his almanac, he began making meticulous calculations while the man waited for the first cry.

But it was slow to come, and he displayed his first sign of apprehension that evening: he stopped smoking and, like a turtle, extended his thin brown neck out towards the curtain and remained motionless thus. Until it came: a sweet squeal, surprisingly full of hope like the joyful sound of water running over a dry riverbed.

A girl, he thought in wonder, even before the midwife's coarse voice announced it and the infant began to cry properly. Quickly, to conceal his joy, for he *had* secretly hoped, he covered the tray of rock sugar that he would have offered the priest if the baby had been a boy, and held out the tray of palm sugar instead. Immersed in his sums, the priest distractedly pushed the offering into his mouth and without lifting his head carried on with his calculations.

The man took up his cigarette calmly, but inside his chest his heart felt as if it was melting. He did not think of how he would feed yet another mouth on their meagre income. Instead, he pleased himself with delightful images of bows on double plaits, glass bangles, and coy smiles. But the priest muttering 'Sudden and immense wealth' caused the man's head to swivel around suddenly, his eyes shining and open to full. The priest, though, was frowning at his notes.

'What's wrong?' asked the father.

The priest shook his head and here and there redid his maths while the father scratched the back of his shoulder, sucked at his teeth audibly, and tapped his fingers on the mud floor impatiently.

Finally, the priest put his pen down. With a sigh, for he hated giving bad news, he raised his head and in his slow, ponderous way explained, 'It would appear that the child is destined to marry a man of truly immense wealth. However, two inauspicious planets, Rahu, the head of the snake, and Kethu, its tail, are situated in her House of Marriage.' He rubbed his chin. 'This means the snake in its entirety sits in her Marriage House. Therefore the subject's marriage will be a disaster.' His eyes slid away as he said the next bit. 'There might also be "disturbances" from other men.'

This was the worst news possible. What was a girl meant to do in life but be happily married? And 'disturbances', what was the man implying? How was any father supposed to hold his head up at this? But the father, idle yes, but nobody's fool, did not appear crushed or in the least embarrassed. Instead, he contemplated the priest with narrowed eyes. Surely there must be a way to negate the malefic effects of the snake.

There was.

The priest suggested that the afflicted child pour milk over the head of a snake statue to appease it while praying to Pulliar, the Elephant God, who coiled subdued serpents about his body as bracelets and belts. If she did this diligently, with concentration and sincerity, all could be well.

'And so she will. Daily,' her father vowed.

After the midwife had tied her bundle and gone her way, and the priest to his temple across the road, the woman took down the blanket curtain and turned it into a hammock for her baby. She hung it with a rope from the middle beam of the house, and rocked it until sleep overcame her. When the man was sure she was properly asleep, he shuffled over on his buttocks to where his newborn hung. Holding up a lamp he removed her covering cloth, and gazed down at the child, naked but for her belly button bandage. Her milky mouth moved and her thin limbs flailed feebly to protest at the loss of warmth, but her nearly transparent eyelids did not lift. A thought struck him. Why, she would probably grow to be a great beauty if she was to win the heart of an immensely rich man. He grunted softly. Certainly nothing like her mother, then.

He threw a quick look at the shapeless figure sleeping on her side, her head resting on the flesh of her upper arm. Weariness made her snore, and the sound irritated him, but he thought it best to let her sleep. Very early tomorrow morning she'd better wash out the disagreeable stench of blood that seemed to have permeated the walls of his house.

He transferred his attention back to the infant, his eyes misting over. His treasure, without doubt the most precious thing he would ever possess. Perhaps she would be like his grandmother. He remembered a hag, but understood that she had once been a beauty of some repute. To his biased eyes the baby did seem to be the most beautiful creature in the world. Maybe he could take the dullest of his sons out of school and offer his services to the cowherd, old Vellaitham. That way, the girl would have her pot of milk every day. And she should begin her praying . . . just as soon as she knew how to hold her palms together. He would make sure of that.

He smiled dreamily. He would name her Parvathi, and just as Parvathi had won the heart of Lord Shiva with her unceasing years of sincere devotion and penance, so his daughter would appease the dreaded snake. With unhurried pleasure he tried to imagine all the priest could have meant by 'immensely rich': horsedrawn carriages with curtains at the windows, fine clothes, large tracts of land, a mansion in the city, servants at his beck and call . . . No, in fact he could hardly picture it, but any one of those things would do, really.

Adoringly, he ran a finger down the child's thin hand; her skin was the silkiest thing his incurably lazy finger had ever known. Unaware of his touch or thoughts, the baby slept on peacefully. He recalled her first cry, nothing like the boys', but fragile and also strangely full of longing. As if her soul already craved all that money. And quite suddenly, without any real warning, came the unworthy thought: if the child was destined to fall and break anyway, then at least let him prosper before that. And as a gust of cold wind will set melting sugar, that grasping thought hardened his heart, changing it for ever.

He snatched his finger away and, mouth pursed, he pulled the old cloth tightly around her body. He must melt down his wife's gold nose ornaments and have them made into little bells for her ankles – that way he would always know where she was. He began to scowl; the door to his house had no bolt, and the house had no fence. He must instruct his sons to build one of those impenetrable walls made from mud and palm leaves. And the other thing he should do was to get the two older boys to cut down the tree that grew beside his house. No boy was climbing up it to spy on his treasure. Disturbances, bah!

And in the sunken eyes that glared down at the child, there remained not even a flicker of tenderness.

Leaving

Parvathi came awake to the smell of a storm brewing. She lay very still until she was sure that all were sound asleep, then she pushed aside her blanket and, sitting up in the pitch black, removed the bells from around her ankles. Holding them in her fist she deftly stepped over first her mother's, then her father's and finally her five brothers' snoring forms. In the darkness her hand touched metal. In the entire village this almost barren hovel was the only one with a bolt on it. It gave way noiselessly. Her face, shaped like a betel-nut leaf, turned for a quick backward glance. All was still well.

She swung open the door and stood at the threshold. She was sixteen years old and she had never ventured unaccompanied beyond that bar of worn wood. Even now, when there was no one to see or scold, it did not occur to her to do so. Perhaps it was because she knew that her father's love, unlike her mother's, was brittle and would shatter with the first hint of disobedience. Or because she believed the myth her father had perpetuated: that there was nothing more important to a woman than her purity, and men (all lustful devils) would snatch it away at the first opportunity. Beyond that wooden bar, alone, protection was not guaranteed.

The sky flashed white, illuminating a shapeless blouse and long skirt – both faded to an indeterminate colour. Standing on the tips of her toes, she grasped the doorframe with one hand, straining her long slender neck and body forward, and extended the other hand as far as it would go. A curious age-old gesture, not that of a young girl trying to catch the first drops of rain, more of a graceful dancer stretching out to pull a lover into her quarters.

The sky lit up again, and a small blue stone in her left nostril glittered as she turned away from the stormclouds and looked to the ancient temple surrounded by coconut palms, their leaves helter-skelter in the wind. In the rain and white light it was simply spectacular.

The temple itself was a shabby thing, but it stood inside a rough enclosure of large upright stones that made it special and powerful. The largest was even believed to be one of the boulders that Hanuman, the Monkey God, had thrown into the sea so that Rama and his army could bridge the straits of India to Lanka. When the moon was full, the faithful from other villages came to touch these magic stones and pray for favours, but during the day children were taught to read the scriptures, write and count there.

Touching the stones reverently, her brothers went in. She did not. Her father thought it was enough for her to learn the alphabet by writing the letters into grains of rice thinly spread on a *muram*. Even so, those stones were not unfamiliar to her. From the time she was four, every day unless they were menstruating Parvathi and her mother took the thirty-one steps from their house towards them.

She stared at the old stones rendered momentarily white. She had never wanted to ask favours of them. Perhaps she was strange or fanciful, but she felt as if she alone understood that there was no grace to be had from their smooth, closed faces. Their smoothness was an illusion. They had not always been so; they had not rolled down mountainsides willingly. A giant monkey had dug his sharpened nails into them and wrenched them away from their mother's womb. Now, they stood as orphans in exile.

She stood looking out at the wall of rain until she judged it almost time for her mother to awaken. Then she closed the door and went back to her place against the wall. She returned the bells to her ankles and lay down on her side facing her mother, listening to her even, familiar breathing. Parvathi knew she would never hear this again. Like the stones, she too would soon be in sad exile. Her bag was already tied and waiting in the corner of the small shack. This was the last time by the wall.

The thought was so large, so daunting, she had to put a fearful arm around her mother's waist. For she was a simple girl who had spent her entire life in her father's backyard alone, daydreaming her life away while her father, one by one, turned down all the local boys. Until four months ago, when the prophesied wealthy suitor finally appeared on the scene.

During negotiations Parvathi was sent out back where she sat with her ear at the door and eavesdropped on the marriage-broker describing the 'boy', a widower of forty-two. Apparently his wife, poor creature, had fallen prey to a mysterious tropical fever. That was, however, quickly glossed over, as there was another death he deemed to be of far more interest – that of the boy's grandfather, whose wealth was the stuff of legends. So much so that, even incoherent with age and sickness, he lay on his deathbed unwilling or unable to part with his lands and gold, until his sons put a nugget of gold and soil into his mouth and held it closed to persuade his soul to leave. Parvathi sat back, astonished at the mean trick.

When again she returned to her post, the broker was describing how the prospective bridegroom had set sail for a distant land called Malaya and, true to the traditions set by his forefathers, he became so immensely rich in the new land that he earned the nickname Kasu (Money) Marimuthu. The marriage-broker's voice rose dramatically. 'Can you believe a man purchasing an island just to accommodate his peacocks?'

Parvathi's eyes opened wide. An island full of dancing peacocks! What an incredible thing that must be! There was truly so much in the world she had no idea about, living within the tiny confines of her father's house. But inside the little hut her father chuckled to show the broker that he too, was a man of the world and appreciated the exaggeration for what it was – a sign of good salesmanship. His mirth was interrupted by the broker asking to see the girl.

'Sadly, my wife has taken her to visit a sick aunt,' her father lied smoothly. 'But haven't you already in your possession the photograph I sent you? That was only taken three months ago.'

The city broker nodded quickly. 'Yes, yes, of course I do, and she is indeed very beautiful, but it is customary for me to check these things out for myself. Some people cheat, you see. And then there is my reputation. Although personally, I could never see the point of cheating since the girl will either end up getting tortured by the mother-in-law, or worse still, will be sent home in utter disgrace. I've even heard of one or two who committed suicide while still at sea.'

Parvathi's father nodded and smiled. A sheep couldn't have been more placid. 'Fortunately for my daughter and your reputation, I haven't the intelligence to be unscrupulous. You can ask anybody, my daughter's happiness is all to me. Her skin is my skin.'

A brief, displeased pause followed.

Finally, coldly: 'When is the lady of the house back?'

'I wish it was tomorrow, sir. It's very hard for me to till the land and take care of the house without my wife. She said she would be back in two weeks, but you know what women are like when they get with their mothers. Every day I put my hands together to pray that she comes home sooner rather than later.'

The city broker searched the eyes of the dried-up peasant in front of him, but they gazed back unflinchingly. If the eyes betrayed the soul, then this man was as pure as he was ugly. Besides which, the broker had come to realise quite early in his career that God did sometimes entrust great beauty in the care of plain folk. No man could be this poor and sly.

Since it was certain the other brokers would be hard at work trying to find the perfect wife for Kasu Marimuthu, he knew he must land this one today. He did not have the luxury of another trip into this godforsaken backwater to sit before this simpleton. This commission could bring him the fame he had always dreamed of. And fortune, he had heard, would always come to knock on the door of fame. Besides which, next week he would be busy with preparations for his own daughter's wedding to a wonderful groom that he himself had found from Colpetty in Colombo.

The broker smiled. 'Your word is good enough for me,' he said, and tipping his head back, poured a stream of tea into his open mouth. Parvathi, crouching in the dirt in her shapeless rags, touched her smooth face wonderingly and asked herself, 'Am I really beautiful?'

'Parvathi, time to awaken,' her mother whispered in her ear, and immediately the girl sat up and began to roll up her sleeping mat. The sound of her bells made her father open an eye and fix it in her direction. In the pitch-black she sensed the eye on her and quickly whispered, 'We're just going to the temple, Apa.'

'Hmmm,' he grunted sternly, and put the eye back to sleep.

They stowed away their mats and went out to the backyard where the men never went. That day there was no need to take the old lamp to the well for the barrel-shaped clay container was overflowing with rainwater. Cloaked in darkness, mother and daughter let their hair down and stripped naked. Parvathi squatted down in the rain and dipped an empty milk tin into the container. The water that sluiced onto her head was even colder than the rain pattering on her skin. She gasped, but her mother made no sound. This would be the last time. They bathed quickly and wordlessly. Then her mother snapped a neem twig in two and they used the exposed strands to clean their teeth.

In unison they stood and made for the side of the house where the thatched roof overhung. There, a set of clean clothes was hanging from a wire line. They dressed with their backs against the wall. It was uncomfortable; their feet were muddy and the bottoms of their garments clung wetly to their calves. Under her breath her mother grumbled softly, but Parvathi cherished the moment. This was the last time dressing together. Wiping their feet as best they could, they hung slippers on them and, huddled under an umbrella, made their way in the squelching mud to the temple.

As always, at the temple entrance Parvathi clutched the small container of milk in her hands and glanced backwards at the greyish stones. As always, they stood very still in their own gloomy shadows. Then she stepped out of her slippers, washed her feet with water from a tiled shallow pool, and after sprinkling a few drops on her head stepped into the temple.

The place was deserted and silent, and the floor chilly under her bare feet. The windows in the apprentice priests' quarters at the back of the temple were already yellow with the light of their oil lamps. Their shadowy shapes moved about, tying top knots, slinging sacred threads diagonally across their bodies, and smearing wet holy ash in stripes on their foreheads, arms and upper bodies. When she was younger she used to look through the windows and wonder about the lives of those young bodies, but as the years passed and she went from girl to woman, she was no longer allowed to even glance in their direction. They, of course, took no notice of the woman and her daughter.

The head priest, sitting on the steps of the temple stringing a garland of holy basil, looked up and nodded briefly at Parvathi's mother, who had put her palms together under her chin. But to Parvathi he opened a mouth loose, empty and stained with betel juice and called in a reedy voice full of affection. 'Ah, so you have come to see your old uncle for the last time, then?'

'Om,' Parvathi said. Om in the land of Jaffna simply meant 'Yes'.

'I've saved some sweet rice for you,' he said with a grin, but Parvathi could not make herself smile back. Turning away, she followed her mother who was already murmuring prayers under her breath as she began her ritual perambulations around the different deities. Three times around each god and nine times past the cluster of demigods. This done, they took their customary positions on the floor and waited for the apprentices to file into the temple. Around the horizon the sky had taken on a pink tinge and, as the big bell outside was rung, the old priest opened the little wooden doors to the inner vestibule that housed the black stone statue of the Elephant God, Pulliar.

He beckoned to Parvathi and she hurried her container over to him. Adding its contents to a large pail already half-full of milk, he began the ceremony of bathing the God. The priest held aloft a many-wicked oil lamp over the newly washed statue, and they lifted their clasped hands high above their heads in prayer.

Unbeknownst to her mother, Parvathi was not praying to the Elephant God at all, but to the little helper snake that waited at his feet, an action the woman would have considered no better than praying to the pot of milk sitting beside the snake. Or that the girl had never felt anything but distant awe for the all-powerful god, and had instead pledged her entire loyalty to the insignificant coil of bronze. And even more incomprehensible, she had not been praying for a good husband and family but for the greatest love in the world, for one who would unthinkingly put his hand into fire for her. One that would die for her. Not that she would want him to, of course, just the willingness to was enough. She didn't know why she should want this as there was no one else in the village who had ever expressed a desire for such an impractical thing, but she did.

Perhaps this thought had fixed itself in her head when she had unbolted the door one afternoon to a mendicant who had smiled knowingly at her and asked, 'My child, what are you doing here when your soul goes out from you crying for *him*? Quickly, wish for it, this boundless love from which there is neither separation nor absence, for God grants every sincere wish.'

How could she have known that he was talking not of mortal love but of godly aspirations?

That morning, with the rain pattering loudly on the rooftop, she told her beloved cobra how much she loved her mother, and beseeched it to take care of her while she was away. 'Let her not be lonely or sad,' she whispered. 'Protect her while I am away and guard us from the wrath of my father when I return. For you see, cobra dear, I might be back a lot sooner than she thinks.'

The priest upended a brass container of red kum kum powder on the black statue, and more than usual fell on the cobra. It turned vermilion – the colour of marriage. A good omen. Perhaps her prayers had been heard after all.

Passage

After the rain Parvathi's uncle arrived to accompany her on her long journey to Malaya.

'Don't forget how we are suffering here. Send money as soon as possible,' her father reminded sternly.

'I will, Father,' she said, and he nodded and moved apart so the rest of the family could come forward to say their goodbyes.

Parvathi saved her mother for last. The woman's eyes were red and swollen. Pressing her lips together to keep them from trembling, she smeared holy ash on her daughter's forehead. 'Muruga, Muruga,' she mumbled softly, so her husband would not hear and be displeased with her, 'please keep this good child of mine safe. Protect her for I am no longer able to.'

Parvathi fell at her mother's feet and kissed them and, though she knew it would anger her father, cried out, 'Ama, don't abandon me now! Don't let them take me so far away from you.'

Her father's thin upper lip curled with displeasure, and her mother suddenly howled, 'Go with God,' and stumbled away towards the open door of their house. She did this because of the black blood that rushed to her head and made her want to claw at her husband's good-for-nothing face. Dashing through the dim interior, she stopped only when she stood in the sunshine of her backyard, where she knew she would not be disturbed. Here, the men never came. Her legs gave way beneath her and she dropped to the ground, a cold heavy mass.

She looked around bewildered, as if seeing her own backyard and roofless kitchen for the first time. She had never really noticed how well-constructed the wall of twigs, mud and palm leaves was. No one could see in or out. And in this prison her daughter, poor thing, had spent most of her life. But then the woman smiled a secret smile to think that, in this at least, her husband had been foiled, for the girl had bored holes into the wall. She had seen out. At first, the woman had been perplexed to see that she had made all the holes at the height of two feet. And then one day she had realised that her daughter was not watching people but the animals that passed.

Her palms pressed into the damp dust, she scrutinised her irredeemably callused skin, the hopelessly knotty knuckles, and the black dirt under her fingernails. Her daughter's hands were smooth, delicate, defenceless. How surprising that the girl in all her perfection had been made inside such a sad, ugly body like hers. Her child was only doing what all girls did: get married. A shiver went through her. It was just that the child was too small to be going so far away. Barely, she reached her mother's shoulder.

Shifting her weight onto one hand, she used the forefinger of her other hand to write in the mud the only word she could spell – her daughter's name. Again and again, until it formed a circle around her, a magic circle. For it was ancient knowledge passed through generations, from mother to daughter, that the circle is a sacred shape; make it, and immediately blessed energy rushes into it. In its charmed space, nothing bad can happen. She stared up into the empty sky. A hand came up to touch the empty holes in her nostrils that had once known gold, and cursed the day her daughter was born. For that was the day her husband's flesh turned to stone. But what of her? She had allowed it. But wait! Long, long before she abandoned the girl, she had abandoned herself. The girl had thought her mother was perfect and to be trusted. No one had told her that on this earth nothing perfect is permitted to exist. She dropped her head onto her knees and in her faded world expressed a passing sound of regret.

None of this might have happened had the priest held his tongue. She made another sound – impatience. And scolded herself harshly. Her husband was right. Women shouldn't be allowed to think. What good could come of blaming a man of God? It was the child's fate. And now the girl was gone and that was that. The woman closed the door to her rusty pain. It was iron and shut with a horrible clang. Let it remain forever shut. She must prepare lunch for the men before she went off to work the land.

She cast a searching eye towards the side of the house. Only one slipper leaned against the wall. Strange. The missing one was nowhere to be seen. Her eyes flickered. No matter. She would simply go on her cracked, crusty heels. Standing heavily she stepped out of the magic circle.

From the moment her mother turned her back on her, it seemed to Parvathi as if she fell headlong into a dream so fantastic that her spirit curled itself into a hiding-place deep within herself. For five days she and her uncle shook and rattled inside their covered bullock cart until the dirt paths gave way to the wide paved roads of Colombo. The city was a blur of busyness. People milled the streets like ants.

At the harbour they climbed into an enormous ship. Quietly, she joined the other women in the shade as the ship slowly, majestically, lifted its massive bulk and forced away from the wharf. It hovered at the crest and then suddenly, with a shudder that rocked it from stem to stern, lurched drunkenly back into the water. Together the women pressed old cloths to their mouths. While they lay groaning and seasick the men cooked in large cauldrons. Overhead, seagulls wheeled in the hot blue sky, and in the water, pods of clicking laughing dolphins came to play alongside the ship. Later, the ship drifted in inky nights amongst stars.

Finally, when she was not expecting it, a bit of brown: land. There was excited shouting and much dashing about. From the upper decks came the sounds of celebration. Green foreground came into view, and the wind picked up. A tin of ship's biscuits was sent down to them. A quarter of a biscuit found its way to her hand. She ate it in three slow bites. The ship drew closer, and Penang harbour came into view. They docked; the sea voyage was over.

She looked around in amazement. Oh! God had not coloured all people in shades of brown. Not at all! In His garden of people

were all shades of pink, white, yellow and black. She had never
suspected. She listened to them make their strange, unintelligible
sounds, but it was a dream after all, and in the umms, ahhs, nods,
and gestures, she understood them.

Odd, that it was the firmness of earth that should suddenly feel
strange. Then, the black iron monster spewing smoke that she
climbed into carried them into the heart of that humid country.

In the house of relatives she watched in wonder as water ran out
of taps, and – her brothers had not played a trick on her after all –
electricity glowed into lamps. Here she found soap that lathered, and
when night came was given a raised platform on legs called a bed; the
mattress so soft she tossed and turned all night to find a hard spot for
her body. How she missed her mother on that soft bed.

The day of the wedding arrived. Her terrified spirit retreated
deeper into its hiding-place, but no one seemed to notice or, if
they did, they cared not. *Oh little cobra, dear. Save me from my fate.
I, who have been so faithful to you for so long, save me.*

Children crowded the doorway to stare with big eyes as
chattering women coloured her hands and feet and dressed her in
the fabulous finery her bridegroom had sent. So heavy, she had to
be hoisted up to her feet by two women and led to a mirror many,
many times bigger than her father's round shaving mirror. She
stared fascinated but they dropped a veil over her face and took
her to a decorated crowded temple where a tall broad man came
to sit beside her.

She was too shy and too frightened to look directly at him. All
she retained was an impression of fierce rolling eyes. In her sight
were his loosely clasped hands. Large and covered in long, dark
hair, and fairer, by far fairer than hers. She sat like a statue, hardly
breathing, aware of the vibrant heat and the silent growl that
emanated from his body. To the accompaniment of drums and
trumpets he turned briefly towards her and she felt the heavy gold
thali fall around her neck as the crowd showered them with rice.

So; she was married.

A cloth was held up and behind it her bridegroom lifted her veil
so the newlyweds could feed each other morsels of banana soaked

in milk. She refused to meet her husband's eye. Luckily, for if she had, she would have seen the strained whiteness about his mouth, and her poor dazed spirit would have become still more terrified.

'Everything went well, a good omen for a long and prosperous marriage,' the priest commented, smiling ingratiatingly at her husband. Everyone was full of smiles and congratulations, but her husband said nothing.

Eyes downcast, she got in the back of a long black car and they were driven through the town and then down a lonely road through wilderness. The air began to change, became drier, smelling of the sea. Beside her, but strictly apart, as if by an unfathomably deep chasm her husband sat, his bulk turned away, cold, silent, furious. She should have become nervous then, but that daze, so useful, kept her safe, cocooned, unreachable.

His house, someone had told her, was by the beach, a beautiful place called Adari, Dear One. Finally, they turned through a set of tall gates. Parvathi looked up at the tall house rising into the clear blue sky and, with a great gasp, was torn from her comfortable sleep.

Adari

Set on the fringe of a jungle, at first glance it seemed to be entirely constructed from precious gems cast in some dark metal, as unreal as something plucked directly out of a fairytale. But as the car drew nearer, different facets caught the sunlight and came blindingly alive. Oh! But if her father had only seen this he would never have dared do what he did. Coming closer, she saw that the house was made from pieces of violet, blue and pink glass held together by wrought iron. Nevertheless, that first impression of a palace made of jewels remained with her for ever.

A circular driveway lined with statuary brought them to a covered porch. Someone opened the car door and, to enter her new home auspiciously, she put her right foot out first. Slowly, for her clothes and jewellery were weighty and cumbersome, she came out fully. People had lined the front steps, and some more stood craning their necks along the balconies on both wings of the house for the first glimpse of the new bride. Nervously, she looked up at them. There seemed to be so many of them, but as she later found out, most were staff, there to serve her.

Her husband came around to her side and together they went up the smooth white steps towards the entrance of the house, where six blue-grey pillars inlaid with white marble creepers and flowers stood. Stretching on either side of them right to the ends of the building were deep verandas made fabulous with arches of stained glass. From their ceilings hung enormous baskets of jungle fern interspersed with grape-like clusters of glass lamps. From the veranda they descended six steps into an open courtyard. There Parvathi forgot the watching crowd and gazed about, wide-eyed, transfixed.

Soaring pillars – this time white, inlaid with blue-grey designs – held up the balcony and roof. But here someone as powerful as God must have said, 'Let there be coloured light,' and there was. Pouring through the stained glass, the sun let fall a myriad of translucent coloured shards onto the walls, pillars, floors, people, animals and the moss-covered pond creature with water lilies and goldfish streaming out of its mouth.

In one section of the vast yard grew an ancient tree. Its ash-coloured trunk was thick and smooth and its leaves moss green. The house must have been built around it, as one of its larger branches was growing through a window upstairs.

On the smaller branches hung many gilded cages, all empty, their doors open while a flock of birds, all of them white or the albino of the species, sat where they pleased on the tree. It was only later that she learned that theirs was not freedom, that the young boy who took care of them strategically plucked their feathers so flight was no longer possible. But at that moment she was entranced when like dreams or ideas exquisite shades of indigo, blue and pink patterns leapt on the beautiful birds as they moved. Tame doves, completely indifferent to the noise and crowds, walked about magically hued on the paved floor. A parrot perched at the edge of the fountain, turned its head sideways and fixed its round eyes on her.

At that moment her bridegroom spoke for the first time.

'You,' he ordered a servant harshly, 'show this lady up to a room in the west wing, and everybody else, go back to your quarters.'

The musicians stopped playing and a hush descended. She had expected this, of course, but perhaps not in front of so many curious eyes. Heat rushed up her throat and face, and her stomach contracted, leaving her quite breathless. She should have stayed in her daze. This humiliation would have been nothing to bear then. This, after all, was the moment she had been dreading ever since the marriage-broker had referred to the photograph of her.

She had not seen the photograph her father sent to him, but she knew it was not of her. No one in her village owned a plate camera. To hear its shutter click one needed to travel to the city,

but the only time she had left her village was when she had made
that image of Pulliar with a fistful of dung from one of Vellaitham's
cows and with her mother as chaperone, had taken it to another
village not far away. There, with other young girls, she had placed
her little idol in a stream and as it floated away had prayed for a
good husband.

Her father had cheated the broker and now . . .

A voice fell softly upon her ear. Eyes downcast she followed
it up a wrought-iron staircase to the balcony. A decorative glass
door opened to the west wing and they stood in a long corridor
where many tall double doors led off on either side. The soft voice
politely enquired if she wanted to choose a room. Parvathi shook
her head, and the first set of doors was opened and the voice
announced, 'The Lavender Room.'

Parvathi entered.

The Lavender Room; but my goodness. Parvathi stood, a dwarf
in that splendid, lofty room and looked with awe at the panelled
walls painted a dramatic aquamarine and then richly decorated
with Chinese birds of paradise, pagodas and weeping willows.
Here too a fine rhapsody of violet, blue and pink light flowed in
through the tall glass windows and doors.

She transferred her amazement to an enormous blue-beaded
chandelier that hung from the middle of the ceiling. Under it, on
a cream carpet, stood a magnificent brass four-poster bed. Its
tasselled mosquito net had been dyed blue and held back with
velvet indigo ribbons. Against one wall was a late-eighteenth-
century French cupboard, close to it a dressing-table and a
delicate stool painted eggshell blue and parcel-gilt. Nearby hung
an open, empty birdcage made of bamboo and coloured with
Chinese ink.

On the wall across from the bed hung a large oil painting of a
white monkey surprised in the act of eating a fruit, pomegranate
peel all around him. She marvelled at how the light in that room
had been marshalled so that the monkey alone was bathed in pure
white light. She stood on the tips of her toes and touched his tail.
The paint was hard and glossy.

A cool rush of wind made the long veil-like curtains billow into the room. Dropping to her hands and knees, she crawled into the balcony and watched the leaving crowd gesticulating and speculating about the state of her marriage.

She hugged her knees and waited as the house fell silent. Soon, her husband would come up, and there would be recriminations; explanations would be required of her. But he did not come up. Instead, she saw him slide into the back of his long car, and it turn off at the gates. Kasu Marimuthu had gone out! For some time she did not move as if it was a trick and the car might turn around and come back, but the road remained empty. Seeing that she truly had been left alone, she stood up and surveyed her surroundings.

The house fronted a golden beach and a very blue sea, and about thirty yards into the water she saw it: the wonderful little island populated entirely by peacocks. There was a small wooden boat in the shade of a thatched roof that she guessed was used to get to it. That afternoon though, the tide was out and the water was so shallow it seemed to her one could have easily waded out there on foot.

She leaned out and to her right and left counted eight balconies in each wing of the house. At the back, unpainted and within calling distance of the back door, were the servants' quarters. Two men stood talking. Between them the carcase of a goat, poor beast, yellow with turmeric and salt, hung from a wire. No doubt part of her wedding feast. Beyond the boundary walls of the house, as far as the eye could see, was nothing but dark green vegetation. It gave the sensation of being completely marooned in wildness, but she took a strange pleasure in that.

She turned back into the room.

Sitting on the edge of the bed, she removed her jewellery and they made a glittering heap beside her. The only item she did not take off was her *thali*, the symbol of her married status, a pendant made by welding together two golden pieces. They were supposed to represent her husband's feet, so that no matter where he was or whatever he was doing, his feet were always touching his wife's heart.

Going slowly to her suitcase she rummaged around and pulled out her mother's battered old slipper. The sight of it almost undid her. She kissed it passionately, closed her eyes and thought of her mother toiling alone so far away, and at that moment missed her so much she could have wept.

Eventually, she put the sandal away and returned to her perch on the bed. On the bedside table stood a porcelain figurine of Scaramu. She ran a finger down his elaborate costume and wondered who he was and why he was there. The ceiling fan whirled lazily and she glanced longingly at the white expanse behind her. The truth was she was completely exhausted. She would lie down for a short while, not close her eyes, just rest her body. She would not be surprised sleeping. No, she'd jump up as soon as she heard footsteps on the parquet floors outside. Curling herself around the heap of gold, she slept.

And came awake in a strange blue mist, instantly on guard. Then it occurred to her: someone must have come in and let the blue mosquito net down. She looked around the room warily. A small wall lamp by the door had been lit. She lay very still and listened. Something had awakened her. In the distance the sea murmured. Then a shrill scream pierced the night. An animal definitely, but too far away to be of any danger. Still, she remained frozen, watchful. Her body had reacted to that sound as if her very survival was implicated in it. There it was again; a clattering. Amplified by the empty acoustics of the house. Someone was moving about downstairs.

Adding her anklets to the glittering pile beside her, she parted the net and slid off the bed. The hardwood under her feet made no sound. The door opened noiselessly into the corridor, lit here and there by the grape-like lamp clusters. She stood at the entrance to the balcony, and through a pink glass petal, looked in wonder at the courtyard below, transformed into an enchanted world. Small lights had sprung up around the green and gold fountain, and the light from inside the surrounding glass corridors had cast lacy trails of seashell lights onto the walls and floor. And there was a tinkling sound like falling silver coins. Surely, otherworldly beings lived here.

But hardly had the thrilling thought formed, than she saw the figure of her husband held up in the milky light of a frosted lamp. Head bent, and apparently only with much help from the banister, he was unsteadily making his way up the stairs. What was the matter with him? Puzzled, she padded to the top of the stairs, where her unexpected appearance startled him and caused him to lose his footing.

Luckily, one of his wildly flaying hands managed to catch the banister, and the face that was exposed to her was so loose and strange that she felt certain he must be ill. She had not discarded the memory of his silent growling or the restless, invisible fear of the man, but she ran down the stairs, her hand outstretched to help him. But he flung out an arm to ward her off, before dropping back heavily on the stairs, his knees falling wide apart as he transferred all his weight onto one hand. He winced. He must have hurt himself in the abrupt manner of his sitting.

In the light from the disturbed water of the fountain she had her first good look at the man she had married. Large beads of sweat covered his nose, and he was holding his head at an odd angle while his bulging eyes seemed to be experiencing great difficulty in focusing upon her.

'What's wrong with you?' she asked, her voice no more than an alarmed whisper, for she had little knowledge of drunkenness so she had not recognised his condition at first. Kasu Marimuthu opened his mouth – his left canine shone pure gold – and laughter spewed forth, bouncing off the walls and echoing mockingly around them. When his mirth was spent he turned to her and said, 'I've left a glass on the fountain ledge. Get it for me.'

She caught the reek of alcohol then, and was so taken aback she couldn't stop herself from exclaiming aloud: 'Oh! But you're drunk.' All the hard surfaces around them acted as cruelly on her voice as they had on his laughter, making it sound shrill, accusing, and so completely lacking in docility that she covered her mouth with her hand in mortification.

The bleary eyes found their fix. The affable mood was gone. 'And why shouldn't I be?' he sneered. 'I asked for a bird of paradise and I'm given a puny peahen.'

Her mother's words came back: 'And when you are far away from me, remember this: if a man harms you only with words, say nothing, do nothing, for words may, when he has gone to sleep, be shrugged off like an ill-fitting garment.' Parvathi dropped her eyes in a show of submission, unaware that this served only to further infuriate her new husband. Absolutely *everything*, he concluded belligerently, about his bride annoyed him. The lack of style, beauty, height, education, sophistication, and now this irritating attack of meekness. The girl was irredeemable. Grimly he muttered, 'Hurry up with that drink.'

Parvathi reached up to the command immediately. He cradled the half-full glass in his hand, and then in great exasperation burst out, 'Oh, for God's sake stop hovering about like some long-necked ostrich, and sit down!'

She sank down a few steps below him.

'I'm sending you back to your father tomorrow.'

She nodded slowly. She had expected nothing less from the moment she had laid eyes on his house. Until then she had cherished a wild, bizarre hope. But really, it was not even her father's fault. How could he, poor thing, living as they did, have any comprehension of what 'immense wealth' really meant? Like her, he must have imagined less, much less. Otherwise he would have understood. Enclosures that kept names like the Lavender Room would always insist upon tall, urbane mistresses.

'You knew, didn't you?' he challenged.

She looked up at him, her eyes enlarged. 'Yes, but you must understand that I had no say in the matter. My duty is to obey my father at all times.'

'What kind of man does this to his own daughter, anyway?'

A tear slipped down her face.

'What will happen to you when you go home?' he asked, and for that small while sounded weary and kind.

She sniffed and wiped her nose with the side of her hand. 'I don't know. If my father will take me back I will help my mother as I have always done.'

He shook his head regretfully. 'Don't think I don't pity you, but no one and I mean *no one*, cheats Kasu Marimuthu and gets away with it. Your father must be a fool or a mad man. Who else would even begin to think of such a harebrained scheme? If he imagined I wouldn't send you back for fear of tarnishing my good name, well, he put his money on a lame horse.'

'Why didn't you just refuse to marry me this morning when you first saw me?' she asked quietly.

He drew himself up proudly. 'Somebody else might have married you then, you mean? I don't care if I am the talk of gossiping women, but there were important people in that hall whom I need for my business plans. I couldn't make a laughing stock of myself in front of them.' And then, as if he suddenly remembered that *he* was the injured party, glared down at her with cold dislike. 'Look to your father if you need someone to blame for ruining your life.'

In the silence that followed he gazed into his glass as if it was unfathomably deep. Finally he looked up and with one bushy eyebrow raised, said, 'We should drown our sorrows together.'

She stared at him in disbelief. The shame of it. She was ruined for life and he wanted her to get drunk with him! She shook her head.

'Why, she said, "no" to a cup of love,' he observed sarcastically, or at least that was how he had intended it to sound, but it came out dispirited and poignant. He looked about him dazedly before laying his head on the cold stone steps and closing his eyes. Oh, but look at the great Kasu Marimuthu now. So rich and so sad. But just as she imagined that he had fallen asleep, he sat up, and in one gulp downed the entire contents of the glass. He set it empty on the stairs and pulled himself upright. 'I'll bid you goodnight then, madam. Be prepared to leave in the morning. Which room are you in?'

'The first room on the left of the corridor.'

'Fine,' he said, as he attempted a half-bow, staggered, and had to cling the banister to steady himself. Clutching it, he went down the stairs. Halfway across the courtyard he stopped, turned back towards her and seemed about to say something . . . but must have

thought the better of it, for he shook his head instead and beat the
air in a discouraged gesture.

'Forget it,' he mumbled, and reeled away.

With his going, Parvathi realised she needed the toilet. She had
seen an outhouse by the servants' quarters and she went outside
through the front door and along the south wing to get to it. A cold
wind was blowing and the jungle looked dark and threatening.
Strange cries and sounds were flung out from its black depths.
Hardly had she finished, when she pushed the door open and,
shaking with terror, fled back to the house. She knew she'd not
sleep any more. She settled herself on the balcony floor to wait.
Let morning come. She was ready.

In the library, Kasu Marimuthu picked up a bottle of whisky by
its neck, and dropped so suddenly into a large swivel chair behind
his desk that he had to hold on to the edges of the table to stop the
sudden backward tilt. He poured himself a drink and was raising
it to his lips when the door opened.

'What do you—' he began angrily, only to stop in surprise.
It was not his unwanted bride who had entered, but a hulk of a
woman holding a circle of light. She paused at the doorway, and
he stared incredulously at the apparition she made. Surely no one
was *that* ugly.

She moved further into the room and in the light of the reading
lamp on his desk he saw with relief that it was one of his servants. His
heart was thumping loudly in his chest. She had given him a scare.
Stupid woman. He thought she might, in fact, be his cook. What the
blazes was she doing in his library at this time of the night?

'What do you want?' he shouted angrily, for that first fear had
still not left him.

Instead of coming to a stop in front of his desk, she came
around the side and towered over him. Now he was really furious.
The impertinence. He made to stand, only to find himself rooted
to his chair. Sweat collected in his armpits and ran down the sides
of his motionless body. He stared up at her, half-hypnotised by
her savage, unrefined features.

'I have come to ask you a small favour, sir.'

He glared at her dumbfounded.

'I understand that you are unable to show the shape of your heart to your wife, but sir, it is not your right to leave the shape of your foot on hers.'

Kasu Marimuthu could not believe his ears. A servant? Forget her place in this manner? It was unheard of.

'Why, how dare you! Get out of here,' he spluttered, and once more tried to rise, but this time she lightly rested her forefinger on his Adam's apple, and conversationally commented, 'This is where man keeps his karma. All the sins he collects through his many lifetimes are catalogued and recorded here. Even the Bible considers it the evidence of man's first sin, does it not?'

That such a low, low woman should be so presumptuous! He tried to jerk away, and found he no longer had any command of his body. Not even his fingers could he move. Had this monstrous woman by some sorcery turned him to inert gristle and bone in his own chair?

His reaction was comical. Never before in his life had he been in such a position, treated thus. He took a deep breath and detected the unpleasant odour of onion or garlic clinging to her hand. And then, without any warning that person who had built an entirely impressive financial empire, that adult who was day and night deferred to and respected, became once more the frightened, confused child hiding in a cupboard and watching his father and uncles close soil and gold into his grandfather's mouth. The ground beneath him felt as if it was shifting and his eyes, already large and frog-like, bulged wildly. But because his servant took no pleasure from his sudden confusion and fear, she did not laugh.

Instead she gazed kindly at him.

'If you could see what I see in your wife,' she said quietly, 'you would fall to your knees in awe. Know that she is an adored soul who has incarnated to experience love in the most unlikely circumstances.'

'I'll have you dismissed and thrown out in the morning,' he said in reply, and with menace, for even paralysed and sloshed, the sharp brain in his head had, rightly, deduced that injury was not coming his way, not from her anyway. This was a simple cook who had forgotten her place and acted out of a misguided loyalty to someone she perceived to be her new mistress. Some of his deduction did not make sense, but he had not sufficient brain cells on duty to navigate the deeper mystery.

She smiled and he saw that she had the big mouth of a dog. Truly there was not an ounce of beauty in the woman.

'You are a good man. If you harm her no more, I promise, one day soon, you'll see what I see.' His eyebrows shot into his receding hairline. The bloody cheek of it.

'Now,' she said gently, 'sleep, and remember nothing of this tomorrow.' And with his eyes still open and staring at her the man fell into a deep, dreamless sleep. Gently she ran her big, powerful fingers over his eyelids and closed them. Then, as regally as she had entered she left, holding her melting candle. Not at all a servant but a Queen.

The Good Samaritan

Kasu Marimuthu came awake lying on his stomach minus belt and shoes, but still dressed in yesterday's clothes. That could only mean that Gopal, his manservant, and one of the other boys had carried him upstairs and put him to bed. God, his head hurt. He extended an arm in the direction of the bedside table and groped around for a cigarette. The approach worked and he rolled over, lit it and took a long, hard drag. As the smoke swirled up he began mulling over the irritating problem of having acquired a wife he had no interest in keeping.

He thought of her – small, dark, plain; a stray – and watched the smoke shudder. The thought of introducing her as his wife to the smart society he kept actually made him cringe, and he cursed the marriage-broker anew. Idiot. Fool. Blockhead. How could he fall for that old trick? But what really made him grind his teeth with fury was the idea that some wretched country bumpkin thought he could get the better of him, Kasu Marimuthu.

Kasu Marimuthu forcibly stopped the direction of his thoughts. He had spent yesterday raging and impotent. Enough of that now. Today he was not only calmer, but also absolutely sure of his next course of action. He had no use for her, therefore the most sensible thing to do was to get whoever had escorted her into the country to accompany her out. And the sooner the better.

He had the inalienable rights of a duped man on his side, and as he had not even – as it was his right to do – sampled the dubious charms of his new bride, he foresaw no hitches in his plan. It would cause a scandal in the Ceylonese community, of course, but what did he care? Let them talk. He'd weathered gossip before. Nothing, Kasu Marimuthu had found to his delight, was irreparable when one had money enough.

He tugged a thick, tasselled cord dangling by his bed and, within minutes Gopal arrived bearing a pot of coffee and a silver drinking vessel on a tray. His manservant did not try to speak to his master, but silently filled the fluted vessel with coffee and put it on the bedside table. Then he disappeared through a panelled door. The sound of water running commenced.

The coffee helped. Kasu Marimuthu's head cleared somewhat, and his thoughts moved to some business matters. But all too soon he was back to his personal situation. He realised that he did not know what would be more proper, to elect someone to take his unwanted bride back to the people she had stayed with before the wedding, or take her himself? Deciding that he did not care for what was proper after all, he opted to drop her off himself on his way to work that morning.

Gopal turned off the tap and came out of the bathroom. Closing the bedroom door behind him, he left as silently as he had come. When he was alone once more, Kasu Marimuthu touched his forehead gingerly. The middle felt odd, throbbing and feverish. It was the drink. As if they had occurred but yesterday, those nights that he had spent in a cold sweat, knowing that he had completely lost control of himself came back immense and complete. He shook his head. He had been wounded then, and mortally too. He wasn't now. There was no longer any void to fill. That whore was completely exorcised, and he whole again. Of that he was sure. He resolved not to touch another drink.

Those two decisions made, Kasu Marimuthu killed his second cigarette, got out of bed and went the same way as Gopal, into the small antechamber of discreet Japanese lacquer and marquetry that served as his dressing room. Carelessly leaving a trail of clothes behind him he walked past an impressive stone bath imported from Cairo, towards what looked every inch an ordinary wall panel, but was, in fact, a concealed door to a tiled cubicle. Kasu Marimuthu did not consider this section of his bathroom fit to be seen by his fine guests. He went in and closed the door.

The room was empty but for a tap and a large container underneath it. Gopal had filled it to the brim. A wooden dipper exactly like the one Kasu Marimuthu had used as a child back in Ceylon floated in the water. He scooped water into it and upended the shockingly cold water over his head. Instantly the headache fled. With gusto, much splashing, and great satisfaction, Kasu Marimuthu finished his bath.

He came out and vigorously towelled himself with a rough cotton towel like the one his father, and his father before him, had used. The decorative fluffy things that passed for towels in the other bathrooms of his house were not for him. He shaved over the bathroom sink and going into the anteroom, dressed in a crisp long-sleeved white shirt and baggy tan trousers. Then he greased and middle-parted his hair. There: Kasu Marimuthu was ready for anything the world had to throw at him.

As he passed the balcony overlooking the courtyard he glanced down and saw a ponderous woman going up the shallow steps leading to the kitchens. He knew she was his cook, but why, when they had never engaged in conversation, should the sight of her bring the vaguely troubling impression that he had crossed paths or words with her? He ducked down to look properly at her, or perhaps solidify the memory fragment, but she had vanished into the gloom of the alcove that led to the kitchens.

Frowning with the effort, he tried to force open the memory, but it was impenetrable, and since he already stood at the door of the Lavender Room, he put the unfinished detail out of his mind. Entering the room without so much as a knock, he found his bride sitting on the floor packed and apparently ready to go. She started and was up in an instant. Good God, a waif if he ever saw one.

Brown, a perfectly awful colour on her. He looked at her narrow shoulders that dreamed of food, any food, and the severely scraped-back hair, and realised that she faithfully described his idea of a servant girl. The thought that he, who could have had his pick of the most beautiful women in the good land of Jaffna, had actually married this insignificant creature made him recoil anew. What a relief it would be, to see the back of her.

'I've put all the jewellery back into the box and left it there,' she said, pointing to the top of the dresser.

Good, he had been about to ask her for it himself. 'Are you ready to go?' he asked crossly.

She nodded.

He opened his mouth to tell her to follow him, but to his utter astonishment he found on his lips, the air between them, and her widening eyes, words that he had *never* intended to say.

'Good, good,' he heard himself saying, 'but there's been a slight change of plan. The person who is supposed to be booking your return passage is unable to deal with it straightaway, so if you like you can spend the next few days here by the sea. Consider it a little holiday.'

That she was astonished by his offer was obvious, but that she wanted to stay was blatantly clear from her prolonged and vigorous nodding.

'You look like you could do with a good meal. Have some breakfast and afterwards a lazy day on the beach, or feel free to explore the house and grounds.'

She smiled shyly. He did not smile back, but walked stiffly to the servant's bell by the side of the bed and pulled it. 'This always brings a servant,' he said. 'Ask whoever comes to show you how to use the toilet. You will be unfamiliar with it. It's a flush system.' He touched his forehead gingerly. It was warm and pulsating gently. 'I'll leave you to it then,' he said shortly, for now that the words he had never intended to voice were out and could not be taken back, he was greatly annoyed with himself. He walked over to the dresser and almost snatched up the jewellery case. Whatever had possessed him to do that?

But, as he went down the stairs he began to feel less and less dissatisfaction with his impromptu invitation. It was certain that when she returned she would be looked upon as the unfortunate wretch who couldn't keep her husband. Why should he punish her? It was not her fault that she was born plain, to a scoundrel. Let her stay a few days. What harm could it do? After all, he would hardly see her. While he was putting the jewellery box back into the safe, his gaze grazed its twin, his first wife's box. Automatically, he averted his eyes. By the time he swung shut the heavy door the other box was completely forgotten, and he stepped out of his study brimming with appreciation for his own munificence. He had done a good deed.

He slid into the back seat of his car and briefly considered sending a message to the girl's relatives about his intention to return her in the next few days, but that didn't feel right even to him – they would wonder at the delay and come to the conclusion that he was taking unfair advantage of the situation. No, he would send a telegram to that fool, the marriage-broker instead. *Wrong girl stop sending back stop let her father know stop.* And the thought of the pandemonium that that telegram would inspire made Kasu Marimuthu lean back into the comfortable seat of his Rolls Royce and smile for the first time since his marriage.

The Good Samaritan Told a Lie

Parvathi contemplated the closed door. Last night he had been utterly set on sending her away at the first opportunity. To what purpose this delay? But, an irrepressible surge of excitement was taking over at the thought of her short reprieve.

Someone knocked on the door, and Parvathi squared her shoulders and called out, 'Come in.'

A woman entered, held her palms together under her chin, and announced herself as Kamala. She had broad hips and thin legs that stuck out underneath the sari that she had tied high up her waist to allow for better movement. She couldn't have been more than thirty, but her mouth had caved in like an old woman's.

'Uh! The master wanted you to show me how to use the toilet,' Parvathi said. 'He told me it is different . . .'

'Yes, Ama, they are different in this house,' the servant agreed solemnly. 'They come from England. They are what white people use, you see. You don't squat, but sit on a bowl, and when you have finished you pull a lever, and water whooshes out of a tank above it into the bowl and, somehow, instead of overflowing out of the bowl, it sucks everything, urine, shit, and water down through a pipe which takes it out to sea. It's a remarkable thing, really.'

Because Kamala was from India she spoke Tamil without rolling any of her words, and Parvathi, who had never known anything but the sweet sing-song accent of her countrymen, found she had to concentrate hard to understand what was being said.

'This way, please, Ama,' Kamala said, pushing open a concealed door in the panelled wall. She led Parvathi through a dressing room into a grey marble bathroom, and Parvathi said a silent prayer of gratitude that she wouldn't have to use the outhouse by the jungle at night again. Meanwhile Kamala had opened a cupboard under the basin and extracted a little wooden dipper.

'White people may be clever, but they are not all that clean. They don't use water to wash themselves like us. Instead, they tear bits of paper from a roll that they specially make for this purpose and use it to wipe themselves. However, I have discovered that this paper has a good use even for the likes of us – if you drop some of it in the bowl, then when your waste falls in, the water will not jump up and hit your bottom,' she said, nodding sagely at Parvathi. Then she turned towards the bathtub and pointed to its taps. 'You can use the water from there,' she said, handing the little dipper to Parvathi. 'All right then, Ama, I'll wait outside for you, shall I?'

There were fluffy towels on a rack and a bar of perfumed soap in a dish. Parvathi squatted in the bath and bathed, catching water in the dipper, and pouring it over her head. Dressed once more, she opened the door and found Kamala sitting on the floor, one elbow on her upright knee, her other leg folded and tucked against her body. She stood up by pressing her hands to the floor and pushing up her backside before straightening. It was exactly the way Parvathi's mother came to her feet, and dull melancholy filled the girl's chest.

'Come, Ama,' Kamala said. 'I'll show you where the eating room is.'

'Thank you.' Aside from the piece of banana soaked in milk behind the cloth, Parvathi had not eaten all day yesterday. She had almost resorted to raiding a large jar full of sweet ladhus by the bedside, but in the end she had not broken the seal for fear that someone would come in and scold her. Kamala led the way past the stairs where Parvathi had sat conversing with Kasu Marimuthu in the early morning hours, to another staircase on the opposite side.

'Did you have a good journey from Ceylon, Ama?'

'Yes, it was fine.'

'Really? When I came it was terrible. The seas were so rough even the men were sick, and then someone died, and they wrapped his body up in a white shroud and threw him overboard, and you'll never believe this; why, even I wouldn't, if I hadn't seen it with my own eyes, but enormous sharks came out of nowhere and lunged for the body before it even hit the water! All the women screamed. Some went absolutely hysterical. To be honest even I was a little frightened, and I'm the brave type. I can never forget it. This way, please, Ama.' They had turned into the corridor that fronted the north wing.

The dining room was the first room on the wing. Respectfully, Kamala stood back to allow Parvathi to enter. Through many tall windows, morning sunlight streamed in. On the opposite side, two sets of double doors led onto an immaculate lawn that gave way to white sands. One end of the long table in the middle of the room had been covered with a white tablecloth and set with chinaware, silver cutlery and all manner of foreign food.

Parvathi turned uncertainly to the Kamala. 'What's all this?'

'Oh Ama, I don't blame you for not knowing. We don't have such things in India either, but this is the food of white people.' She moved towards the table and uncovered a silver container. 'See, this here is their bread, quite nice actually. Delivered fresh every morning from a bakery that the master owns in town. In the evenings they bring all the buns that don't sell, and we get to eat them. I like the coconut ones best. Honestly, Ama, I can't tell you how happy I've been, living in this house.'

She stopped speaking while she folded a napkin into a small basket and began to transfer some slices of bread from the silver container into it. 'You know, Ama,' she continued, 'before I came here, I was so poor I once pushed aside a dog to get to a bit of rotting food in a dustbin. My husband was a very cruel man. He's the one who knocked all my teeth out. He beat me even when I was pregnant. I didn't want to lie with him and bring more and more children into the world, but every few months the pains came and I had to leave the fields to give birth. Three times I drank poison. Yes, Ama,' she emphasised, 'three times. God knows, I was so unhappy, I did not even think of the children. The pain was indescribable. Your entire insides burning as if on fire. I can never again eat spices. They make me very ill. But living here is like being in paradise. All of us have our own room, a raised bed to sleep on, and a cupboard to keep our belongings in. What luxury this is, I cannot tell you. And the master is such a good man he has ordered that a big iron pot of milk be hung over embers by the kitchen so the staff have access to warm milk all day long. Never before have I come across or even heard of such generosity. I'd give up my life for him. And now he has gone and married you, Ama, and I can tell that you too are such a good person. I'm never wrong about people. It makes me so happy I could cry.'

She sniffed loudly, and lifting the edge of her sari, pressed it to her dry eyes.

'Anyway, this here is strawberry jam, made from the fruits of a tree that grows only in England,' she informed inaccurately. 'The other one there is marmalade and that is made from a kind of bitter orange that I believe grows only in cold climates. In that brown pot you will find honey which Kupu the cowherd gets from the jungle, and under this lid here is butter. That over there is cheese, but I have to warn you that it is white man's cheese, so it tastes nothing like our *paneer*.' She pointed to a silver pot. 'In there is coffee, and in that round pot, tea. However, both are without milk or sugar. You add those yourself, according to how white or sweet you like them. Mmm . . . what else? Ah, yes, if you want eggs, tell me how you prefer it, and Maya will make it for you.'

'No, no,' Parvathi said, shaking her head. 'This is more than enough.'

'All right then, Ama, I'll just go and get this bread toasted for you. It'll only take a minute,' she said, and left carrying the basket of bread.

Parvathi chose a seat facing the beach. She looked out to the sea sparkling in the sunlight and knew that all her great and beautiful dreams were a repulsive lizard on the ceiling of someone's house. It was time to relinquish her childish fantasies of passion and love, for she understood now that such a love did not come to look for puny peahens. Until her bridegroom said it, she had not guessed. It had seemed to her that she was just like everyone else.

There wasn't a renowned beauty in her village. Everyone was just ordinary.

She thought of going home to face her father's wrath and shame, and felt a shaft of terror. If only Kasu Marimuthu would somehow let her stay, even if it was only as a servant like Kamala. In fact, she'd stay for food and shelter alone. But she knew he wouldn't relent. It was obvious from his expression that even the thought of her as his wife sickened him.

Kamala returned with two racks of toast. Parvathi took a slice. It was still hot and it smelled so good her stomach growled with hunger. She put it in the middle of her plate, and in a semi-circle around it, she put a spoonful of jam, a bit of honey, and a pat of butter. Then she tore a corner of the toast off with her fingers and was about to dip it into the jam, when she not only heard but also felt Kamala's wilful silence. She looked up and the woman was staring at her as if she might explode if she wasn't allowed to say what was on her mind.

'What?' Parvathi asked.

'Ama, that's not how you're supposed to eat this kind of food.'

'Oh!'

'Using a knife, you have to first spread butter on the toast, and only then jam. Honey goes directly on toast. The master's first wife used to have nothing but a scrape of butter on her toast, she was watching her figure, you see. And then she would hold it between her fingers like this,' and she daintily held her thumb and forefinger close together in front of her loose mouth, 'and take small, neat bites out of it. For she ate as she did all things, beautifully. And she always, always kept her mouth closed while she was chewing. Apparently all white people do. They don't even talk with food in their mouth. They think it is bad manners, you see. And that folded cloth beside your plate, that's a napkin. She used its ends to dab the corners of her mouth now and again. And you know what else is not done at the table? Nothing can be poured directly into the mouth. Small sips must be taken from the lip of the cup. Imagine if you did that in India though. All the different castes would have to start carrying their own drinking vessels with them everywhere they went, wouldn't they?'

While Kamala laughed heartily at her own joke, Parvathi did as instructed. Chewing with her mouth closed felt strange and uncomfortable, but not enough to prevent butter and jam on Western bread being quite the most delicious thing she had ever tasted.

'Shall I pour some coffee for you?' Kamala said.

'Yes, thank you. Would you like a cup?'

'Oh, how magnanimous of you. May God grant you a long life. I'll just go and get my mug.'

'Use one of these cups,' Parvathi said quickly.

'Aiyoo, Ama, are you sure?'

Parvathi nodded.

'You are extremely kind, Ama. The first wife would never offer, let alone allow me to drink from these expensive cups.' She stirred two teaspoons of sugar into her coffee. 'I heard that she was from a bad family, that when they decided to move homes, all the plants that had not flowered for years suddenly went into bloom. She was an Anglo-Indian, very proud, and godless. Why, the whole time she was here I never once saw her step into the prayer room and . . .' Kamala's chin rose at her own blamelessness. '. . . I've seen her eating tinned beef. If I had not seen it with my own eyes during one of her famous dances I would never have believed such a thing. The shame of it!'

'Famous dances?'

'She called them "balls". Grand affairs where people came to eat, drink and dance in the great hall at the bottom of this wing. And how they drank. By the end of the night, hundreds of bottles of wine and spirits would have been consumed. I used to sit in the bushes and watch the guests arriving in all their finery. Sometimes they wore masks, wonderful things studded with jewels and feathers. The first wife always wore a satin wolf mask and a red velvet ribbon tied around her throat. I once heard one of the guests say she gave the best balls in all of Asia. Even the state royalty used to come. You could always tell them apart. When they were present, nobody else was allowed to dress in yellow or white, and they always came with big entourages of people who hung on their every word.'

The woman paused to slurp noisily at her coffee.

'Those were the only times I ever saw her laughing and really happy, otherwise she was bored. She never came downstairs before ten in the morning. To be fair, I suppose there was simply nothing for her to do during the day other than paint her nails and flip through Western magazines looking for designs she liked so she could ask Ramu, he's the tailor, to make copies for her, but never exactly as it was in the picture. She hated it if anybody else owned the same thing as her. Do you know that the most expensive sari in the world was made for her? It had real gold thread, and was embellished with so many precious stones that more than fifteen thousand jacquard hooks were needed to hold them all in place and it took three thousand hours with ten boys working around the clock, to make it. And I heard that one of them even went blind because of it. What a sin to wear such a sari!' Kamala shook her head sorrowfully.

'It wasn't even as if she needed such ornamentation. For she was as fair as a Bengali and very, very beautiful. Anything she wore suited her pefectly. You won't believe me if I tell you, but she would come down in the morning in her housecoat, and she glowed that much you would think Goddess Lakshmi herself was coming down the stairs. I could have sat and watched her for hours. But what good is such beauty? I ask. Tsk, tsk, the poor master. He didn't deserve that. Not at all. And nearly it killed him too, but never mind all that now. I'll wait outside for you, shall I, Ama?'

'Wait. Um . . . would you like some breakfast?'

'Oh Ama, but how very good of you! You really are too kind. I don't usually eat in the mornings, but well, since you have offered, I suppose I could have just one slice of plain bread to dip into my coffee.' She reached for a slice of toast. 'Actually, it'll be so good with a bit of butter on it, won't it?' She buttered the slice liberally. 'Butter has such a nice taste,' she enthused, and casually taking another slice, buttered that too. 'I just love it. In fact, I do believe it might even be my most favourite food in the world. I suppose it's just like our ghee, only more salty.'

Parvathi invited Kamala to join her at the table, but she shook her head vigorously, genuinely horrified by the suggestion, saying, 'Oh, I couldn't possibly! Anyway, I'm not one for sitting at tables. I'm used to eating on the floor. I prefer it.' She retreated to a patch of sunlight by one of the tall windows and squatting on the floor, folded a slice of toast in half before greedily pushing it into her mouth.

Of course it was wrong to gossip with the servants, but . . . 'What was it you said that nearly killed the master?' Parvathi asked.

'Aiyoo, Ama, why do you ask? Such a scandal it was, everyone knew about it. Honestly, she dragged the master's honour through the mud. What woman does that, I ask you? I don't blame him for burning all her photographs and forbidding anyone to mention her name in his presence. But then he took to drinking, Ama. Every night he would get drunk. Sometimes he would finish all the alcohol in the house and go in the middle of the night into the cellar looking for more drink. And sometimes, Ama, he would shout and curse like a man possessed. We could even hear him from our quarters. We were all so worried for him. Then one day Maya secretly began to slip medicine into his food and about half a year later, he suddenly stopped. And now he has become so strong-minded that he lets all the bottles of whisky remain in the house, and at his lawn parties, and there are many of those held in this house, he serves his guests but never touches it himself. Maya has said though that if he ever went back to it again, there would be nothing she can do.'

Parvathi sat very still. Some of the words Kamala used were unfamiliar to her and it was obvious some had a slightly different meaning, but was it possible that the Ceylonese word for 'leave' meant 'die' in India?

'What actually happened to the first wife?' she asked.

Kamala's mouth became a gaping cavity of masticated breakfast. 'Didn't anyone tell you?' she asked incredulously.

Parvathi shook her head.

'*Aiyoooooo*, Ama, that woman, can one even call such a one a woman, ran away to Argentina with a polo player. I heard he had come to coach the Prince's team, but I know they met at one of her balls. A tall, very handsome man. At first, he used to come to the master's parties, and then he started coming during the day when the master was not in, and they would go to the beach together. He was teaching her to swim, you see. They used to laugh a lot. But if she had asked me, Ama, I would have told her to be careful. These white men, they are not like ours. They are easy to get, but they are also very easy to lose. I know all about them. I used to work for a white family in Delhi, you see.

'I was there for nearly a month. Then one day I was going out to hang the clothes and I fell into the pool, and nearly sank to the bottom. Luckily, the gardener was there and he fished me out with a long pole. After that the memsahib told him to drain the pool and clean it out, and when the Sahib came home he gave me my full wages for the month and told me to leave. I think they were afraid I might fall in again and drown in their pool.' She grinned suddenly. 'But thanks to them I can speak some English now,' she said, and launched into a choppy monologue of foreign sounds. '"Take that silly mask off your face. Pick that up now. It's too damn hot in this country. Be a dear and fix me a G&T."'

Parvathi put her slice of toast down and dabbed the corners of her mouth calmly, but she had stopped listening. Kasu Marimuthu's wife was not dead from a mysterious tropical fever. She had run away with a white man!

'Kamala,' she called suddenly, interrupting the woman's chatter. 'What's a cellar?'

'It's the large room underneath this house where all the costly bottles of alcohol are kept.'

'Do you think I could see it?'

'It's always locked, but I think Maya has a key. Why don't you ask her?'

Parvathi nodded. 'I will. Who's Maya?'

'Oh, Maya's the cook. But she's more than just a cook, much more. She's a medicine woman.'

'Really?'

Kamala nodded gravely. 'I cannot say more about her. You have to see for yourself,' she said, and lapsed into an uncommon silence.

By the time Parvathi had eaten her second slice of toast Kamala had slurped two cups of coffee, chomped through five slices of bread; three with butter, and two with honey and jam. Parvathi slid out of the chair and Kamala put herself upright.

'What would you like to do now, Ama?'

'I'm going to look around for a bit.'

'Shall I show you around the house?'

'No, you go ahead and carry on with your work. I'll be fine on my own.'

'Are you sure, because I've been in this house even longer than Maya, and I know everything there is to know about it. Even the littlest details. For example, all the stained glass came from England, but the architect and builders were all from India. And the architect had to sign an agreement that he would keep no copies of the plan, so neither he nor his family could ever use the design anywhere else in the world.'

'Thank you, but I might just wander around by myself for a bit,' Parvathi said, and turned away.

'Ama.'

'Yes?'

'You won't tell anyone that I spoke about the first wife, will you? We're not supposed to mention her any more, but I just thought you should know.'

Parvathi smiled. 'Don't worry. I won't tell the master. By the way, do you know what kind of business the master does?'

'Well, of course he has the bakery and the provision shop in town. He also has rubber estates all over Malaya. I also know that he has great tracts of land in Ceylon and India both. There was once even talk of investments in England and America. And Gopal says that a nice portion of his income comes from the monopoly contract he holds with the Sultan to manufacture and distribute *toddy* in this entire state.'

The Medicine Woman

There were forty rooms upstairs, twenty per wing, ten fronting the sea and ten overlooking the jungle at the back, but only some would open to Parvathi's hand, and even those she strayed into distractedly, registering them only vaguely. Her hands lingered over bone, horn, china, onyx and Venetian lacquer, but her head kept the dizzying thought, *Kasu Marimuthu lied; his wife is not dead*, while her eyes searched ceaselessly for evidence of the woman.

In the drawing room she stopped in front of a cabinet full of Venetian glassware and wondered why drinking vessels came in so many shapes and sizes. She did not know then that each beverage demanded a shape of its own. She gazed at a jar, unlike any she had seen, a marble bird designed to hold cold water. There was so much to marvel at. Medallion chairs, Chinese punch bowls, leaf-decorated armoires. All so marvellous.

In the music room she sat on the purple velvet stool of a pale-green and yellow grand piano with sheets of music on it. Pressing its keys, she was delighted to discover, released pretty sounds. She left it reluctantly and came to a set of grand doors, the entrance to the great ballroom. Moving into the dim echoing space, she discovered the light switches and watched in amazement as five massive chandeliers came ablaze. The walls were a jigsaw of coloured glass. It was very beautiful, but somehow sad, as if it held onto a memory of happier times when royalty had stood in it. She closed its doors and carried on with her exploration.

The walls of Kasu Marimuthu's library were painted dark green and the room smelled of tobacco. When she entered it fully she saw that it was a repository for thousands and thousands of leather-bound books on shelves that went all the way up to the ceiling. Here, she did not expect to find her predecessor's picture, but perhaps learn more secrets about the proud man who, by some incredible quirk of fate, had been tricked into becoming her husband.

She might have gone behind his large desk and sat in the huge dark chair or even tried to open its drawers, but for the big painting behind the desk. She stood rooted to the spot and stared at it. Later she would learn that the strangely painted man with his arm gently draped around the curving neck of a swan was called a clown. His job was to make people laugh. But his bright hard eyes were such that she began to edge away, and his eyes, as if alive, followed her retreat.

On her way towards the kitchen she came upon the prayer room. Fragrant smoke was wafting out of it. Its walls held pictures of deities, and on a raised altar stood a gently smiling, five-foot white marble statue of Mahaletchumi, the Goddess of Wealth. Coins poured out of her skin and clothes. Parvathi remembered her mother saying that every house should have a 'sitting down' Mahaletchumi, since it was believed that a 'standing up' goddess is a goddess about to leave and take her bounty with her. But what could her mother, living in a mud hovel, teach the great Kasu Marimuthu about wealth?

Parvathi touched her forehead to the floor. When she raised it she came face to face with an eight-armed goddess, six inches tall, coarse-featured. Six snake hoods were spread over her head. Two of her arms had broken off and they lay beside her, ridiculous little sticks of clay and flaking paint. There could have been no greater contrast between the exquisite marble goddess and that cheap ornament, but it was immediately apparent that someone loved her, and very much. Real faith was required to pray to such a thing.

Parvathi knew immediately that this idol alone, in that whole house, did not belong to her rich husband. She wondered who the owner was and felt a strange affinity to that person; she knew what it was to stand before a huge impressive god and want instead to worship the small insignificant thing at its feet. She smeared holy ash on her forehead and left.

On the floor of a spotless kitchen an enormous woman sat with her legs stretched out in front of her and crossed at the ankles. Her large powerful hands were busy sorting a pile of leaves into three sections. A cheroot was clenched in her teeth. At Parvathi's approach, she placed the cheroot at the edge of a cracked plate that she was using as an ashtray, and turned her fleshy face upwards.

There were gold discs the size of coins in her ears and nostrils, and a shell strung on a black string around her throat. Turning to her side she rose easily and with surprising agility for a woman of her size. Standing in a Malay sarong and a washed-out blouse, she was an impressively ugly, towering mountain of a woman. Parvathi looked up into her big, dark eyes and knew she had found the owner of the broken idol.

The woman's teeth flashed red-brown. 'I hope you don't mind, I've finished all my work and I was just taking a short break,' she explained.

Quickly Parvathi said, 'That's all right. Who are you?'

'I'm Maya the cook,' the woman said.

Ah, the medicine woman. 'Is that goddess in the prayer room yours?'

'Yes. The master gave me permission to leave her there since he hardly ever enters that room.'

'I don't recognise her. Who is she?'

'That is Nagama, the Snake Goddess.'

'What happened to her arms?'

'Oh, when I was only a child a holy man gave her to me. Everyone thought he was mad because if anyone spoke to him he would smile from beneath his dreadlocks and wave his nails – twisting, disgusting grey-brown things, each almost a foot long – at them. He lived under a tree and as I passed him on my way to school he would nod at me. One day he called to me and told me that he had a very special gift for me, but that I must come to him before the afternoon shadow touched a nearby rock the next day or he would have to go away without giving me my gift.

'When I arrived the following day, he pointed to a nook in the exposed roots of the tree where he had put the Nagama statue amongst the roots. He said he had made her himself and told me that I must travel the world with her until the day one of her arms fell off. And there I must wait until her third hand fell off. When I said I would, he called me to come nearer and held his hands up with his palms facing me, like this.'

Maya held up her hands with her fingers well spread out.

' "Approach and entwine your fingers with mine," he said, but I didn't want to. They were really horrible fingernails and I stepped back instead. He whispered, "Come" and looked at me in such a way that suddenly all my disgust vanished and I went to him willingly. I knelt in front of him and he threaded his fingers with mine. His skin was incredibly soft, like flower petals. It felt like only a few seconds, but I must have fallen into a deep sleep or a trance, and it was only when he slumped forward that I woke up. All the revulsion I felt before returned, and with it also fear, for the dead weight bearing down on me. I wrenched myself away and his body struck the ground. I ran all the way home. That night I was delirious with fever. I thought thousands of insects were running all over my body.'

Maya stopped for a moment. 'I was ill for a week, and by the time I was better they had buried him, but there amongst the roots was the goddess. I took her home. It didn't happen suddenly, but by and by I would look at someone and know what ailed them. Or I would see a plant or some weeds growing by the river and know immediately what diseases they would cure. Soon the desire to leave struck me, and my Goddess and I began our travels, all over the world, without money or direction. I would be simply standing at a harbour looking out to sea and suddenly a man would run up to an important-looking person and explain how his daughter was too sick to make the journey, and that important person would turn in my direction and say, "You girl, yes you, would you like to work for me."

' "Yes," I'd say, and I'd be off to Egypt. In this way I travelled the world until the day I arrived in this house and the first arm broke off.'

'Why here?'

'I don't know, but I do know that this house is built on sacred ground. There are only a few other places like this on earth.'

'And the second arm, when did that break?'

Maya looked at her with an impenetrable expression. 'It broke yesterday. After you arrived.'

'Oh! What does that mean?'

'I don't know. We'll have to wait and see.'

They stared at each other. Then Parvathi, because she was used to sharing pauses only with her mother, rushed in and broke the moment. 'What did you have to leave behind in India?' she asked.

Maya's great ugly mouth opened and she laughed unselfconsciously. 'Only a mud house with a coconut-leaf roof.'

'What about your parents?'

'My mother died when I was very young and my father married another. She was happy to see the back of me.'

Neither spoke while Parvathi struggled with the question uppermost in her mind. 'Is my husband a . . . I mean, does he still drink a lot?'

Maya's eyebrows rose at the speed of Kamala's tongue. She looked at her mistress thoughtfully for some time. 'Actually, yesterday was the first time in more than a year.' She smiled suddenly, vividly. 'But you are not to blame. If he reached for the bottle it was because he was looking for a reason. If it was not you, it would have been something else. Be patient. He is a good man. He stopped once. He can stop again if he so decides.'

Parvathi stood awkwardly on one foot. Once more she was discussing her husband with a servant, and this woman had answered her with such an awesome majesty that her inquisitiveness seemed worse and even more disgraceful. Now she saw clearly that she had been foolish to sit listening to Kamala adroitly criticising in the guise of lavish praises. She should have been more dignified. To begin with, none of this was her business. He did not even want to be her husband. He would be furious if he knew she had rewarded his kindness by digging around in his private affairs.

As if she had caught the change in Parvathi, Maya rolled her dark eyes towards the stove and said, 'I'm making *varuval* with goat's blood for your dinner tonight.'

'I don't eat meat,' Parvathi said.

Maya smiled. 'Just for the master then. I will prepare something very special for you. Will you be going down to the beach today?'

'Yes, I think I will.'

'I will send a tiffin for your lunch,' Maya said in a tone suitable to that of a servant addressing her mistress.

'Yes, that will be good. Thank you,' Parvathi said distantly, belatedly assuming the role of mistress of the house.

'It will be wrapped in a cloth but be sure to keep the tiffin hidden at all times. The monkeys around here are excellent thieves and the males can be very fierce.'

'I will,' Parvathi said, and left the kitchen through the back door. Turning left she came upon the servants' quarters. Alongside was the dairy. They were making cheese or ghee and the smell was very strong. On the other side of the dairy, many lines of washing were billowing in the sun. Towards the edge of the property she came upon the generator room, a square brick building. An awful racket came from within.

A man in rubber boots was skulking near it. He had a long scar running down the length of his left cheek and his eyes were small, moist, without cunning. He lifted both his hands deferentially up to her and said his name was Kupu. As he spoke, his right eye twitched. Ah, the cowherd, honey collector. But he told her his real job was the upkeep of the generator and ensuring there was always enough petrol in its engine. Backing away, he disappeared into the noisy interior. Shading her eyes against the sun she saw cow stalls further away and a man with a pail of milk balanced on his head heading for the dairy.

She looped around the side of the house past a greenhouse filled with rows of exotic orchids, some as high as her.

At the front of the house, a barefoot girl with her long skirt tucked into her waist was sweeping the tiles with a broom made from the spines of coconut leaves. Soapy water cascaded down the stone steps. When she saw Parvathi she put the broom down and came forward to greet her much the same way Kupu had. Her bent head was so close Parvathi noticed the lice running through her hair. Then the girl raised large injured eyes to Parvathi and smiled sadly, reverently, as if Parvathi was not human but a goddess, to whom she was silently pouring out her troubles.

Parvathi nodded and walked away quickly.

She passed the gates, guarded on either side by life-sized bronze bulls. Yesterday she had not even noticed them, big and shiny as they were. She glanced back at the house shimmering in its skin of glass and light. Soon she would be gone. At the beach she kicked off her sandals; the sand was already lovely and warm under her feet. She walked up to where the ground was crusty and broke with her weight, and then along the waterline until she came to the fringe of a little fishing village of small wooden houses on stilts. Yards and yards of red fishing nets were laid out to dry on the sand.

A child covered in a white shroud was chasing a small group of boys who were scattering in all directions, screaming, '*Hantu, hantu!*' They stopped suddenly at the sight of her. Approaching her, they spoke shyly in Malay, but unable to communicate they resumed their game and Parvathi retraced her steps to the house. When it was within sight she sat down under the shade of a tree beside a patch of pretty purple flowers. Idly she plucked one. To her surprise its leaves shrivelled up right before her eyes. Very lightly she touched another leaf and it too instantly wilted. She wondered how such a delicate plant managed to survive at all.

In the blue sky swallows were enjoying the upwind. She lay back, closed her eyes, and clearly saw her disgraced return. She'd be the talk of the village. Everyone would laugh at her father for being fool enough to try and cheat using a switched photograph. Even Parvathi in her sheltered existence had heard of that. And even in that story the girl had been sent back in such disgrace that she had committed suicide. She opened her eyes and stared at the ocean, so grey and dazzling it seemed to be molten metal. The sun grew fierce, and in the shade she grew drowsy. She would not go home. There must be other big houses around in need of servants. That way she could send money home every month and no one need ever know the truth.

When she awakened, it was nearly lunchtime. Someone had brought her a tiffin carrier of food, complete with water, and covered it so it looked like a shapeless bit of cloth beside her. She ate hungrily. As she was closing the lid of the container she noticed a magical thing: the leaves that she had thought dead had been restored to their proper selves. For a while she amused herself by touching the leaves and watching their filaments close up on themselves, and in time slowly stretch out again. When she tired of the game, she plucked a handful of the purple flowers, tied them into one end of her sari, and set off in the opposite direction she had taken before.

She walked for a time, the sea on her left and impenetrable forests on her right. Up ahead there were big grey boulders. She climbed to the top and stood watching the waves crashing white underneath. The spray that hit her face was cool and refreshing. She stood there a long time, not wanting to miss it later.

She came upon the house and saw what she had not before. From a branch of a spreading tree a rectangular piece of wood hung on two ropes. She recognised it as a swing from the stories her mother used to tell: the seat where the heroine sat while dreamily waiting her lover's return. Holding on to the ropes she lowered herself on it and pushed away with her feet, first slowly and then, as she became more confident, faster and faster. Quickly, she knew to stretch out her legs on the way forward and bend her knees on the way back. Tipping her head back she saw the green canopy above, and through it patches of clouds and blue sky. Never mind that she had to return. Never mind that she would never marry and have children. *Never mind. Never mind.*

Soon she was going higher than she could ever have imagined. For the first time since leaving her home she forgot to be frightened, or nervous, or worried and began to laugh from sheer exhilaration. It was twilight when she finally slid off the seat. Her arms ached and her legs felt odd, but it was not an exaggeration to say that it was the best time she had ever had in her life.

Maya met her in the courtyard and gave her a glass bowl to put her flowers in. She placed them by her bed and was pleased with them. That night she ate alone in the large dining room.

'Eat with me,' she had said to Maya.

But she explained that she was fasting and ate only one meal a day, and that no later than sunset.

After dinner Parvathi wandered sadly out to the veranda. It was a dark, moonless night. So dark not even the foam of the waves was visible. Her mother once said it was on nights such as these that Goddess Kali mated with Lord Shiva.

Maya was smoking in a rocking chair in the furthest corner, and had automatically started up at Parvathi's approach, but her new mistress hurried towards her and placing both hands on the woman's wide lap, knelt at her feet and in an ashamed voice cried, 'Please, I don't want to pretend any more. I feel so lost and alone and you're the only one I can speak to. I'm not your mistress. Nothing could be further from the truth. I'm from a very poor family. We live in a ramshackle hut with a leaking roof that my father and brothers are too lazy to mend. By some strange trick of fate, my father was able to cheat your master with a switched photograph, but now that he has seen that I am dark and ugly, he has begun the necessary arrangements to send me home. In no time I'll be gone.'

Maya's large hand came to rest on Parvathi's head. It was not heavy but infinitely gentle. Oh, how frightened and sad she really was. She sobbed on the woman's knees while the wind murmured in the trees and the woman made sweet little sounds that ended with that word 'da'. When used on a boy or a man it was disparaging and rude, but used by Maya on her, it became the most affectionate endearment and Parvathi never wanted to leave that soft, giving lap.

Eventually the woman said, 'You are so young and beautiful, and to them the gods give special gifts.'

Parvathi's head shot up. 'But I'm not beautiful.'

Maya smiled. 'Beauty, my child, lies in the eye of the beholder. Your husband has convinced himself that there is only one type of beauty. In fact, you are very beautiful.'

'I am?' Parvathi said, confused.

'You are. You do not yet know because you have been sheltered. But soon you will see it in the eyes of men.'

'You don't understand, Maya. The master doesn't want me. He has already said that he is sending me back. There is no question about that. And he is right. How can an uneducated peasant girl like me ever be the mistress of such a house? But at the same time I cannot return or my father will become the laughing stock of the entire village. You don't know what he is like. He will never forgive me. To make me suffer he will punish my mother. He will blame her for not bringing me up well enough to keep my husband satisfied. The only way out of this that I can see is if I run away and become a servant. There must be other houses like this. I was hoping you would know some place where they might need domestic help. I can cook and clean as well as anyone.'

Maya chuckled. 'Child,' she said, 'have faith. Remember I told you that you have arrived on one of earth's few power spots? This here is the centre. Time as you know it does not exist. Here, eternity can be found in a moment or it can pass so fast it is gone in the blink of an eye. And though you may have relinquished your great dream for the moment, you have actually come here to seek that which is to be, and so, cannot leave until you behold what you have come for.'

'I don't understand what you want me to do.'

'This is my advice. Forget the transient beauty of this house, and sit instead with your back firmly to it. That way, none can move you. Even the sun, the moon and the stars can only wheel around you. Be very still in this sacred space and your call will be answered.'

The big grandfather clock in the house ticked loudly and Parvathi looked at Maya without comprehension. What on earth was the woman on about? How was she to sit with her back to the house? She needed something more solid than that. From the blackness an owl hooted.

'What's that?' Parvathi asked.

Maya smiled and began to sing in an unexpectedly sweet child-like voice.

> *You are the bright one.*
> *You are the bright one,*
> *You are walking now,*
> *but soon you will dance.*

There was silence when she finished and she said quietly, 'Remember that every woman has inside her the skill to attract any man she wants. A man is born with the ability to push and a woman to pull. She pulls men to her body and with their seed she pulls life itself into her. Stay still and you will pull to you all that you want. Off you go to sleep now. I must wait here for the master to return.'

Parvathi rose obediently, but at a pillar, stopped and turned back. 'What time will my husband return?' she asked softly.

Maya did not turn her head or take her eyes away from the dark distance or stop her slow rocking. 'Today he will be late, very late,' she murmured.

'What will you do until then?' Parvathi asked.

'I will sit very still,' Maya answered mysteriously.

Parvathi turned away and went through the courtyard; all the birds were silent and sleeping. She let herself into her room. The small lamp by the door had been switched on. She moved onto the balcony and stood for a long while watching the tip of Maya's cheroot glow in the darkness. Then she lay down on the bed, her eyes open, no wiser. She turned her head towards the sea and it lulled her to sleep. Her last thought was that she would be anything he wished or wanted, if only he would let her stay.

The God of Sex

She dreamed that she knew exactly how to sit with her back pressed against the house and call out to her greatest desire. And from the sea, he came. Shining in the sunlight. A god. She could not see his face, but knew he was beautiful beyond compare. The hand he put on her face was cool and firm. '*Hold nothing back*,' he whispered in a voice like music.

It was nearly dawn when she opened her eyes and found him at the end of her bed, wearing Western clothes and smelling of drink, but not drunk. Not like the night before.

'Is your name really Parvathi?' he asked.

'Why do you doubt it?'

'My first wife was called Parvathi and I wondered if your father . . .'

'No, it's my real name,' she said, so very quietly he had to move closer to catch the words.

He looked at the bowl of touch-me-nots, without comment. Silence fell over their still figures. Only the curtains moved, letting in the sea breezes.

'I'm really sorry my father tried to cheat you,' she whispered finally. 'He is not a bad man. We are just so very poor. Someone like you couldn't imagine what it is to be so desperately poor.'

But he carried on looking at her with cold, unforgiving eyes, and she cried out, 'Have you never done anything wrong in your life then?'

He jerked away as if she had struck him. 'You're nothing like her and you don't deserve such a name,' he spat viciously. 'She was tall and fair, a dazzling beauty. I will never use her name on you.'

She stared at him in amazement. He wanted her to believe that he was still so much in love with the woman who had run away with another man that he could not bear to call her by the same name. What kind of upsidedown world had she fallen into here?

'In ancient stories, inconsequential characters are known by more than one name. And since you are obviously not the heroine of this story, for the rest of your stay here you will answer to the name Sita,' he said.

She had been sitting on the bed with her knees bent and her elbows resting on them, but she shifted slightly, and one heel became exposed; her husband's gaze altered, became suddenly hungry. Why, there was youth again, calling. In the smooth skin he saw all the beauty and innocence he had lost, and he wanted it back. She pulled cloth down over the paradise he had glimpsed. It made him transfer his gaze back to her face. And it came to him then, that he might have been too hasty that morning to dismiss such a round and full mouth as ridiculously childish. Glossy, it was a glossy pout the girl wore. And her swan-like neck was, if he was fair, a thing of real beauty. And that extraordinary voice of hers. Well . . .

Well, he was entitled to, after all.

'Sita,' he called softly.

'Yes?'

'Show me your heels.'

'What?'

'Show me your heels,' he said again, in a different voice.

What bizarre thing was this in the upsidedown world? Not taking her eyes off his face, she lifted the edge of her sari a little and while the bells of her anklets sang, exposed her heels to his gaze. He inflated his lungs to full and his big hands pulled her towards him.

The shock of his unexpected advance made her struggle, but he was much stronger, very much so. She stopped resisting him and lay very still, as she had seen her mother do, as still as Maya had said a woman should, to pull everything she wanted towards her. And she remembered the only advice her mother had given her – there might be blood the first time. Burying his mouth in the hollow of her throat he breathed in the scent of her; Attar of Nothing. 'Hold nothing back,' the Sea God had said. 'Sita,' he had called her. Yes, she could be Sita, for a while or for as long as it took. And what a relief – it was not unendurable. Afterwards he put her knees back together and rolled away.

She waited until he was snoring gently before she crept around to the other side of the bed. For a while she stood looking down on him thinking, knowing: *Your wife didn't die, she ran away with someone else.* She stood for a moment longer over him, young, sore, secretive, triumphant. She had pulled him to her body! But some part of her being that was not quite wholly woman yet, could not sustain the potency of her new conviction and needed more. She knelt down, folded her hands on the bed, and resting her chin on them, watched him attentively.

For a very long time she remained so, while he slept on, lost in a deep dream where there was nothing but blackness, and in a place so far away from her that she could never hope to go. He left her clueless. She thought his skin might be the bridge, and ran a gentle nail against the growth of hair on the back of his hand. He was that far away, he did not stir. She watched the way the hairs lifted and fell back. And then she followed with her finger its lie, and it was silky, like pelt. A pet. But, presently untamed and requiring caution.

He was angry. No doubt, rightly. Perhaps too he was a good man, but he and her father had in one uncaring stroke ruined all her dreams. A gust of wind lifted the curtain and it fluttered sadly, and suddenly she felt the fragility of her destiny in this proud man's callous hands. She shrank away from him and felt afraid of that house and its heartbreaking secrets, of Maya and her mysterious words. Already she knew the nights in this house were different. Something happened. A door to a parallel dimension opened and through it came invisible night spirits, masters of disguise to cast spells of semblance, but even they knew they were unable to truly change things so they always hurried away before the clear light of morning. She knew her husband would wake up, dry of drink and magic, and once more his eyes would fade her clothes and call her ugly. Every night she must fight to win him back. With her body.

Those she trusted, they who should have rushed to her with open arms in pity, had betrayed her and pushed her into this impasse. How could she pretend otherwise? 'Have you forsaken me too, my beloved Snake God?' she whispered. But at the sound of her own voice, so helpless and alone, she went down on her hands and knees and began crawling chaotically away from the sleeping man, tripping on the ends of her sari, landing hard on her elbow, crying out, looking back in fear, shuffling backwards on her bottom, pushing with her hands, until her back hit the corner of the room.

She brought her knees close to her chest. From the tight coil she had made of her body she stared fearfully out at him. Whimpers, pitiful animal sounds escaped her. Their loudness horrified her. She slapped her hands over her mouth, but the heaving sounds set themselves to a louder pitch and tore past the flimsy barriers she had erected. But she needn't have worried for her husband snored blissfully on even after she began to sob and call for her mother.

Afterwards, she sat in an exhausted daze and listened to the hollow sound made by some metal part of the roof that had become loose and was banging in the wind. She began to convince herself that it would be all right. Her father had not betrayed her. He had done the best he could. He was not to blame; no one was. It was her fate. She would sit still and wait. See what the goddess Nagama had in mind for her.

Eventually, it must have struck five, for she heard Maya come back to the house to cook the sweet rice offering for the gods. She felt sore and empty and strange and hungry. Very hungry, actually. Rising stiffly she went to wash away the blood and tears. Then she climbed tiredly into the other side of the bed. She dreamed that her mother had fallen into the well. Naked and shivering, she was sobbing for Parvathi, but Parvathi only leaned over the edge and told her that she could no longer answer to any other name but Sita, whereupon her mother cried, 'Have you so soon brought shame upon our family, my daughter?'

Measuring a Vipala

Parvathi opened her eyes to glorious pieces of coloured light on the walls and ceiling, and told herself that she was glad she had not awakened to his eyes. It was better if they met only during the magic of the night. Both could then pretend. 'Show me your heels,' he had said. She kicked the blanket away and looked at her feet. They did not seem remarkable. Must have been a clever illusion of the night spirits. But even they had not been able to persuade him to say, 'Stay and be my wife.' She must wait for the night. See if the deepest night would bring to him a need of her.

Then she remembered it was nothing to be used. That other girl too had known her husband. Only, shame and sorrow had caused her to miscarry on the return voyage.

After breakfast Parvathi went into his library. Avoiding the direct gaze of the clown she walked towards the leather-bound books. They seemed hardly touched. She pulled one out of its space and opened it. It was full of a great many tiny words. She put it back and pulled another out. It had pictures of trees. She sat down on a chair to look at them.

'Can you read?'

She shot up guiltily. She thought he had gone to work. He was frowning, but he had said she could explore the house and grounds. 'No,' she admitted, stepping away from the book. 'I was just looking at the pictures, and I was being very careful.'

'Ah,' he said, and coming forward, looked at the page she had been gazing at. 'I have decided that you should stay until your next period. Just in case there is a baby involved.' He shut the book and looked at her curiously. 'I don't know what you do all day. It must be very boring.'

'No, it's not,' she said, and shook her head vigorously.

'Have you ever been to school?'

'No. My father thinks schools are only for boys.'

'Would you like to learn something while you are here? I could get a tutor for you.'

She couldn't believe her ears. Her own teacher! A professional! She had always dreamed of going to school to be taught by a proper teacher instead of making do with her uninterested brothers teaching her far less than what they themselves had learned that day. She nodded enthusiastically.

'What would you like to learn?'

She remembered Kamala rattling in that foreign language. 'English,' she said. 'I should like to learn English.'

Kasu Marimuthu seemed amused. 'All right,' he agreed mildly. 'I shall arrange for a teacher to come tomorrow.'

She smiled shyly. 'Thank you.'

'See you at dinner about eight,' he said, and left.

Kasu Marimuthu knew of course that it was a waste of time, but he thought it would be interesting to see how much she could pick up in a month. She didn't seem too bright, but she was certainly eager. He laughed softly to think of the peasant's reaction to his daughter speaking English.

Parvathi stood uncertainly at the dining room entrance, eyeing the knives, forks, spoons and other unfamiliar utensils on the table with great apprehension. Kasu Marimuthu arrived at a quarter past eight. Maya was nowhere to be seen but a manservant hovered behind him.

'You can remove my wife's cutlery, Gopal. She will eat with her hand.' Turning to her he said, 'Tomorrow you will learn to use cutlery so that for the time you are here at least, you will be civilised.' Then he took his place at the head of the table. She stood somewhere in the middle of the room, unsure of what was expected of her. A wife was supposed to serve her husband.

'Sit,' he ordered curtly, and indicated the seat beside him. Food was served by the man whose conversation never progressed beyond a respectful nod.

'Does he not speak?'

'Yes, but I prefer it if he doesn't.'

'Oh,' Parvathi said nervously.

'Are you a vegetarian?' he asked, glancing at the dishes on her plate.

'Yes,' she said quietly.

'Why?'

'I became one when I was five. They were killing a goat a few doors away, and its cries were so much like that of a child that I found it impossible to eat any kind of meat after that. My brothers were happy to accommodate.'

'I'm sure they were,' Kasu Marimuthu said grimly.

Surreptitiously she watched him neatly load small pieces of food onto the fork, fit them into his mouth, and chew them behind closed lips. As he had said, it did all look rather civilised.

'What have you done all day?' he asked, cutting up more food to gather on metal.

'I spent it on the beach.'

'What, the whole day? Well, I suppose you had nothing better to do. Never mind, I expect your English teacher will keep you busy tomorrow,' he said dismissively

She bit her lip. Where was the skill to entice this man? How to sit with her back to this house and make the moon, stars and sun circle around her? She bent her head.

'I was really scared today,' she told him. 'A cow named Letchumi came towards me and I thought she was going to butt me, so I screamed and nearly ran, but the women in the dairy shouted for me to remain still. She only wanted to lick my hand. I didn't know their tongues were so rough.'

Kasu Marimuthu laughed. She stared at him. Suddenly he looked younger, this stranger who disapproved of her. Seeing her eyes on him he stopped suddenly. This man didn't want to be charmed or enticed. 'It's the peacocks you should heed. A bad-tempered lot, them. Never take the boat out to the island,' he advised, before returning his attention to his food.

'Did you know that Maya is a healer?'

He looked up, clearly surprised. 'Maya?'

'The cook.'

'My cook, a healer?'

'Yes. This afternoon a queue of sick people turned up, and simply by placing two fingers on their wrists she seemed to know exactly what was wrong with them. She dispensed a whole load of medicine too.'

'Medicine? What kind of medicine?'

'Roots and herbs, I think. She looked really impressive, sitting there with all these people bowing and so grateful. She must be good.'

'Really,' he said disapprovingly.

Parvathi faltered. 'Yes. To one she gave seashells and showed her how to lay them on her body with the spirals pointing inward. This, she said, would clear away the invisible shadows that caused the woman's pain.'

Kasu Marimuthu shook his head in wonder at the madness of these people. He signalled the hovering manservant who immediately refilled his glass. In the silence Parvathi realised that she had made a mistake to tell him this. Quickly she rushed on. 'There was a man too who came because he was having trouble with his crops, and she told him to look in the cobwebs and bring the insects he found there. Then she would tell him what to do. Isn't that amazing?'

He swivelled a haughty head in her direcion. 'These people, they didn't come into the house, did they?'

'No, no,' she said immediately, chastised by his forbidding stare. 'Everything happened under the Angsana tree.'

'That's all right then,' he said after a moment, and to her great relief, returned to his food.

And she too shut her mouth, glad that she had not told him about the ginger tea that Maya had distributed for free. They ate quietly to the ticking of the grandfather clock in the living room until he said suddenly, 'So, what do you think of the house?'

'It's really very beautiful.'

He smiled carelessly. He had not expected her to say otherwise.

'What does it mean, that painting of the clown?'

He put his fork down and looked at her as if surprised or impressed.

'What do *you* think it means?'

'I don't know.'

'Ah.' It was a sound of disappointment. He raised his wine glass, took a sip and regarded her from above the rim. 'You're not supposed to ask the meaning of a painting. Not even to the artist. Paintings are secret languages spoken between hearts. Every artist will try to show you the contents of his soul and it is bad form to show him he has failed.' He leaned forward on his elbows and looked at her curiously, his fork forgotten on the plate. 'What does it make you *feel*, Sita?'

She dropped her eyes. She did not want to seem ridiculous. 'Nothing really,' she said.

He straightened away, his lips twisted. 'From the urn comes wine, of course.' She looked down at her plate in confusion. He was annoyed with her. But then, he must have reconsidered. Her simplicity, her artlessness was not her fault. 'Go,' he said, 'and stand so close to it that the shapes stop deceiving the eye and it becomes what it really is, parts of the human body.'

After dinner Kasu Marimuthu retired to his study and Parvathi climbed the stairs alone to her bedroom. She was almost asleep by the time he came to her. In the dark the illusion had spread further, for his wine-scented breath murmured in her ear, 'You have the most beautiful neck I have seen in a woman.'

The next morning she stood in front of the mirror and looked at her neck. It rose out of her narrow shoulders, thin and long and not at all noteworthy. She went back to stand before the painting, as close as it was possible to go before the colours started to blur and run into one another, and still she saw neither the parts of a human body nor hidden meanings. Maya came to stand beside her.

'What do you think, Maya?' she asked. 'Do you feel anything when you look at this painting?'

But Maya only shrugged. 'To me it's just a painting, like any other,' she said, but she did come up with a useful suggestion.

'Shall we take it down and see if there is a date or title behind it?'

Parvathi had no idea there might be something behind it. They took it down, but there was nothing at the back. Kasu Marimuthu was right: 'Either you got it or you didn't.'

'Perhaps there is no hidden meaning. Perhaps it's just a painting of a clown and a swan,' she said and, disappointed, went to wait for her English teacher. He arrived at 8.00 a.m. sharp.

Ponambalam Mama was bespectacled and must have been at least seventy, but he had walked the entire five miles from town, and planned to do so every day except Sundays. He had a cataract growing over one eye but otherwise there was no one brighter or bushier of tail.

He faced her in the music room sternly, as if they were adversaries sizing each other before the battle.

'Before we begin I'd like to say that the white man has invented some great things and built some admirable institutions. His cities are grand, his laws fair and well thought out, his music occasionally sublime, and his poetry well constructed. But before you start assuming the white man's superiority and begin to slavishly ape him, consider this. The Indian has not always lounged on the ground drunk on cheap toddy; he is lying in the gutter only because he has forgotten the soundness of his credentials, the incredible exactitude and brilliance of his ancient systems.'

Parvathi stared silently at him.

'To give just one example; the division of time into various subdivisions. One kalpa is 4,320,000 years. It takes four yugas to make one kalpa. One yuga or day of Brahma is one thousand years of the gods. One day and one night of the gods are equal to one human year. One human year has six seasons – spring, heat, rain, autumn, winter, coolness. So each season is two months, a dark lunar month and a light one. One lunar month is twenty-eight nakshatra. One nakshatra is twenty-four solar hours. Twenty-four solar hours is thirty-one muhurta (forty-eight minutes). One muhurta equals two ghati (twenty-four minutes). One ghati equals thirty kala (forty-eight seconds). One kala equals two pala (twenty-four seconds). One pala equals six prana (four seconds). One prana equals ten vipala (0.4 second). One vipala equals sixty prativipala (0.000666 of a second).'

'How did they measure 0.000666 of a second?' Parvathi asked.

'There is a good probability that we will never have the answer to that. And since we are here, please remember that while history records that the white man was first to fly, the only language with a word for aircraft is Sanskrit. This language also stores detailed instruction on how to man, maintain and even crash land these machines. That much has been lost to time forever is the Indian tragedy.' He stopped a moment to savour with evident satisfaction her surprise before saying, 'Now that we have established that the white man is no smarter than the Indian, let's start on his practical, whimsical, rather wonderful language.'

With all those big, complicated words that she could hardly understand, Parvathi should have been mortified, but instead she grinned broadly at him. He was exactly the kind of teacher she had always dreamed of. They began with the alphabet. She noted down everything he said in an exercise book. At the end of the lesson he gave her a children's book that he had brought for her, and said, 'We will start on that tomorrow.'

Parvathi remained in the music room and revised her lesson for the day while he ate a solitary lunch in the dining room. Immediately after, he left on the back of the gardener's bicycle, his thin hands clutching the metal seat, his brilliant white dhoti flapping in the wind. Parvathi sat in the shade of a tree on the beach and recited her alphabet aloud. Who would have thought it? She was learning English!

That evening, she had her bath and joined Maya for prayers. Afterwards, she sat in the music room and filled twenty-six pages with each letter. Her husband did not return for dinner and when next she saw him, it was at the breakfast table. The wireless was on in the background and he was reading the newspapers.

He looked up at her entrance. 'You are awake. How was your English lesson?'

'I am learning the alphabet,' she informed him enthusiastically.

'Good place to start,' he commented shortly, and bending his head to his paper, completely ignored her. When his coffee cup was empty, he pushed his chair back and bade her good day. Parvathi, who had stood until he left the room, resumed her seat and told herself to be patient. In the daylight the magic did not work. After breakfast she went to the music room to revise and wait for her teacher.

At eight sharp Ponambalam Mama walked through the door. 'Good morning,' he greeted her in English. She returned the greeting, and they began the lesson. When he realised that she had learned the entire alphabet by heart, his bushy white eyebrows rose, and his one good eye shone with approval.

'Very good,' he said, and opened another book he had brought with him. 'Let's learn how to spell some nouns first. Nouns, by the way, are words used to identify people, places, things and ideas.' So she came to know that A started the noun for apple. B for boy, C for cat, and D for dog. Time flew in Ponambalam Mama's company. When it was time for him to leave he pulled out an English to Tamil dictionary from his cloth bag and told her to learn ten randomly picked words a day.

As she was seeing him out, Parvathi saw Maya getting into a car with two Chinese men who drove her away.

'Kamala,' she said, 'where are they taking Maya?'

'This is the Chinese month of the Hungry Ghost. You can't walk in the town for all the ashes everywhere. They burn things for their departed ones, paper cars, houses, clothes, even servants. The smoke carries these things up to the spirit world where their relatives can make use of them. They are taking Maya to do prayers for them.'

'What? Maya does prayers for Chinese people?'

'Oh yes, Ama. Maya is very famous. People come from all over to see her. There is nothing she cannot do.'

Parvathi went in and sat down to the lunch that Maya had prepared. There was plum pudding out of a tin for dessert.

God Comes

It was a clear starry night and Parvathi was on the balcony when she saw the civet cat, the tip of its tail shining silver in the moonlight. It had found something to eat on the edge of the beach, but it must have heard a sound for it stopped, listened and grasping its meal in its mouth, took off in the direction of the jungle. Parvathi ran through the house to the balcony facing the jungle, where she saw its bushy tail disappear into the dark wall of jungle just as Maya opened the gate that bordered it and went into the pitch black without a lamp! Either the woman had excellent night vision or she had imagined it.

There was a concoction of taro and medicinal leaves boiling in sugar on the stove, and Maya was chopping something when Parvathi walked into the kitchen.

'Maya, did I see you go into the jungle just before dawn today?'

'Yes, Da, I often go into the jungle pre-dawn to collect the shoots I need for my medicine.'

'But in the darkness, without a lamp?'

'Yes, Da. It's better that way. When you carry a lamp you are seen before you can see. Besides which, in the dark a lamp only serves to blind you to all but its feeble circle of light.'

'Maya, can you take me with you the next time you go?'

The large woman was silent for some seconds. 'Perhaps not next time. You are not ready yet, but I would have thought soon, very soon.'

'Is it because of tigers and wild elephants?'

Maya smiled. 'I was thinking more of scorpions and centipedes.'

Disappointed, because she had looked forward to entering the jungle, Parvathi walked up to the rocks and sat on the edge of one. While gazing out at the white surf, something cast its shadow on her face. She looked up and saw a huge butterfly with wings of white velvet and a body of coal dust. With a slow swoop around her head it landed on her hand. It fluttered its wings once and then snapped them shut and waited. She remembered her mother saying, 'When a white animal approaches you it is a sign of grace.' A moment later, it made for the air once more. It sailed away and she saw Kupu running towards her.

'Ama! Ama!' he called.

She stood up and waited for him. He stopped in front of her, his body gleaming with sweat and his eyes shining with some great excitement. 'I think I've found some ancient structure in the jungle,' he panted.

'What is it?'

'I don't know, but I've never seen anything like it. And it's old, very old.'

'Will you take me there?' she asked eagerly.

He hesitated, glanced down at her flimsy sandals. 'It's quite a way in and the path is not so easy. Maybe it will be better if I clear the way first.'

'No,' she said quickly. 'I can manage. Really, I can. Please Kupu. . . .'

'All right,' he agreed.

Parvathi felt a thrill as they went out of the gate that Maya had only that morning said she was not yet ready to go through. They walked past the wild banana trees growing at the edge of the forest and suddenly they were inside that dim world of wonder, at once frightening and enticing. She had imagined it to be cool and sweet-smelling, but the opposite was true. It was hot, damp and smelled of decaying deadwood and the fungi that lived on it. Many layers of fallen leaves made the earth underfoot a living ground. Sometimes her step released clouds of black spores. Ahead, Kupu swung his machete at the tangle of undergrowth in graceful arcs. Every time he glanced back she assured him she was all right, and they pressed deeper and deeper into the twilight world.

There were pitcher-plants winding themselves amongst the bracken, and trees with their bark hanging in tatters – underneath they were scarlet. Others had patches of white mould growing on them. Giant ferns brushed her arms. Nestling in a thicket of bamboo were birds so vibrantly coloured they were like jewels. Kupu's scythe slashed away, even beautiful trailing berries as big as grapes. Sometimes there were low-lying branches and they had to duck. Then louder than the incessant sound of insects, monkeys and birds, came a loud barking. She had heard that sound before. It started every day at mid-morning and became a booming song that even the billions of leaves in the jungle could not muffle. 'What's that?'

'It's an ape called a Siamang. That's the female,' Kupu said.

The bark was followed by song. 'And that's the male,' Kupu said. 'You might be able to see them. They live where we are heading.'

They came to a place where either side of them the wall of vegetation seemed impenetrable. From the branches of giant trees hung great creeper stems, sometimes with long wiry shoots and fish-hook spines as thick as a man's calf. Here, Kupu ran up tree trunks like a monkey and held them aside for her. Small animals suddenly shot up the overhanging branches to disappear out of sight. But once he caught in his hand the back legs and tail of a lizard that seemed to fly at him in fury. He flung it away from him contemptuously. It crashed without voice into the undergrowth.

'Was it poisonous?' Parvathi asked.

'Poisonous and wicked,' he confirmed, 'but I am used to catching them. I make nooses out of palm-leaves and lasso them.' By a moss-covered stone near a hill he stopped and turned to look at her. 'It's just here,' he said.

She looked around. 'Where?'

He pointed to a fallen tree, its roots completely uprooted. 'It must have fallen in the storm the night before you arrived,' he explained, and she saw that it had ripped away at the hill and exposed a doorway. He stood at the entrance and lit a match.

'It's empty,' he announced. 'But if you prefer, I will go in first.'

She looked at the opening in the hill and was astonished to see just above it the big white butterfly. It fluttered upwards and disappeared where light broke through the leaves. A bird suddenly flew out of a mass of leaves towards her head. Stifling a scream she ducked and scrambled through the small opening into a small windowless space. The air was absolutely still. In that rare silence she heard Kupu enter behind her. His breathing was even and soft. She forgot that they were in the middle of a jungle alive with sound and activity. In the silence she heard the scratching sound of his match and in the faint light she glanced around curiously. It was indeed empty, but such a thick layer of earth had collected on the ground that although she could stand upright, Kupu had to bend from the neck.

'Look,' he whispered, and she saw that all the walls were covered with hieroglyphs, and in the centre of the wall facing the entrance was a carving of two upright entwined serpents.

'Do you think this temple was built to venerate a Snake God?'

'I don't know,' Kupu replied, and both looked at the other and said, 'Maya.' When the fifth match burned out, Kupu did not light another.

'Let's go,' he said in the dark.

The first drops of rain brought on an unfamiliar smell: moist, earthy, intoxicating. Millions of leaves began to shiver. Animals, Maya had told her, didn't like wind; it parted their fur and the cold got to their bodies, but they didn't mind rain. True enough, the undergrowth came alive with their calls. Parvathi replayed that time alone with Kupu, of how strange it had felt. She wondered if he had felt it too. There had been something unfamiliar in the voice with which he had said they should leave.

It began to rain steadily. The tree trunks dripped with moisture and the ground became slippery. Once Parvathi slipped, tried to hold onto a log, and screamed when her hand went right through the bark, for the whole section was rotten and slugridden. She retracted her hand. It was covered with yellow and green juices and some sticky black mess. She looked at it with horror. Kupu took his vest off and gave it to her to wipe her hand with. She began to thank him, but he shook his head as if it was nothing, and they carried on. Another time by a tall tree with half its roots exposed, she skidded on some wet leaves and fell, hurting her hip. Then he twisted his body over the roots and held out a helping hand.

'Are you hurt?' he asked worriedly. 'I should never have brought you. Now the master will be angry with me.'

'I'm fine,' she assured him.

His eyes fell upon her arms, all thin and scratched. 'I shouldn't have brought you,' he repeated.

And she looked at the tense sinewy body curving towards her and marvelled at how effortlessly he kept the fine tension of his balance even though he had forced his legs, body, and hands into unreasonable places. She did not take the proffered hand. Instead she looked down his wet throat to his shoulder where the rain pattered onto his skin and bounced off in little droplets that then fell to his chest and ran down his flat stomach. She thought of it collecting in his black rubber boots.

Then a thought, unconnected, intimate. Did he ever suffer from backache? Did he go to his room and rub an aromatic oil on his neck and run it down the length of his back looking for hard knots underneath the lean, tough sinews? She took a deep breath, and could not distinguish between the scent of the jungle and him. In the hissing rain he had become a part of the jungle, mysterious and dangerous. At that moment no one else existed but them. When her naïve gaze returned to his face, rain was using the scar on his cheek as a riverbed; the rivulets splashed on her skin. She stared at the purple frosting on the outside of the gash; the scar itself, light brown, tough, more shoe leather than skin.

'What happened to your face?' she asked.

He blinked, the wet eyelashes sticking together. 'I was mauled by a tiger when I was a child.'

'Oh.'

Rain had made her clothes cling to her body, but his eyes as they looked at the girl on the forest floor did not darken or fill with lust. In fact, there was nothing to be seen in their opaque depths. Neither surprise nor condemnation; not even the instinctive recognition that he had unwittingly awakened sexual curiosity in another being. Nothing had registered. Luckily, but impossible, surely, after the wanton way she had stared at him. Hot blood rushed up into her confused face. It must have been his excessive humility and lack of social understanding that had prevented him from guessing her shameful thoughts. Lacking the ability to ridicule, he would have been overwhelmed if he had known.

'Come, we must carry on. There is some way to go yet,' he said.

Parvathi put her hand in his and he hauled her up easily. She kept her eyes on the ground after that.

They arrived at the kitchen door a bedraggled, sorry pair. Maya came towards them. 'What is it?' she asked.

'Kupu found a ruin inside a hill in the jungle. It must be a snake temple. It has snakes carved into the wall. Come on, Maya. You have to see it now,' she said, tugging the woman's fleshy hand.

'Come inside first, child.' And taking the cheroot out of her mouth, she burned off all the fat black leeches stuck on Parvathi's legs.

As soon as it stopped raining, they re-entered the jungle. Maya had to crawl into that low space. They heard her draw in a sharp breath. 'My God, this is no ordinary snake temple. This is a stargate,' she gasped. Parvathi and Kupu waited in silence as Maya shuffled over to the wall on her knees and held up a kerosene lamp to the strange shapes on the wall. She turned an astonished face to them.

'And it was not dug into the hill. The hill settled around it. This is thousands of years old, ten, maybe even fifteen thousand years. You have no idea how sacred and special this place is. A people highly evolved, with an extraordinary knowledge of the skies and possessing inner spiritual vision, gifts which we have now forgotten, constructed this. The holiest men of today know these gateways made it possible for the ancient ones to connect earth to heaven and converge with God while still in the physical form, but the knowledge of how to do it is lost for ever.

'Amazing,' she said, shaking her head in wonderment. She touched the drawings on the walls. 'And look at all these sacred symbols. How fortunate I am to be able to see so many in one lifetime. Ah! The two dancing snakes you spoke of, they symbolise serpentine energy. There must be a round tower somewhere underneath all this earth. Towers are the best way of harnessing swirling energy.

'This hill must also contain an astronomical observatory, for this advanced race studied the planets, stars and galaxies. See these lines?' she said, pointing to a drawing that looked like fish bones. 'It is a faultless calendar able to predict solar and lunar phenomena with extraordinary accuracy. It is read using either the moonlight or the sunlight coming in through that porthole window. I'm sure if we dig around here we will find bones, perhaps even human ones.'

She caught Parvathi's look of horror and with a gentle smile said, 'Our past often fills us with loathing at the thought of what we were, have been, and what we suspect still remains in us, but these people cannot be held by our morality, for morality is not fixed and equal at all times. For the moment our new higher, more refined culture decries sacrifices as cruel and inhuman, but these earlier civilisations had a different concept of energy. They knew the soul was indestructible. So there was no real sacrifice involved. All that was being offered was the willingness to give up the mortal body. Abraham's apparent willingness to sacrifice his own son was enough, but Jesus had to offer His body on a cross.

'You see, these people were bartering. It was an ancient belief that during a total eclipse, in those few minutes when the world is dark, a tunnel, or a sacred pathway opens, and a rare and powerful opportunity to communicate with the gods is possible. But the times when the tunnel is open to the gods is also a time when demons plunge head down through the same tunnel. They have to be fed. Sacrifice was an exchange of energy. For profound connection they gave life force. So consumed were they in the flames of their faith they would have given their own flesh and blood if necessary, and often did. But as time went by people forgot the true meaning of sacrifice and began to offer what was not important to them, ten fatted goats, their neighbour's daughter, the hearts of their enemies. And as this lack of commitment and fidelity in our ways of welcoming God changed, so also our ability to meet our Maker as they did.'

Maya turned around to face them, her face large and hideous with moving shadows from the lamp that swung in her hand. 'It will be very interesting indeed to actually lay eyes on all that is inside this hill.'

Both Kupu and Parvathi nodded.

'Now you know, Da,' Maya said quietly, 'why the goddess dropped her arm for you. See what your coming caused.'

Parvathi beamed happily at the thought, but that evening she sat on the edge of her gleaming bath and wondered if Maya could be wrong, after all – that it was just a simple coincidence. Her period had come. She was not pregnant. And Kasu Marimuthu was now certain to return her to her father.

Changes

Kupu stood in Kasu Marimuthu's study with his shoulders hunched up close to his neck and his arms folded submissively. Out of his black boots his bare feet were a much paler colour than the rest of him.

'Well then,' Kasu Marimuthu said. 'Tell me all about it. I want to hear it straight from the mouth of the first person to enter the temple.'

'Actually, sir, I was not the first one to step into it.'

Kasu Marimuthu frowned. 'I was told that you discovered it.'

'That's true, sir, but your wife was the one who went in first.'

'What?'

'Your wife said she wanted to come, sir. I couldn't not take her, but I didn't think it was my place to enter it first, sir. I did light a match first to make sure that it was completely safe.'

Gopal, who had been leaning against a bookcase in the shadows, spoke up. 'It is the new mistress, sir. She has brought luck to this household. The tree uprooted itself during the early-morning hours of her auspicious arrival.'

Kasu Marimuthu addressed the voice without turning. 'And this is exactly why you are not to speak unless spoken to. Don't let me hear another word from you.' To Kupu he said, 'Is it in my property?'

Kupu's one eye shivered uncontrollably. 'Yes, sir.'

'Are you absolutely sure?'

Kupu raised his hand self-consciously and touched his madly twitching eye. 'Yes, sir. It lies less than a mile before the stream that makes the boundary.'

Kasu Marimuthu nodded, satisfied. It was a good thing he had bought up the extra land. But even if the man was wrong and it happened to be out of his property, he would simply buy up more land from the Sultanate. 'What kind of temple is it?'

'I don't know, sir. It is not a mosque, a church or a Chinese place of worship, and it is most definitely not one of ours. It is not really possible to make the whole shape of it out at the moment. Too much earth and vegetation covers it. But it seems to be constructed using very large white stones, all cut and put together so precisely that I couldn't get my knife-blade between them. If you wish, the boys and I can excavate it for you, sir.'

'How long do you think it will take you?'

'Perhaps a few weeks to tear away the vegetation and cut the earth, but longer to wash down the stones. We will need to carry water from the stream or failing that, bring it from the house.'

'All right, start the clearing tomorrow. I will bring in bulldozers and two hundred men to help you – work them in double shifts. I expect it will take many months to unearth, but I want to see it as soon as possible.'

Kupu touched the middle of his chest and bowed his head once. When Kasu Marimuthu nodded, he backed away respectfully.

'You too,' Kasu Marimuthu said, and Gopal slunk away noiselessly.

Kasu Marimuthu sat back in his chair and swivelled it around to face the French windows. Far away, the gardener was tying a gunnysack around a jackfruit to stop the squirrels and the fruit bats from getting to it before it fully ripened. It was already nearly a foot long. A boy was driving the cows back into their stalls and the evening air was loud with their bells and his cries of *'hrraah, hrraah, hrraah'* when the timid knock came on Kasu Marimuthu's door.

'Come,' he called.

Parvathi came in and closed the door behind her. He looked at her, saying nothing. She was wearing that same brown sari he had taken such a violent dislike to that first morning. Her hair was wet and loose down her back. Idly, he reflected that he had not realised that it was quite so long.

She stood in the middle of his study and with halting embarrassed words told him that her period had come. He saw her little speech to its end and then carried on watching her nervously wring her hands, until he came to the bizarre realisation that he had no wish to be married to her, but neither did he wish to relinquish her. Generally, he was not a superstitious man, but even he could see that his marriage had so far been propitious. On the day of his marriage he had been given the opportunity to acquire three 500-acre estates, one on the way to Pekan, one in Jerantut, and another in Malacca. And he had not forgotten that first morning and all those unplanned words. And, after all these years to unearth a temple on his land! He should have felt resentful and trapped in a situation not of his choosing, but oddly, he was in point of fact, totally indifferent to his situation. He waved her away absently.

And he was not drunk that night when he went into her bedroom and purposely stood his long shadow over her sleeping body until she opened wide, frightened eyes to him. When he saw that that first fear had passed, he moved close to her ear and whispered, 'Let your father know that he will not get one cent from me. Ever.' Straightening, he left.

The next three days passed for Parvathi in the study with the English teacher, while in the jungle Kupu revealed an unexpected talent for excavation. He knew exactly when to stop the big tractors and bring in the shovels. He had such a fine instinct that not even one of the standing stones suffered a scratch.

And then:

'I've got a letter from home, Maya!' Parvathi cried joyfully, skipping into the kitchen. 'And look at the postmark. They must have sent it almost as soon as I left.' She ripped it open excitedly. 'My older brother has written it for my father. He sends his best wishes . . .' And then her face closed up and she read the rest in silence. When she raised her head once more, her eyes were bitter. 'I was supposed to send money as soon as possible,' she said. 'My mother has fallen ill because she has been missing me, and since she has not been able to work, the family is in terrible difficulties. My father borrowed to pay for my travel and my wedding trousseau. And now he needs that money back'.

'Wedding trousseau? What wedding trousseau?' Maya asked.

'Anyway, my father is very angry and thinks that I have forgotten my family after all they have done for me.' And looking at the letter again, read a part of it out loud.

'Remember, my daughter, while you are seated at your husband's fine table eating delicious meals that there is hardly a full plate of rice to share between us. And when you get down from your horse-drawn carriage I want you to keep in mind that your mother has lost a slipper and with no money to replace it, goes barefoot. Twice now she has cut her foot on stones and thorns.'

Fresh tears welled up in Parvathi's eyes. She had never thought her mother would not replace it. 'I have been so careless and selfish. I must do something, but what? I have no money. Should I ask my husband?'

Maya shook her head gently. 'No. No good will come of that, Da. Write to your father and tell him your husband is furious at his deception. That you are no more than a prisoner here. It is often like that with bullies, they will dominate only those whom they perceive to be weaker than them, and your father, forgive me for saying, is one, so he will bend from the waist to Kasu Marimuthu's will at all times. He will tend to his wounded hopes of an indulgent life quietly and will not bother you for a time. Things will settle down here, and then you will be able to send some money home for your mother. But for now I will give you some money, not enough to satisfy your father, of course, and your mother will be no better off for it, but we will send it with a pair of slippers for her.'

'How can I take your money?'

'I have renounced all worldly desires and sensual pleasures. What use money to me?'

'I will only take it if you consider it a loan.'

'As you wish, Da.'

⋆   ⋆   ⋆

One week later, Kasu Marimuthu went to inspect the site. Parvathi did not go with her husband. Instead she waited until Maya had finished cooking lunch and went with her. The women stood back and watched in awe at what had been uncovered in so little time. The hill had become a horseshoe shape holding inside it a complex of structures. The hexagonal room that they had been so excited over now seemed small and insignificant compared to the main structure beside it, a tall round tower. On the outside steep, narrow steps circled it all the way to the top, but Kupu had said it was still not safe to climb. The men had also exposed stones arranged in half-circles, and, grouped in twos and threes, perfectly crafted spheres two to three feet high.

'Everything here has been carefully measured and planned. There are extraordinary secrets hidden in every pattern, marking, surface, length and weight. Even they,' Maya said, pointing to the standing stones, 'are neither dead nor dreamless, but waiting for the day when one enlightened enough will wake them up again. And though the mysteries of sacred geomancy reveal themselves to the uninitiated only very reluctantly, and the time when pure, irreproachable men could look upon gods in their full divinity is gone, I dreamed last night that they might not be waiting in vain.' She stood pensive for a moment.

'Even now these stones speak to each other. See that upright tongue-like stone over there? It is a very special stone, a communicating stone. It will speak even to humans. In my travels in the Americas a shaman, he was three hundred years old when I met him, told me that legend has it that if you put your forehead to them they will take you into their world and show you things.'

Maya raised her hands and pointed to the cupmarks on the stones.

'See those round marks gouged out of the surfaces? Streams of good energy should be pouring out of them, nourishing all they touch. But not all earth energy is good.' She gestured to the floor of the doomed room in which they were standing. 'These rings are inverted silver bowls buried beneath the ground. They are speaking to the bad energies, keeping them from rising up, saying, "Come not upon us, east or west".'

'How do you know all this?' Parvathi asked.

'I feel it, but there is one way to be really sure and that is to use divining rods. Let's come back tomorrow and follow the energy lines that lead off from that main stone over there. We will see where they take us.'

Maya and Parvathi were back early the next day with divining rods that Maya had made with bits of metal and wood, to begin mapping the energy trails emitted by the stones. As Maya had predicted, streams of them led away from the stones. Mud sloshed around their ankles and ferns came up to their armpits as they followed their divining rods. But without warning and for no apparent reason, Parvathi's suddenly began to weave sharply from side to side even though Maya, a few steps ahead, continued to follow the line without any interference.

'Maya, something's wrong with my rods.'

Maya stopped. 'How is that possible?' she said. Retracing her steps, she took up Parvathi's rod and immediately it began to move as it should. Maya swung around to look at Parvathi. 'What were you thinking about?'

'Actually, I was remembering my mother.'

An expression impenetrable to Parvathi crossed Maya's large face before she turned away, saying briskly, 'It is enough, what we have done today. I have to start preparing dinner soon. Let's mark the spot and return tomorrow.'

'What did you do today?' Kasu Marimuthu asked without curiosity as he lifted rice and mutton to his mouth.

'Well, Maya and I used divining rods to follow one of the energy lines flowing from the standing stones at the temple.'

Kasu Marimuthu shook his head in disbelief. 'What a ludicrous idea Since there is a vast range of natural and artificial energies always present to some degree on all of earth's surface, dowsing for energy is an errand without any intellectual agenda. Anybody could claim to trace a "pattern" using their meaningless results. Unless you are dowsing for water or minerals, then you are both wasting your time. What about your English lessons? Have you lost interest in them then?'

'No, of course not. We only spent a couple of hours or so doing that, but if you prefer I will stop.'

For a moment Kasu Marimuthu considered her seriously. Then he smiled, a mean, mocking little smile. 'No, do carry on. Let's test Baudelaire's theory that only paganism, if properly understood, can save the world. Yes, in fact, I am very curious to see this rotten world as my mad cook beholds it.'

But as it turned out, Parvathi did not carry on, because when she went that night to sit with Maya they had their first and last argument.

'Maya,' she asked, 'why did the divining rods go cold in my hand?'

At first Maya had tried to evade the question by saying, 'Don't worry about it. It can happen sometimes.'

But she had grasped the woman's hand tightly in her own and insisted, 'But why did it happen while I was thinking of my mother? And why did your face change so? I must know. Tell me, please.'

Even then Maya had hesitated, but Parvathi continued to nag her until eventually Maya pressed her purplish lips together, and said, 'The divining rods can go haywire if the person working them thinks of someone deceased. The more recently departed, the more quickly they will go cold.'

Parvathi threw Maya's hand away as if red hot. 'What a cruel thing to say!' she cried. 'My husband is right. All of this is nonsense. How can we pretend to map energies when the entire earth's surface is covered with them? And how can you possibly know anything about people who died thousands of years ago, anyway? My mother is not dead. Do you hear me? She is *alive*.'

And she fled from Maya and did not see her until the next night when she was cold and formal with her. 'I would never have said such a thing to *her*,' she fumed. 'How could she? She shouldn't even have thought it, let alone said it.' Maya for her part did not seek out her mistress and remained in the kitchen. And later in the

afternoon, from a window upstairs, Parvathi watched as she went
about her affairs under the tree. But in truth she missed Maya
sorely. And yet she was unwilling to forgive her unless she took
back her unkind words. If her mother was dead, she would have
felt it somehow. Of that she was sure.

Two days later, Kasu Marimuthu came home early from work. He
interrupted her English lesson and sent the teacher home. Then
he sat in front of her and told her that her father had sent him a
telegram. Her mother had passed away.

'Passed away?' Parvathi enquired politely.

Kasu Marimuthu nodded. 'Nearly a week ago.'

'Oh.'

There was a pause.

'Did my father say anything else?'

Kasu Marimuthu's eyes slid away from his wife's. 'He asked for
some money.'

Parvathi felt nothing. She brought the palms of her hands up to
her chest. 'Will you give it to him?' she whispered.

'Yes,' he said quietly. 'My lawyer has already drawn up a letter.
Your father will get a lump sum, a rather large one, and in exchange
he must never attempt to contact you again.'

'Oh.'

'If you want, we can go to the temple today and have the priest
do some prayers for your mother.'

She looked up into her husband's face. 'Did my father say what
sickness?'

This time Kasu Marimuthu did not flinch away but looked her
directly in the eye and very slowly and clearly said, 'She hanged
herself.'

Parvathi stood suddenly, and as she backed away from him,
whispered hoarsely, 'I'm all right. Really I am. I just need a bit of
time. If you don't mind.'

'Of course,' he said.

She turned and walked quickly out of the room. Her feet took
her to the front door. Funny, how she didn't remember the trip

to the door. She stood at the entrance steps for a minute. She must be alone. The sea. She would go to the sea. She ran towards the beach. She was already at the edge before she realised she was there. She was losing bits of time. How strange. She thought of the rocks, and found herself at the foot of them. By the time she climbed to the top her breath was coming in great gasps and her chest was tight and burning. She stared out into the horizon. Below, the sea roared and crashed.

She seized her head with both hands and tried to remember her mother. And to her great surprise found she could not. Instead, she could only see her father's face, scornful and displeased. She hit her forehead with the palm of her hand. Repeatedly. *Stupid. Stupid.*

Suddenly her skull yielded that beautiful woman. She came back to her, not blue, not purple, but unscathed and in no way diminished. All of her was still there. She remembered her, in the market tipping a bottle of honey upsidedown to check if it had been diluted. She had a way of turning the bottle so the honey journeyed down in swirls and rings, dripping only from the middle. But when the bottle was brought home Parvathi could only make the honey slide down the sides.

She must have done it on the centre beam of the house. But how could she? Parvathi thought of how Kamala had once said, 'Committing suicide is easy. It only takes a minute to decide. And afterwards, if it is a failure, you are sad and ashamed that at that moment you were so selfish you did not even think of your own children. But at that moment it is easy.'

Parvathi howled then.

Back in the house Kasu Marimuthu poured himself a large measure of whisky. She would come back when she was ready. She had asked for time. He would give her that.

The sun was almost disappearing behind the house, and her voice was lost with sobbing when Maya came and sat beside her. They sat staring out towards the restless sea as the moon rose over it.

'I've finished tracing the energy stream we were following,'

Maya said gently. 'It enters the river, crosses it, and travels towards the house. It encircles the house, to form something of a protective energy bubble before entering through the back door and exiting through the windows. Taking the path of least resistance, the streams then come to these rocks before going out to sea towards that island.' And she pointed towards an island in the distance.

This said, they sat together in perfect silence.

Hours later, Maya broke the silence to ask if she would like some food. Parvathi shook her head slowly. And a few hours later, Maya asked if she would like to go in. Once more she only shook her head. Eventually, Parvathi laid her exhausted head in Maya's lap and Maya covered her curled body with one end of her sari so she would fall asleep. But every time she nodded off she would jerk awake with a startled cry. Once she whispered, 'How long has she been hanging there?' And another time. 'For pity's sake untie that woman.' It was the early-morning hours when dreamless sleep finally came to claim her.

Waiting at the French windows with a glass of whisky in his hand, an inebriated Kasu Marimuthu stared with a mixture of disbelief and awe at the fantastic sight of the large dark shape of his cook coming up the slope, carrying his sleeping wife in her enormous arms as if she weighed no more than a garland of flowers.

Kasu Marimuthu allowed a week to pass before he called his wife to the library. When she came in he was behind his desk. He picked up a bunch of keys on a chain and held them out to her. She took them from him, but when she hesitated and did not seem to know exactly what she was to do with them, he came around and fixed them to her waist-belt, and in an ironic voice said, 'Now that you are officially the mistress of Adari, it is time you introduced yourself to the ladies of the Black Umbrella Club. Your predecessor found their pursuits too provincial, but I do believe you might find their friendship eminently suitable.'

The Black Umbrella Club

As it turned out, the Black Umbrella Club was not a club, merely the weekly gathering of the wives of seven men who had left Ceylon to fill the lower ranks in the departments of the British government of Malaya. The women took it in turns to host their assembly, held mid-afternoon when their chores were done and their men were still at work. Since they lived within walking distance of each other, each one would arrive depending on the weather, either under a black umbrella, or with it tucked into her armpit.

The housewives' agenda was, as Kasu Marimuthu's first wife had snootily dismissed, provincial to say the least. They met to talk about the meals they had cooked for their families, gossip about the doings of the rest of the Ceylonese community, discuss events being organised at the temple, and show off their handiwork – things they crocheted, sewed or knitted.

Nervously, Parvathi dressed for her first meeting. Had they come by the gossip of how she had become Kasu Marimuthu's wife? Would she be compared unfavourably to her sophisticated predecessor? Anxiously, she went into the kitchen where Maya, bless her, told her she looked beautiful, which helped a bit.

All the neighbours came out of their houses to admire the Rolls and stare at Parvathi. Self-consciously, she walked towards the wooden house standing on low concrete stilts. Her hostess, a plain, matronly woman, was waiting at the top of the stone stairs. With a sinking heart Parvathi noted that she was dressed in a well-starched cotton sari and a plain white blouse, with her oiled hair coiled at the nape of her neck. Parvathi guessed that inside the house there wouldn't be a jewelled belt or a gold hair ornament to share between all the other members.

'Come in, come in,' her smiling hostess welcomed.

Parvathi joined her slippers to the others and climbed the steps. A hush fell inside the front room of the house as the other cotton wearers turned their assessing eyes towards Kasu Marimuthu's new wife. They had not impressed the first one. She had been openly scornful of their sheltered lives and had queried in her proud, Westernised manner, 'Your *husbands* go to the market for you?' And indeed they must have seemed a mean lot to her, living in government quarters and counting every cent. The women had looked at her diamond earrings and consoled themselves by saying, 'What does she have to worry about? Her husband lends money to the royal family.'

All their money had to be carefully spirited away to pay for their children's education. They had been brought up to be great believers in education. As a race they reserved their greatest esteem for learned people, lumping all commercial enterprises under the vulgar charge of 'keeping shop' or 'doing business'. Unless, of course, the man in question touched the giddy heights that Kasu Marimuthu had. Him they called Kuberan, the man that God Vishnu himself had approached to finance his lavish marriage.

The women were introduced. The Ceylonese community was famous for its nicknames. No one seemed to escape it.

Manga Mami (Mango married lady) because an abundant mango tree grew in her backyard.

Kundi Mami (Buttocks married lady) because she had a very large rear that stuck out noticeably.

Negeri Sembilan Mami (Negeri Sembilan married lady) because she was the only one there from the state of Negeri Sembilan.

Padi Mami (Steps married lady) because hers was the only two-storey house in the area.

Dr Duraisami Penjathi (Dr Duraisami's wife) who was given the due respect of being a doctor's wife and although a Mami wasn't referred to as such.

Melahae Mami (Chilli married lady) who was so fierce and hot-tempered even her husband dared not open his mouth in his own house.

Velei Mami (Fair married lady) because she had the much-admired golden colouring of a young mango.

As their nicknames were made known to her, Parvathi earned hers: Rolls Royce Mami (married lady with the Rolls Royce).

Parvathi smiled and took the seat that had been left vacant for her. The women leaned forward, curious about the daughter of the man crafty enough to cheat such an incredibly important man as Kasu Marimuthu. Kundi Mami began the inquisition with the grave business of Parvathi's family background. What was her father's name? Who was her grandfather? She told them. No, they shook their oiled heads slowly in unison. No one knew of him. Which village was she from? Vathiry. Ah, that was the neighbouring one to Manga Mami. Everybody turned to look at her, but she shook her head regretfully. No, she had definitely never heard of Parvathi's family, but she knew a Tangavellupilai? Did Parvathi know of his family? It was Parvathi's turn to shake her head regretfully. She never left the house much. They nodded approvingly. Girls shouldn't run about like boys.

What about the name of her relatives in Malaya? Sokalingham? Which Sokalingham? Was it the one who worked in Public Works? No, not Public Works Sokalingham. Oh ... Sokalingham from Kuala Lipis. In that case they would not have heard of them either. None of the Mamis knew people from there. Even Negeri Sembilan Mami shook her head gravely. Never mind all that, what about her family? How many of them? Five brothers. Would they be coming to Malaya too? No? They should. This was the land of milk and honey. If they were doing nothing better than tilling the land, she should send for them. Surely Kasu Marimuthu would be able to place them somewhere in his empire? 'A tycoon' Padi Mami called him. 'I suppose my father and my husband will decide whether they come or not,' Parvathi said. The Mamis nodded sagely.

Kundi Mami's children returned from Tamil school and she sent them straight to the kitchen. Without moving from her chair or turning to look in their direction, she knew when they had chewed their last mouthful, and imperiously ordered them into their room to do their homework. Eventually, the Mamis' great curiosity ran out and they turned to their handiwork. Quiet pride came into their voices. This was their joy. This was what they did for pleasure alone. They showed her what they were making. Kundi Mami was knitting little flowers that she was going to join together to make into a poodle or a doll, she hadn't quite decided. Dr Duraisami Penjathi was embroidering a set of pillowcases, and both Velei Mami and Padi Mami had undertaken to produce tapestries of peacocks. They were almost finished and Parvathi was impressed with their efforts. Melahae Mami spread out her unfinished patchwork quilt blanket and Negeri Sembilan Mami showed the intricate pattern of beads she was sewing on her daughter's wedding sari.

'And what would you like to do?' They looked expectantly at her.

Parvathi hesitated. There was no doll, poodle, pillowcase or tapestry she could make that would be beautiful enough to display in Adari, and certainly none of her saris were fine enough to bother embellishing. But she had been to the tailor's room and there were many bolts of cloth and remnant pieces of cloth. She would make a blanket. A luxurious narrow blanket for her father, for the monsoon months, for when his pains and aches kept him awake.

While tea and cakes were served the sound of monotonous thudding began.

'What's that?' Parvathi asked.

'That's old Vellupilai pounding my spices and chillies. Why, who comes to work your pestle and mortar?'

'I don't know,' Parvathi confessed. The other women looked at each other. Despite their lack of education, their inability to speak the local language or earn money, they were forces to be reckoned with in their households. Not knowing absolutely everything that went on under their own roofs was incomprehensible to them.

'So,' Negeri Sembilan Mami asked, 'how many servants do you actually have?'

'I don't know,' Parvathi admitted.

Now the women were well and truly shocked. They did not have servants. Only Padi Mami, on account of her bad back, had a woman in from India to clean three times a week. She paid her ten dollars a month, but had nothing but horrible things to say about the woman. She was a drunk, she talked back, she was dirty, she smelled bad and ate too much.

'Never mind,' consoled Melahae Mami. 'You are still young and beautiful. You don't have to cook hot aubergine curries just so he will rush home to you.'

The other Mamis guffawed heartily.

As she was leaving they asked her if they could have cuttings from the pots of Japanese roses in her house. Parvathi was glad to oblige.

Then Padi Mami smiled at her and said, 'It's a very good thing your husband married you. His first wife was no good. Look what shame she brought him. But what can you expect from an *Indian* woman? They can be used only as servants.'

'Far easier to trust a cobra than an Indian,' said Melahae Mami.

'It is always a mistake to marry outside your own kind,' agreed Negeri Sembilan Mami quietly.

Parvathi said nothing, but when she reached home she headed immediately for the kitchen.

'How did it go?' Maya asked with a smile.

Parvathi touched Maya's arm and pulled it downwards. Maya sat on the floor and Parvathi lay down beside her with her head in the woman's lap.

'Maya,' she said looking up into the face hovering over hers, 'do you think Indians are very different from Ceylonese?'

'Ah,' Maya said slowly. 'People who keep prejudices in their hearts do not know that it does far more harm to them than to the people they express it to.'

'I don't want to go back there. The way they spoke of Indians made me angry. How can I keep going back to them if they speak like that about your people? I feel disloyal to you.'

'Don't grieve on my behalf. Their recent ancestry is from the land of Jaffna, but take it back far enough and they will turn into dreaded Indians right before their eyes. So you see, my people are their people.'

'Even if I go back, I will have to set them straight.'

'But why say anything at all? In arguing, you will lose not only their friendship but more importantly, your precious energy. And anyway, they have been incarnated into a certain race to experience all the lessons and opportunities that that race offers. So if they want to marry inside that race and have children of that race, who are you to tell them otherwise? Shall I accuse them of being racist because they don't want to leave their race for mine? Leave them be. Why ruin their illusions of superiority? By resorting to prejudice they reveal their lack of confidence in their own worth. Wish them well. It is not for you to judge. Don't do what they do. Don't look for differences. Look for the similarities.'

For a long while Parvathi remained silent and thinking. She did not cook for her husband, she had no children, and didn't think that she could get too excited about a bit of needlework. The Mamis were all older than her. They dressed differently. And it was certain they had never lain in the dark and wished for a man to be willing to die for them.

'There are no similarities,' she replied finally.

'There are,' Maya said firmly, 'You just haven't found them yet. Don't give up so quickly.'

'Maya,' Parvathi asked after awhile. 'Who pounds our spices and chillies for us?'

Maya looked surprised. 'Old Vellupilai,' she answered.

Parvathi laughed. 'Oh Maya,' she said and laughed again. She did have something in common with the other members of the Black Umbrella Club, after all. Maya was so right. Now that she had found the first similarity, suddenly, many rushed upon her, their shared accents, ancestry and femaleness. Weren't they full of hopes for the future, and didn't they desire happiness for themselves and their families?

'One thing though,' Parvathi said with a frown. 'All of them run their own households and I felt like a silly girl today for knowing so little about the running of mine. I don't even know how many staff we have.'

'That's easily remedied. We have twenty-two servants.' Slipping her hand into her blouse Maya fished out a purse from her chest and gave it to Parvathi. 'And if you like you can start learning about your household by going to the beach with Amin this evening to buy some fish.'

Parvathi opened the purse and looked at the foreign notes. 'Straits dollars,' she said, and giggled; she was going on her first ever shopping expedition. Maya smiled.

There were already people waiting on the beach. Women in drab clothes and old cloths loosely tied around their heads squatted in semi-circles and talked. Upon the sand beside them a baby or two lay asleep on a sarong. Old men kept brass boxes of betel leaves and black tobacco beside them while they played draughts. Children splashed at the water's edge. There was no notion of time as anything but the comings and goings of the tides. The crescent-moon-shaped boats got closer.

As the fishermen jumped into the water their families made for the shallow waves and peered excitedly into the boats at the catch; the old men, their shoulders covered with faded cloths, nodded with satisfaction. Then three generations heaved and pushed the boats ashore, using rollers and bamboo poles, while the women stood with their hands on their hips and waited at the water's edge. In the evening sun the straining, bunched calf muscles of the fishermen gleamed like polished wood. And as the waves withdrew, the boats, the men's legs and their colourful sarongs created a beautiful mirror effect on the water and wet sand.

Amin and Parvathi moved closer to one of the stranded boats. Inside were shimmering fish. Some were still. Others, braver and more resourceful, had made it to the bottom of the boat where some seawater had collected, and there they struggled and vainly beat their tails. But even they must have felt the sand beneath them, and one by one with small belly-flops, they too became still. Parvathi took a few steps back. Amin looked enquiringly at her and she signalled for him to carry on. Plunging his hand into the boat he began to choose the fish he wanted. He pointed to his selection, a pile of mackerel.

'How much?' he asked in Malay.

'Four cents,' the fisherman replied.

Amin pushed his watch with the thick silver strap that his employer had given him on his last birthday higher up his arm, and made a disbelieving face. 'Less, less,' he admonished.

'Three cents,' said the fisherman.

Amin made a convincingly incredulous face. 'Three cents! For these few?'

Parvathi had the impression Amin was showing off because she was there and that four cents was a very fair price indeed. The fisherman turned his leathery face as craggy as stormwaves to the new mistress of the great mansion on the beachfront. Their eyes met and held for a few seconds. His had endured much hardship; they were full of loneliness, patience, waiting. It was as if he had spent so many days and nights alone out at sea that he had become the sea. And now he, more than other men felt the salt in his sweat and the ebb and flow of blood in his wrists. He knew secrets. In his deep unfathomable eyes lay the knowledge that he was alive because the sea favoured him, but the day might come when it would reclaim him for its own. Then his wife and children would stand for hours at the water's edge scanning the horizon incessantly, uselessly.

He imagined her to have access to unimaginable amounts of money. But that served only to disadvantage him. He was poor and the poor must always defer to the rich. It was a privilege to sell to the rich to count them as your customers, even if they robbed you in the process. And yet he was not a trader, not in any way that counted. For he believed in *rezeki*, the will of God gives. That one should always work hard and be grateful for all God's mercies large or small. If God was willing only to part with two and half cents then so be it. He sighed his defeat.

'All right then. Two and a half cents,' he said.

Parvathi looked at the man's burned toes half-submerged in wet sand, the ripped long-sleeved top, and the cloth he knotted around his throat to protect his arms and the nape of his neck from the fierce midday sun and the cold night air. She looked at the triangular hat that had not stopped his face from turning deep bronze, and at that terrible poverty that she recognised in his opened palm. Without thinking she moved forward and thrust into his hand her five-dollar note. The fisherman began to shake his head, he had no change on him. But Parvathi shook her head and it suddenly dawned upon him. He was being *given* money.

The simple man opened his mouth to protest. It was far too much. He could not possibly accept. He held it out, but she smiled and, beckoning the gaping Amin, began to walk away. Amin was saying something in a whining voice but she did not listen. Her heart was full of joy. With her back to the house she had done something good.

The moment they returned Amin ran to tell Maya that they shouldn't let the mistress out on any more buying expeditions because she hadn't yet learned the value of the Straits currency. But Maya told him that she did not have the authority to stop the new mistress of Adari from doing anything she wanted to. However, she added, if he was in a position to do so, he should definitely curtail her. With a shrug of indifference Amin slipped out of the back door.

The New Mistress of Adari

Two days later, the men came running in to tell her they had found the skin of a large snake by the stairs to the tower; they thought it might be a king cobra. They advised her not to go to the site until they could trap and kill it. In the most imperious voice she could manage she forbade them to kill any snakes on her husband's land. Instead they should leave eggs and a bowl of milk for it.

'It could bite us,' they cried in unison.

Parvathi said she would feed the cobra herself. Every day, rain or shine.

'What if it comes to feed while you are up there? You will be trapped with no way out.'

'Snakes loathe climbing stairs,' Maya said with a smile.

Finally the tower was declared safe for the women to enter. However, the steps were without railings and so steep that it was vertiginous to look down. A third of the way up, Parvathi found herself down on her hands and feet, crawling slowly. At the low entrance they bent to enter. An oil lamp threw its sickly glow on the small chamber, empty but for a coffin-shaped granite box. It had no lid. Inside were traces of white grains.

A tense silence hung in the air and Parvathi rubbed her arms to dispel a strange sensation of being watched. If a god had once lived here, he could not have been the friendly sort.

'Where are the gods?' she whispered.

'This is not the temple,' Maya said, and they climbed the stairs to the top where there was a platform. 'This is the temple.'

'This?'

Maya nodded.

'What did they do here?'

'Here they met the gods that wander in the winds.'

'What was the little room in the middle for then?'

'There they prepared themselves to meet their gods. That was the room of secret rites where they fasted for weeks, and sometimes even tortured their bodies in the hope that their egos might become so fragile that they would shatter and their soul could shine forth ready to catch whatever energies or vibrations could be caught from the heavens.'

Over dinner, that night, Kasu Marimuthu said, 'So you've been to the site today? What did you think?'

'Why do you call it a site? It's a temple complex.'

'There is nothing in it to suggest it was that. With it being so close to the sea it could have been an observation tower, an early warning system of sea attacks.'

'An observation tower? But what about the room in the middle?'

'Probably a storage room of some kind. Possibly even the lodgings of the poor bugger who manned the tower.'

'How strange that you should say that. Just thinking of that room makes my skin crawl.'

'Why? It's an empty room.'

'It was not always empty. Maya says nothing is ever lost, even walls will retain every thought and deed that occurs inside them. Layer by layer, all is recorded. And the walls there are shocked.'

Kasu Marimuthu stared with astonishment at his wife. 'What do *you* think happened in there?'

'I don't know. Maya says people were tortured in there.' She paused. 'Repeatedly.'

He gave her an odd look. 'I hope you won't go around saying such things to anyone else, or they'll think I'm married to a madwoman.'

She shook her head hastily, and he changed the subject. 'They must have been exceptional stonecutters though, amazingly precise. I've never seen anything like it.'

'Maya says those are not stones. They were poured into shape,'

'Sometimes I wonder at you,' Kasu Marimuthu snorted in exasperation. 'At how you take everything that uneducated woman says as gospel truth. Concrete, my dear wife, was not discovered until recently. So it was not "poured" it was cut by very skilled stonemasons. Besides, concrete is not supposed to be able to last hundreds, let alone thousands, of years.'

Parvathi remained silent, but she remembered Ponambalam Mama telling her that aircrafts already existed thousands of years ago, which could only mean that man had forgotten that once he knew how to fly. Man must have also forgotten that he already knew how to make stone that could last and last.

They finished the rest of the meal in silence.

When Parvathi went to the temple the next day, the bowl was empty; the egg eaten whole, so neatly there were no broken shells. Up on the platform she could see the crowns of many trees, and it was then that she noticed the family of Siamangs. The parents, a teenager, and a baby clinging onto its mother.

They had stopped doing whatever they usually did and were all lying on their backs or fronts on the branches watching her. Even the baby had popped its woolly little face with its big shining eyes out of its mother's fur for a quick peek at Parvathi before vanishing into it again. She waved at them but they did not respond. Then the male suddenly blew up his throat pouch to almost the same size as his head and emitted a high-pitched scream, which then became a thunderous display of his powerful vocal cords which then became a melodious duet. Sometimes the teenager, who did not sit still but like a trapeze artist swung about from branch to branch on his long agile arms, joined in the performance. Parvathi, believing it was for her benefit, felt pleased.

As soon as the English teacher left the next day, Parvathi set off for the jungle with a comb of ripe bananas for the Siamangs. She stopped to watch a flying lemur sail gracefully from one tree branch to another, and quite suddenly became aware of a dark flash from the corner of her eye. Her head whipped around and she saw a huge male monkey bounding towards her. The bananas. She should have thrown them to the ground and run, but she was too shocked by its open mouth, and its long canine teeth; two if not three inches long. Already he was so close. Unbelievable! There it was danger, rushing, flying towards her, and she watched as if it was happening at the end of a long tunnel. She understood that everything was happening at incredible speed and yet it seemed to her in slow motion. The slowness meant she saw and heard it all in stunning detail: the way the animal's fur lifted off his body and flew up into the air when his legs left the ground, and settled down while he was still airborne, only to rise up again with his next leap. The deafening thud of his progress and his scream, so savage, so full of threat. *Withdraw. Leave. Give.*

Then, something unexpected – a ball of guava leaves, a tailor ants' nest, whizzed towards the ape and hit him square in the face. The ants vented their fury at their destroyed home immediately. The brute screamed with pain and rage and ran howling back in the direction he had come from. Parvathi turned her frozen face towards the guava tree and Kupu nodded respectfully to her.

'Ama,' he said, coming to stand in front of her. 'It's not safe to walk around with food in your hands.'

She nodded and then her knees gave way and she slid to the ground into a sitting position. He crouched next to her. She looked from his dripping wet clothes up to his face. 'You're wet,' she observed in a wobbly voice.

He jerked his head at the guava tree where he had dropped his gunnysack on the ground. 'I've been gathering seaweed from around the island for Maya.'

'Oh,' she said. Now she understood. He had come out of the sea, and with lightning quick reflexes plucked an ants' nest from the guava tree and flung it at the charging beast. She was not surprised; she had seen him catch a flying lizard in his hands. She looked down at her own hands. They were grasping the bananas tightly. If the monkey had got to her . . . She opened her fingers and the fruit fell into her lap.

'Where were you going with the bananas?'

'I wanted to feed the Siamangs.'

'They are not hungry,' he said slowly. 'There is enough food in the forest.'

'I thought I could make friends with them.'

A thought, intelligent and highly skilled, flashed across his eyes. There was more to him, much more. The dullness was a pretence, a cover. 'There is a better way,' he said, and with his teeth held together and his tongue pushed up to one side of his cheek he made a grunting nose that he ended on a whine. 'Try it.'

She did.

'Lower,' he said.

She tried again.

'Better,' he said, 'but make the end sound last a bit longer.'

She gave it her best shot.

'Perfect.'

'Will it work if I use it on other animals?'

A ghost of a smile came to his lips, making him look childlike. 'Not all, but it'll work for the Siamang.'

'Where do the Siamangs nest?'

'They build no nests. In the daytime they roam their territory looking for food, and at night they go to sleep in the forks of tree branches sitting upright, their heads between their knees.'

'Thank you,' she said, 'for saving me.'

'Shall I take you back to the house?'

'No,' she replied. 'I'm going into the forest.'

'Would you like me to come with you?'

'No.' Maya had said going into the forest was no more dangerous than crossing the road. As long as she thought like it, became it, it would always welcome her into its fold and care for her the way it cared for all the animals that lived in it. 'I'm all right now,' she said to Kupu. 'You go ahead.'

She watched him gather up the seaweed that had spilled to the ground. Still dripping seawater like the semi-amphibious being she believed him to be, he went towards the generator room.

She stayed where she was for a time. Then, taking a deep breath, she pushed herself off the ground and went towards the jungle. At its mouth she turned back to look towards the generator room and saw Kupu already in dry clothes, leaning against it, watching her. She waved and he waved back; with a silent prayer, she stepped into the forest. She did not see him slip into the jungle behind her or realise that never once was she out of his sight.

From the top of the tower she could see the Siamang family sprawled lazily in the shady branches. She named them, the father she called Humpty, the mother, Mary; the intrepid youngster had to be Jack, and the little one was obviously a Jill. That day, she had her first encounter with Jack. She made her clicking whining sound and after a few minutes he swung off a branch and dropped onto the platform. Standing on two legs, he scrutinised her warily. On the tree branches, both parents tore off their lethargy and turned resolute attention to the manoeuvrings and goings-on on the roof tower between their offspring and the human.

Parvathi stayed very still as he walked towards her, his long hands held high above his head to balance himself. Three feet away he stopped and dropped to his haunches. His father munched pensively on a leaf stalk, but his mother gave a coughing bark – a nervous warning. Ignoring her, the reckless adolescent pursed his lips and sat down. His reddish-brown eyes fixed on her, innocent, vulnerable, intelligent. But abruptly, he broke eye-contact, looked up and caught something small, an insect, which he ate.

Hoping to re-engage his attention, Parvathi made the sound again, and froze. She had the attention of the Siamang, but something else had caught hers. She rose and went to one side of the platform where creepers hung from a tree like a thick wall. Nervously, she parted the green curtain, and found Kupu, his dirty brown hair well camouflaged amongst bark and leaves.

'What are you doing here?' she demanded.

'You were making the sound incorrectly,' he said sheepishly.

'Did you follow me here?'

'Yes.'

'I thought you said I was safe with the jungle.'

He smiled lopsidedly. 'I wasn't so sure the jungle was safe with you.'

Parvathi had to bite her lips not to laugh out loud, but in truth she didn't like the thought of being spied upon. So she said very sternly, 'I do not need to be watched like a child. However, since you are here you might as well get out of that tree and come and sit with me.'

He landed on the platform in a single leap. His skin smelled of the sea. She looked away. 'Tell me about the battle with the tiger.'

His hand went up to touch the scar. 'It was no battle. I was working in a circus as an errand boy, and feeding the animals was one of my duties. One day during feeding time, which is when the tigers are at their most ferocious and unpredictable, one of the cages that had not been properly locked, suddenly swung open. One moment I was standing there with a bucket of raw meat and next, the tiger's claws were in my cheek and his jaw a clamp around my neck. But there was no pain. For those few seconds nothing existed but his glowing yellow eyes, fiery breath, and the deep, low growling that seemed to come from the very depths of him. It was as if he had done magic on me, paralysed me. Then the trainer was there cracking his whip and he leaped off.'

'Did they put the tiger down?'

He turned to look at her wryly. 'In India even the small animals are more precious than the workers. They told me to leave. I was too careless.'

'What happened to you?'

'Oh, then came the burning pain, and many days of fever. Again and again, dreaming of that tiger. I dreamed it suffocated me to death, but I was not afraid. Sometimes I would talk to it. I told it, "Hurry up Akbar, this pain is insufferable."'

The sound of men approaching floated up, and as if startled out of a dream Kupu sprang up and slipped behind the curtain. The suddenness of the movement caused Jack to cartwheel backwards, leap into the air and, hooking his hand around a branch that must have been more than twenty feet away, engage in the most clownish of hyperactive acrobatics. Parvathi heard a movement in the adjacent tree and knew Kupu was gone. Going to the edge of the roof she looked down. The men had brought a tall cage with a round hole at the top so only the snake could get inside to eat the eggs.

As time passed, Parvathi came upon garlands of flowers, camphor and incense. No one ever saw the big snake, but perhaps someone had made a wish that had come true, for the men had begun to call it the wish-fulfilling tree. Then when it was no longer enough to simply feed their god, they built him a shelter. A simple wooden structure with a concrete base and a low altar, but what else did those poor people know. She found their belief touching, their shelter, a sun-dappled square of peace and quiet. Every garden, she thought, should have such a sanctuary, a mellow place of worship.

But her husband shook his rich, educated head. Still, what did he know of real, unquestioning faith? Nothing. He thought it should be obvious to anyone with half a brain that the Siamangs were simply putting their long hands to good use, and helping themselves to the eggs. Otherwise there should be some pieces of broken shell left behind.

The local women did not know better. What fortunate people. They came to clean the lean-to, bringing their bells, their cloths, their oil lamps, their clackers, their garlands of mango leaves and eventually their ecstasy, and the place became a holy shrine. All hours they went to pour oil into the solitary hanging lamp and so intimately intertwined their lives with the shrine. Simple peasant women are special people. Their tales are not idle. In no time the intensity of their prayers turned it into a place of pilgrimage. If she were a god, she too would come to wait in that little haven of devotion.

It was there that Parvathi met the gardener and asked him for a small vegetable plot. He allocated a corner plot lying fallow and she began growing long beans, tomatoes and chillies. As she worked the soil with her hoe she imagined harvesting the long beans while they were still unripe and tender. Her back was sore but even at sundown when her husband arrived she was still working. He got out of his car and came towards her. She straightened and waited for him with a hand pressed into the small of her back.

'Come and see how much I've done all by myself,' she cried out joyfully to him, when he was close enough to hear her.

'You've grown even darker,' he said grimly.

And suddenly she felt the mess that her hair was, the sweat that made her clothes stick to her back, and the streaks of dried mud on her face. Taking her unresisting wrist in his hand he looked at the blackened nails and brown calluses – they had been pulling up roots. He raised his eyes to hers.

'You are the mistress of Adari. Why do you want to look like a servant?'

He dropped her hand and she used it to scratch a mosquito bite. They stared at each other in the gathering dusk, strangers. In the distance Kupu was standing by the generator room, one leg twisted around the other, watching them. She dropped her head in shame. She'd not work the land again. She knew Kasu Marimuthu was waiting for her to speak, but she remained mute. If only she could say she didn't want to be always perfumed, colourful and studded with hard gems, but she knew she mustn't. She must wait. This was still the sober capitalist who addressed her, and she almost never had the right thing to say to him.

In a little while, dark would descend and the hard-headed businessman would go away and strong drinks would bring forth the poet who would go out to the hawkers in town and return with packages of food carefully chosen to contain no meat. And they would sit listening to concerts on the wireless.

When the moon was full, they ate in the garden. She would carefully fill the beautiful seventeenth-century Ming vase with water and he would drop into it a handful of orchids that he had cut himself. He refused to arrange them, preferring instead to haphazardly throw all the different types and colours together. Years later, when she recalled him, she remembered the moonlit orchids dazzling in the blue and white vase, and his slurred voice reciting poetry. Great Indian works and sometimes Blake. Rolling out of him from some unknown depth to surprise her. How strange that this immensely practical man should by night turn into a such deep and eloquent lover of beauty.

The undrinkable brew – for she had tried the whisky – must be a secret door to another world, one infinitely more beautiful than the one he lived in during the day. Every night he opened it and they walked through the darkness to a storehouse of grandeur. Once there he carelessly used and discarded the gifts he found. She ran behind him to pick up the priceless items as they dropped from him. She knew that when dawn came, that world would disappear into thin air. And then it became once more a parade of blame, cold regard, and the deliberate negation of her very existence. That only while they stopped there it pressed upon him, his wishing her better.

Then they would go indoors into the dim library and amongst his countless books he attempted to educate her; poetry, art, literature, music . . . He flicked the gramophone switch.

'This is Wagner,' he said, slumping untidily into a chair, a glass held loosely between his knees, as rich, primal music filled the spaces between them. 'See the way he refuses to find resolution to these chords?'

Although she closed her eyes and listened very carefully, she never could hear what she was meant to, what was daylight to him.

'Do you hear it?'

She opened her eyes and looked into his waiting, watching eyes. She did not want to disappoint him, really she did not. But. 'No,' she confessed sadly. She was tone deaf. She could not even differentiate between the flutes and violins.

To his credit he showed neither disillusionment nor displeasure. He nodded thoughtfully and stood up to select another record. 'This is Verdi. Listen to the change in colour.'

Colour! She let the soft luxurious sounds swirl around her.

'Hear the difference now.'

She bent her head in concentration.

'Now,' he said, 'that!' That? 'That, that lower sound. There it is again.' Where? 'And again.'

But slowly, night-by-night with the grandfather clock ticking loudly in the background, she thought she began to hear sounds so rich they had to be finished by another lower sound. They left

Offenbach behind, and he put Mozart on. Clean, unsentimental, accomplished notes sprang from the machine. She looked up at him.

'Do you hear the rich chords now?'

Chords? That day she thought she could endure it no more. She must stop the humiliation. 'Yes,' she said.

He fixed her with his eyes and smiled a slow, tired smile. 'There are none. Mozart was too good to resort to such excesses. Good night, Sita.' He stood but not to put on another record. To leave. And not come back. So she would understand that she had not disappointed him until that moment; that he had relished her honesty. Gods and men shouldn't meet each other. Both will feel the same dismay.

If she had no ardour for the sublime, so be it; he would punish her with the prosaic. He would teach her to hostess. Just as well. She had feared the advent of the lawn parties and the glamorous dinners when Kamala and the girls would have to take down the silver gilt dinner service so all the great and good of the state could eat off it.

In exchange for an obscene amount of money, Kasu Marimuthu hired Madame Regine to bring his wife up to high shine. Parvathi waited for her in the piano room. She had a 'past', you could tell from one glance. A woman of indeterminate age, dressed entirely in black, stepped in and glanced wearily at the expensive décor. But when her eyes fell upon the nervously fidgeting girl she had come to tutor, she stood for a moment expressionlessly studying her. Then she stepped forward and with an amused gleam in her eyes said in the deep, heavily accented, smoker's voice, 'It is always a pleasant surprise when a husband underestimates his wife's charms rather than the other way around. It makes my life that much easier.'

After this rare moment of approval Madame Regine proved a very difficult customer to please. She did not appreciate spicy food, complained about the suffocating weather, griped about the depraved locals who, she complained, 'gawked incessantly' at her, and her pet hate, the untrained servants in Adari. In an effort to impress the formidable lady, Kasu Marimuthu opened a bottle of Château Lafite Rothschild 1904 at dinnertime. He toasted her time in Malaya and they all sipped at the best of Kasu Marimuthu's cellar.

'Mmmm,' savoured Kasu Marimuthu.

'Vinegar,' rasped Madame Regime. 'Must be this unbearable heat.' Then, turning towards a hovering servant, ordered without the least charm or polish, 'Soda water.'

But during the day she took Parvathi into a different world, a world of perfect taste. One far and away more dangerous than the jungle, full of booby traps and concealed pits for the unwary – for those who did not belong. Here the society was exclusive and exacting. Besides the soup bowls, the finger bowls, and complex rules about cutlery, there were unexpected things like not cutting bread with a knife but breaking it off, a tiny piece at a time, and these crumbs had to be passed between the lips with the fingers. This was followed by all the grim niceties of fine dining, the goblet for red wine, the flute for champagne, the large balloon glass for brandy, the tall glass for gin and tonic, the short straight glass for whisky, small glass for sherry. Sour sorbets for between courses and the sweet ones for afters. Pets, social kissing, napkins – nothing, it seemed, was too trivial not to matter.

Delicately sponging her forehead with iced vinegar, Madame Regine turned to deportment. Parvathi learned that just turning her elbows by the slightest fraction in towards her body could tremendously improve her silhouette. With books balanced on her head they negotiated what seemed to Parvathi to be hundreds of unimportant details in a woman's appearance or behaviour, but that assumed monumental proportions if effected incorrectly. Apparently a cultured woman's goal was to immediately turn every word, action and object into an ornament. And so Madame Regine taught refinement as a jaded sophistication of a time gone by.

Until, that is, the day she looked slyly at her pupil and said, 'Maybe now you learn . . . how do you say it, "to flirt" a little.' This, by the woman who had never sat long enough in the sun to know about voluptuousness. She did not know that voluptuousness comes slowly through the generations on the mother's side. It rises into cinnamon bodies from the friction of sand between the toes, the sound of faraway drums in the wind, salt crystals on bare skin.

'Blink slowly. Expose your wrists. And,' said the spinster to the island girl, 'when you are with that one you adore, you must immediately forget everything I have taught.' And quite without warning, eating with one's fingers was no longer unhygienic or disgusting, but entirely desirable. 'On the tips of your fingers bring the food directly to your mouth. Hold it to your lips, like so. Wait a moment. Look into his eyes as your lips caress not only the food but also your fingers.'

Parvathi thought it best not to inform Madame that there was no occasion to put such advice to use, for her husband hardly looked directly at her, preferring instead to address the space six inches to the left of her face.

But Madame Regine then surprised her by winking and saying merrily, 'Use it for when you decide to take a lover.'

The Red Lotus

Parvathi remembered that the Mamis were admiring embroidered pillowcases one afternoon when Padi Mami mentioned the Indian gypsy dancer, recently arrived from the temple of Pandharpur, in the state of Maharashtra. Apparently her beauty was such that even a trip to the well would be cause for another youth to fall irrecoverably in love with her, but renouncing all, she had devoted her life to dancing for Lord Krishna.

'They are all red lotuses, these temple dancers,' Kundi Mami said firmly, but on the way home Parvathi decided that she wanted to see the dancer perform. It might be her only chance to see a truly beautiful woman.

'Maya, what does it mean when someone is referred to as a red lotus?' she asked, as they sat tying rose garlands.

Maya did not look up. 'She's a hussy,' she said briefly.

'Oh!' Parvathi exclaimed.

'How's your Siamang family doing?' Maya asked, for she disliked the scent of gossip.

'There is something wrong with Jill. I think her right leg has become infected from a cut. She is so weak she just about manages to cling to her mother's fur. Her mother often peers closely at that leg, always careful not to touch the raw wound, but it must be getting worse because yesterday she dribbled saliva onto it and rubbed it with her index finger. I really hope that Jill doesn't die. If only I could do something.'

'I'll give you some medicine. Take it with you and call gently to the mother. If she is desperate enough she will come.'

Over dinner Parvathi said, 'There is a famous gypsy dancer who has come from India. Padi Mami and her husband have been to her performance and they say that she is very good. Shall we go too?'

'Why not?' her husband said. 'Find out when the next performance is.'

For the occasion fruiting banana trees had been cut and tied to either side of the temple entrance. The Chairman of the temple committee came out to the street to greet and garland them while the priest hovered at the entrance, and Parvathi remembered Melahae Mami saying, 'I remember in the good old days in Ceylon when the priests used to go up to ordinary people and say, "Come in, come in. Sit down and eat." Nowadays they only care about people with money. Only to them are they kind.'

Inside the temple special lamps had been lit. At the end of the temple a blue statue of Lord Krishna holding a flute to his mouth had been erected and richly decorated. A large crowd segregated by sex was already seated on the floor. A place had been reserved for Parvathi in the front of the women's section. Looking around she saw that none of the other Black Umbrella Club members were present.

She came in then, this temptress, with painted eyes and reddened mouth, and a hush fell upon the crowd. Without acknowledging her audience she went directly to the statue and threw herself at its feet. Moments later she came up upon her hands, her back arched dramatically. With a fluid, undulating movement, she rose. Striking her feet on the floor she began to dance, her eyes darting from side to side, her lips smiling and chanting her Lord's name incessantly, as if in an ecstasy of devotion.

Red lotus! There was nothing more pious or God-fearing than this woman's dancing. Her anklets did not just chime, they laughed, they cried, they spoke. With her hands she made the gesture to depict the great feet of Krishna. For she was Ratha anxiously preparing for Krishna's arrival. Her costume rustled and whispered. Though unsure if he was coming she applied *kajal* to her eyes, rubbed sandalwood paste on her breasts, and put flowers in her hair. Suddenly, she stopped her ministrations and her hennaed feet began to run in circles – distress. Worrying about what kept her lover away. Even in the painfully bright lights of the temple, Parvathi accepted her distress. And when she turned her face towards the breath of the Yamuna River and began to mime the silvery movements of tears, Parvathi felt the back of her own eyes begin to burn.

The dancer's eyes grew enormous, the cymbals crashed, her eyebrows rose – surprise. Her devotion had been rewarded; a spell had been cast, and now she could see her beloved everywhere – in the walls, in the flame of the lamp, in the sky, the trees outside, the chair, the bed. Everywhere. He fell on her like rain. She lifted her hands to catch him, pure joy flitting across her face, and began to dance rapturously. Her dance drove her mad and she experienced God's touch. Light, bliss, grace, all came to her simultaneously. Finally, she came to a standstill in front of the statue, panting, utterly spent. She did not look to the crowd for adulation, but ran behind a wall and disappeared.

Behind Parvathi someone said, 'Only a gypsy could dance like that.'

To which her companion sniffed and answered, 'Only a gypsy would wish to dance like that. It shouldn't be allowed in a temple. God lives here.'

But Parvathi sat frozen with admiration. Never had she seen anyone dance, let alone so beautifully, and with such energy. This woman actually loved with complete abandon. This was the kind of love Parvathi had dreamed of all her life. If only she could love in that way. People were stirring, getting up to go, but Parvathi, heavy with unfulfilled dreams, remained seated.

Her husband came and said, 'Shall we go?'

She rose and followed him out. They did not speak in the car and when they arrived in the porch, she said, 'You go ahead. I'm not tired. I'll come in a bit.' He must have looked at her curiously but she had already opened her door and stepped out into the cool night air. The ropes of the swing crushed her sari. She pushed herself off the ground and keeping her legs straight out in front of her, let her head hang back. Between the leaves of the tree the moon and the stars shone brightly.

That morning, Mary had come onto the flat roof. At first she stood where she landed, eyeing Parvathi warily. But Parvathi spoke to her gently and she had approached cautiously. Sitting down, she pulled her sick baby away from her shaggy body and held the soft ball of dark fur out to Parvathi. It weighed no more than a potato. Tenderly, with her mother watching, Parvathi bathed the wound in Maya's liquid. It whimpered once and then lay passively. The poor thing was so weak it was more dead than alive. She bandaged Jill and gave the baby back to her mother, who carefully stuck the black ball of fur back on her body and swung off the roof.

The stars and wind rushed at Parvathi. If she could only keep her back against this house long enough, she would find forever in a moment. The curving night sky became her whole world. She lost track of time and was startled by the crackling of something underfoot. She turned her head sideways. Her neck hurt. She had not realised how stiff it had become.

'Come in now. It's late,' her husband said.

She let her feet touch the ground, dragged them.

'Maya is cooking sand crabs for you tomorrow,' she said.

'That will be nice.'

The swing came to a halt.

'Do you know the name of the dancer?'

'No, but I can ask the priest if you want to know,' he offered, kindly, as if he pitied her.

'No, no, it doesn't matter. It was only a passing thought.'

'I'll see you upstairs then,' he said, and turned his back to her.

Sitting in bed she opened her favourite book, *Beauty and the Beast*. Beauty too had sacrificed herself for her father. In the illustration Beauty had a little heart-shaped face very much like hers, but she had brown hair and enormous emerald eyes, while Beast was depicted with paw-like hands and a leonine face, but not entirely ugly. There were no pictures of the beautiful palace where Beast lived, but Parvathi envisaged it looking something like Adari. She imagined him saying, 'I've been waiting all my life for you. I built this jewelled palace for you. All I want to do is please you.' If she closed her eyes she could hear the corridors whispering what he could not say; 'Be mine. Set me free.' And she heard herself saying, 'I love you. I am yours.'

It was time for Madame Regine to leave. She behaved splendidly, but her delight to be gone from the heat, the badly trained servants and the lack of civilised conversation was beyond concealing.

Parvathi still could not remember whether one spoke to one's neighbour on one's right during soup, fish and entrée, and the person seated on one's left during roast, sweet and savoury, or the other way around. Nevertheless, Madame informed Kasu Marimuthu that his wife was ready to charm and be charmed by the most sophisticated of societies. He in turn informed his wife that he was planning to throw a lawn party, a very English affair.

Parvathi sat on her bed alone that night looking into the dictionary and found her new word for that day: Anglophile [*ang-gl*Ofil]: *n* and *adj* (person) well disposed to England and everything English.

The Anglophile

Parvathi awaited her first party with nervous anticipation, for she believed herself unprepared. In fact, she felt certain she was going to commit some grave faux pas. Still, she had her strategy – she'd not eat, drink or do anything until she had seen someone else do it first. After that she'd simply copy the action in its entirety.

Her strategy hit its first snag when Kasu Marimuthu came to an abrupt stop at her door and barked, 'Is *that* what you are planning to wear?'

She had no glittery merchandise for her shop window.

'Show me all your clothes,' he ordered, moving briskly into the room.

She opened the cupboard and stood aside as he surveyed the cheap saris her father had bought for her wedding trousseau. Incredulous, he turned around to consider the woman he had married. 'Is that all?'

She nodded and remembered Madame Regine saying, 'I will not help with your costumes as I know nothing about them.'

'What a funny little thing you are,' he muttered, turning back to confront the dowdy contents of his wife's cupboard, brown, bottle-green, grey and dirty yellow saris. And it shocked him too to think that he had paid so little attention to her that he had not noticed her cheap, ugly clothing. 'Well, it's too late to do anything about it now,' he began, and then stopped.

'Or maybe not—' Snatching up her wedding sari blouse, and making a sign over his shoulder that she should follow him, he left on such big strides that she had to run to keep up. They crossed the courtyard, and made for a room she had not yet entered. When she had first explored the house it had been locked, and since then she had become more interested in the goings-on in the jungle. He stopped outside the door and impatiently signalled for the bunch of keys that hung from her belt. Hurriedly she pushed it into his waiting hand and he opened the door to his first wife's bedroom.

Parvathi looked around the soft green room. A day bed stood on an emerald silk carpet. Above it hung an exquisite painting of a white hummingbird rising into the air from an orange tree. And how strange, but this famously sophisticated woman who used to shop in Bond Street had a doll collection that entirely filled one wall of the room. Parvathi thought she could never have slept watched by the blank eyes of hundreds of Victorian dolls in full costume, some quite big, sitting in rows on shelves. On another wall hung her trademark, the satin wolf mask. Kasu Marimuthu threw open the doors of a mirrored cupboard.

'She had a wonderful figure so her blouses will not fit you,' he said, unconscious or careless of any hurt he might be inflicting, 'but let's see if we can find a sari to match your blouse.' He pulled out a green sari, embellished with fine threadwork and obviously very expensive. 'This,' he said, and held it under her chin.

'But they don't match,' she said.

He smiled sardonically. 'To have style, my dear, you have to know the rules, and then be prepared to break some.'

She stared at his face, perplexed. He wanted her to break rules? How could she? She had been brought up to conform – to listen and at all times do what she was told. One thing was sure – none of the other Mamis' husbands were telling them to break rules.

But Kasu Marimuthu was not finished. In the library, he opened a wall safe hidden behind a picture, and rifled quickly through its treasures. 'Aha,' he said, when he found the velvet box. 'Open it,' he commanded, handing it to her. A bespoke ruby necklace with a matching belt lay inside. While he fastened the starburst necklace he told her to instruct the tailor to alter all her predecessor's sari blouses to fit her.

'Well, what are you waiting for?' he asked impatiently as soon as the clasp clicked into place.

Parvathi raced up to her room and looked at herself in the mirror in amazement. Her husband was right. Apparently green and orange did go well together when Kasu Marimuthu decided they should. So well that an Englishwoman came up to her to comment on the combination. 'I never would have thought, Mrs Marrymuthu,' she gushed, 'but how lovely, mint and orange.'

'Thank you,' Parvathi said, looking down at her sari. So: this was not just any old green, but mint.

After that first time, all the parties blended into each other: guests gathering around a stage where a live band played, and on the breeze the smell of a pig hunted down in the rubber estates using spears, dogs and pit traps turning from red to brown on a spit. This was a favourite of the Chinese businessmen.

They were an enigma to her, those badly dressed men who responded to all queries about their business with dour, downturned mouths and a universal claim that, business was '*bo ho*', no good, or if they spoke English, with the words, 'just surviving'. And yet her husband told her that they were immensely powerful and some of Malaya's richest. He also said that, to these men, the subject of death must never be brought up; even the word made them nervous. 'It is a race thing,' he said. 'To be born Chinese is to be inherently terrified of death.' They wanted no part of it.

But it was the women they brought with them that intrigued Parvathi. Always it was a third or fourth wife, or sometimes a concubine claiming the status of fifth wife. With the narrow flat bodies of adolescent boys, all their sex was in their faces (which were often very beautiful), their blue-black shining hair, and their smooth, shapely legs. But around them Parvathi found an invisible, impenetrable wall.

The Malays she liked. A charming race who always came with a small gift that literally translated as 'a gift of the hand'. The men were exceedingly polite and their women graceful and voluptuous. There were not many of them at Kasu Marimuthu's parties, for they were not natural businessmen.

Then there were the white people, mostly British, tall men and women who smiled kindly down at her, the little woman struggling with their language. The first thing they inevitably did was find another Imperialist face to whinge about how much they missed the meat pies from their butcher back home, proper fish and chips, Sunday roasts, reading the broadsheets, etc, etc. There they were in Kasu Marimuthu's beautiful grounds, enjoying his lavish hospitality and asserting their cultural superiority. Once Ponambalam Mama accused her of naming the Siamangs with European names because she thought the white race was better than her own.

'Aren't they?' she had replied.

'Can't you see they are convinced of their superiority only because you are?' he countered in frustration. 'Do you know that when the white man first came to India, he mixed only with royalty and therefore convinced of their superiority he went native, copying their language, customs, habits, and even marrying their princesses. So you see, our value and riches we hold in our own hands.'

Parvathi shook her head in disagreement. 'You're not actually going to deny that we are woefully backward compared to them. We don't think like them or invent like them. Do you know that everything in this house was designed by them?'

Ponambalam Mama sighed and said something about the cycles of human evolution, about the Egyptian civilisation that had built things that could not be replicated even today by the most advanced white man.

And though she had stayed silent after that, Parvathi retained the opinion that the whites were, in fact, different. Even their children were not submissive like Asian ones. Disobedient, bold, and full of curiosity and always asking, 'Why?'

As if aware of Parvathi's growing inferiority complex, once while they were watching a crow search the ground for worms, Maya said, 'When you sit quietly and listen to their chatter, do not forget that in other lives you have already been white. And when you were that colour you too spoke as if that alone made you superior to your fellow men of different colours. Do you know, that crow sees black as white and white as black? So to it they are all black and you are white. Your reality is an illusion of your perception.'

The crow cawed harshly and Maya added. 'On the day you hear that as a song, you will know that you have found that your reality is not solid. If you change your perception, you will change your reality.'

Unconvinced, Parvathi did not try to change her perception, but continued to secretly eavesdrop on the white women's gossip. They hardly noticed her, partly because she remained so still, and partly because their smugness prevented them from ever suspecting that her vocabulary had long since surpassed theirs. From them she learned that Kasu Marimuthu was 'nouveau riche', Adari was 'Versailles meets Hollywood' and she was the 'botched replacement'. But she bore them no ill-will. If anything, she was utterly fascinated by them.

She could have listened to them for hours talking about their children, shopping at NAAFI, the unbearable heat, their thieving servants, the absence of a good school system, reminiscences about their country cottages, their rose gardens in spring, and gossip about people they knew. They seemed to reserve their most catty remarks for India Jane Harrington, the Headmaster's wife. Often she was criticised for letting the side down, while the other women moved closer and shook their heads disapprovingly.

'Honestly,' said Mrs Adams, 'the woman's quite enough to make one ashamed of one's own race. She's now gone from fast to dark.'

Parvathi began to watch Mrs Harrington covertly. She had a different accent that favoured the longer 'a'. She also chain-smoked and drank like a fish, but with her glinting green eyes, scarlet lips and a slinky, pantherine body she looked every inch the glamorous film star. Her star was not even dimmed by an insipid querulous daughter called Kakoo, whom Parvathi once overheard asking her mother, 'Is that his pet?' of a fly buzzing around a waiter's head. At which point her mother, and not without irritation, said, 'Must you always be so silly?'

Anyway, it was soon apparent that it was not the women who spurned her company but she who maintained the cool distance while openly seeking the company of their husbands. But there was neither 'fast' nor 'dark' behaviour present. True, she danced with many men, but so did the others, and in exactly the same way as she did. The men placed their hands on her back, but never raised them beyond the point where cloth gave way to flesh. Sometimes their fingers were almost flush with the material, but never, ever over. Propriety was faultlessly observed. Parvathi concluded that the women were just jealous.

Then one day she was standing at the French windows in the music room for a moment on her own when she heard in the corridor the voices of Mrs Harrington and Major Anthony Fitzgerald. It was a split-second decision to sidle up behind the curtain. They entered in a rush; he closed the door, locked it, and turned towards her. And then it was as if they were dancing, he leading, pulling, she running towards him and their mouths joining breathlessly in snatched kisses. He pushed her into a corner. Her scarlet nails curved around the back of his red neck, and in an instant his grey trousers had pooled around his ankles.

Parvathi was as curious of their manoeuvrings as she was of the dogs outside her father's compound. She listened to the wet slapping, panting and grunting, and watched Major Anthony Fitzgerald's lily-white buttocks shake and jiggle loosely as if made of coconut milk jelly. There was no question of an intrusion of privacy, for these were surely another species in the jungle. For it was different, completely different between her and Kasu Marimuthu. Not just the wilful prolonging of the act that could be over so quickly, but the way *both* abandoned themselves to it, and the audible enjoyment the female took from it.

Then India Jane Harrington did a surprising thing, she tensed up, and with her face contorted, but not, Parvathi was startled to discover, with pain but pleasure, screeched and suddenly went quite limp. Pleasure! But her mother had always borne it in silence, a duty.

After that India Jane turned her face away from him, and drawled, 'Hurry up, Anthony.' And as if he had been waiting for just such an order he looked to the side of her and quite comically panted, 'Yes, yes, quite so.' Facing away from her, and as the mating dogs outside her father's compound often did, he gave a last great juddering thrust and sagged into her. They remained joined for a few seconds more, then the Major pulled out of her, and turning slightly away, began to put order to his clothes.

From a pocket he produced a very large handkerchief with a blue border. He pushed it into his crotch, and in the blink of an eye, had pulled up his trousers, and stood ready to go. But instead of going he dithered, pulling at the handkerchief, looking around diffidently.

'You can go now,' India Jane said, still leaning against the wall, her voice returned to its usual cool and superior tone. And he did; scurrying away with a furtive backward glance, as if leaving a crime scene. The dogs had been more dignified. Parvathi was left alone with her quarry.

The woman moved her knees further apart, and in a fluid movement swiped her bare palm between her legs from back to front. Then she straightened and coolly walking over to the expensive silk curtains, wiped her hand on them. There was a mirror across the room and she went and looked dispassionately at herself. She was beautiful and bored. Ten chicken-pie-eating Majors would not have satisfied her. She should never have married the Headmaster. She was obviously too good for him, for the world in which she now found herself. She had imagined different, more glamorous.

Wetting a finger on her tongue, she smoothed a sulky curl by her cheek. Her evening bag yielded a cigarette which she lit. She took a long slow drag. Then she walked over to the drinks cabinet and poured herself a drink. Outside, the band had started playing the most flirtatious music in the world, the *rongeng*. And on the lawn white men were trying to dance but, without the innate rhythm or instinctive style of the Malay professional dancers.

India Jane moved to the tall windows; standing hardly two feet away from Parvathi, she watched the dancers. Her reflection on the glass showed a scornful twist to her lips. Eventually, she moved away, put out her cigarette and retrieved her underwear by the desk. She did not wear it, but stuffed it into her handbag and left the room.

Parvathi came out of her hiding-place and went to the curtains where Mrs Harrington had smeared her juices. The smell of their coupling hung close to it. The curtain had absorbed it. A peelable layer, a thin memory of India Jane Harrington's moment of pleasure. Parvathi stood where she had stood and looked out at what she had looked out on. What a shameful, disrespectful, contemptuous woman. No wonder the other women did not like her. And yet, how brave she was to take what she wanted without caring for the consequences. The woman became more precious and perfect in Parvathi's eyes. Without touching anything or leaving any sign of her presence, just as if she was in the jungle, Parvathi left, side-stepping the ash Mrs India Harrington had left on the expensive carpets.

On the lawn Father Marston approached her.

'If you don't mind me asking, what's your religion?'

'I'm a Hindu,' Parvathi said, turning to look at his thin, tired face. He had been fever-stricken too often, but he had a calling and now his eyes burned with a bright light.

'Ah, so you must have your favourite deity then. Let me guess . . . it's Ganesh, the Elephant God, isn't it?'

'Actually, I pray to the little silver cobra that serves him.'

The priest reared back as if a cobra had shot out of her mouth and made directly for him. 'Goodness!' he cried, genuinely horrified. 'I've never heard of such a thing. How do you know he is God? Who told you?'

Parvathi shrugged.

'Mrs Marimuthu, do you know that it was because people were praying to idols and worthless images that God sent His only son down to earth to tell us all who He really is? His son was called Jesus and He died on a cross for us. But there are still some of us who insist on praying to snakes. In Christianity, the serpent is the one who tempted Eve and first caused man to sin. How can you pray to a symbol of evil?'

Parvathi had no answer.

'I will come by tomorrow and drop off a Bible for you. Please read it and tell me what you think. I would really be interested to hear your opinion. I know without a shadow of a doubt that God is definitely not a snake.'

That night, Parvathi sat on the veranda with Maya. 'Maya, have you read the Bible?'

'I have. Why do you ask?'

'Well, a Catholic priest asked me how I could pray to a symbol of evil. He said God cannot be found in a lump of clay or a carved stone, no matter how beautiful it is. And to carry on pretending to do so after God sent His only son to earth to tell us so is simply heathen.'

Maya sighed. 'Could you say that the one slipper of your mother's that you keep with you is her?'

'No.'

'It is just one tiny aspect of her, and yet to you, it represents her so completely that it is enough for you to look at it to bring the whole of her back to you. You could just as easily have brought an old blouse, a piece of jewellery, a comb with missing teeth, or anything that reminded you of her.'

'Yes.'

'To encounter divinity in all His fullness would be impossible for man, so he sees a light, a burning bush, an angel, an apparition on a cross, and he calls it God. But with the usual arrogance of man, he then starts believing that that small part he has taken is the All. The carved stone is a symbol. Anything you worship can become God because God exists in every living and dead thing you see. He is everywhere and in everything. If one believed enough in a piece of rock, that rock will one day open its eyes, and show the God that lives in it. It doesn't matter if one decided to worship a stone, a man, a tree, or a snake. Believe and it will be.

'God will manifest Himself to you in whatever form will fill your eyes with tenderness. What difference to God if it is a dying man on a cross or a serpent that is used to remind his devotee of Him? It is important only to love Him with all your heart. True,

He will never appear as a serpent to a Christian, but He will come to you thus.'

Downstairs, Kasu Marimuthu, with no thought for his young wife's spiritual concerns, raised his glass and drank. Steadily more and more through the years. The bottles arriving in crates from England.

Temptation

Parvathi stood at the top of the steps that led down to the party, dressed in the most expensive sari in the world and high-heeled slippers studded with yellow topaz and tiger's eyes. Her beautifully made-up eyes swept the lawn where waiters in starched uniforms and white gloves served elegant guests. Gracefully, she began her descent down the sloping lawn. Who could picture her origins now, the one-room shack, the two-change wardrobe? There was almost nothing left of the original her to betray this new self. Here, all was bright and glittering: the past dared not come. It hung back like a bewildered ghost. Why, there was not a woman present who did not envy her wealth and position.

The band was playing something fast and catchy, and there were couples dancing. On a long table with a white tablecloth many crystal bowls and platters held nuts, dates, finger sandwiches, curry puffs, slices of imported fruit cake, garishly coloured local cakes, Chinese biscuits, imported chocolates, and savoury titbits. The central flower arrangement was incredibly exotic; the gardener had cut away the centres of certain flowers and fitted them into the calyxes of others. The deception was so skilfully executed it was impossible to tell. Not far off, a wild pig was slowly revolving over a fire. The whiff of burning wood and roasting flesh reached her, and she turned towards a sea breeze. It made her sari billow and all the jewels on it glittered in the dying sun's rays.

She sipped at the pretty cocktail created specially for her: a transparent green creation with rose petals and a salt rim. Being non-alcoholic it had not become popular, but it didn't dim the fact that she was somebody special, she was Kasu Marimuthu's wife.

People wanted to talk to her. Even the waiters had been taught to address her as 'madam'.

A lady came up to speak to her. She had eyes like the dolls in the first wife's room. Green with a starburst inside. But unlike the dolls she had webs of lines around her eyes. When Kasu Marimuthu caught Parvathi's eye and waved her over, she excused herself politely and moved on.

He introduced her to a business acquaintance. She nodded graciously, never forgetting that time she had answered a question with the words, 'Exactly that have I,' and the displeased glance he had flicked in her direction. After the guests had gone, he said, 'Brevity is your ally. You are a genius until you open your mouth.'

Parvathi bent her head and daintily licked the salt off the rim of her glass, and looked up directly into a pair of intensely blue watching eyes. For a while she was caught, claimed by the boldness of the man's stare, and then she remembered herself, and her eyes slid away. She kept her distress from showing. But she had done a wrong thing. She tried to think of who she had seen do that first. Ah, India Jane Harrington. She should have waited for one of the others to do it before copying the gesture, for she realised now that it was an excessively voluptuous one. She would not do it again.

When next she saw him he was in conversation with someone, and stood with his head slightly inclined, listening attentively. He was different from Kasu Marimuthu's usual guest, definitely not English, anyway. More than the deep tan or square jaw, there was a tense impatient quality to him.

A gong sounded; it was time for the lion dance to start. As people began to gather around the stage, Parvathi took the opposite direction towards the edge of the lawn. She stood for a moment where the higher beach started and wished the monsoon would come. Then it would be clothes snapping wildly on the washing lines, coconut trees bending in the strong gales, and between the wind and the lashing rain every last speck of dust would be washed out of the air, so that it became so clean it was possible to see everything in its brightest, most pristine state. Possible to see even the spiders' nests that sparkled between the coconut trees' leaves and the grains of sand on the beach. And where she stood would be filled with fallen coconuts and green grasses.

The sun had already set behind the house casting its violet shadow on the sand and that last eerie orange light that the villagers called *mambang*, hovering spirit, floated over the darkening water. On the verandahs, the servants had begun the twice-daily ritual of watering the hanging ferns and lighting the lantern lamps in the balconies. This was her favourite time of the evening.

Walking to where the soft sand began, she slipped out of her high heels and, going past the tiny holes that hermit crabs had made, stood for a moment at the water's edge.

Then, lifting her sari almost to her knees, she stepped into the sea. The water was warm and she wriggled her toes in the sand. A seagull flew above. Mesmerised by the way the sun turned the ends of its wings translucent red, she was startled by the sound of someone joining her in the water. She turned around. It was the stranger. He had rolled his white linen trousers up to his calves. They were golden. He came and stood beside her. Without her high heels she barely reached his chest. Her eyes swung up to his face. He had ocean eyes.

'You're very unhappy, aren't you?'

She opened her mouth to deny the ridiculous observation, but the breath was pulled out of her in a rush. Her mind went blank and she couldn't utter a sound. They stared at each other. This ocean wanted her. Involuntarily, her hands opened, and the most expensive sari in the world fell into saltwater. At the base of her belly a wave of the bluest white broke and her entire body became as intensely alive as the deer that scents a predator in the wind. Suddenly, she was aware of everything; the deeply pink sky behind his head, the wind revealing his body through his shirt, the hundreds of gold hairs that dusted his skin, the smell of his cologne, the taste of the salt in the air, the waves sucking at her feet, the cry of the bird above, and that fantastically tiny fraction of a movement both their bodies made towards each other.

Oh! How she wanted him. She wanted to press her entire length against his tall body and beg him to do, in the orange light, the things that her husband did to her in the dark. For some inexplicable reason, the memory of the time she had sat at one of the holes in her father's wall and spied on two dogs came back. The bitch crouched down, her tail waving, calling. Then, as if they had known all along they both ran towards each other, bumping and circling one another, shivering, panting, emitting guttural sounds. They even rose on their hind legs and licked each other's muzzles. Then the dog mounted the female. At first she whined and moved under his weight, but then both became so still Parvathi wondered if they had fallen asleep. But a quarter of an hour later they moved apart and stood for a moment side by side, then first the dog and then the bitch moved away.

In an effortless, dreamlike movement of great sensuousness her hand came up towards his face, as if to caress the lean cheek where a muscle throbbed. Her bangles brushed against each other and made their sweet sounds.

Sita.

Her hand halted. Someone had called her name. She turned her head towards the sound, used that stilled hand to wave, and then abruptly stepped away from the man and walked back to dry land. An instinct deep inside her wanted, pleaded to be allowed to go back into the water, but the façade of her life reasserted itself and now her mind stepped in, furious and unforgiving. She was Kasu Marimuthu's wife, impeccably turned out, deeply mysterious, and unquestionable. What was this comparison to dogs? They were not dogs. Certainly, she was not.

Was it possible that he had thought her hand had gone up to ward him off? Yes, yes, that was what she had been about to do. Her guilt turned into a cold rage, and no longer directed at herself. She was blameless. She had tried to ward him off but he was practised at that sort of thing. That man was mistaken: she was neither Kasu Marimuthu's first wife nor was she the Headmaster's wife. Rude fellow. Did he think that Kasu Marimuthu's wife was that cheap? She was decent, a good woman. She did not have affairs. How dare he? She retrieved her slippers and holding them in one hand, began to run towards the house. Does not the loser always run off with his tail between his legs? The wet sari stuck to her legs. Dear God, the sari! She had ruined the thing that Kamala said a little boy in Jaipur had probably gone blind to make. He had sacrificed his sight for nothing.

What should she do now? She rushed around the side of the house. Maya would know how to save the sari.

As she reached the back door she began calling out, 'Maya, Maya, look what I have done.'

At the doorway Maya glanced down at the sari edge and then back to Parvathi's flustered, breathless face. Tendrils of hair had escaped from her chignon and they lay helplessly this way and that around her long neck. She wondered what had happened to make the child suddenly have to struggle with women's emotions, but there was no expression on her face as she said calmly, 'It's six yards of cloth, Da.'

Parvathi took a deep breath. 'Please, Maya, help me to save it.'

'Of course. Take it off and give it to me.'

Maya dipped a bucket of water into the clay jar beside the back door and poured it on Parvathi's feet, and Parvathi stepped into the kitchen. She stripped off quickly, and ran upstairs under the cover of an old blanket. In her room she headed for the mirror. What she saw there shocked her. Her hand came up and touched her trembling lips. 'I'm not unhappy. I'm very happy,' she told her reflection, but at the final moment her eyes, so strangely glittering, slid away.

Turning, she walked out to the balcony. The man was still in the water, his hands pushed deep into his pockets, staring at the horizon. And, the Headmaster's wife, drink in hand, was picking her way towards him. An unbidden image of the woman's legs entwined around him flashed into her thoughts. What did she care? 'Let her have him,' she said aloud, but her voice sounded unfamiliar and angry. Who would have thought it? She was jealous.

She went in and began to dress. 'Actually it's good that I saw them together. They deserve each other. Both are alike,' she told herself, and this time she was relieved to note that she sounded like herself once more. Expertly she retouched her make-up and repaired her hair. In the mirror a poised, detached woman looked back. She went back down to the party.

'Oh, you've changed,' someone said.

'Yes, I spilled something,' Parvathi replied civilly.

'Sita,' her husband called.

'Yes,' she said, and turned with a smile.

Kasu Marimuthu was standing with the blue-eyed stranger. Parvathi's practised smile did not falter.

'Samuel, my wife, Sita. Sita, Samuel West. He's an American. If all goes well we might be doing some business together.'

'Hello, Sita,' said Samuel West. His eyes were friendly, and his touch warm and firm, but brief. It was as if that time in the water had never happened.

'How nice to meet you, Mr West.'

'Please, call me Samuel.'

'All right,' she agreed distantly.

'You own a beautiful stretch of beach. Are the waters safe to swim in?'

'Sita doesn't swim,' Kasu Marimuthu stated.

Samuel West's eyebrows rose in surprise. 'Oh!' he said, and was about to say more, but someone across the lawn called, and Kasu Marimuthu excused himself and left after promising to return.

She looked at Samuel West. 'Come with me. There's something I believe you'll enjoy.'

'Sure,' he said, and followed her. She took him to the barbecue pit where many people were already gathered, and asked one of the young boys tending to the fire for a plate of the new dish Maya had concocted: giant prawns marinated in dark rum and spices. Samuel refused to bother with a fork or knife. His straight, white teeth bit a prawn cleanly in half. What a beautiful man he was. Perhaps the most beautiful she had ever seen.

'This is really good,' he enthused. 'Food in Asia tastes so much better.'

For this she had an answer from her stock of small talk. 'It is the sun,' she said. 'Everything tastes better when it is sun-ripened.'

'Mmmm.'

She watched him eat. It must be nice to be so confident. To know that whatever you do is or will be right. Never to have to look at someone else to know how to behave. It must be wonderful to be a small child and be taught that you are a superior race. That there is no need to bow or bend to anyone. There was nothing effete about the way he pulled the napkin across his mouth either. A man's man. Handsome. He was handsome.

Samuel West glanced up suddenly and caught her watching him.

'Would you like me to teach you to swim?' he offered.

Before Parvathi could think up a suitable reply, the Headmaster's wife stood beside them, pelvis thrust slightly forward, drink in hand, and leaning seductively to one side. Her voice was light and flirtatious. 'You're wasting your time, Sam. The locals believe there are dangerous spirits lurking in the water waiting to carry off the unwary. They congregate on its beaches, paddle about in the waves, but they never swim.'

Samuel West turned flinty eyes towards her. 'You know, Mrs Harrington, it's a fine thing we are not in Arabia, for the Arabs take a very dim view of the guest who insults his host.'

India Harrington turned an unrepentant face towards Parvathi although her body remained slanted towards the male. Her eyes flashed, but not with malice. She just wanted the man. Who could blame her? He was such a dish. 'I wasn't insulting anybody. It is true, isn't it, Mrs Marry-muthu? The people in this country *are* afraid to go into the sea.'

Good news, Mrs Harrington. This man's not for me.

'I wouldn't know, Mrs Harrington,' Parvathi said. 'I am not from this country either. However it might be useful for you to know that,' she paused a moment and turning so her face was half-hidden from Samuel West, winked and continued, 'in my country we like to keep a box of tissues in the first right-hand drawer.'

It took but a second for it to register, and then India Jane Harrington smiled, a slow, splendid smile. 'I wondered who it was. I knew it had to be someone small. I nearly spoke to you,' she said.

'You should have. It was too hot inside the brocade.'

Mrs Harrington threw her head back and gave a shout of laughter. 'Oh, but you are precious.'

'Now you must both excuse me. I think I see my husband beckoning,' Parvathi said lightly. As she walked away she heard Samuel West ask, 'What was all that about?'

To which India Harrington drawled, 'That is a story infinitely better left untold.'

Eventually, he came to say goodbye. In the lamplight his eyes did not shed light, they were almost all pupil.

'You must come again, Mr West.'

'I will. It's turned out to be a most interesting evening.' Purpose and strength flowed in his voice. This man had never wanted anything badly; everything always fell into his hands easily and quickly. He was an American abroad. Nothing stood in his way.

'Good night, Mr West,' she said, and smiled politely.

'Good night, Sita,' he said, and for reasons she did not comprehend, did not smile back.

That night she dreamed that he came to her, and she told him, 'Don't touch what you have not paid for yet.' But he only laughed and said, 'Don't you know, to be stylish you have to break a few rules.'

'I won't run away with you,' she warned.

'But I don't want you to run away with me. I just want what you promised on the beach,' he said, and reached for her sari. But Maya, smiling ghoulishly, appeared suddenly. 'Let's see what you can do to God's child,' she crowed. And what happened to Draupadi when the evil King tried to strip and ravish her in the story of the Pandavas happened to Parvathi. The more the blue-eyed man pulled at her sari, the more cloth unravelled until a whole mountain of sari rose beside him, but Parvathi remained totally clothed and chaste. 'I told you I was not like the Headmaster's wife,' she said.

But suddenly she was in a courtroom and Kasu Marimuthu in a judge's robes and wig and holding a cucumber sandwich said, 'I can't accept *this* as evidence. What I want to know is what happened to the first sari?'

'Maya has it,' she replied.

'Not true,' said the clown, holding the swan in the crook of his arm. 'It is ripped and torn to bits.'

'I knew it. All women are faithless!' cried Kasu Marimuthu. 'Sita stood in a fire and did not burn. Prove your chastity in the same manner.'

And as in all her nightmares, out of nowhere, her mother appeared to ask, 'You haven't shamed us, have you?' And suddenly the ground under Parvathi opened up and she felt herself begin to fall into the dark earth.

She awakened with a start. It was nearly 2 a.m. Covering herself with a blanket, she went out into the balcony and stood under the stars. It was a cold night and even with the blanket held close to her body she shivered. Out on the sea, a lone fisherman was in his boat fishing with the light from his lamp. The wind blowing in an east-west direction brought the smell of Maya's cheroot smoke.

Normally she would have gone down to the woman, but that day she wanted no company. Instead, she stood for hours gazing up at the sky while her mind incessantly replayed that unguarded moment when her hand had lifted of its own accord to touch the blue-eyed stranger. When the lights of Kasu Marimuthu's car turned into the driveway she moved back into the shadows, and waited until she heard Maya shut the front door before she returned to bed. When she heard his loose rambling footsteps in the corridor, she turned on her side and pretended to be asleep. But his footsteps did not stop at her door. He hardly ever came to her any more. But if he had she would have closed her eyes and pretended it was the blue-eyed man.

In the light of a single lamp Maya sat by herself painstakingly removing the waxy covering of seven lime seeds with a small knife. What she found inside she turned to paste in her pestle and rolled into little balls to give a mother who had come to her that evening in tears because her daughter was an insatiable nymphomaniac. 'Help her. Help her, before her father kills her. There must be something to dampen her sinful appetite.'

The Dog

When she came downstairs the next morning the sari was hanging in the shade of the big tree in the courtyard looking no worse for its time in the sea. But when she went closer, she saw that a faint wavy watermark remained – the most expensive sari in the world was ruined. She stepped away from it. Let it be a lesson to her. Never again would she allow herself to be alone with him. On that she was resolute. The man seduced with his eyes. It was the existence of men like him that made men like her father imprison their daughters.

Anyway, those strong wayward feelings of yesterday had faded down. Now she knew that it had been a kind of madness, but fleeting, unimportant, and unlikely to be repeated, if she kept away from him.

She had realised something else that morning too. The man was not a dog, but a civet cat, killing for the sake of it, the urge to kill triggered by movement or sound. Her loneliness must have triggered that instinct in him, and he had moved in for the kill even though he was not hungry and did not particularly want to eat.

She was walking in the rain along the water's edge lost in thought when a man suddenly fell into step beside her. She whirled around, her hand flying to her heart. 'Oh! Mr West,' she gasped. 'You scared me.'

He grinned, an attractive tactic. 'I like the way you get it wrong all the time. It's Samuel.'

She stared at him. He was soaking wet. As she was. There was no wind and the rain fell straight like needles. A drop of rain must have fallen into his eyes because he blinked suddenly, unbearably beautiful. And there it was again that mad urge to touch him. And not in any kind or gentle way, but to tear uncontrollably at him. It was dangerous here. There was no one about to stop her. She moved a step back.

'I've got to go,' she said, and turned away.

'Wait, Sita.'

She turned back slowly. 'My name is not Sita, Mr West. It's Parvathi.'

He looked at her quizzically. 'Parvathi.' He said it beautifully. She wished he would say it again.

She nodded. Why had she told him?

'It's a good name. I like it.'

'So do I,' she said, and smiled.

Tall, proud, unaware and almost certainly uncaring that 'dark' behaviour such as his was causing the likes of Mrs Adams to be ashamed of her white skin, he smiled back. And it came again as soon as she relaxed, that desire to wrestle him to the ground. To bite his mouth. To lick his face. To rut with him right there on the sand, the water lapping at their crazed bodies. No pleasantries, no apologies, no pretending. Raw. Primitive. To screech with pleasure like India Jane Harrington. But had not India Jane shown her that that was a momentary thing, of little worth? She could not give up what she had breathlessly dreamed of all her life, the path with a heart. What would he know about a path with a heart?

'What are you doing here?' she asked coldly.

'I came to teach you to swim.'

How unimaginative, Mr West.

'I've really got to go now,' she said, and took a step back determinedly, but he grabbed her hand. And because it so closely resembled the kind of violence in her thoughts, a charge of electricity shot up her arm. But when she looked between the wet eyelashes she could tell instantly that he had not felt it. It was not like that for him. Just underneath his skin, he was not screaming. In her mind's eye she saw herself tearing at the buttons of his shirt with her teeth and his astonished face saying, 'Why do you have to tear, when you can take it off in a civilised way?'

He had come into her territory without the necessary qualification, in short sleeves, looking for a holiday romance under palm leaves. *Have another look at this plant you have brought to me. A weak insipid thing with poisonous leaves and bitter, seedless fruit.* She already had that with Kasu Marimuthu. *Learn from the dog when you want to approach a bitch.*

'Listen,' he shouted urgently, but when he had her attention, he went and diluted the moment with ordinary, everyday words. 'I know it is crazy, and I feel like a damn fool, but I can't get you out of my mind.'

For a while she stared up at him, into those vivid eyes, trying to see behind them. What was really going on? How could she tell him that she had been waiting all her life and was still waiting for a love that knew no bounds, a thorny, musk-scented weed that waited for the raging monsoon to bloom. And this wild weed, she wanted to tell him, it lived for ever. It was without boundaries, vast, and unending. *Get back, Parvathi, Get back. You won't find it here.* She twisted her arm out of his grasp. In her mind he refused, even the idea of letting go for a moment, unthinkable, but he released her instantly. This was a holiday romance, a weak plant, after all.

Look at him. He was already sorry he had been so forward, so impulsive. An apology was waiting on the tip of his tongue. *Good man, don't make it worse.* Then again, it was hardly his fault; no one could blame him for not pouncing on her. It would have been most inappropriate, loutish even.

'I'm sorry, Mr West. You can't teach me to swim.'

'Why not?' he shot back passionately. 'You're not in love with *him.* What happened between us in the water doesn't happen often and I've never done this, waited in the rain for a woman. I have a wife back home. I thought I loved her until I saw you.'

He had a wife. Of course he did – a pale woman in a cold country waiting for her husband to return from distant lands. Could this man be trusted to put his hand in the fire for her? Unlikely. The wind had picked up and rain began to fall sideways right into her face, stinging her eyes and lips. She shifted her body and he made the answering shift in his. How perfectly aligned their bodies were.

Yet their minds were in parallel worlds. Now that she had stopped walking she felt cold. A shiver passed through her.

'You're cold,' he said, but he did nothing. There was nothing he could do. They stood facing each other helplessly. He was one step away, but that was one step too far. Their bodies hungered and circled each other, but their spirits already knew there was no happy ending to this.

Parvathi hugged herself and looked down at the sand, thinking of Kasu Marimuthu, the world's greatest pretender. There he was, pretending to be white, pretending to be sophisticated. But underneath all the trappings of good china, silver cutlery and Venetian crystal, the man liked nothing better than mixing together rice, curries, a mashed banana and yoghurt on his plate and making it into soft balls before putting them into his mouth, and all this with a hand unadorned by cutlery. And while he chewed these food balls he was not above making small humming noises of pure pleasure. She thought of his proud face. What would he do if he found out? Pretend to all that like his first wife, she too was dead of tropical fever? And ho! What a juicy piece of gossip for the community.

She looked up at Samuel West, desire in her belly, a dark chasm at her feet. Yes, he was extraordinarily handsome, but she was not going with him. Not even because of Kasu Marimuthu or the gossiping community. But because he brought awake some violent impulse that ordinarily lay peacefully asleep inside her. Something she didn't want to look at. Something that could only bring shame and disgrace. She wanted to be pure and demure. She wished to be what everyone else wanted her to be. She wanted to be like the other members of the Black Umbrella Club. Safe.

'I'm sorry but I can't,' she said, and walked away quickly. He called to her. She did not turn around, but broke into a run.

He did not come after her.

She looked and found inside her no regret for what she had done. She had closed that door. He would find another or go back to his pale wife. And she must get dressed and attend a meeting of the Black Umbrella Club. In fact, she was quite looking forward to seeing the doll that Negeri Sembilan Mami was making out of straws. And so she would smile and compliment their efforts and the other Mamis would do the same with her blanket. And no one would ever know that that morning on the beach, she had turned down the most beautiful man on earth.

It was her birthday, she was eighteen years old. Maya had begun a week-long fast in honour of it; Kamala and the other girls had brought in flowers; Kupu gave her a beautiful pure white coral; Kasu Marimuthu bought jewellery, and Samuel West sent his gift through her husband.

'Sam said this puppy needs a home. Do you want it?' Kasu Marimuthu asked.

She scooped it up in her arms and with foolish trusting eyes it reached up and licked her face. 'Do I want it? I most definitely do.'

'He's quite unusual for a Dalmatian, liver spots instead of black, but he's deaf in one ear so he is unacceptable for the show ring or breeding.'

'Why does he shiver so much?' she asked.

'Mixture of excitement and fright, I should have thought. It's his first time away from his mother and siblings. Put him in a box in your bedroom tonight.'

She looked up at her husband. 'Will you thank Mr West for me?'

'Thank him yourself. I've invited him to the barbecue tomorrow.'

He came dressed in a white shirt, his throat a strong, brown column, but she did not stare. 'Hello,' she greeted cordially.

'Hello, Sita,' he said, to let her know that Parvathi was their secret. She smiled and thought it was good that he was a foreigner. They could always be depended on to be discreet. He had brought rubber grooming gloves, jumbo-size guillotine nail cutters, metal nail files, smoker's tooth powder, Epsom salts, Germolene, gripe water, a bottle of kaolin, and an anal thermometer.

'Goodness,' she said, opening the bag. 'Well, thank you for the dog and now this. How did you know I wanted one?'

'I didn't. He needed a good home and I couldn't think of any place more suitable,' he said pleasantly.

'I'll have him brought down,' she said, and rang the bell.

'Have you named him yet?'

'I'm calling him Kalichan.'

'A good name,' he approved, and she was suddenly pleased. He paused a moment. 'It is fall in the States now and I must leave next week.' He stared at her with the same barely leashed longing of that time in the water. 'But I'll be back.'

'Have a pleasant trip,' she said lightly and smiled, but sadly. Mr Samuel West was a kind man, after all.

And then Kasu Marimuthu was slapping him on the back and asking, 'What will you have, old chap?'

In the kitchen, Maya was infusing dried anacyclus pyrethrum leaves in coconut oil over a slow fire for a man who had come to complain that he could not sustain an erection.

The Child

The years came and went but Parvathi remained childless, and Kalichan, who had become ridiculously attached to her, behaved as if he was her child. But sometimes she lay on the beach with the dog, watching the daredevil boys cleaning the stained glass while hanging onto the high ledges by their fingertips, and realised that the house was like a beautifully maintained mausoleum. It wept for the voices of children.

'Maya,' Parvathi asked bitterly, 'am I to be not only displeasing to my husband but also barren? Is this all my life is to be, to endlessly entertain people I don't care for?'

Maya had a surprising suggestion. 'Adopt a child,' she said. 'The same way that a common stone may be turned into a priceless ruby by a change in its environment, a small change to the household could make your husband's seed take.'

Parvathi didn't find the idea displeasing. So when the Pulliar temple priest brought the tragic news that the gypsy dancer had died suddenly, and asked if they would be amenable to adopting her three-year-old orphan, Parvathi did not hesitate.

'It would be an honour to raise her child,' she said, the image of the beautiful dancer running in distressed circles, wondering why her lover did not come, still fresh after all these years.

Her husband was much slower to react, and when he did, it was only to nod, the sadness of a childless man hiding in his eyes. The two men left to fetch the girl. Parvathi shut Kalichan in her bedroom, since he had become large and boisterous and could overwhelm the child. Then she went to stand at the top of the veranda steps, and wait.

Kasu Marimuthu opened the car door, and out climbed the most enchanting creature in the world – above a round red mouth enormous peacock eyes, and over those a bouncing riot of curls. Dressed in a short dancer's blouse and a long puffed skirt that ended just above her ankles, she surveyed her surroundings boldly.

Parvathi went down the steps smiling. 'Come,' she said in Tamil, and held out her hands in welcome, but the child clenched her fists into little paws and shrank back until she was up against Kasu Marimuthu's legs and then said very clearly in English, 'No.'

The dancer's daughter spoke English!

Parvathi sat back on her heels, stared into the child's mutinous eyes and knew without the slightest doubt that this was no gypsy dancer's orphan. This was her husband's daughter. The dancer was only the earth to which he had entrusted his seed. And there she was again, the gypsy dancer, but no longer distressed. Late, after the performance, after the crowd had gone, her lover had come, after all. And to him she must have said, 'Keep this for me after I die, for that which is foul desires to become pure.'

Truth be told, Parvathi was not shocked. She might have pretended even to herself that she didn't, but she had always known the dancer was his mistress. Of course she knew; from the moment she had asked her husband the dancer's name and he had feigned ignorance. She thought of the Mamis, their afternoons without her, eating muruku and sneering at her driving around in a Rolls, the mistress of a household that included a tailor and a dhobi and consumed a sack of rice a day, but what a poor, ignorant fool not to guess at her husband's other life.

Come to think of it, he had been sadder than usual two days ago. He had cried while reciting his poetry. She had never seen him cry before. He must have loved the dancer well. Poor man. To be so unlucky twice. Never mind, the child had a father, the house had a child. And she, the stone that could turn into a ruby.

'Sita, this is Rubini,' her husband said from above. 'And this, Rubini, is your new mother. Just as you call me Papa you must call her Ama.'

But the child dashed a clenched fist rebelliously to her face and burst into tears.

'No,' Parvathi said gently, withdrawing her hand. 'Let her call me *Mami*.'

'Come, come, my little Queen,' her husband coaxed the child.

'Papa,' sobbed the adorable child, apparently inconsolable. He knelt beside her and gently massaged her fat little fingers one by one. The sobbing stopped. 'Again,' she sniffed, and suddenly, irrepressibly, grinned. Oh, cheeky little thing. Who could refuse her anything?

'Aha,' said he, and began all over again. An old game then. When he turned his face to speak to Parvathi, the child put two hands on either side of his face and possessively turned it back towards her. Her father was hers, and hers only. She had lost one parent, and she had no intention of relinquishing the other. Kasu Marimuthu laughed easily, wholeheartedly. Upon which the child turned to Parvathi, her eyebrows brought so low they were almost a straight line above her round eyes, and straightening her mouth into another stern line, slowly, deliberately raised the forefinger of her right hand in a warning gesture. Parvathi's hand fluttered to the middle of her chest. There was no mistaking it. The dancer's child disliked her intensely.

Even so, the child blew through the house like a morning breeze, fresh and unsullied. The patter of her innocent feet was a wonderful thing. It lifted the heart. And just like that, all became well at Adari. The disused ballroom was opened and her tricycle put inside. Kasu Marimuthu brought gardenias for her hair. She made him pin them in.

'Pitty or not?' she asked coquettishly, tilting her adorable little body to one side for she was vain about her looks. Kasu Marimuthu's shout of laughter echoed for a long time in the vast, hollow space. No matter how many times he heard it, he never ceased to be as enchanted by her inability to pronounce her 'r's as when he first heard it.

'Yes, very,' he said adoringly, when he could bring himself to stop laughing.

And it was the same with everyone in the household. No one could resist her, and she in turn seemed to be genuinely fond of them. Parvathi, it seemed, was her only enemy. It was careless shrugs to any questions Parvathi directed at her and resentful glances whenever she found herself alone in the same room as her stepmother. Her rejection was so total and unremitting that it was baffling.

'What am I doing wrong?' Parvathi asked Maya.

'Nothing. Her rejection of you is not personal. You perceive this experience as a celebration of your own kindness so you don't realise what a traumatic one it is for her. A child who loses its blood mother even when it is deemed too young to remember, is wounded in a way that cannot be measured. Just because she runs and plays and appears normal on the outside, does not mean she is not mourning for a loss to which there is no redress. No replacement is possible by anyone. Her trust that she can ever be safe is gone for ever. So is the belief that she is worthy of love. Love will always be associated with being abandoned. Poor mite, she cannot even turn to God, for wasn't He the one who allowed the first tragedy to occur?

'When she seems to be pushing you away the opposite is true, she is only testing your commitment to her. To see if you too will abandon her. To see if she was right not to trust you. To see if that thing she fears most, inevitable desertion, will happen. For the thing she wants most is to connect to you, though you are the most dangerous candidate to bond with – a potential abandoner. And due to the matter of loyalty to her real mother, your position in her life becomes even more ambivalent.'

'Should I play no role at all in her life then?' Parvathi asked.

'You can make a big difference by always being caring, loving, and nurturing, and whenever she is provocative, unreasonable and aggressive, let her be – she is grieving. Then one day she will come to trust the permanence of her tie with you and realise that love is not always dangerous and then the anger and hostility will fall way. That day she will attach to you. And then separating will become an even greater problem.'

Late one night, cries from Rubini's bedroom brought Parvathi rushing in. Damp curls were plastered to the girl's flushed face and her eyes were closed, but she appeared to be in great distress – tossing and turning, her arms and legs flailing. Gently, Parvathi shook her awake. She opened her eyes and for a second looked at her stepmother fearfully without recognition, and then seemed to come to her senses and appeared briefly relieved, but as she came awake properly, she pushed Parvathi's hand away and twisting out of her hold, scrambled to the far end of the cot, where she curled against the wooden bars and regarded her suspiciously.

'You're missing your mother, aren't you?'

She nodded, her eyes large with confusion and pain.

'I can't bring her back for you, but I promise to take care of you just like she would have,' Parvathi whispered, and using her index finger, gently stroked the child's thumb, until a shadow fell upon them, and with a new sob the child raised both her arms and sat up. With infinite care Kasu Marimuthu took her dear little body in his arms and tenderly rubbed eau de cologne on her wrists to calm her down. As she drifted off to sleep he kissed her face and hands, and whispered again and again, 'You can trust me. I won't abandon you.'

The moon had begun to wane and Maya set about filling the house with dark green objects. She took pieces of green fabric and some green seeds outside and cast them into what she called the Tibetan autumnal winds so that they were scattered far and wide. In this way she spread the power and blessing of the season.

The Little Darling Dancer

It must have been in her blood, like the instinct to eat and procreate, this tremendous desire to perform. It began one night after dinner when Kasu Marimuthu told the story of the unicorn that saved India from being invaded and razed to the ground by Genghis Khan.

When he finished, the girl slid off her father's lap, tied peacock feathers to her ankles, and announced that she would dance the story back to her father. Parvathi stared at the eyes in the peacock's tail and held her breath. The girl began by putting her forefinger to her forehead, and though she took it off almost immediately, a long horn had grown so that all who watched her that night saw it. With that small, almost insignificant act she was transformed, no longer a child, but a unicorn living deep in the middle of an enchanted forest where neither flowers nor leaves ever died. Where it was always spring. Rubini cupped her hands and smelled them – the fresh cool smell of spring. She pulled her forefinger down her cheek and let it rest on her chin – the unicorn was thousands of years old and yet she was beautiful. Rubini covered her eyes – but no human could see her unless she deemed it.

Rubini turned her face attentively to one side – the unicorn was standing in the bushes listening to the conversation of woodcutters. Squaring her shoulders she played their parts as they spoke about the coming of the great conqueror, Genghis Khan, and shook their heads in despair and fear. Then pulling her shoulders towards her chin, she became the unicorn again. Her tail switched, her long mane tossed – India laid to waste! Her temples burned down! Her gods and goddesses smashed! Leaving the cool shade where she had lived all her life, she ran for days until she came upon the ruthless conqueror. He had just finished his prayers to the lake, the moon, the sky, and was just beginning his salutations to the sunrise. Kneeling down before him, she began to whisper – but of course, no one will ever know what the elusive magical creature told the great conqueror. She turned her back resolutely to show that it was the only time in the mighty warrior's history that he retreated from his purpose.

The first time the dance teacher came to Adari Rubini was four and half years old. Parvathi showed him into the large music room and left the door ajar so she could watch from the other room. He began to count the beat, '*tei, taka, taka, tei*' and the child began to dance, but perfectly. She had inherited something one did not, could not learn, a fluidity, a purity of movement that lived inside her being. What could this man teach her?

Then she made a turn and caught Parvathi watching. Immediately she ran to the door and shut it. But that was not dislike. That was the consummate artist who wanted only the end result on show. Still Parvathi could not help herself. She hid in the shadows of the veranda and watched through the window as the girl laid one palm over the other so the webs of her thumbs touched, snaked her hands in figures of eight at waist level – fish. Or holding one hand, the thumb and index finger touching and the other wriggling high, over her head. Her shoulders twitched, and that high hand made jerky, striking movements, but her head was still, so still; it had no function – peacock. And Parvathi would swear that she could see the muscles in the child's back shivering as the spirit of the proudest peacock came to animate her.

Amongst the long white-headed grasses on Peacock Island, a miniature stage with flowers painted on the sides and gilded decorations on the roof was built for her. In the evenings when there were parties, Kupu took her out in the boat to the island. The red velvet curtains parted to reveal her small figure standing alone against the scenery. As the guests raised the opera glasses that the waiters had handed out to them, she put her hands together in greeting. The music struck up, and she smiled and began.

She was not like her mother, tragic and full of longing. No, no, she was a tiny, fiery figure in bright purple, her little legs in dark slacks leaping energetically in the air, twirling incessantly, her skirts rising up to slap her waist. Her body dipping, hands flying, heels meeting, feet stamping, and the peacock feathers at her ankles shimmering, shimmering, shimmering.

The sky turned red as the setting sun's light fell on the water, and she became only a silhouette, restless all the same. Kasu Marimuthu watched with growing pride and love. What a joy she was to him. Oh, how he loved her! The man with the long flute stopped his music and she took a bow. Everyone clapped and commented on how well she danced. A victorious result.

'Her mother was a famous dancer from India,' Kasu Marimuthu said proudly, garlanding her with white flowers. And somewhere in an unseen place the dancer smiled. *Keep this after I am gone.*

One day upon a whim the girl decided to do a rendition of Artenadiswaran, the dance of the half-man, half-woman God. Difficult to do, and done well by so few. The control that was needed for the dance made it an extraordinary choice for someone of her age to attempt, but she did it. For the entire duration of the dance one side of her strutted and swaggered, and the other strolled with grace and softness. The applause was thunderous. She became famous for it. Watching her, even the servants forgot that this was the same demanding little madam who flew into uncontrollable tantrums for the slightest reason. Her faults became necessary complements to her prodigious talent.

And so it came about that everyone was united in the care of this prodigy. Her every wish became a command. If she lost something, the entire household came to a standstill until it was found or replaced. The only person the child did not dare bully was Maya. Maya alone was able to make her eat, clean up a mess she had made, or apologise for unruly behaviour.

An artist from England was commissioned to immortalise the child wonder. He lived in the house for two months. The completed portrait was unveiled in the library, a polished, dashing composition against a purple backdrop. In all her finery she stood at a feast. Beautiful, innocent, openhearted, glowing. Not yet touched by peace, so of course, mysterious. What did the future hold for this child, so rich with food and celebration?

'Tremendous,' said Kasu Marimuthu.

'Stupendous' was the considered opinion of her dance teacher. She was indeed his best pupil. He expected her to be distinguished some day. There was no doubt in his mind about this. He said it willingly and often. As a reward Kasu Marimuthu decided to take her with him on a little trip, but he brought her back the next day.

Parvathi stood in the doorway as Rubini, ignoring her, skipped up the steps and disappeared into the house, calling for the dog.

'What happened? Why are you back already?' she asked.

Her husband shrugged. 'She cried all night because she was worried something might happen to you.'

Parvathi said nothing and remembered Maya's words. 'And when she has finally attached to you, she will still continue to keep you at a distance while you are around her, but she will cry to leave you for any length of time. It is an anxiety that comes from a fear of further loss and desertion.'

A Baby Comes

To help her theory that a common rock could be turned into a precious stone in the right atmosphere, Maya began adding more eggs into Kasu Marimuthu's diet to turn his seed less bitter. To nourish Parvathi's womb she gave her ashoka leaves to chew, and three days before her periods, three white flowers of the Adhatoda Vasica and three of the Morinda Coreia, ground and added into a cup of human milk to drink.

Nearly a year later, Parvathi gave Kasu Marimuthu the good news. He smiled broadly. A happy surprise indeed.

'Let's celebrate,' he said. And reached for the whisky bottle.

The months passed dreamily, slowly. She drank the concoctions Maya set before her and her body made its changes. She began to crave tosai with grated coconut. While Maya made and drizzled them with sesame seed oil, Parvathi sat on the kitchen floor listlessly waving a paper fan at her face and neck and Kalichan rested his head on his front legs and watched her.

'The gardener found a hornet's nest in my vegetable patch today. He showed it to me just now,' Parvathi said.

'How many entrances did it have?' Maya asked.

'Only one, I think.'

'That means it will be a boy,' Maya predicted.

And so it was.

He came in the night while Kalichan stood outside the door whining, scratching, and eventually howling at being separated from his mistress at her time of distress. Added to the commotion, suddenly and inexplicably, all the cows began lowing at the moment of the baby's arrival. She could hear them from her room. And through the haze of pain she heard Kupu singing to them.

They put the infant into her husband's arms. He was dark, but what had displeased Kasu Marimuthu in his wife, now brought an outpouring of love. Gently, he caressed the boy's skin, and scooping him to his face, breathed in the sweet, sweet fragrance of a son. *Let him be called Kuberan.*

Astrologers were sent for. They spoke as one – the boy's star did not agree with his father's. Either his ears must be pierced as if he was a girl and would therefore be no longer malefic towards his father, or symbolically sold to a temple for a bit of sweet rice, as if he was no longer a son of his father's. They did both, but it did not help. Kasu Marimuthu's ox-like constitution and frame, that had seemed unshakeable until then, suddenly showed the first signs of damage.

'Why do you have to drink so much?' Parvathi asked.

'Ah you,' he mocked cheerfully. 'Always in the tavern. Come once to find me in my temple.'

She looked at him, reduced, vulnerable, and inconceivably distant. 'How do I find your temple?'

'First look at me without reproach. Because I've crossed over. I've crossed over, and now I exist only in an old song no one remembers any more. The only way to join me is in a glass.'

She shook her head. 'I can't. I have to pray in the morning.'

He laughed. 'Don't you know, you should offer everything at the altar. God accepts all, especially the morning fumes of the alcoholic's obedient, pure-hearted wife.'

She held out her hand for the drink and sat on the floor beside him. He laid his head in her lap tiredly and was soon asleep. Gently, she pushed a lock of hair away from his forehead. Then she bent down and kissed the tired, lined skin she found underneath. The truth was he drank because even with all the money in the world, he was just not happy. She looked up and saw Rubini framed in the doorway.

'Is he sick?' the child asked in a frightened whisper.

'No, he's just tired. He'll be fine in the morning. Go to sleep now.'

The girl turned around unquestioningly and went back to bed. Parvathi watched her small figure go up the stairs. She had thought Rubini would be jealous of her brother, but from the first moment she had walked in with her father, she had gently touched her brother's cheek, and with pride and love called him, 'My baby.' As it turned out, it was Kalichan who was insanely jealous of the new arrival. He growled menacingly whenever Parvathi picked up or kissed the baby. If Kasu Marimuthu shouted him down, he would stop growling, lie back down with his chin on his front legs, but unhappily.

Kasu Marimuthu warned Parvathi never to leave the child and the animal alone, but Parvathi refused to take his warning seriously. Instead she told him a story she had heard on her mother's lap about a man who left his pet, a mongoose, to guard his firstborn. He came home one day and found the mongoose, its mouth dripping blood, standing over the crib. With a horrific cry of rage, he cut the mongoose in half, but in the crib, he found his son gurgling beside a dead cobra. 'See, even a mongoose can be trusted . . .'

But Kasu Marimuthu frowned impatiently. He had no time for folk tales.

'Look,' she appealed, 'Kalichan's always been a bit slow on the uptake, but it's only a matter of time before he gets used to the baby and accepts him as part of the family. Look at him now. See how he is smiling.' For Kalichan had a way of pulling back his lips when he was happy. It looked like a snarl but it was not.

'God! Not more nonsense,' Kasu Marimuthu muttered, and strode away. He did not believe dogs could smile.

Afterwards, she watched Kamala sit on a wooden stool and lay the baby on her thin legs. And while Kuberan screamed without respite, she oiled and bathed him so vigorously that Parvathi sometimes feared her son would slip right out of her grip. Afterwards she stuck her thumb in his mouth and pressed it into the roof of his mouth and with the other hand yanked at his nose.

'What are you doing?'

'This will make his nose nice and sharp like a Bengali's.'

Maya shook her head, but Kamala swore by it. She had done the same to all her children and they all had high noses.

One Sunday after his bath Parvathi came into the room and felt her knees give way. Kalichan had her baby by the shoulder, close to the neck. Though his teeth were bared, they had not yet broken the skin. She dropped to the ground and spoke gently to him. She explained that the baby was only little. She told him he was her first love and that the baby was only a little thing. She asked him not to hurt it. She promised to love him until the day she died, and Kalichan let go the crying baby and stepped back. The baby was squalling with terror, but she did not move to pick it up. Instead she held out her arms to the dog. 'Come here, you silly thing,' she said, and he trotted up to her and stood shamefaced inside the circle of her arms.

'Don't do that again,' she said, and he looked so sheepish for what he had done that it made her want to cry. He began to shiver and whimper with fear and remorse, and Kasu Marimuthu who had been waiting at the doorway, ran in to snatch up the baby and rock him gently in his arms until his cries ceased.

'He isn't hurt,' Parvathi pleaded, but Kasu Marimuthu, his face a thundercloud, would not even look at her. Wordlessly, he gave the baby to her and called to the dog. With a dejected glance at her, Kalichan followed him. She held the baby in her arms and stared out of the window. He was going to punish the dog. Poor Kalichan, he hated being locked up. She must be very careful from now on. She'd not leave them alone until the boy was a bit older. She nuzzled her baby. 'Don't be frightened,' she said, 'The two of you'll be the best of friends one day. He didn't really mean it, otherwise he'd have drawn blood; easily. He won't be able to help loving you, you'll see.' She buried her face in the baby's neck and breathed in the scent of the boy and dog, and thanked God she had walked in when she had.

The sound of the shot went right through her unprepared being.

She went rigid with shock, and must have squeezed the baby, for he began crying again. She held the blaring bundle in her arms dumbly, not rocking it, or in any way attempting to comfort it, until Maya appeared before her, and she held her son out to her. The baby transferred, Parvathi turned and ran down the glass corridor, down the white stone steps, out of the house, and halfway across the lawn before coming to a sudden halt.

Kasu Marimuthu was walking back towards the house, holding the gun loosely in his hand, his shoulders slumped forward and his face grey with the terrible thing he had done. When he saw her, he stopped and waited. Behind him, Kupu and the gardener were moving towards a flash of white on the ground. She had polished Kalichan's fur with the palm of her hand only that morning, using dew she found on the grass. She raised that hand – it was trembling uncontrollably – towards her eyes. There were no tears, just this searing fury. The fury was indescribable. It focused on the metal in his hand. Her hand itched for that cold grey invention.

'That dog was not yours to shoot,' she would say calmly as he fell clutching his miserable chest, his face incredulous. It would be sudden, and that suited her just fine. She dragged her hand down her face, and her foot took a step towards him. Her face was strangely mask-like, only her eyes were pools of black hate.

He had killed the dog because he was a big man. And it was imperative that a big man always undertake the big gesture. He could not have segregated the dog and the child, or waited, or even given the dog away. No, he was a big man. But she? What was she? What was this cold thirst to see his blood spilled? At heart revenge was so meaningless. The wrong cannot be undone. No matter what. No, she shouldn't get any nearer. She knew that. She took a step backwards. Her husband, impetuous fool, stretched a shaking hand out and took a step forward. Turning away, she ran back around the side of the house towards the gate, and into the jungle.

In the temple, she sat, her hand covering her mouth, remembering what Maya had told her when she first arrived. 'Sit very still and you will pull everything you want towards you.' So she did, her eyes closed, not thinking, not moving a muscle. How long she stayed like that she could not have said, but eventually she heard a shambling sound, dull thuds on the stone floor. She felt neither fear nor worry. The sound came closer, but still she did not react. But when it came to a stop right in front of her she opened her eyes; and blinked. Why, it was the old female, Mary! She was so old. There was grey in her coat. Parvathi had not seen her for three years now and thought she had died, shot by poachers trying to capture her baby. Oh, what great joy it was to see her again! Shame there was no strawberry jam sandwich for her. And with that thought she began to cry helplessly, tears pouring down her face.

Mary put one hand on Parvathi's lap and raised a leathery index finger to touch the tears on her cheek. And then the ape did the strangest thing. She moved her face closer and simply looked into Parvathi's eyes. Parvathi stared into her small amber eyes. Unlike human eyes they had no discernible thought behind them, and that made them seem timeless and depthless, without beginning or end.

All of a sudden it happened: Parvathi felt her reality – and she would use this very word later to describe the feeling to Maya – 'wobble', as if the air had turned to water. Then her mind was taken over by a swirling vortex of black wind. She experienced this as a total loss of solidity, a quality of weightlessness, of moving in an arc, but strangely not upwards, but downwards, being pulled through a narrow gap that led into the depths of earth. She was not frightened until somewhere inside her she suddenly registered emptiness, loss, and terrible regret.

A man's voice shouted, 'No!' in her ear and she jerked her head back, and the sudden movement caused the ape to leap away. For a long moment both ape and woman looked at each other in astonishment, and then Mary backed off, slowly and without a sound, passed out of sight.

When Parvathi told Maya what Mary had caused to happen, Maya said, 'It's not the ape. It is the ground that allows energy vortices that cannot normally be seen, heard or felt, to be discerned as a feeling. I told you before that this ground is very powerful. Because in your moment of sadness you forgot your petty little worries, hopes and wants, and connected on a deep and meaningful level with another creature of nature, an energy vortex allowed you to feel its presence, and let you into a secret. It told you that not only your past, but also your future is gathered around you, waiting to manifest. That time is not linear but spherical, and because it is so it can be changed today, now. In that moment of connection it let you see what was standing around you, what your present is calling towards you.'

'But it was a sensation of unspeakable regret.'

Maya remained expressionless.

'You must tell me, please. How I can change the future if I don't know what to change?' Parvathi urged.

'You are here because you wanted to experience love in all its many manifestations. Your son volunteered to test your idea of love.'

'What do you mean?'

'Because you held him in your belly you will never be indifferent to even the smallest indignity towards him, but he will bring pain to you.'

'Why? What can you see in the future?'

'I can't see into the future. Nobody can for certain. Nothing is set. No one can say for sure. We Asians are too fatalistic with our fortune-tellers and sighs of "But it's all fated". The future is a set of probabilities. Every moment we are changing the future with our thoughts, choices and deeds. In fact, there are ways even to change the past if one knows how to. Even the smallest change in a person can have big ripples in his future, and sometimes the entire future of mankind can be changed by one small decision by a single person in one tiny part of the world.'

Parvathi felt a flash of resentment sweep through her. 'If that's the case, how can you sit here and so calmly claim that a sweet newborn who has done nothing wrong yet, will cause me grief some day?'

'His stars indicate it, but the concept that you or anyone is a victim is an illusion. Nothing that happens to you is bad, ever. Everything has been carefully chosen to test you, to see if you are ready for the next level. People do not realise this, but to go up we only have to respond to all our challenges from the heart. Since unconditional love is not an emotion, it doesn't pass through the body subject to certain conditions being met. It is a powerful, unchanging, eternal, limitless energy, and like fire it has the power to transform. You and perhaps even him.'

'What if it doesn't change him?'

'Then that will be the perfect outcome of your love. It is difficult to grasp, but everything is already perfect. You see, the universe is made up of only three forces, positive, negative and balance. When does peace come to a pendulum? When it stops swinging either way, and stays exactly in the middle, exactly in balance. Understand that that is what everything is trying to do, come into perfect balance. Whenever you see any kind of chaos or trouble, see it as something that is looking for its peaceful middle. Be it a human being, an animal, a situation, a country, or a planet, the same cosmic law is at work.

'It is not for us to judge the path anyone else has chosen to walk. Remember, they who are angry, frustrated, disillusioned, or in places where they are killing, cheating and lying are already as divine as they will ever be; only they have not come into balance yet. Allow him to come into balance in his own way. But whether we take a thousand lifetimes or one to come into balance, we all will.'

That night, Kasu Marimuthu did not come home for dinner and Parvathi lay in bed tormented by the sight of the scratches the dog had made on the door during the times she had locked him in her room. It was the early hours of the morning when her husband returned. His footsteps stopped for a moment outside her door before he turned the knob and came in, but when he saw that she refused to open her eyes even though he stood for a long time over her, he put something on the bedside table and went out.

It was a shell full of touch-me-nots. She touched the soft flowers. Kasu Marimuthu was sorry. There was a clumsily folded paper amongst them. She opened it and saw diagonally, across the paper, his untidy scrawl. *He did not struggle. He gave himself up to his fate with a* smile. *It was almost sweet.* She shivered.

When she saw her husband at breakfast the next morning, he had already finished and was getting up to leave. He pushed back his chair and dismissed himself by saying briefly to that space six inches away from her face, 'Good morning.'

The February rains that were necessary for a good mango harvest had arrived and she turned her head to look at the deluge outside.

Illness

Kasu Marimuthu was 52 years old when he suffered a stroke. At first Parvathi thought she had dreamed his great shout, and did nothing, but his voice came again, louder, more urgent. She rushed out of bed and found him lying with his eyes rolled up into their sockets, his mouth pulled down on one side, and his left hand twisted under his body. She ran for Maya and stood back nervously while she crouched over him, and held his wrist between her thumb and first finger.

'Do I send for the doctor?' she asked.

'No,' said Maya. 'Give me an hour and a half. Since Western medicine has no treatment for his paralysis, a delay will not make a difference to them. But in these first crucial hours I can take away this stiffness.'

'All right,' Parvathi agreed immediately, although by the increase in the unintelligible noises Kasu Marimuthu emitted, it was obvious that he had strong objections to Maya's plan.

'Wake Kamala up and tell her to heat two handfuls of salt crystals and one of black pepper.'

Parvathi ran to her task. When she returned, Maya was using her thumb and middle finger to flick the pads of Kasu Marimuthu's fingers. Then she used a safety pin that she found on her blouse to prick them and squeeze them into bleeding. While Kasu Marimuthu continued to babble and shout with fear and pain, she did the same with his toes. Next, she massaged his fingers with firm upward movements. Kasu Marimuthu groaned softly.

Kamala hurried in with the salt and pepper wrapped in a white cloth. Maya asked for piper longum seeds. As Kamala turned to do her bidding Maya held the hot compress to the crown of

Kasu Marimuthu's head and he gave a great cry of fury. Parvathi cringed and Maya spoke soothingly to him, but she did not stop her painful ministrations. In fact, she called for Gopal to hold down his flailing hands, and began moving the compress down to his forehead and onto his struggling, shouting face, paying particular attention to his twisted lips, moving the compress down to his neck and chest. From his armpits she moved to his body, hips, the backs of his knees, and finally to the soles of his feet. Huge droplets of sweat that had gathered at Maya's forehead and temples ran in rivulets down her throat into the dark valley between her breasts, and the back of her blouse was soaking wet.

Kamala returned with the piper longum seeds. Prising open Kasu Marimuthu's mouth, she slipped them under his tongue. When the compress lost its heat, Kamala was sent to reheat it. Kasu Marimuthu groaned while Maya flicked his toes, beat his wrists, kneaded his stomach, and bore her entire weight down on his back. Then all over again, deaf to her patient's cries, she placed the hot compress on all the areas that were stiff and unmovable.

'Call the berloedy doctor,' Kasu Marimuthu blurted out suddenly. And as if on cue his eyes rolled back down, and he stared at Maya in shock. The enunciation was a little off, but he could speak. The root doctor's treatment was working!

Maya smiled. 'It is spring now and all things can be healed. I will cook his food without salt, oil or meat, and massage him for another ten days, and you must bathe him in very hot water and dress him in red.'

When the doctor arrived he found Kasu Marimuthu sitting on a chair, weak and aching, but back to normal. They were mistaken, the doctor said; it was impossible that Kasu Marimuthu had actually suffered a stroke or had been half-paralysed two hours ago. It must have been a temporary contraction of the muscles, perhaps a fit of some kind.

He looked at Maya with all the power and authority of his profession. He was, after all, one of society's gods. 'It is not possible to cure paralysis with the application of hot compresses and an hour and a half of massage, no matter how vigorous.'

'One hundred years from now, most of the things that you are doing in the name of medicine will be considered barbarous,' Maya said, drawing herself up to her great height.

The doctor looked at Parvathi sternly. 'In future, call me immediately. I have seen the harm that these uneducated witch doctors do even with the best intentions.'

Opening his black leather bag he fetched a gleaming stethoscope to listen to Kasu Marimuthu's chest. Satisfied with what he heard he busied himself with other routine checks. Finally, he shut his bag, declared that there was nothing physically wrong with Kasu Marimuthu and left.

'You may stand now,' Maya said, but Kasu Marimuthu refused. 'I can't. I've just suffered a major stroke,' he said.

'You haven't,' said Maya. 'If you had, you would have crumpled to the floor with not your left but your entire right body affected and I would have treated you with a cold compress on your head and made you vomit but even then you would have had to to drag your right leg, but you would still have been able to walk.'

In the days that followed, despite the doctor's prognosis and Maya's assertion that there was absolutely no reason why he shouldn't walk, Kasu Marimuthu did a strange thing. He ordered a wheelchair and confined himself to it. He also purchased a silver cane that he hung behind his wheelchair and never once attempted to use it. And then because he loathed being carried up and down the stairs he hired Chinese builders to build a lift for him.

Attired in his dressing-gown, he said to Parvathi, 'I don't know why it should be, but I feel just like a writer.' In actual fact, he had no interest in writing. His real passion was reading. The first time he asked her to climb up the mobile winding stairs in the library and get him a book he wanted was when she realised that he actually knew where every single book was kept. It was no random collection after all. He had selected the thousands very carefully indeed.

Early one evening while he was reading quietly on the veranda, he saw his son peering into the flower bushes at the far edge of the house. The boy had found a bird's nest. Kasu Marimuthu was about to call out, to tell him not to touch the chicks or the mother would abandon them, when something silenced him and he watched his son with growing horror. He saw the boy take a chick from its home and hold it in his cupped palm. Then he straightened out his palm exposing the shivering, loudly chirping creature. It tried to stand, and tottered unsteadily. He brought it up to eye level. Then he caught its tiny head between his thumb and index finger and deliberately twisted its neck until it chirped no more.

As Kasu Marimuthu's eyes bulged at the careless cruelty he had witnessed, Maya came into his vision. As if in a dream the boy raised his head and looked up to her. She carried a heavy hand up to his face and lovingly stroked it until he fell into a kind of trance. Gently she touched his Adam's apple and Kasu Marimuthu's hand went instinctively to cover his own. He had the uneasy feeling of having had a similar experience.

She gazed into the boy's blank face and said, 'You can be better than this. I know you can. Don't make your mother's heart bitter. I have seen the future and it is not pleasant, but it is not set in stone either. Nothing is. You can change it. You can be different. You only have to decide to change. You came here to master yourself, remember?' And then she took the carcass from the boy's frozen hand and moved away. The boy stood alone, and it was very slowly that he came out of his trance-like state. For a moment he looked about him in confusion, but then he shrugged, picked up a stick by his feet and threw it at nothing before running off in the direction of the beach.

Kasu Marimuthu stared thoughtfully into the distance, and remembered Parvathi saying, 'Maya is in this world but she is not of it. She is special.'

That evening, when Maya came to give him his massage, he said, 'Is it true that you can look into a person's left eye and see the animal that they most closely resemble?'

Maya spared Kasu Marimuthu a brief glance. 'Yes,' she

answered, and returned to carefully grating a small twig as if every speck of it was precious.

'Well then, tell me what you see in my daughter's eyes?'

Maya smiled to herself. 'Now that she is young she is a peacock. Beautiful, vain and sure of herself, but in time she will grow kind and be full of love.'

'And my son?'

'He has the narrow shoulders of a wolf and the ungrateful eyes of a crocodile which will cause him to eat his own mother's heart.'

'What can be done with him?'

'Nothing. In God's plan he is the perfect vehicle of his own evolution.'

Kasu Marimuthu looked astonished.

'You cannot understand now and I cannot explain.'

Kasu Marimuthu closed his eyes. Soon he would be gone and any little discipline the boy had would die with him. He must call his solicitor the next day, amend his will, give his wife greater authority.

'Will you tell me what you see in me?'

'A tiger. Alone, wounded, frightened, lashing out.'

'What about Sita? What animal does she keep in her left eye?'

Maya looked up from her task. 'What do you think?'

'A deer. Sweet, innocent and gentle.'

Maya laughed outright. 'Oh sir, you have not known your wife at all. She is not a deer. She is a snow leopard. Elusive, brave, mysterious, unknowable.'

Kasu Marimuthu sucked his tongue against his upper front teeth to express disbelief. 'No. How can that be? She is always so quiet, so shy, so still.' And, he thought to himself, even when I climb on top of her.

'You have seen her but not recognised her.'

'The way she allows the boy to boss her about is not very unknowable or predatory, is it?'

'That is a privilege her love has accorded him.'

Kasu Marimuthu fell silent for a while. And then he asked the question that his heart wanted to know. 'And the dancer?'

'She was a broken-hearted swan. Her mate went and left her.'

Kasu Marimuthu closed his eyes to hide his pain, but it seeped into his mouth. 'I still love her,' he whispered brokenly.

'I know,' Maya said, and he had never heard her gentler or kinder.

Last Days

Maya dipped her fingers into thin rice-flour paste and drew patterns on the floor just inside Kasu Marimuthu's bedroom door.

'A pentagram?' he observed, after a while.

'Ah, so that is what it is called. I didn't know its English name.'

'What's a Western symbol of witchcraft got to do with Hinduism?'

'If it is known to you as a symbol of witchcraft then the male energy that has ruled this planet for this last thirteen thousand years has done its work of imbuing yet another feminine symbol of power with a negative connotation. These interlocking triangles are a symbol of unconditional love.'

Kasu Marimuthu laughed shortly. 'Why might a great and secular body like the Government of the United States of America want to use the symbol of unconditional love as the logo of their military might and stamp it on every tank, fighter plane, and missile they produce?'

'Makes you wonder who those men in power really are, doesn't it?' Maya smiled. 'Anyway, it is there because the men who put it there understood its limitless power. In times of great sages and pure-hearted men, an arrow shot after a mantra had been whispered into it could unerringly hit a target many miles away. But the unscrupulous rule the world now, and if their parasitic existence is to be maintained not only can they not admit that such symbols have any powers, but they must also set about destroying their reputation, and suppress their use by others.'

Kasu Marimuthu frowned and crossed his arms. 'Why would a sacred symbol avail itself to misuse, anyway?'

'The human race is conditioned to sit in judgement, universal laws do not. A law is a law. Does gravity differentiate between a criminal and a saint? All sacred symbols are governed by universal cosmic laws; they are there to all who seek them, and will lend their power equally to heal or destroy. There is an ancient story about an evil king who performed unfailing penance for many hundreds of years until eventually Lord Shiva appeared before him and granted him a boon, anything he wanted – wealth, power, immortality ... But from the Great Destroyer God, the King needed only one thing – the power to turn to ashes everything he touched! To test his new power, the King expressed the desire to touch his benefactor's head.

'What could Shiva do but turn and run, with the King in hot pursuit. Watching from the heavens, Vishnu, The Preserver, turned himself into an irresistibly beautiful woman and appeared on the path of the King. It was love at first sight. "Marry me," he cried. "Swear it upon your head," said the siren coyly, and in a great unthinking rush the King touched his head and turned to ashes.

'The figures are of course, allegorical, but Shiva is a force, that can no more deny an evil king than he can a saint who has performed the same penance. Likewise the energy that is inherent in the pentacle will grant its boon to whoever uses it.'

'Good God, I can't believe I'm actually having this discussion with you. You don't even listen to the radio. What do you know about what's going on halfway across the world?'

'I am ignorant of world affairs, so perhaps you will tell me, where does the Statue of Liberty come from?'

'It was a gift from the Freemasons of France.'

Maya looked up from her drawing. 'Well, well; not one of those Western secret societies, surely?' she said, and laughed. 'In her right hand she holds aloft fire, the symbol of her consort, the Sun God, because she is, in fact, a Goddess Queen of the Babylonian religion, right down to the spikes around her head.'

Kasu Marimuthu looked at Maya sharply. The woman was mad. 'To what point all this nonsense, anyway?'

'To concentrate the power of a cold, rigidly pragmatic, ancient bloodline, which is not completely human.' At this point Kasu Marimuthu's eyebrows shot up sceptically, but Maya carried on regardless. 'They already own most of the earth's wealth and are unimaginably powerful, but remain so shadowy, they almost don't exist. Their aim is exclusive control: world domination, a one-government world. In this aim they never take chances. Behind the scenes you will find their money influences everything, the ruling party as well as the opposition, heads of state, governments, world bodies, central banks, the food and pharmaceutical industries, the media, and all secret organisations that spy on people. Subtly the masses will be hypnotised into a semi-stupor through the education system, and a steady diet of entertainment designed to titillate the senses until even the most hardcore pornography will not be enough. Caught up in distractions, people will not realise that their power is being systematically stripped away and their ability to awaken to their true potential has been suppressed. In less than a hundred years there will be something called globalisation that will further concentrate the power in fewer and fewer hands so that eventually the few can completely control the many. They will begin with a central government for Europe.'

'Hold on a minute,' Kasu Marimuthu said, greatly amused. 'Seeing it's you I'm willing to stretch to alien-humans, but a central government in Europe; that's lunacy. They hate each other. You do know that there is a war going on in Europe to stop just such a thing happening, don't you?'

'War is nothing more than an opportunity for the right people to profit. The European one-state will come into being and then America will merge with Mexico and Canada.'

'The Americans will never stand for it.'

'The United States of America is where the earthly war between good and evil will ultimately be fought. The Declaration of Independence – equality, freedom, and fulfilment – drawn up by the Founding Fathers, was the beginning of a sacred vision that was meant to one day transform the entire world. But mischievous forces have taken hold. One day the son and grandson of a convicted Nazi war criminal will become American Presidents, and the world will know a permanent war economy; a policy of secretly fuelling both sides with weapons that keep the world profitably warring. And oil, ah! What will they not do for that? That is when they will find a useful thing: "terrorism". And so the men in power will attack their own people and blame it on the terrorists. In the name of security, draconian laws will be legislated, turning the freedom-loving American people into one of the most massively controlled people on earth, all the time marching towards their goal of a global government, a ferocious global army, a cashless one-currency society, and the employment of a tagging system with chips inserted into the body. Mankind will become no more than a herd of sheep.'

'If we are all to be no more than manipulated animals, what hope is there for the future?' Kasu Marimuthu asked, with mock horror.

'For us there is always the law of karma, another fine example of a law that shows no discrimination. All actions have consequences. Let them beware. Misuse always brings ashes. The system will crack. Dark always serves the light. All of humanity is evolving into shamanic consciousness, and we *will* awaken to our own power. One day men will do the right thing, without caring for the consequences to themselves, and that day we will all become free again. Perhaps not in our time, but certainly before Rubini's time is up we must all become conscious or all be damned. For we are all one, all invisibly but inseparably connected, and as long as there is even one person who is lost, so are we all.'

God Comes

The trunk of books of 'everything Japanese' that Kasu Marimuthu had ordered arrived. He picked out the ones he thought most important and urged Parvathi to read them.

'Know thy enemy,' he said.

But she turned the pages desultorily; history. Dry stuff about Emperors, shogunates, samurais and boring port treaties. Discarding them, she crouched beside the trunk and selected a book on Japanese art. She looked at the unfamiliar landscapes made with a few simple brushstrokes, but without the cultural sensitivity to appreciate such austerity, she put it aside and chose another, skimming over pages until she came upon a photograph of a geisha. She stared at the bone-white face with only the middle of her lips painted scarlet. As if compelled to, she touched the strange face. Her finger was very dark in comparison.

Was it the eyes of that unknown woman, so cold and far away, or was it the idea of a human face turned into a mask that made her feel an affinity for that sad creature? She read the paragraph underneath. Anonymous geisha, nineteenth century, it said simply. Geishas, the author was at pains to point out, were not prostitutes but extremely accomplished women who served and entertained men in tea houses. But how did one entertain men if not with the body?

Eventually, her hands came upon a collection of love letters geishas had penned to their lovers. Nothing high-minded about them, but they were her first taste of romance on a page, and hence commanded her complete attention. It seemed as if in the end they were all ill-fated that fell in love in Japan. Always the geisha was left broken-hearted or committing suicide. She looked again at the picture of the unknown woman. 'Did you kill yourself too?'

At the very bottom of the trunk she found a sex book euphemistically named 'selling spring'. It was full of cartoons of men and women engaged in lewd acts. Utterly shocked but also riveted, she studied them minutely. The pictures got more and more lurid until the pages were crammed with awful people with rolled-back eyes, writhing and twisting under unnaturally enormous genitals.

There was one more hideous than the rest. A woman in the embrace of a giant octopus, but this octopus had also put its beak-like mouth between her legs and seemed to be eating her. But what was confusing and intriguing to Parvathi was that the woman did not seem terrified, revolted, or in pain. In fact, her expression was one of pure ecstasy. What a thoroughly obscene race, she decided. But then she found herself tearing out the page, folding it into four, and tucking it into her blouse.

'Remember Samuel West?' Kasu Marimuthu said.

'Yes, why?'

'Big scandal, he's getting a divorce.'

'Oh!'

'He rather fancied you, I thought.' And when he saw the sudden unguarded expression in his wife's face, asked drily, 'Does the plot thicken?'

But she recovered herself, looked him square in the eye and replied, 'With flour it might, not otherwise.'

'Anyway, he might be back,' he said enigmatically, but Parvathi did not pursue the remark.

Three months passed quickly, and though Parvathi was still struggling with the basics, Kasu Marimuthu already had a good grasp of Japanese. But he was also turning a strange, waxy yellow. He complained of nausea, fever, chills, vomiting, abdominal tenderness and pain. His body had begun to pass mercaptans directly into the lungs. The doctor called it a late sign of liver failure, Maya called it the 'breath of the dead'. But even then the craving for alcohol was sometimes so strong and so uncontrollable, that it was impossible for anybody to approach him, but Parvathi.

'Hold my hand. I'm afraid,' he whispered. Parvathi took his big, dry hand in hers and held it until he went to sleep.

Downstairs, Maya was sitting in her rocking chair. 'Is he asleep?' she asked.

'Yes,' Parvathi said, and sat down on the swing opposite. It rocked gently and her eyelids fluttered down tiredly, until a great shout shattered the peace. Parvathi came upright – Kasu Marimuthu was awake and needed help.

But Maya stood. 'I'll go,' she offered.

'Are you sure?' Parvathi asked, already falling back into the soft cushions.

Maya opened the door and saw the man flushed and restless in his bed. She pushed aside the mosquito net and he turned his face to stare at her, large, calm, not a hair out of place. Her powerful hands moved towards the glass of water by his bedside. She dipped a finger in it and pulled the moisture along his parched lips. His tongue, coated with white and yellow sediment, came out to lick the coolness.

'Let go,' she said. 'You need not this rotting body in your new environment.'

His eyes and mouth opened in fear. A film of sweat glistened on Maya's upper lip as she reached down to his stomach and with long, slow strokes began to rub his mottled skin with sesame oil infused with herbs. Under the solidity and weight of her hand, the fear and suffering relented. His eyes closed.

'I know,' he said. 'I am not like my grandfather. No one needs to feed me soil and gold. I am prepared to leave all this behind. It never brought me happiness, anyway.'

She nodded slowly and carried on with her firm, steady movements until he fell asleep.

On 25th August Kasu Marimuthu took to his bed permanently. Teams of doctors came but none of them appeared confident of his chances of recovery.

'Parvathi,' called Kasu Marimuthu.

Parvathi stared at him. He had called her by her real name for the first time.

'I want you to know that I am glad I married you,' he said. 'I was a fool to chase after beauty. It's a handful of air. When I am gone, do not wear the white sari of the widow, and whatever you do, do *not* try to run the shop. Sell it immediately, or your family, who did not care enough for you to protect you from my wrath, will come to squander away all that I have built.' She looked blank, hearing only that he had loved her out of pity. He grabbed her hand urgently. 'Do not be a fool. You must believe me. They will all come to cheat you. One by one. Promise me you will sell it immediately. I have left more than enough for you and the children to live very well on for generations to come.'

'I promise,' she said, and at that time she could have sworn she meant to do it.

'The Japanese are coming. They are uncaring and inhuman.' She thought of the woman with the octopus. 'You will be safe as they do not care for dark skin.' The white-faced geisha flashed into Parvathi's mind. 'But do all you can to protect my daughter. Cut her beautiful hair. Blue is not her colour, dress her in it. Get the tailor to make shapeless shirts out of old cloth. Turn her into a boy and hide her as much as you can. Send her not even to school, for they will be there too. Teach her yourself at home. Install a huge portrait of Mahatma Gandhi in the entrance of the house. They are known to be kind wherever they find his face.'

The head priest from the Pulliar temple came with a group of Brahmin priests. With top knots, and bulging stomachs, they had come especially from India to perform a *yagna*. To propitiate the Gods so they would bless the sick man, they gathered around a large brick pit at the entrance of the house, and made their sacrificial fire. The head priest lifted his thick wooden spoon. And so it began: between dollops of the purest ghee, fruit, seeds, nuts, spices, coconut pieces, sweet rice, flowers, roots, paper money, honey, milk, and salt were offered to the flames.

The fire became hotter and hotter, but they fanned it still further with their incessant chanting. Secret Sanskrit mantras that ended with the word *swaha*. Their voices were all different, deep, shrill, high, low and yet it all came together beautifully and began to rise to a crescendo that trembled so powerfully even the hair on her hands stood. Someone said, 'Feed a piece of jewellery to the fire.' So Parvathi removed her bangle and the priests offered that to the fire. They continued to feed it for a day and a night. Dark clouds closed in, thunder cracked the sky, and it rained torrentially, the Gods had accepted the offering. Everyone seemed suddenly hopeful of Kasu Marimuthu's recovery.

Until the servants found the steel cap of one of Kuberan's imported shoes in the ashes. Wringing their hands in great consternation they ran to tell their mistress. Who could have done such a blasphemous thing? Parvathi felt her hands go clammy. Kuberan was called down. At first, he denied it, but then Maya was called in from the kitchen. He was afraid of her. She stood before him with folded arms and stared down at him until he confessed. He had not meant it in a bad way. He just wanted to see his shoe burn. Anyway, he spluttered, he had only thrown it into the fire after the priests had finished their prayers. The assembled servants gazed wide-eyed at the boy's audacity. Then Rubini went out and came back in with a cane. She held it out to Parvathi.

'Papa is too sick to punish him, so you must,' she told her stepmother.

Parvathi gripped the thin rod in her fist and stared miserably at Kuberan. She had never disciplined him before. He looked back at her without remorse. She bit her lip. She knew everyone thought that he had done something unforgivably disrespectful in desecrating a sacred ceremony, but she didn't see it that way. True, he was demanding and spoilt and could bring the entire household to a standstill if a toy he cared nothing for went missing, but to her he was simply a mischievous child. Boring holes into the outhouse walls and peeping at the servant girls at their toilet, and once even creeping out of his bed in the middle of the night to paint all Kasu Marimuthu's rare white birds bright green. She moved to stand before him. Though he had not meant to, he had ruined the *yagna* and then lied about it.

'I'm really sorry, Ama,' he said, his bottom lip quivering.

The sight worried her heart. But servants were watching. Some discipline was necessary. Her voice was stern. 'Hold out your hand.'

He stretched a hand out. It seemed small and defenceless to her. She raised the cane high above her head, and he snatched his hand away about the same time that she brought the cane down hard on a table nearby. Her heart was beating fast. Kuberan was looking at her curiously, the lively glint back in his eyes. He would, he must, grow out of his wild ways.

'You should have caned him,' Rubini said into the silence. Then turning blazing eyes to her brother said, 'And you shouldn't have done it, Kuberan.' But the little devil grinned at her.

For a moment his sister stared at him, bewildered. 'If anything happens to Papa it will be your fault,' she cried, and rushed away in tears.

Parvathi ordered everyone to leave.

'Why?' she asked the boy who looked up fearlessly at her.

Kuberan thought for a while. Then he shook his head. 'I don't know why,' he said glumly.

'But you knew that *yagna* was for Papa, didn't you?'

He nodded slowly. Maybe even sadly.

'Don't you love your father?'

His eyes swam suddenly with tears. He had not thought of the consequences of his behaviour.

'Go to your room and don't come out until I tell you to.'

At the door he stopped and turned back. 'If Papa dies it won't be my fault, will it?'

'No,' she said softly. Upstairs Kasu Marimuthu steadily weakened.

Two days later the enemy landed on the shores of Malaya. News came from the plantations in Malacca that they could hear the vibrations of the bombs, not Japanese ones, but the British destroying their own strategic posts behind them. The managers began moving out of their bungalows. *Leaving for Johor stop*, came the first telegram. Soon all of them were gone. The British had deserted the sinking ship. The planes flew overhead three at a time. Parvathi never knew if they were British or Japanese. Only that they should all make for the shelter stairs.

Kasu Marimuthu pulled Parvathi's arm so her ear was close to his mouth and asked, 'What's the Japanese word for "friend"?'

Parvathi shook her head. She had forgotten already.

He pulled her down again, 'To-mo-dachi,' he whispered.

'Tomodachi,' Parvathi said, and he smiled tiredly.

'The pain is gone,' he said. His eyes were full of peace and his face glowed. He had never looked better.

Parvathi was cleaning out the oil lamp in the prayer room when she heard a faint tinkle, looked up, and saw that Maya's little statue had lost another arm. For a moment she stood, shocked, and then she ran out towards the kitchen calling, 'Maya, Maya.'

From the kitchen Maya began to run towards Parvathi's voice. They stopped within sight of each other.

'Another of Nagama's arms has fallen.'

'Then it must be time to leave.'

'You can't leave us now!' Parvathi cried.

Maya shook her head. 'It is not I who will be leaving, but you. I will only be following you.'

'What are you talking about?'

'Let's just wait and see what happens.'

Kasu Marimuthu began to vomit blood. The earth that bore him desired him back. He would not survive the night. To facilitate the separation of the etheric sheath from the physical body, Maya lit an orange light and burned sandalwood in his room.

'Pease don't leave us, Papa,' Rubini sobbed.

'Don't call him back, child,' Maya admonished gently. 'Or he will be caught between two worlds. His mission here is complete and he must leave the old behind. A doorway has already opened and beautiful beings are coming through it to escort him back. Sing him across, child.'

In the early-morning hours he became frantic. With his eyes he motioned Parvathi to him and when she was close enough, he grabbed at her and brought her to his wretched face. His bristly cheek rubbed against hers, and his hot fetid breath fanned her neck. This was his last surge of strength. Very soon, minutes, he would be no more. His words were barely a whisper, '*This is important. Don't cut your hair, Parvathi.*' With those last unfathomable words the richest man in Kuantan was gone, into death's arms.

Her son was given the lighted torch to carry around the coffin, and that made her cry. Not because she was heartbroken, but because the future that called was bleak and uncertain. True, suttee was dead but a Hindu widow's lot was meagre. Had she been a Brahmin she would have had to shave her head as well; nevertheless, custom still required that she become invisible, less than nothing. No longer allowed to wear kum kum, colourful clothes or jewellery. At twenty-seven she was the woman people did not invite to weddings or auspicious occasions. And even at her own children's marriages she could not bless them or partake in any of the ceremonies. In fact, a good mother would absent herself altogether, for she symbolised bad luck.

The funeral was a huge affair. The house was crowded with people, a great many of whom Parvathi had never before laid eyes on. A dark, thin woman with five small urchins clinging to her, fell on the floor beside the coffin and sobbed so desperately that Parvathi sent a servant to find out who she was. Her husband was a rubber-tapper, a no-good drunk, who beat her mercilessly. If not for a monthly stipend from Kasu Marimuthu, she and her children would have starved to death. In the following hours, seven other women came surrounded by their own clutch of pitiful children to mourn a generous benefactor.

Parvathi removed her thali, kissed it and put it into the coffin. Later, Kasu Marimuthu's oldest friend brought it back to her from the cremation ground and dropped it into her open palm. As customary, she donated the locket to a temple.

That night, Parvathi was roused by the sound of bells.

Chum, chum, chum, came along the empty glass corridors, down the stairs, through the courtyard and towards the study, becoming fainter and dying away in the study. Parvathi lay unafraid. She knew they were only dancer's bells, Rubini's bells, but what on earth was the girl doing at that time of the night? The first notes of classical Indian music played too loud startled her. The lights of the stage on the island came on. Parvathi slid out of bed and went onto the balcony. Rubini was rowing out to the island. Parvathi reached for her opera glasses. Illuminated by bright lights, the girl made for the stage and immediately surrendered to the music. Ah, Rubini, swelling, wanting to burst, dancing for her father. Dressed in her mourning attire, Parvathi attended Rubini's best and last dance recital.

The portrait of Gandhi arrived at the same time as the solicitor. While the boys hung it up facing the entrance, she faced the solicitor with her two children huddled on either side of her. He told her that her late husband had left everything to her, save Rubini's dowry, a large settlement and a house in Bangsar, Kuala Lumpur, and to pay for the boy's education a piece of land. The wisdom to divide the wealth between their children at the appropriate time had been entrusted to her. There was a sterling account in Coutts with sixty thousand pounds in it that would automatically transfer to her. Copies of the deeds to all the land and estate that she now owned were given to her.

After he left Parvathi hid the entire clutch of legal papers behind the books in the vast library. That same night she and Maya took all the jewellery that was in the safe and buried them under the flame tree.

On the third day the visitors stopped coming.

Wearing a white sari, she went to feed the cobra. As she crouched at the altar to pour the milk she heard a sound behind her, the mango leaves being set aside. She turned, not quickly, but slowly – how long she had waited for this moment. A huge cobra with a golden ridge down the back of his head was slithering from the rafters into the wooden enclosure. Her god was so big!

Years she had been going there to feed him, and look how large and magnificent he had grown. No one had ever encountered him before. He was hissing and black as the night, and yet she was frightened not at all.

He did not come forward to drink the milk, but stayed in the shadows by the edge of the temple, coiling his enormous body. Slowly, majestically, he reared his head high above the ground, opened his hood to full and regarded her steadily, her god. With clasped hands she dropped to her knees. For a long time they gazed at each other until eventually he closed his hood and came forward, moving so close to her that his body brushed hers. While she watched, he drank the milk and ate the eggs, grasped them gently in his mouth before cleanly closing it over them. When the eggs were all gone he left, the same way he had come, quietly. She sat back on the floor, light-headed with joy. What a privilege. God had heard her prayers. She must have remained there for hours, thinking she was now surely safe from all harm.

Samuel West arrived that afternoon. Restlessly he paced the veranda. When she appeared at the door he looked at her with surprise. 'I have never seen you like this.'

Unconsciously her hand went to cover her bare throat. He had always seen her painted and decorated. 'A widow does not adorn herself.'

'I must talk to you,' he said urgently.

She looked into those sea eyes. He had retained all his beauty. 'Of course, Mr West.' And she led the way to the courtyard.

He looked around. 'Somewhere private,' he said.

She closed the study door behind them and turned to look at him.

'The Japanese are coming,' he said. 'You need to leave here as soon as possible. I have reserved return flights from Singapore back to the States for us. I'm not as rich as your late husband, of course, but I can support you very handsomely.'

She was astonished. 'No,' she said. 'I can't go with you . . . There are the children and Maya to consider.'

'The children and Maya can come too.'

'Even so, no.'

'Why?'

'Don't you have segregation in America?'

He looked at her strangely. 'I'm from the North.'

'What will I be in your country? Won't they still stare and point and laugh?'

He had the grace to look shamefaced.

'I could never do that to my children.'

He took in her set face, and said, 'Then I'll stay too.'

'You mustn't. It is not safe for foreigners. I will be fine. Go, please, Mr West. We'll meet again after the war.'

'Is there nothing I can do or say to change your mind?'

'No.' She smiled to soften the rejection.

'But we *will* meet again after the war,' he insisted stubbornly, and there was such determination in those sea eyes that she was surprised. Why, he did care, after all. Temporarily at least.

'Have a safe journey, Samuel,' she said.

'Even without any adornment you are beautiful,' he said gruffly, and strode away without a backward glance.

The Japanese arrived in Kuantan.

Parvathi found Rubini in her room. She was at her desk and looked as if she might have been crying, but she stared at Parvathi sternly, holding her pain, refusing anyone's sympathy. She had already made it very clear that she was not going to accept her stepmother's authority.

'Rubini,' Parvathi said, 'we have to cut your hair.'

Rubini stood in her shapeless blue-grey smock and looked at Parvathi's white sari scornfully. 'When my father was alive, sometimes I had to stop myself from saying exactly what I wanted to you, and the effort used to make me tremble so much I had to leave the room. Now at least I never have to do that. You are not my mother, so don't tell me what to do. Just consider yourself lucky that we are not in Africa. There, widows have to drink the water their dead husbands have been washed in.'

Parvathi gasped. 'You don't understand, do you? They are already here. It is no longer safe for anyone. We must cut your hair now. It's what your father wanted.'

'Cut yours if you want to. Oh, and another thing, you can cancel my dance lessons. I don't plan to dance ever again.'

'Why?'

'Because I hate it. I only danced to please Papa, to be the perfect daughter for him and live up to his expectations of me as my mother's daughter,' she said, and left the room.

In her clinic under the tree Maya told a woman who hobbled up to her on painfully cracked heels to soak her feet in her own urine for fifteen minutes at a time. 'And you will see that they will close up in no time at all.'

Tomodachi

Kupu was sitting on the ground sharpening his sickle and Parvathi was on the balcony when the car turned into the driveway. Its doors had been wrenched away and three swords stuck out on the ready. Parvathi recalled reading that no one who has seen a Japanese sword can fail to be impressed by how shiny its blade is; made for beheading, they were to bone what knife was to softened butter.

The car stopped in the porch and its occupants jumped out, the thump of their boots uncivilised, brutal. Their utterances to each other were guttural, a series of barks.

Parvathi ran to the top of the stairs and saw that in the courtyard, the servants had begun to gather like frightened sheep behind Maya.

'Where's Rubini?' she asked.

'In the jungle,' Maya mouthed silently.

And although she had been apprehensive about her ability to face the uncertain future alone, Parvathi rushed down without a second thought and positioned herself in front of Maya. The enemy barged in, ludicrously small men in sweat-stained singlets, soft caps with flaps around the ears and neck, and boots pulled up over baggy brown trousers, but in their faces naught was funny. Hard, impatient, furious, looking for trouble, each an extension of his shining sword.

They came to a sudden standstill and gazed about them. From their open mouths came sounds of wonder, 'Oh, hoh, oh ho.' But they soon remembered themselves and reverted to pointing, grunting creatures. From his frame Mahatma Gandhi smiled his tranquil, benevolent smile. Resistance without violence.

With her hands clasped behind her back, Parvathi bowed very low. '*Ohayoh gozaimasu.*'

Uncouth people; they did not respond. Instead, they grunted and gestured with their swords. She had heard that it was better that they do that, for it was impossible to understand their rotten English, and they were quickly infuriated by anyone who did not understand their needs. And incomprehension turned those shining swords from their vertical positions to fast-moving horizontal ones. But, as it turned out, she had no trouble understanding their crude actions. It was simple really, in the name of their Emperor they wanted the house.

Her late husband had guessed correctly that their home would be appropriated for the greater good of the Empire. In the event he had already made provision for his family to move into the accommodation above the shop, unless the Japs wanted that too. If so, there was the back-up plan; a small house in the middle of a rubber estate on the way to Pekan. 'Take the car,' he had said. 'There, they will never go. The Japanese are frightened of our jungles.'

Immediately, she shape-shifted into that hated creature, nodding vigorously, crawling in the dirt to please. '*Hai, hai,*' of course, at once, certainly, sir. The moment of taking and giving interrupted only when the children, the boy sobbing, the girl white-faced, were herded in by a grim solider. Parvathi couldn't believe her eyes. After everything her husband had said, was it possible that they were this unprepared, this naïve, this open to destruction?

'Mmmm,' one of the soldiers said, but he made this harmless sound from so far down the back of his throat that it held onto its status as a sound, and not an actual act of violence by the thickness of a sapless leaf.

One of them went over to Rubini, grabbed her by the hair and forced her face up. Twitching his nose, he uttered sounds that could have been 'oh', 'hoh', or 'ho'. One of the servants gasped audibly, but the girl screwed her eyes tight shut and refused to blubber. Parvathi began to shake with dread. There was nothing she could do. These were not men. These were beasts. Another soldier came to stand on the other side of Rubini. He did not laugh or make bawdy comments, but leered at the girl. In the excitement of their find, none had heard the sound of a truck driving up.

When a door slammed the men looked at each other in surprise. A soldier rushed in and stood to attention. Immediately the men flung Rubini aside, and came to attention in a row, their hands raised in a salute. A man strode in, a lackey trotting at his heels. He wore a belted army uniform decorated with badges and medals on his chest and shoulders, and a peaked hard cap. There were gold stars on his collar. He too had a sword but it was sheathed at his side. He had a regal, erect bearing and a flat, closed face. It was instantly clear he was not one of them. There was irritation and fury in the quick eye he ran over the situation.

He walked up to the row of men and in true Japanese fashion, slapped them one by one, so hard that they reeled backwards. But he did this with a control that was more ferocious than the unruly bestiality of his men. Their cheeks were bright red, and one had a muscle ticking furiously in his jaw, but all of them stared ahead without a murmur. Within minutes he had reduced to incompetent minions the men who strutted around with human heads stuck to the ends of their swords.

The air bristled with the absolute power this man had over his men. He said something very quietly, and suddenly the language was no longer uncivilised barks but a collection of menacing hisses. She understood one word, *bakairo*, a swear word to the tune of 'fucking idiot'.

'Yes, sir,' they agreed in one voice.

And then this coldly controlled man turned his eyes, the smallest, blackest, most chilling eyes Parvathi had ever seen upon her. Real fear gripped her, a cold metal claw in her belly. She bowed. It took her even lower than before. Who would have thought she could go this low. Another few inches and her head would have been resting on the floor. Polished black leather shoes – different from the coarse boots of his men – came into her vision. Nothing was said so she didn't raise her head.

'It is considered disrespectful to prolong a bow,' he said in clipped but perfect English.

His fluency startled her and caused her to lose her balance and land on her hands. Her first good look at him was from that servile position. His colouring was milk and saffron, his nose flat, his cheekbones high. There was a dull flush of colour on them. His upper lip was thicker than the lower, but they were both drawn into a straight line. And as for the black eyes; there was just one word for them: impenetrable. All in all, it was a breathing mobile mask of a comprehensively suspicious xenophobic.

He had a view of the West as unheroic; a soft, sickly, corrupt civilisation addicted to decadence and personal gratification. Merchants with no ideals, no moral sense, or spirituality and no honour. But there he was wearing European dress, influenced by French architecture, employing British naval strategies and relying on Western weaponry, come to eradicate the disease of Westernisation from the entire world.

But suddenly what the rishis claim to be true became true: it is possible to look into a man's eyes and to see right through to his very soul. She looked into the kill now, ask later, eyes and saw not a fascist tyrant, but a door, one that opened to admit her. Inside that darkness was everything there was to know about him, everything that was important, anyway. So, while she couldn't know his name, or where he lived, or how he liked to while away his time, she knew that once he had worked with his hands, doing something gentle. She knew that he was harsh and exacting, but she also knew that once he had been kind and good-hearted. That this ruthless, merciless behaviour was not inborn but learned.

Then the moment was lost. The door closed. In the blackness of his eyes, like that of a horned beetle something else was preparing.

'I must apologise for my men. I'm afraid vanguards are not picked for their sensitivity.'

'They have not harmed us.'

'Very well. If they have not already made clear. You have twenty-four hours to vacate these premises. You may take your personal belongings, but must leave behind all furniture, cars and servants,' he said, as if he had every right to go about taking people's property. But *that*, she could tell, was not all he wanted. He wanted something more, by far more precious.

Her eyes slid down to Rubini. *Ah, Baby look at you, all curls and eyes. You should have listened to your father. You should have let me cut your hair. I should have held you down and shorn you. What do we do now?*

He had followed the direction of her eyes to the girl on the floor, but the words that left the dagger-cut mouth were not meant to destroy the child.

'If you wish to spare her, you may take her place,' he said softly.

Her eyes opened and her lips parted in disbelief. The fathomless eyes bore into her.

Yes, she had known he was about to strike; even so, she had not expected this. Her husband and the Mamis had declared that their kind wanted only the fair-skinned, and even then only to rape and use the once. Her brain reeled stupidly. Perhaps, she had misunderstood his meaning? 'I'm very sorry, General, sir,' she said. 'I didn't hear you. Could you please repeat?'

'You heard.' No mercy, no smile of encouragement. Nothing. Just a blank wall asking her to be his *ianfu*, his comfort woman. She had begun life in the white sari of a widow only last week.

'Be quick. Time is precious,' he snapped impatiently.

'I can't. I'm a widow. My husband died only last week,' she said.

The stiff face slit open and from it issued soft words spoken pleasantly. 'Do not misunderstand me. That was not a request.' And she saw something in his eyes that she had never seen in her husband's or Samuel West's. Behind a pretence of coldness lay desire, raw, so raw it was bleeding. This man wanted her badly! And not just for the once. She had the sudden knowledge that there was nothing he could hide from her. They were connected at some bizarre, primal level. Or she had known him from before. Had already tasted him.

She dropped her eyes. What was the matter with her? She blinked and he turned to look at Rubini, this time meaningfully. Their voices had been too soft for anyone to have heard.

Everything had an unreal quality to it. 'Asking your favour, sir, would it be possible if my children, and the servants . . . and

my friends, ... my community do not know of this ... ah ...
arrangement.'

He frowned blackly. 'You ask too much. You want this, you want
that. Enough. When you meet a Japanese, do not ask so bluntly.
Say in a gentle way, "If you don't mind, could I please ask?" And
only one thing at a time.'

'If you don't mind, could I please ask something, General,
sir?'

'Of course,' he said, inclining his head.

'Would it be possible if no one was to know?'

A flicker of something passed in his eyes. 'I believe it can be
arranged.'

'That would be really too kind. Thank you very much, sir.'

He bowed; a formal, stiff bow. There was nothing scornful or
impolite in it, but when his eyes met hers again his were different,
sly, verdant. As if by her request for secrecy she had engaged him
in a game. He was the smiling desert that allowed the merchants'
caravan to cross. Halfway through he might stop smiling. They
risked it for profit. She did it for the child. It was a sacrifice. What
was the alternative?

'Will you require assistance to move?'

'No, sir,' she said. 'I will live over my husband's provision shop
in town.'

'You may keep some of your personal belongings in one of the
rooms. Every time you need something, you may come here and
collect it personally.'

She nodded slowly. In a daze. Her eyes on his moving mouth.

'I'll send someone at midnight tomorrow for you,' he said, and
the desire she saw in his face was so intense she dropped her eyes
with shame.

'Ask him to come to the back of Marimuthu's General Store on
Wall Street,' she said.

He nodded curtly and left. The chastised men did the same after
hanging up banners at the entrance of the house. The servants
began to pack while Parvathi stood on the balcony and stared
unseeing out to sea. She had been standing like that for some

time when she heard a movement behind her. It was Rubini, but so pale and strange. Her beautiful hair was loose and unadorned, without the coloured bits and pieces that she liked to weave into it. This time she had escaped. What would happen the next time? She might not survive unsullied.

'What is it?' Parvathi asked.

Rubini held up a pair of scissors. Her eyes were blurry with hate and fury. 'That man,' she said fiercely, 'I smelled the faeces under his fingernails.' Oh, poor, poor child. Now she understood that she must stand in line to make herself ugly.

Silently they carried a chair onto the balcony and Rubini sat on it. Parvathi plaited her hair and then taking a deep breath she cut it close to the neck. 'I'll have to neaten it a bit now,' she said, giving the thick plait to Rubini. The girl put it in her lap and placed both her hands over it.

'You know,' she said, her voice wobbly, 'I have to fight not to react every time you touch me.' Parvathi's hands stilled. The girl carried on talking. 'And every time I see you I think of myself asking my mother for Papa and her answering, "He's gone home to his wife. We can't be selfish. We have to learn to share." Then I remember that night when she supposedly died of fever. I was there. I saw her drink the weed killer. They think I don't know. I cannot forget her burned mouth and chin, and the way she rolled and rolled on the ground. And before it, how she cried. "Always remember," she said, "I'm not leaving you. I'm doing this, so you won't be the dancer's bastard child." So I could live in my father's house. She was being unselfish. But I would have been happier as the dancer's bastard child. She shouldn't have done it. It was not worth it.'

She turned her tearstained face up to Parvathi. 'I know you're a good person and it's not your fault at all. And I'm really sorry, but I feel so angry with you all the time that sometimes I just have to strike out. I even used to feel as if you had manipulated this whole thing and you had stolen my mother's rightful place in this household and me from her. Even now I sometimes catch myself thinking that if not for you, she would be alive in this house with me. I have behaved unforgivably towards you and I feel guilty and ashamed because I know you don't deserve it.

'No matter how rude or obnoxious I have been, I can't remember a time you have raised your voice to me. I don't think I can ever love you, but I promise to try my best to be as kind as possible to you from now on.'

When the last black curl was on the floor, Parvathi closed the scissors and put them on the table. 'I'm sorry about your mother,' she said. 'I once saw her dance and she was the saddest and most beautiful woman I have ever seen. And though it may sound strange to you, I too wish she was still alive.'

Rubini walked to the mirror and stopped aghast. It was as if she was looking at someone else. Her face crumpled, and she ran from the room.

That night, Parvathi dreamed she was at her husband's funeral. They had already closed the coffin, but she asked them to open it again. Inside she saw that Kasu Marimuthu's corpse was not bloated and mottled but as healthy and vigorous as he had been when they first married. As she peered down, he suddenly opened his eyes and sat up. Taking his garlands off impatiently, he asked, 'What the hell is wrong with all of you? I'm not dead yet.' She woke up then and lay quietly in the dark.

The Japanese general had touched her with his eyes.

But she must not forget that it was nothing special that he should want her. She had come to understand that men had 'needs'. Even the Japanese authorities with their draconian ways and methods had had to maintain the bedding of foreign women as a deplorable but necessary evil. But then again, didn't Maya say that, in this world, what you want wants you. Light attracts light. A good woman will bring a good man to her. The beautiful will seek out the beautiful. What had she brought to herself? *A thief comes for a thief.*

Unable to go back to sleep she got out of bed and wandered around the house, room by room, passing quietly in the moonlight. Then she walked out to the beach, and sat, watching the sand flow out of her hand. That was how she felt. Everything was flowing away. The harder she gripped, the faster it flowed. She listened to the waves until the light in the kitchen came on and she knew that Maya was awake.

The Anglophobe

The town had only two streets in those days, Main Street and Wall Street. Both had rubble on them, but not so it obstructed their progress. The shop was on the corner lot of Wall Street. It had wooden panels that slid out. On auspicious days, the entrance was decorated with ropes of jasmine flowers. Inside, it was dim and full of sacks of dried peas, nuts, lentils and rice. Immediately to the left was a table full of mahogany boxes peaked with spices. On every wall, floor-to-ceiling shelves held riches of camphor, soap, toothpaste, tins of imported food, scourers, incense, washing soda and clay lamps. The till was a simple compartmentalised wooden box. A man in a white veshti sat beside it calculating bills. Above it was a prayer altar with garlanded pictures of Mahaletchumi and Pulliar. At the back of the store where it was dark there were big bananas, slowly ripening.

Upstairs were two bedrooms, a living room and a bathroom. The children were quiet and subdued. They put down their bags and went to look out of the window at the street below. Suddenly Rubini screamed: there was a rat in the room. The workers shook their heads dolefully and said there was no getting rid of them. They had tried everything, but hordes came and went as they pleased. Cockroaches enjoyed the same courtesy. They were so plentiful, it sometimes rained cockroaches. Human hair was their favourite landing destination. Rubini opened an umbrella and did not close it until she was inside the mosquito net.

Parvathi wanted Maya to share her room, but she refused. She would be too disruptive. She kept odd hours with her praying and preparing of herbs. Finding a bench downstairs, she said, 'That'll do,' and set it up in the storeroom. Then she went into the adjoining kitchen, and was still cleaning it at 4 p.m. when the *vadai* seller came carrying his wares in a basket on his head.

'Ama,' he called mournfully at the back door.

Maya went out to him.

'Today I've got very good *vadai.*'

She bought four for half a cent, and brought them upstairs with a pot of tea.

By dinnertime the most wonderful smell was wafting out of the kitchen. The men down in the shop were pleased. Rightly they had anticipated that delicious treats were soon to mark their days.

There was no electricity, but Maya found an old kerosene lamp. They lit that and sat around its glow, Rubini under her umbrella. The six o'clock show at the cinema across the street ended and by nine o'clock the street had fallen eerily silent. Maya went out on an errand, but was back by ten. She retired to her room and closed the door.

By half past eleven Parvathi was already waiting behind the door. A thunderstorm was about to break and frogs were making a racket in the drains and she feared she might not hear the knock. There were flashes of white lightning and thunder in the sky. Soon the rain would come. At the first soft knock she opened the door. The driver and she bowed at each other.

She got into the back of the car. They came to a stop. Not a word had been spoken. She climbed up the entrance stairs, her heart in her mouth, turned the door knob and became a guest in her own house. It was the same, and yet, as rain changes every aspect of the desert, her absence had in some strange way nourished it in her mind. There were new shadows and a new kind of silence. There was grandeur too. She had lived here once, and taken it all for granted.

She went to the study and knocked quietly.

'Enter.'

He was sitting behind the desk without his coat or sword, wearing the Japanese military-issue white shirt for officers. The two gold stars on his stiff collar glimmered. There was black ink in a bowl. A glass paperweight held down a black and white map with red dots and crosses. He rose and inclined his head towards a chair. She moved to it.

'This house,' he said conversationally, 'is full of every kind of Western luxury and absurdity.'

She said nothing and he let it go. He went to the window and with his back to her said, 'Your late husband must have been a very strange man to keep nothing but a bunch of worthless papers in his safe.'

She looked at him. He was the enemy, one of the men that her husband had said were coming to show Malayans the difference between arterial and venous blood. The bright and the dark of it. *Trust them not. They are only pretending to bring light. Never forget they are not coming to liberate, but to take without asking.* He turned slightly towards her. His face was stern, even in the shadows. They stared at each other in the blue flashes of light.

'Which one is your bedroom?'

'The first bedroom in the west wing.'

'And the room with the dolls?'

'That was the first wife's room.'

'I see,' he said, and came forward, and she was caught by the way he swung his arms as he walked; unattractive. He stood directly in front of her. 'Take me to your room.'

There was nothing worth saying and what was could not be said. She turned and led the way up the stairs. Her feet were bare and silent on the stone, but his boots made a hollow sound. She would remember that sound until the day she died. It began raining hard. She opened the door and went into her old room. He followed her in and closed the door behind him. Outside, in a flare of lightning coconut trees were bent in the wind, their leaves wildly blowing to one side. The windows were open and rain was coming through. She went to close them.

'No,' he said. 'Rain blesses.'

'For us too,' she said, and let her hands fall to her sides.

He took his cap off. Oh! He was shaven-headed. 'What if I told you your daughter was always safe, will always be safe. Would you still lie with me?'

She looked at him uncomprehending. 'I'm sorry, sir. I don't understand you.'

He shrugged. 'I never wanted her. She is a child. I need a woman. Stay or go as you please. There will be no repercussions either way.'

'Do you mean it?'

'You have my word.'

She knew that he was telling the truth. She was free to stay or go. She felt a flare of excitement at having evaded capture so easily.

'Thank you so much—' she began, but he had stepped back and with exaggerated courtesy held the door open for her. Hardly able to believe it, she began to walk towards the door. He let her pass. There was no expression on his face. She ran through the corridor of glass doors and down the long staircase. But halfway down she came to a sudden standstill. Who was she running from? He had let her go without a fight. And she remembered what she had seen in his eyes that first time. Once, he had been gentle, before he was taught to be merciless. And then she thought of Beauty with her little heart-shaped face and emerald eyes. Dimly lit, this house in her mind became the home of Beast. And there was Beast upstairs waiting for her to rescue him. The corridors whispering what he could not, '*Save me. Save me.*' But she was going back for a darker, more intriguing reason.

Because she wanted to.

She turned around slowly and went up the stairs and found him by the windows, standing very erect, his hands clasped behind his back, looking out at the rain. He turned around; neither surprise nor pleasure showed in his face.

'Undress,' he said flatly. This game was to be played cold. Tenderness would imply romance, substance, emotions. He did not want her to think she was anything but a momentary pleasure. To know that after he had enjoyed her, he would not look back. But the request itself surprised her. She had seen countless cartoons in the 'selling spring' book and in all of them, although in various stages of strategically explicit undress, no couple was ever entirely disrobed.

She went to turn down the light. 'Don't,' he said. The windows were open. Anyone standing on the beach could see in. Sometimes the gardener liked to sleep with his orchids, but it was raining and he would be indoors. There should be no one on the beach.

Even so, sex had always been done in the dark. Quietly, quickly, furtively, as if some unspeakable sin was being committed. That sensation was so convincing that she hesitated in the middle of the room. Take her clothes off? While this stranger *watched*? He made an impatient sound inside his closed mouth.

Her hands went to the back of her left shoulder. Fumbled. Awkward. But she had done this a million times. She tugged the brooch off. With a tearing sound the pin dropped to the floor. She unravelled the sari and pulled the pleats out of the underskirt in a bunch. Unglamorous. This could not have been what he wanted to see. The material fell in a ring of white at her feet. There were buttons on her sari blouse. Inside she was bare. Here she hesitated. Surely he did not expect her to undress fully? Even her husband had never requested it.

He was watching her intently, but she knew this only by the way he held his head, tilted at an unnatural angle, for his black eyes were completely in shadow. The last button relinquished its hold on the material and she shrugged out of the white garment. She worked the tie of the underskirt. It came off. There, she was nude. But ashamed, so ashamed, the blood rushed into her face and throbbed loudly in her temples. Still, it was not her body she wanted to hide behind her shaking hands, but her face. He came for her then. She was surprised by his breath. The lack of alcohol in it. He put one hand around her waist and perhaps because of the storm she felt a spark of electricity at his touch. He must have felt it too. His eyebrows rose.

He touched her cheek. 'Tears?'

'Rain,' she lied. She did not know why she was crying. She looked at his fingernails. They were cut very short and clean.

He did not undress fully, only his trousers. Then he put her on the bed. She watched his expression, flared nostrils, the quickly breathing open mouth and the centres of his eyes that were no longer clenched but had opened like darkly endless tunnels – where they went it was impossible to tell. Then, before she could begin to enter them, came the familiar gasp, to tell her everything was over. It had been even quicker than with her husband. But with this one she was sorry it had come to an end.

For the first time she had been enjoying the friction, the body of a man moving inside her. For a moment he slumped to the side of her, breathing hard, his weight on his right elbow, his hand resting lightly on her belly. Accidentally, her hand brushed his forearm. Oriental silk and underneath, tightly bunched muscles. It was unfamiliar. She had known only the flaccid flesh of her husband. Instinctively, her hand closed over it. He levered himself up and looked at her. They stared at each other silently. Wordless, he withdrew and dressed.

'Come back tomorrow,' he said, as he walked through the door.

She lay on the bed listening to his boots go down the stairs and out through the front door. She sat up, blew out the lamp, and went to stand on the balcony. The moon was very bright. It was still raining, but he wanted no umbrella. He walked fast. Suddenly, he stopped and looked up at her. His face was pale in the moonlight. They stared at each other.

Minutes ago their bodies had moved together and now they were in different spaces, different places. Hers warm and dry and high up, his cold and wet and exposed, yet her position was weak and indefensible, and his superior and powerful. What did he see? Not much probably, perhaps a shadow, or an outline. It was dark. Even for her, he was no more than a pale oval, but suddenly she knew the mystery of the clown in the painting. He was as discomfited to be discovered looking out of the frame as she was into it. It was the moment when the watcher becomes the watched, and the line of watching becomes blurred. She wanted to shrink back, but found she could not. She was trapped by the eyes of the man she thought to secretly observe. It was like a challenge. If she looked away first, she lost.

He looked away and disappeared in the direction of the beach. It was not rape. She had consented but she had expected more from him. She knew he had imposed himself on her in that way deliberately. He had wanted her to feel soiled, like a common whore. She pulled away from the window and went into the bathroom. For a long time she let the water flow over her. Her cries were all silent. *What now?* Because she had lost the protection of one man, she by default became the property of another? *But you chose to,* a nasty voice in her head mocked.

She dressed quickly, unlocked the front door and went out into the night. The driver was nowhere to be seen. There were guards on the grounds, and at her approach they swivelled their heads and raised their guns, but when they realised it was her they turned their faces away immediately as if she did not exist, as if she was a ghost.

The rain had stopped, but the ground was wet and full of puddles, and soon the hem of her sari was soaked. But she did not feel it. She walked to the beach and sat on the wet sand. The moon came out and to the lone man on the edge of the beach she must have made a sad vision, sitting alone, her head bent. Where was she heading? Who would believe that the high and mighty Rolls-Royce Mami could fall this low? The scandalised Mamis gathering in around their handiwork, murmuring, 'What? Kasu Marimuthu's widow the whore of a Japanese soldier? Ah! The money that man didn't have.'

A hand clapped over her mouth, which was a good thing or she would have screamed; his arrival had been so sudden and without warning. Quickly he bent his head and ran his tongue up her neck to her ear. She had felt it as a delicious fluttering in her belly. And when her rigid body relaxed he brought his mouth to hers. She was startled. She had never been kissed. Perversely, she thought of the Mamis. Had any of them been kissed like this before? She had held her lips closed, but with his tongue he prised them apart. She forgot the Mamis.

He pushed her back onto the sand and undressed quickly. His body was pale and very smooth. In fact, it was a shock to see that he was almost completely hairless. She touched the fine skin. Underneath her fingers steely muscles rippled.

And then she discovered that she knew nothing about making love to a man. In one smooth movement she was no longer under him, but on top. She watched him watch her as he moved her against him, until pleasure as she had never known came to take her. It was shocking to think that from that place where she knew only the inconvenience of her monthly cycles, the discomfort and the ensuing soreness of her husband's thrusting while she was still dry, and the pain of childbirth, came these unfamiliar sensations.

From the base of her they came, the unfamiliar, delicious waves that spread and ended in her fingertips, and made her think she had lost control and was floating away into a vortex of darkness, and that she must be dying. She became afraid. He is killing me, she thought, and pushed her knees against the ground, away from him, opening her mouth to cry out. Either he was prepared for her reaction or he was very quick off the mark, for he cupped the back of her neck, and kept the other tightly clamped over her mouth.

'If you shout, the guards will come, and though the servants are forbidden to leave the quarters after dark, they will hear you, and you don't want them to know, do you?' She heard his whisper, but as if from far away, over her own muffled shout and hammering heart. The servants, the guards. She had forgotten them all. This way, locked, and with widened eyes, she had her first orgasm.

Still joined she lay on top of him.

So . . . now she knew how the ecstatic woman felt in the giant octopus's cunnilingual embrace. Now she understood. Then she realised that there had been no release for him. Oh, the iron control of the man. She raised herself a little and opened her mouth.

But he did not let her speak. 'It is time for you to go,' he said. Did he know that the need for a woman to love is so extreme that she would give herself even to the most unfamiliar, the most fearful. Someone should have told him that once a man touches a woman the way he had her, she will start to see, hear, taste, smell and feel with her heart. And the heart is blind to even the most vicious humiliation.

*   *   *

Parvathi stole back into the shop house like a thief. She felt guilty and ashamed at how shamelessly she had responded to his touch. How she had opened herself to him so easily, so eagerly. Covering her burning cheeks with her palms she knocked softly on Maya's door. Maya opened it and let her in. Parvathi perched on Maya's bench unable to meet her eyes. But she had to get it off her chest. She could hardly keep a secret of such magnitude from Maya anyway.

'I unhesitatingly accepted the love offered by life. Was I wrong?'

'You saw a poisonous cobra as God. Who can blame you?'

'But he is the enemy.'

'Does not God himself say, "Love your enemy for he is me"?'

Before Parvathi could reply, Maya raised her finger to the young woman's lips and shook her head. 'Just remember this,' she said. 'If we are born again and again and mostly with the same people, once as daughter, then mother, another time son, or uncle, only to return again as wife, or even forbidden lover, wouldn't that make sex an irrelevance in the big scheme of things? When all is said and done, Da, only love matters. Sex is a biological function, like eating. It is man who has imposed all these taboos on it, for surely it would be chaos if father slept with daughter and sister with brother. Have patience with yourself. You are growing and learning. All these little steps you are taking that you imagine to be insignificant, they are vitally important to your soul. Each is a miracle in itself. Use them to stretch out for greatness. Stop wasting time with regret, grow past all shame and embarrassment, and instead welcome every experience. Let your life have the quality of a magnificent celebration. You don't realise it, but you are a god experiencing corporeality.'

The next day passed in a dream. She could not stop thinking of the night before. She heard Rubini plead from inside the mosquito net, 'Maya, can you not do something about these horrid cockroaches?' And Maya's answer, 'I can try to negotiate with them, but insects are, in fact, the rulers of this earth and if they refuse to go, there is not much I can do.'

And then she heard her son say, 'Ama, you're not listening.' He had been talking to her and she had not heard a word he had said. She smiled guiltily at him. At least he would never know. He did not care enough to wonder if she had any needs other than being his blindly devoted mother.

By ten she was in bed, lying fully dressed under a thin blanket listening to the sounds of the night. There were children hidden in drains all the way to the Japanese sentry. They were there to hear the dreaded sound of boots or the click of a sword on the pavement and warn their fathers who were gathered around a radio in someone's house. She was waiting to hear that same sound on the concrete outside so she could go as quickly as possible to her lover.

Adari was in complete darkness when she arrived. She went to look for him in the study, which was lit by two kerosene lamps. He was wearing a kimono. A light garment. And over it a silky white thigh-length jacket. His pale arms were concealed inside the wide sleeves and he looked, to her eyes, rather beautiful.

'What happened to the lights?'

'There is something wrong with the generator.'

Parvathi stifled the laugh that bubbled up with a small cough. She had lived there for ten years and the generator had never seen a day off. It was Kupu's little rebellion against his new masters.

'There is fish in the kitchen. Cook for me.' Passion did not feed on soft words and pretty songs.

She took a lamp and went into the kitchen. The fish were wrapped in a sheet of newspaper by the sink. With the tips of her fingers she unwrapped them. They stank so. She could not begin to imagine how his race ate such a thing raw. It made her feel quite ill to gut and wash them, but she did. She did not know where anything was kept and she had to hunt around for the rice, spices and oil. She knew the Japanese were unaccustomed to chilli, so used only turmeric and salt to marinate the fish. While the rice was boiling she went down to the cellar to look for a bottle of sake. They had plans for the cellar; all the wooden racks had been pushed to the sides of the walls. The place seemed empty and horrible.

She set the table with a bowl and wooden chopsticks. The house was very silent. The door to the library was closed when she passed it. In the kitchen she made some tea for herself, and sat down to wait for the rice to cook. When it was nearly ready she began to fry the fish. Then she carried the meal to the dining table and knocked softly on the closed door. There was no answering call. She was about to knock again when it opened and he came out. He led the way not to the dining room but to the music room where all the furniture had been removed and there was only a low table and some cushions on a mat. He sat on one of the cushions while she hovered uncertainly in the greenish shadows.

'The food,' he grunted impatiently.

Quietly, she brought the food and served it to him on the low table. She filled his glass with sake.

He raised his eyebrows at the sight of it, but when he tasted it said, 'Horrible.' He opened his palm to the cushion next to him. She sat. He picked up the bottle and made to pour it into another glass for her.

'General,' she said. 'Thank you, nevertheless I don't drink.'

'Do not refuse me,' he said politely, and poured the sake. He raised his glass. 'To your health.'

She drank (Oh! but no lazy drink that.) He waved his hand towards the food. Ah, so, he wanted her to join him.

She bowed. 'I am a vegetarian.'

'It would please me to see you eat,' he said softly and putting a slice of fish into his bowl, pushed it towards her.

She looked at it and in her mind she could still see it all slimy with its flat dead eyes. She looked up to him. He seemed mildly curious. She picked it up with her chopsticks and brought it to her mouth. It smelled so disgustingly fishy she simply could not put it into her mouth. She put it back into the bowl.

Slowly she raised her eyes to his. He was watching her sadistically, and she felt a gnawing ache, an emotion she could not name. She must not be the bride who wore no flowers to her own wedding.

Breaking off a morsel she carried it to her mouth. The smell made her gag, but she put it in anyway. There, it was done. And there, that something in his eyes was gone! But chewing, she found, was an entirely different matter. It released the oily taste and smell trapped in the fibre of the animal. She should have just swallowed it. Her stomach began to heave and she had to rush away to the toilet. She washed out her mouth, and she looked at her watery eyes in the mirror over the sink. He'd picked the wrong woman to challenge. She'd show him. This was war.

When she went back to the dining room he had finished eating and had unwrapped some red bean jelly.

'Have some dessert with me,' he invited cordially.

Holding his gaze, she picked the jelly up with her fingers and put it into her mouth, her fingers brushing her lips, her lips enclosing her fingers, her finger caressing her lips. Madame Regine would have been proud of her performance. He became very still. She chewed the jelly slowly, though it was bland and unappetising, her eyes never leaving his. She licked at her lower lip. Yes, this was war.

'Come,' he said, standing up, and wordlessly she followed him.

Afterwards, she lay beside him, so utterly spent that she was without even the will to move. How many times had he imposed himself on her? Lazily she tried to remember. Three, no, four. One day he would return to his country where he would go back to pretending that all foreigners were uncivilised barbarians, and no one would guess how insatiable he really was, how he simply couldn't get enough of one uncouth foreigner. She felt her eyes close. She was drifting off. There was a weeping willow by a bridge on the lane they had chosen to walk upon.

'What is this perfume you put in your hair?' he asked softly. His eyes were closed. He too was exhausted, not entirely present. She had vanquished a man of war.

'I smoke it in myrrh. It takes too long to dry, otherwise,' she said. Her voice was soft, unfamiliar even to her. He opened his eyes and confessed that he did not know the meaning of the word. He had studied in America, but English would always be a second language forever waiting to overwhelm him, in harmonics, grammar or vocabulary. They looked the word up in her dictionary.

'Ah,' he said, a smile dawning. 'Of course. I recognise it now.'

Suddenly she felt close to him. Yes, she became certain then; this was the beautiful soul she had been longing for. She smiled back, open, trusting.

But that seemed to sober him up. He shifted away from her. 'I have a wife and a daughter in Tokyo,' he told her quietly.

She didn't know why she did, but she cried. It was so silly.

He touched her shoulder awkwardly. 'This is strange for me too,' he said.

It was still dark when she left. On the grounds where Kasu Marimuthu had entertained lavishly, soldiers in white vests were just beginning to assemble for their morning training under the flag of the rising sun. Back in the flat she lay down inside the mosquito net and realised there was no sound of rats dropping off their perches or cockroaches flying into nets. Maya's appeal had met success.

Need

While the other Mamis were selling their gold chains an inch at a time to pay for oil and rice, Apu was actually making a profit trading with the stuff that people came to sell at the store in the flourishing black market. Parvathi, however, remained oblivious of his entrepreneurial skills or the healthy state of the long, narrow accounts book that he handed over every Wednesday evening, and that she dutifully returned the next day, without having looked at it. How could she, when she lived only for the nights?

During the day while the children were at school she slept or sat at her upstairs window endlessly daydreaming about him, conjuring up unlikely scenarios. They meet in the street and go down an alleyway and have furious sex between dark doorways. They see each other by accident in a public place and he comes up to her, caresses her hand openly, and says, 'You are mine. I'll kill any man who comes near you.' More and more she took risks to see him. She knew it was dangerous, but she didn't care.

The only time she ever felt a frisson of fear was the one occasion a week when she sought her black umbrella and walked through the town to sit with the other Mamis. Here she was forced not only to listen but also join in the vociferous cursing. Beasts. Monsters. Raping, taking, killing. And now the disgusting creatures were urinating on the streets! Vile. Unspeakably hateful.

Once, Padi Mami looked at her slyly. 'You must have a very lucky star shining on you. They never come to disturb you or your shop, do they? Not even the bandits' (those days the Communists were referred to thus) 'raid your shop.'

A hush fell upon the group.

Parvathi answered Padi Mami, but she understood that she addressed them all. They were of the same opinion. 'The Japanese have taken over our house, our estates, our bakery and our cars. Is that not enough? As for the bandits, it is common knowledge they never come into town.'

The women nodded sympathetically, but in fact, they were inwardly pleased that the occupation had somewhat levelled out the financial differences between them.

Kundi Mami stood up, pulled the loose end of her sari over her steadily growing posterior, and uncovered a tray of tapioca cakes. 'Come,' she invited hospitably, 'let's not talk about that race that doesn't know better than to eat rice with sugar.'

But she was wrong about that, anyway. Rice and sugar was not the usual diet of the Japanese man. Parvathi knew because she cooked for one. She used to watch Maya pluck a chicken and wonder how, being a vegetarian, she could bring herself to do that. Plucked chickens used to remind her of babies, certainly too pitiful to cut. Haughtily she used to claim that her conscience would never allow her to kill one. But now she knew that she could because her lover liked chicken curry when it was not spicy. And that was not all; she was willing to prepare the other things he fancied too, shark, alligator, lamb (although she still couldn't stand the smell of it while it was cooking), and the other day, how shocked Kamala would be, beef.

There were other things he liked too – Maya's mango sambar that he ate as if it was soup, in a bowl with a spoon. Or that Japanese peculiarity, green tea poured into a bowl of cold rice and eaten with chopsticks. At first she had found it bland with a bitter aftertaste, but he had assured her that it was a favourite with most Japanese. She learned that it was an acquired taste, and that she did like it, after all, especially with boiled soya beans. And when the gardener dug up sweet potatoes, they had those boiled too.

'This would be so good with grilled octopus,' he said, as he devoured them cold.

Her thoughts were interrupted by Apu sprinting up the stairs to announce breathlessly that a Japanese general wanted to see her.

'Don't admit to anything. They can prove nothing,' he whispered, blinking violently. He imagined his black-market mischief had brought in a General.

'Show him up,' she said, and listened as Apu clattered noisily down the wooden stairs. Maya had gone to the market, the children were in school, and she was alone. But they were not supposed to meet during the day. This was against the rules, forbidden. She stood and waited, her hands clenched at her sides.

He came forward, uniformed, dashing. Voicelessly he released her hair from its bun.

'I dreamed of you,' she whispered, and the General took her as a man does a woman he desires intensely. The widow came arching her spine, her lover's hands tightly clamped to her hips. Turning her over, he gently stroked her face. He did not know that all his passion had not touched her like his hand on her face. She looked up into the slanting eyes. 'Why did you come today?'

'I wanted to see your beautiful face,' he said.

'I am too dark to be beautiful,' she answered; she had not forgotten the white-faced geisha.

'Yes, in my country white is revered, but I have since learned that a flower is no less beautiful because it is standing in the shade.'

She stared at the man; outside the beast, inside dazzling light. Her hand reached out, grasped his belt and tugged him towards her. He came willingly. Her other hand brought down his mouth and kissed it, but violently, capturing his tongue, sucking, desperate, greedy, wanting something she could not have. He let her. When she pulled away, her mouth was throbbing. She released his belt abruptly. 'Don't forget me,' she said, and turned away.

He pulled her so hard she slammed into him. His face blurred as his mouth plunged down, crushing her lips against her teeth. It was not without pain, and yet she would have had it go on and on, that heartless assault. Not so. Without warning, as suddenly as it had begun, it stopped. She tasted salt and blood in her mouth.

'Nor you me,' he said brusquely, and left her.

Veiled behind curtains, she watched his erect figure climb into the waiting jeep. He did not look up. She went to stand before her

mirror. Who was this dishevelled, swollen, desirable woman in the
mirror. She stared into her eyes. Really, who was this wanton? The
woman smiled, a seductive, knowing smile. Some control must be
maintained. With shaking hands Parvathi tied her hair.

At the back door of the shop Maya, returned from the market, was
telling the father of a drug addict, 'When the cravings come, salt
some sliced onions and give them to him to eat, and the irresistible
need will recede as surely as I sit here before you.' And looking
him in the eye, she said, 'Do the same whenever you need to sober
up after drinking.'

Hair

Comfortably attired in a white cotton kimono, he sat in the music room, at peace with himself and the world. He looked at her and immediately she lifted the jug of warm sake from the low table and refilled his bowl close to the brim. It was not that she wanted to encourage him to inebriety; it was just that he was normally so tightly bound by such a rigorous code of conduct that when he drank it was with the intention of getting thoroughly drunk, for to be at the bottom of a bottle was to be excused of everything, allowed even human emotions. Relinquished from his doctrine of constant conformity and discipline, he told her things, sometimes even confidential military things. Things not to be mentioned on the morrow. Once she made the mistake of referring to something he had said the night before, and his face had hardened with cold disapproval.

'We can win this war. Discipline will always overcome decadence. We have secret reports from 1935 commissioned by the British Government on the condition of their armed forces. It concluded even then that its Army and Air Force were in poor condition, and its pride, the Navy, was considered to be incapable of adequately defending British cities from attack, let alone the rest of its empire. And it strongly recommended avoiding war against Japan, Italy and Germany simultaneously.'

'What glory is there in killing the defenceless then?' she had asked.

He had looked at her disdainfully. Proud, how proud he was. 'The most famous samurais smelled of the blood of hundreds, sometimes thousands of men. They had no mercy in them.'

She had gazed at him without words. At first it had surprised her to see a human being who could kill without a second thought.

But now she knew the Japanese had learned to venerate merciless men. And duty gave them a clear conscience. Not once did he awaken in the night with nightmares. It was the training given in the Japanese army. Everyone was treated with brutality until it seeped into him, and even if he had arrived abhorring violence, he left their grounds if not revelling in it, then accepting that it was the only way to treat the enemy, the foreigner, the stranger.

It gave them the conscience to impose the most disproportionately savage sentences for minor offences.

Once she heard a long wail come from the depths of the cellar, and had frozen, but the sound had stopped as suddenly as it had started, so she pretended that she had imagined it. Prisoners of war. What could she do? Wait for when he was full of good food and flushed with drink to ask, 'Why is this torture necessary?'

'It's war,' he replied unperturbed, as if that explained everything. As if it was natural for one man to steal from another, to torture him, and be so careless with his women because he had conquered at the point of a weapon. But that was what war did to the victor. It made him more powerful than was good for him.

But there were those rare times when he gave up extravagant, ornate facets of himself. Like that time he said, 'Because they fall, we love them.'

'Women?' she had hazarded.

'Cherry blossoms.'

And she had the sensation of trying to hold on to something that was slipping away.

Or that time she stood him before the painting of the clown and said, 'Tell me why this painting disturbs me so much.'

'For the same reason it will disturb everyone who sees it.'

She stared at his rigid profile. 'It did not disturb my husband. He liked it.'

'He was a liar then, your husband. He bought it because it disturbed him and he put it here, in a room where his chair backed on to it and his visitors faced it. He wanted to see their reaction, their discomfort. He wanted to know he was not alone in his fear.'

'But I know a woman who does not tell lies and she told me she did not feel anything when she looked at the picture.'

He looked down at her. 'Then she is a lucky woman. She has no worldly desires to be ashamed of.'

'I don't understand.'

'Whoever looks at the painting sees themselves in the clown, miserable with the desires they have acquired or plan to. When I look at this picture I am the clown and you are the swan, but when you look at it you will be the clown and I will be the swan. Always when we take something, its freedom is gone. I have taken from you what I should not have, but you have imprisoned me too.'

With new eyes, his eyes, Parvathi looked at the painting. Yes, of course, it was not right that such a proud and fierce creature should be so subdued inside a man's grasp. That was what had bothered her. Even more than the desolation in the eyes of the clown who knew the hidden cost of his desires.

'Actually, I've been meaning to say this to you for a long time,' she said. 'I'm very grateful to you for what you did for Rubini. If you had not come when you did . . .'

'The men would have used her,' he said flatly, and she shuddered.

'Why did you pick me?'

'Because of your hair. It was the first thing I saw. So long it reached your knees. Wig-makers say Chinese hair is good, but Japanese hair is better. They have not seen or touched yours.'

She looked at him in astonishment. 'My hair? But it is straight. Not beautiful and curly like Rubini's.'

It was his turn to look surprised. 'We have noodles in Japan like that.'

How strange that what her culture considered beautiful was undesirable to another. He took her hair in his hand, let it slip through his fingers, sighed and fell silent. 'It was so beautiful I had to move towards it as if my past was calling. You see, my father was a famous hairdresser in the Geisha quarter of Gion. He used to say that there was a time when you could tell everything about a person just by looking at their hair. What kind of work they did,

which part of the country they came from. There was even a
different hairstyle for every class.'

'What would you have done if I had not come back that first
night?'

'I only wanted a woman, but when you arrived dressed in white,
your face unadorned, I became frightened the way a man fears a
thing that could destroy him. If you had not come back, I would
have found another and she would have done just as well, and the
same man that arrived on these shores would have left it.'

Much later, she climbed in through the unlatched downstairs
window and went towards the kitchen where a light was burning.
At the doorway she stood and stared, too engrossed by the scene
to sense she was intruding. Rubini, in her nightdress and bare
feet, was curled up in Maya's lap. There was a plate of half-eaten
coconut milk and green beans *apam* on the table. With her head
resting on Maya's breast, the child was gazing up into the woman's
face and Maya was singing to her in a voice that Parvathi had
heard only once before; that night at the beach when she heard
the news of her mother's death. She had completely forgotten the
voice until now; hearing it again broke the memory. What had
actually happened on the rock boulder? Fragments, snatches came
up: the wind, the restless waves calling her, the moon coming up
over the water, and the terrible, terrible sorrow that wanted her to
drown in the cold, dark water, until this same voice had come to
rescue her from those unimaginable depths, whispering, 'Sleep,
all will be well.' She searched her memory. What else was said?
Nothing else emerged.

Calmly, Maya looked up and said, 'Rubini had a nightmare, and
since you were not in your bed she panicked, even though I told
her that you often went for walks at night and always returned
home perfectly safe.'

Rubini scrambled off Maya's lap and for a second seemed
confused or lost, looking from one woman to the other. Then she
turned on Parvathi angrily. 'Don't you know it's dangerous to
go out at night? Something could happen to you, then what will

happen to all of us? But you don't care, do you? And anyway, how did you get into the house? You didn't use the front or back door, because I've been listening.'

'Come here,' Parvathi said, and impulsively, still full of her lover's scent, she stepped forward and hugged the small, raging body. First, the child went rigid in her arms, and then she immediately began to wriggle and squirm in earnest. Parvathi let her go and the girl hurriedly stepped back. Always, always, she had to keep the greatest distance between her and her feelings.

'I am here now, and nothing is going to happen to me or any of you,' Parvathi said gently.

Rubini stared at her, biting her lower lip, while all kinds of conflicting emotions chased across her face, but unable to voice any of them, she turned suddenly and with a tearing sob, raced up the creaking stairs.

Maya pushed the glass of milk on the table towards Parvathi and said, 'Here, don't forget to take this with you for her.'

The Kimono

He slid a flat cardboard box across the table towards her.

'For me?'

He nodded. So she lifted the lid. Textured handmade paper was tied with pale blue ribbons. Carefully she undid them. The Japanese, she knew, took the giving and receiving of presents as a serious matter. A light-hearted approach was an insult to the giver. Inside, another layer of tissue paper. And then – a silk kimono, a beautiful, understated thing in shades of quail's-egg grey. She stroked it, the finest, most luxurious silk, so fine it was almost transparent. She lifted it out. White grasses; the stitching beautiful, and the texture that of a living animal. It had a plain mauve *obi*.

'Except on stage, a geisha must not be gaudy,' he said.

'It's beautiful,' she said, and let the fabric brush her cheek.

'It is a very special kimono,' he continued gravely. 'Its design is of autumn grasses, but it is made of the lightest silk to be worn in the summer. Traditionally, a geisha selects a kimono with the appropriate flowers, plants, insects or birds of that season. Sprigs of pine on deep purple for January; plum blossoms in February; cherry-blossoms in spring; frogs, rain, or small trout in June; cicadas in high summer; maple leaves in autumn; roses on slate blue for October; and snowflakes in the winter. Naturally since no geisha would dream of wearing autumn grasses during the summer, this garment can only be worn by a foreigner.'

He made her take all her clothes off. But she had learned to be nude. At first, it had felt so strange. She was from a culture that thought a body without clothes was indecent, unless, of course, it was without life. But now she no longer needed or wanted to cover herself. He moved behind her and very slowly, very meticulously, licked her from the nape of her neck all the way down her spine. She wanted to turn towards him, but he sighed softly, and said, 'Don't move.' She heard him walk away from her. She stood in the middle of the room like a hatchling, vulnerable, exposed, trembling, and wet.

She heard him return to her body. Something cold touched her back. From the corner of her eyes she saw a pale brush loaded with white paint. With slow precise strokes she felt his brush make the shape that looked like the fork of a serpent's tongue on the nape of her neck.

Then he came around the front and applied a thick layer on to her face, neck and chest. His face was a mask of pure concentration. It was called *kata*, the proper way of doing things. The aim, whether it be a garden, a poem or an ink painting was perfection, always. With feathery strokes he made her eyebrows as black and straight as moth's wings. Then he outlined her eyes in red, extending the line out at the corners, and blushed pink around her nose. From a stick of red safflower paste a tiny half-crown of intense red was licked on her lower lip. Most disconcerting.

'When only the lower lip is painted it is the mark of a novice. The world will see that you are still a baby,' he explained.

Next, he turned to her hair.

'Your hair is so long and plentiful I won't even need yak hair to hold everything in place,' he said, and used curling irons repeatedly on her hair until it was smooth, shiny and incredibly straight. While oiling a small tortoiseshell comb with bintsuke oil, he explained that it was the same oil that was used by sumo wrestlers to keep their topknots firm. He combed in more globs of the pomade and pulled his second and middle finger along the hair in a practised, professional way. It was what those hands were made to do.

When her hair was extraordinarily flat he pulled back his sleeves. 'Ready?' he said, and taking a section of hair from the crown of her head, tugged so hard to make a ponytail out of it, that she cried out. 'I know, *Anata*,' he consoled. 'The crown of every geisha's head is bald for this very reason.' Carefully, he wound the hair around a roll of paper. He swept that forward to form the central knot. The hair at the back of the head was then brought up and over, coiled into a stiff loop and held in place with a piece of lacquered wood. Then came the touch that made the Japanese topknot different from all others, the two side wings, stretched round with wax, and tied with a string to the central knot to sit on either side of the face.

The front was teased into a bun, pinned, and black paper inserted to keep its bouffant shape. By now her head felt uncomfortably tight and heavy, and she could feel an ache starting at the crown of her head.

'Hair decorations,' he announced, and slid black combs into the wings and a few behind her ears. The beads that hung from them reached down to her chin. Some brushed her shoulderblades.

'In Japan there are no more geishas. They are wearing smocks over indigo-dyed peasant trousers and working in factories sewing parachutes.' There was regret in his voice.

Finally, cloth came to touch her skin. The under-kimono was peach-coloured, light and cool. A relief. He brought the piece around the front to envelop her. And then the real thing, heavy and cumbersome, with a train that swirled and eddied about her feet like water. He tied it so that a flash of the under-kimono was visible at the sleeve and the hem. Sex appeal to the Japanese man had all to do with mystery, a hint of the disreputable under layer upon layer of fabric. The sleeves hung to her hips.

After he had tugged, pulled and patted the costume into place he began wrapping the *obi* – weighty, and longer than a sari – round and round her waist, all the while tucking in pads of stiffening and a cushion at the back to give extra bulk. It was hard work and he began breathing hard. His forearms glistened with sweat, the muscles underneath straining as he tied her in. Only when she was completely cocooned did he stop, wipe his brow and announce, 'Done.'

For the final romantic touch he added a narrow white silk cord, the ends dangling to the floor. He gave her a paper fan shaped like a gingko leaf, inscribed in exquisitely brushed black characters. 'What does it say?' she asked.

'Fumiko,' he said.

Fumiko? The owner of all this sumptuous finery and this beautiful oiled paper fan? A former lover? But she asked no more. What for when the bamboo was withered, its stalks eaten at the base by insects? He squatted beside her, slipped a pair of *tabi*, white, toed, linen socks on her feet and put on the ground clogs. She stepped into them. Camellia oil was brushed behind her ears and he walked away from her.

He switched off the lights, lit some candles, and scrutinised her minutely in the soft glow, before nodding approvingly and pointing to the mirror. She picked up the train.

'Left hand,' he reprimanded severely.

The clogs were uncomfortable to walk in. They clattered. But he wanted her to take small mincing steps as if underneath her clothes she had something very tight on, that ended in the middle of her calves. He said, even when opening a screen a woman must never allow her knees to be more than a few inches apart. 'Kneel, sit on your heels, bend from the waist to serve, whatever, but always with your knees together.'

In the end she shuffled over, the *obi* swinging heavily behind her. Undignified in this dreamworld he had so painstakingly created.

'*Mutae, mutae*,' wait, wait. 'You have to slide your feet. The kimono and the normal way of walking don't go together.' She stopped and waited. He came back with a piece of string. He parted her kimono, slid his hands up her calves and tied her knees together.

'Now walk,' he said. Ah yes, now it was possible to glide. Slowly, from side to side like the greatest, grandest geisha of them all. And it was as if she was suddenly standing on a rickety balcony in the pleasure quarters, peeping over, looking past the winding lanes crowded with wattled roofs of small wooden houses, far into the heart of a city, where there were slender-pillared temples, vermilion palaces, theatres and gardens full of lovers gazing at the moon. There were people mixing incense and others mixing art and beauty. Exactly like the nineteenth-century woodblock prints she had seen in the books from the trunk.

The mirror. Oh, but this woman was not her! She stared at herself with astonishment. Look at her, all tied up. The white face and neck that seemed to come out of the dark were that of a doll or a butterfly woman, remote, aloof, mysterious and yet enormously erotic. A fantasy created to drive a king or a great warrior mad with desire. This woman knew how to snuggle up intimately, but never lose her head or her heart. He had purposely misrepresented her but she liked it, and understood that this seductive creature was made only for the darkness or uncertain light.

She raised one hand. Even her movements were more languid, charming, and polite. What on earth had happened to her? Had she become part of those passionate tales of samurai warriors, villains and whitely beautiful temptresses – in which too often the hero and heroine die?

He met her eyes in the mirror. 'See, how beautiful you are,' he said caressing the small unpainted area at the nape of her neck.

Hidden beneath the sumptuous finery she could pretend all kinds of things. After all, this time was without repercussions; she knew there was no crossover into the real world. The sun surely returns to cut off the head of every dark night. With a sidelong glance she breathed his name. Even her voice was different – higher, a coo. It felt as if she was no longer speaking the same language.

'We must find you a new name,' said the General.

And the geisha nodded shyly. Yes, she would like a new name. For when she shuffled down streets lit on either side by paper lanterns.

'Sakura.'

'Yes, I like it.'

'Come, let us take tea.'

The *obi* was stiff and made her sit up straight. He made the tea, a series of precisely choreographed movements performed with a strange mixture of concentration and an economy of movement so the impression was one of stillness. He put the bamboo whisk down. She held the bowl of foaming green tea up to her lips and sipped slowly.

She folded herself onto her knees and placing her hands in front of her, flat on the ground, she touched her head to them and remained motionless. And in this way she prepared to serve her master.

In the middle room of the round tower Kupu lay on the floor and looked at the stars through the porthole window. He dreamed about how far away they were, what their bodies were made of, and who lived on them. He closed his eyes and might have dozed off, but became suddenly aware of light outside his closed lids. Light? In the middle of the jungle? At night? He rushed to the window, to witness a most unlikely scene.

A group of about twenty men wearing hooded brown robes and carrying burning torches were gathered in a circle around the communicating stone. It was not possible to see their faces, but their complete stillness was sinister. And something else about them was not quite right either – they did not seem completely solid; their edges were uncertain, wavy.

One of the ghostly figures left the circle and went to the wall of the tower where the stairs began and struck it. Then he looked up to the window where Kupu stood and beckoned to him. There was no face, only deep shadows cast by his hood. Kupu felt a chill run through the entire length of his body. The figure returned to the group and resumed his place. Then all of them slowly faded away.

For a while Kupu stood at the window, shocked by what he had witnessed, and then he turned around and saw his body still asleep on the floor. For a frightening moment he thought he was dead. Slowly, he walked, well, floated towards it, and kneeling over himself, stared at his prone body. He had never seen himself from this angle before, and he was even less pleased with himself than on the rare occasions he had chanced upon his image in a mirror or a watery surface. When he tried to touch his inert body, he found himself sucked, and quite painfully, back into his body. He sat up, confused and in a daze. Had he dreamed it all?

Nimbly, he ran down the steep, banisterless stairs towards the place where he had seen the figure hit the wall. He struck it with the heel of his own hand and the entire block began to resonate like a tuning fork. He stumbled back in amazement. It sounded as if a whole flock of birds were beating their wings in preparation for flight, and he knew instinctively that the sound symbolised flight into the unknown. It was as Maya had said: not a single stone was without purpose or secret.

May arrived and Maya, ignoring the yellow bulbs of garlic on the market floor, brought only the whitest home, and then that year ran out too, and it was January again.

The Gift

She came upon him standing on the balcony, gazing out to sea, and for a long time she simply stared at him, his back ramrod. Eventually, she called to him, and he turned, bitter and full of hatred. 'We shall kill many Americans,' he rasped, but his voice betrayed some terrible inner weariness. He too must have heard the fatigue for he repeated himself, and this time she heard only the unemotional statement any general of war following the aristocratically simple policy of a 'master' race might make. They had already done it successfully once in Korea.

He jerked his hands violently towards her, and held them palms up, the fingers spread out – 'I have killed so many.' Very gently, with the edge of her sari she began to wipe the tense hands as if removing a stain while he watched her, at first fiercely and then sadly. He laid his forehead on her left shoulder. 'I have a present for you,' he said.

It was in a plain, unwrapped box.

The anger was instant, uncontrollable. She had never experienced anything like it before. The box fell to the ground as her accusing eyes raced up to meet his. 'Where did you get this? It's stolen, isn't it? Don't you know, I've had far more than this and I cared nothing for it?' she lashed out. She flung the necklace away so hard it hit a wall and broke.

'Of course,' he said quietly. But she saw the great hurt she had inflicted.

Immediately she threw her arms around his neck and said, 'I'm sorry, I'm so sorry. I just don't want you to taint yourself for trinkets.

Don't become like the rest of them.' She slipped her hand into the rough material of his uniform and found his heartbeat. 'This, bring me this. Nothing more,' she whispered fiercely. She took his hand and together they ran to the beach. Both desperate to erase what had just happened. Both needing to lose themselves in each other. To feel pleasure coursing through them again. To know that nothing had been lost in the exchange. Wanting to be one again.

They swam in the dark, their bodies slipping against each other. Their laughter muffled, their hands cleaving the water like oars, silent in the dark.

The air became cool, while their bodies became warm and wonderful. They made love in the pouring rain lying on the seaweed that had washed to shore. The rain stopped. The sky filled with thousands of stars and an almost full moon.

Warm and dry in bed afterwards, she turned to him lazily. 'Are you all right?

'Hmm.' His voice was always stern, but she knew it was his way to be thus, even in bed. Once, just once, he had said, '*Suki desu.*' But it only meant, 'I like you', a poor expression of affection, and even confessing that had made him awkward and uncomfortable. He preferred to communicate his feelings with his body.

She stared up at the ceiling. 'I wish you could meet Maya.'

'I've met her.'

She came up on her elbow, her face surprised. 'You've met her! When?'

'That first night before you came to me. I had gone out for the evening and when I returned she was waiting behind the door. It was a reflex action, to aim my sword at her stomach. But the thing about that incident that I remember most is that I wounded her, there was blood on my blade, but she didn't even blink. "If you hurt her, I will cut you down while you sleep," she said. Who knows where that illiterate foolhardy woman got the idea to threaten a Japanese soldier? If it had been any one of my colleagues they would have had her head on the spot. After she had delivered that extraordinary statement she backed away slowly, but never taking her eyes off me. Quite creepy actually.'

Parvathi was speechless. She thought of Maya sitting humbly on the kitchen floor taking the marrow out of mutton bones with a hairpin and her son opening his mouth to take the dark red offering dangling from her hairpin. What streak of steel was that woman made of? It was not as if she had not seen the heads rotting on poles everywhere in town or heard of the merciless brutality of the Japanese soldier.

When she returned to the flat she asked Maya about it.

'What is a sword in my belly? Death is nothing. I'm not attached to this body. It is only a vehicle my soul needs to reach higher levels of consciousness and light. Human beings are all confused – without death, how will the deathless soul continue its journey?'

A New Thali

It was the last days of October 1944. While Parvathi was draping herself in her customary white sari, Rubini came in. She sat on her bed and said, 'Mami, you always looked nice in red. Why don't you wear a red sari just around the house? No one will see except us.'

That night, Parvathi went to him with flowers in her hair and a coloured sari. He stared at her in surprise.

'It's actually a wedding sari,' she said softly, but his face changed and he turned away from her. Tentatively, she touched his curved, rejecting back. The muscles twitched under her hand.

'Why?' she asked.

'I don't know. It seemed you were mocking me. Telling me you'll never be my bride.' He sighed heavily. 'This is all a charade anyway. The imperial headquarters have been deceiving us. We are losing the war.' He sighed again. 'What a mess it all is!'

His words brought swift pain. She had known it was coming, and it was as he said. The Allies had to win and he would have to go back to Japan in shame. She wanted the war to be over, she wanted her children to go to proper schools and for sanity to return, but the thought of parting from him was unbearable.

In a dip on the beach they sat to their midnight picnic. Afterwards they lay beside each other. The quiet was broken by a sudden commotion at the cowshed. She rolled over and saw Kupu running out of the servants' quarters towards the shed. Laying her chin on her wrist, she watched him from her concealed position. A patrolling soldier called out to Kupu, who stopped and waited. They spoke briefly, then Kupu carried on to the cowshed.

'What's going on?' asked the General, without the least concern in his voice.

'One of the cows must be calving,' she murmured.

Through the smoke she saw Kupu light a lamp, all his movements beautifully fluid and concise. He bent his head towards the cows, and hidden behind the wooden slats, was lost to her sight. She tried to imagine him speaking to the cow, gently coaxing, and that moment in the jungle when she had thought him beautiful and wanted to touch him came back to her. She still thought him beautiful, but now that desire did not want or need to be satisfied.

'What are you thinking about?'

'Nothing,' she said, returning to her old position.

He sat up. 'In front of this empty gourd of sake, these chopsticks, and these leftover bits of food, will you marry me?'

His face was full of black shadows. She could not see the expression in his eyes. For the Japanese army it was not sex that was taboo, but love. It was the unspoken rule. They were not to take wives. They were not to leave progeny.

'Won't it destroy your career?'

'A woman's beauty must be judged by the men she destroys.'

She closed her eyes. But the tears squeezed through anyway. 'Yes, I will.' It was only a whisper.

'Come, we will go tonight to your temple. Let your gods be witness that you are my chosen woman.'

'But I have no *thali*.'

He wrenched off his signet ring. 'Will this do?'

That night they travelled to a temple far away. So far away that the existence of Kasu Marimuthu or his widow was unknown there. It was a small Murugan temple, her mother's deity of choice. As she stepped into the temple Parvathi noticed that the floor was dirty, and felt ashamed. We should keep our temples cleaner, she thought. We should house our gods better, and she glanced at Hattori San. Surely, his temples were cleaner.

They took the priest from his slumber and he came out in a hastily tied *veshti*, his hair an untidy knot, terrified. His eyes darted every now and again to the sword hanging so casually from the Japanese General's belt.

His hand trembled when he reached for the burning camphor. The couple exchanged garlands. The General put vermilion powder on her forehead. The priest fed the fire and brought it to them so they could hold their hands towards its warmth. In the light of the camphor, his pearly face shone. He smiled at her, but she cried. Why? Because it was not real. Nothing that happened in the night, in secret, was real. Only fools and people in love would attempt them.

With his thumbs he rubbed away her tears, but they would not stop so he pressed a finger to her quivering lips. She lifted her eyes to his then; the tears became stones in her throat. Locked in his gaze she saw a sad, hopeless longing for tomorrow, for more memories, for this to be a beginning. Fiercely, she told the stone statue, 'I love him. I truly love him.'

She did not know the statue had seen it all before. Lovers who staked everything on nothing. Her hands wandered to the garland of jasmine flowers. She was married. Yet this was not a marriage, not really. They were the doomed lovers of Japanese legends: as the shining bells toll at the coming dawn, they take their own lives.

'I am happy to be your husband.' Light overflowed from his eyes as his arm stretched to encircle her waist.

Her husband! Yes, husband. This man who should have smelled of blood, how she loved him. Who would dare to tell her otherwise? This was no dream either. No, the pebbles under her bare feet hurt.

She looked back one last time. The snake smiled. *Everything you asked for*. And yet, what about *for all time*? Had she lost some meaning?

The priest called goodbye, but halfway to the car he came running after them. 'Wait!' he called. 'You forgot your umbrella.'

The frogs were still croaking, but it had stopped raining. 'You keep it,' she said. Twilight was coming in, they must hurry back. She looked into his curious eyes. He was a good man. He wanted to go back inside where it was warm and safe. 'Pray for me,' she said.

He looked at her with pity. 'Of course,' he said in Tamil. 'You have sacrificed yourself for the community.'

She wanted to tell him that she had not, that she loved this man, but the words stuck in her throat. Her love was not the marvellous thing she imagined, after all. She nodded and turned away.

'Go with God,' he called out. Until they reached the car she did not acknowledge the guilt, but as the door was held open for her she said to her husband, 'Wait for me a minute.'

The priest was a silhouette standing at the edge of the temple.

'It is not a sacrifice. I love him,' she said to the shadowed face. It seemed important to say it. At least to the priest, not to be a hypocrite, to be bare. To God's representative one shouldn't have to lie.

'I knew that,' he said, 'but for the sake of your pride I pretended.'

'Bless me, I love him,' she said.

'You are in God's hands now, child.'

She ran back to the waiting car.

Her husband looked at her. 'What was it, *Anata*?'

'I just wanted to thank him properly,' she said.

In the flat above the shop Maya was awake and tending to a clay pot on the stove. Inside was medicine that had been cooking non-stop for two whole days.

'How much longer?' Parvathi asked.

'Anytime now the pot will break and the medicine will be ready.'

Parvathi nodded distractedly. 'Maya,' she said, 'if I was looking for a beautiful soul to fall in love with, why didn't I just fall in love with Kupu? There can hardly be a soul more beautiful than his.'

'What is that game called with all the oddly-shaped pieces that you have to put together to make a picture?'

'A jigsaw puzzle.'

'Yes, that's the one. Each of us have come to this earth with a few pieces to a jigsaw puzzle as big as this universe. Each time we meet someone, we unconsciously show them our pieces to see if they have pieces that will fit ours. If they don't they go their way, and we have no more to do with them. But if they do, ah . . . that is when the attraction, hate, jealousy, love, heartaches and lessons begin. Kupu has not the pieces you need. But don't underestimate him. He has other pieces, other things to do, important things. Being an ordinary householder is not one of them. Though he may seem a simple being, sometimes more wild creature than man, he is complex, very complex, with unexpectedly large and ageless thoughts.'

'I married the General today,' Parvathi blurted out suddenly.

'Well! Are you happy?'

'Yes, but it won't last, will it?'

'There is nothing in this place of decay that can or will last. Even stones will crumble to dust. Everything changes. The trick is to immerse oneself completely in the moment, live it, and when it goes, to have not an ounce of regret or a backward glance. To know it will go and not mourn for it. To let it be,' said Maya.

'That's a hard trick to learn,' Parvathi said.

'For sure,' Maya murmured.

Parvathi hid her *thali* in her cupboard. Not because she was ashamed, she told herself, but because it was too special to be soiled by even a passing jealous eye.

Deep in the jungle in the light of the moon Kupu sat, alone and mateless on the temple steps, a look of great sadness on his face. A gentle breeze lifted a lock of his hair. The leaves shivered with it. He lifted his gaze so that he would not see the graven piles of dead bees around his feet. His dazed eyes reached for the communicating stone.

It lay uprooted and face down. He thought of the Japanese soldiers who had wreaked this damage. A wholly enigmatic race, their souls covered with night light; deadly, ill-pleased men who would cut down a tree for a coconut and blow up a whole nest for a comb of honey. Today they had come to unearth the silver bowls as large as temple bells and cart them all away.

But they had no idea what they had done.

He shivered; the stone underneath him was communicating, something hard and rejecting. It did not want to bear his weight.

He stood slowly, tiredly. He must not further burden the stone. And then he jerked and froze: he knew this jungle and its inhabitants intimately and he could not imagine what could have made that single depressed sob.

He remembered Maya saying, 'Man has hardly any friends among the other life forms on earth because he has used them all so badly.' There was a rumble of disquiet inside him. In fact, after that sound, the entire place had become pregnant with a quiet waiting dread, asking for wounds. Maya was right. The bowls had kept away bad spirits and now without them, the energy that was nourishing and protecting had turned 'black'. He could feel it – a silent silky menace, getting ready to destroy.

Losing

The children had come down with chickenpox and were fractious. Maya tied together bunches of neem leaves, and when their skin itched Parvathi brushed them with the leaves. To make the scabs fall she and Maya rubbed castor oil on their bodies. The days and nights passed slowly. It was more than a week before Parvathi could creep away. As the car drove up she noticed that the impressive iron gates were gone, presumably to be smelted down in munitions factories in Japan. The house too was blanketed in darkness, but this time it was not Kupu's doing. There was hardly any oil left for the generator. The war was going badly wrong.

She watched the candles slowly burning down. Some nights he hardly spoke at all, but she had learned not to ask questions even when she longed for his voice. That night though she wished he had stayed silent.

'I killed a snake today,' he announced. 'A huge black cobra. More than thirteen hands long. I cut its head off.'

Parvathi thought she was breaking into little pieces and floating away, but he appeared to have not noticed anything amiss.

'Shocking, isn't it? To think that such a huge animal could live in this area.'

To conceal the horror in her voice she whispered, 'Where did you find it?'

'Well, that's the strangest thing. I saw it from our bedroom window, simply lying on the lawn below. I rushed downstairs and at first I wasn't even sure if it was still alive, because even with the noise of my boots on the ground it did not prepare to defend itself or escape. In fact, it did not stir at all. It just lay *looking* at me, as if it understood what I was about to do and welcomed it.' He shook his head. 'It was really odd. I felt sorry afterwards. It was a beautiful thing.'

God was dead. But that it should be he who had done it! Now the divine force that had brought him to her and protected them all this while was gone. She knew then that the time had come for him to go away from her.

'What is it?' he asked.

'Nothing,' she said. 'I'm terrified of snakes.'

'Well, it's dead now.'

She made herself smile although she was dying inside.

The next day she went to the goldsmith's and asked him to make her a snake statue, coiled and open-hooded.

'In gold?' he asked.

'Pure gold.'

From under untidy grey eyebrows he regarded her shrewdly. To the best of his knowledge there were no rich locals left. 'How big?'

'Maybe six inches.'

'That will be very expensive,' he warned, 'and I can't accept banana money. It will have to be British currency,' though he knew well that it was a capital offence to transact in any currency other than the worthless Japanese notes.

'I have money,' she said.

'I'll need it in advance.'

In a week it was ready. He carried it out from a back room and put its gleaming form on the glass case.

'Yes, it's perfect,' she said, and took it home. While Maya watched, she took down all the other framed pictures. She would give them away. And so the little gold snake came to stand alone on her altar.

When she arrived at Adari that night there was someone with him in the study. She sat in the music room and listened to their voices in the next room. Then she heard a man's voice say, 'What did you say? Do you wish to die?' It was not a roar, but a quiet threat. When they left he came to find her. He looked weary.

'That was the Kempetai,' he said. 'Japan is in grave danger. She is beyond the help of lowly commanders like me. I know now that my country has embarked on a war that we have neither the technology nor the manpower to win. Japan is a prosperous land, and the Japanese are nobles, but this war is wrong. It is not "co-prosperity" at all: the internment camps are rife with tropical diseases, and the locals hate us. No, it should all end. To that effect I have released all the prisoners-of-war. The Allies should win and yet if they do, I can neither remain here nor take you with me.' He rubbed his hand over his shaven head in a gesture of exhaustion and defeat.

'There is nothing left to do but get drunk,' he said flatly. So they did, on vile local *toddy*. Now she knew exactly what her husband had meant when he said, 'I need it.'

'I finally understand,' he said sadly.

'What?' she asked.

'That odd poem:

An old pond,
the noise,
when a frog jumps in.'

'An old pond, the noise . . . when a frog jumps in,' she repeated slowly. In precision and economy it was what she would have expected of his race. Quickly she had been brought to the green water disturbed. But enigmatic – to what purpose?

He fixed his eyes on her. 'The frog is given to the old pond.' He paused, remained contemplative. 'No, not even given. Lent temporarily. This is what it means. Despite that eagerly swallowing noise, is the temporary frog really worth the loss of stillness? Are *you* worth it? Really?'

He passed out on the cushions and Parvathi stayed awake, watching him.

Unable to sleep, she went to stand at the window and saw Kamala sitting on the porch of the servants' quarter. Suddenly she knew a longing to listen to her incessant chatter, the comic inaccuracies in her knowledge. She slipped across the lawn noiselessly and very gently laid her hand on Kamala's shoulder. The woman jumped up with a strangled yelp and shrieked, 'Oh, Ama! What are you doing here?'

'Shhh,' Parvathi said, hiding a smile. *I've been coming here for years, I just didn't let you see me until now.* But what she said was, 'I came to see the house.'

'Ama, don't you worry about the house. I am aware that all the window-ledges of the upstairs windows are encrusted with pigeon droppings, but very soon the white man will win the war and you will come back, and then the daredevil boys can clean up, can't they? For the moment, the girls and I will do the best we can.'

Parvathi sat on the edge of the cement by the drain.

'How is Maya? Is she well?' Kamala asked. 'The other day I had a pain here.' She placed her hand under her right knee, 'and I wished she was here. She would have cured me straight away. I really miss her.'

'Maya is very well.'

'And the children – how are they?'

'The children were down with chickenpox but they're better now. How are you?'

'I miss corn bread. Since the bakery closed we only get the bread that comes in the trains, and it is always hard and stale. It is difficult for me with my teeth, you know.'

'How are they treating you here?'

'Oh, I'm scared of them. They are so fierce. They never smile or talk, and sometimes they hiss at me when I cannot immediately understand their gestures. They spat my cooking out the first time, too hot for them, so I started adding a lot of coconut milk and they don't spit and snarl any more.' She paused and shook her head. 'But terrible things are happening in the cellar. People are being tortured down there. A few times the cellar door has been left open and I have heard screaming. Cheh! They carry out dead bodies from there, even in broad daylight. And now unquiet spirits have moved into the house and I am afraid to set foot inside at night any more. Sometimes I hear the ghostly sound of a woman

singing, and once I think I saw her. She was very beautiful and as
white as rice. She wore a long gown and wooden clogs, and she
carried a paper fan. She was simply standing on the beach looking
out to sea. Ama, I don't mind telling you, I've never been so afraid
in all my life. I ran and hid in my room. But don't you be scared.
When you move back here, Maya will know just what to do to
get rid of these ghosts. Other than that it's all fine,' she said, and
flashed Parvathi a brilliantly toothless smile.

   Parvathi left her old servant and walked on the beach for hours,
then, following a foul scent, came upon a dead turtle. She shone
her torchlight at it. Its mouth was full of black blood, sand and
bluebottle flies. It was gone the next day. The fishermen must have
buried it.

To Change a Prayer

She knelt, and sat on her crossed heels, while he put a record on the turntable and went to stand by the open window. The wind blew his white kimono away from him. The voice of a woman singing in a high-pitched voice to the accompaniment of a lone string instrument filled the room. Strange, and to her untrained ear, displeasing.

'I'm afraid I don't have a good ear for music,' she said. 'My first husband had to give up on me.'

He came towards her. 'Listen, but this time, do not use your ears.' He put her index finger into his mouth. The wet finger he held up over her head. 'Listen with your skin. Forget what you look like. Open your mouth and taste it with your tongue. It has drama. Fall in love with it. Let it possess you. Be possessed. Listen,' he whispered. 'Hear that sound? That is the *shamishen*. It is an instrument that requires great skill. No giggling *maiko* can play this. Only the oldest and most accomplished of geishas can pluck it like this.'

She listened to the twanging sound. Hollow. Sad. Lonely. No rich chords here. The famous Japanese restraint?

'It is made from cat's skin. Only the skin of a female virgin kitten is used because if a cat is mounted even once by a tom, he will leave scratches on her skin that will affect the perfection of the sound.'

The lonely sound continued, scratchy, even without the tom.

'You must hear it in your heart or turn away from it for ever.' He faced her. 'Did you hear it?'

'No,' she said. He returned to the window and stood with his back to her.

'It is nearly all over. In secret negotiations with the US via the Vatican last spring our Emperor has already agreed surrender terms. But the US is stalling, while devastating Tokyo with B-29s. They goaded us into making our first bad move, attacking Pearl Harbour, and now I think they *want* to invade Japan. Try out that new atomic weapon of theirs on a live target,' he said.

She said nothing. What could she say?

And then she stared at his back, aghast as he explained in a flat, unemotional voice that dying was an infinitely better destiny than surrender. In Japan, it was the way of the honourable Samurai to fall as purely as the cherry-blossom does. The act of clinging to life instead of choosing the rush of death for great ideals was a cowardly bourgeois habit. Ancient warrior codes instructed their members that when in doubt whether to live or die, it was always better to die. Had he himself not briefed his men with the words, 'No half-measures now. All of you come back dead.'

And there was another good reason to choose death. She remained without words while he spoke of *giri*, honour, an utterly blind and uncompromising obligation towards the family, the group, the employer. In silence she learned another word, *giri-ninjo*. The obligation to one's wife, children, parents. In comparison with this obligation, the call of love was a trivial matter. They could never be together.

There was a pause. Then: would she like to join him in committing a double suicide? *Shinju*. Like Hitler and Eva, but not as an act of war or rebellion, rather an expression of atonement.

But she had seen a picture of this double suicide that he referred to. It was horrible. The man lying over the woman. A sword sticking out of his back and she open from ear to ear, as if she was grinning hideously, triumphantly. Crumpled blood-soaked cloths around the dead couple. A terrible picture, but then again, all the doomed lovers of the best legends committed suicide.

The cult of an honourable suicide was a facet of *his* culture; but how could she take her own life? What would become of her children? They would never live down the disgrace of it. Good families would not want to marry into hers. 'Bad genes,' they would say and shake their heads. And what of her soul? She thought of it wandering who knows how long, a spirit or devil, lost and in torment.

Her eyes turned up to him, full of begging. She opened her mouth and quick as a flash he thrust out his hand and covered it. Her eyes widened with the suddenness of the movement, the violence of it. His fingers moved; he caressed her cheek, gently massaged the area around her mouth. She stared at him: the calmness in his eyes the sternness of his mouth. The music stopped. He took his hand away.

'Do not worry yourself. It is not important, after all. Get some rest,' he said, his voice unseasonably gruff. This was him at his most tender. But this was also his final word. She could follow him or not. But he must die. It was the only way for him. He smiled at her. She wouldn't smile back. Even through her shock she saw that this was the very thing she had prayed for. *Let him be willing to put his hand in the fire for me, let him be ready to give up his life for me.*

The Snake God had delivered.

And what does a woman do if she realises she does not want what she had asked for? Should she still bow and accept? What would happen if that woman changes her mind and does not want to accept?

She lay awake beside him until dawn and then went back to the shop house. She did not know what to do. Her skin felt clammy. For a long, long while she rested her forehead on the tips of her fingers and meditated. And then she decided. *If that woman does not accept she goes back to the altar.* She looked at her coiled serpent and said, 'I was a child before. I did not know what I asked. Forgive me. I am a woman now, and I ask that he be spared. May none of his bandages carry my name. Let him live, even without me. Bless him. Let him live.'

He joined her inside the henna-dyed mosquito net.

'The chrysanthemum season would be upon me if I were in Japan now,' he said quietly. She gasped. Had he already left her behind and returned to his motherland? She let the book she was holding drop out of her hand and heard the thud of it hitting the ground. A cool breeze blew in onto her hot, damp flesh. Her hand fell heavily on his shoulder. The smell from the gas lamp was strong. Outside, a peacock called. The wind rustled in the trees. The generator was silent. She remembered it all. Every little detail captured like a living, breathing photograph. She had thousands of them. They were all beautiful, precious secrets, like buried treasure.

8th May 1945. The war in Europe ended and London, the radio said, was awash with intensely patriotic parades and street parties. High overhead, American bombers were passing on their way to Singapore. The Mamis said, 'Very good. The Japanese won't be around too long now.'

6th August 1945. The BBC broadcast that the first atomic bomb had hit Hiroshima. General Hattori stood ashen-faced on the balcony and looked blindly out to sea.

8th August. The second fell. The city of Nagasaki became a sea of rubble. Parvathi remembered the sweet-seller in Ceylon who had, without any warning, gone mad one day. He rushed out into the street with dishevelled hair and gave away handfuls of his sweets. When his sons came to find him, he was sitting at the doorway eating an onion, and laughing for no reason.

15th August. Emperor Hirohito was forced to deny on the radio that he was God. Japan had 'endured the unendurable and suffered the insufferable,' he said.

2nd September. Japan surrendered to General Douglas MacArthur. The war was over, but not in the Malay Peninsula, not until 13th September 1945. Japanese officials drove in with cars bearing white flags. The crowd jeered, but the officers did not react. The surrender document was signed by both parties. As the names of the officers were called out, they performed the ritual act of handing over their samurai swords to denote the total disarmament of the Imperial Japanese Army.

To the woman who came to Maya with PMT she said, 'Throw away the Gregorian calendar you keep in your house. Your body is simply confused because it knows that there are thirteen months in a year, not twelve. Just follow the cycles of the moon – recognise the new moon as the first day of the month, the full moon as the middle of the month, and the black moon as the last day of the month – and you will never again suffer pains or depression before, during, or after your periods.'

Without

Her drawers were full of banana money. She gave them to the children, Rubini played shop with them, and Kuberan, the destructive little monster that he was, burned his in heaps. Burning money! It should have made her shudder, but she was glad not to profit. It was tainted. What would the Mamis do with theirs, she wondered. With tears in their eyes, fold them into origami flowers and little dogs? Adari. She knew it had been bombed, of course, she had expected it to have suffered, but that jagged silhouette that met her ... All the glass had been shattered, the roof had caved in, and what remained cast long shadows. In the middle of the ruin was Kasu Marimuthu's metal cage. It alone had survived intact. She recalled his anxiety about being trapped in it if there was a fire. Strange, what he had worried about.

She thought of all his thousands of dust-covered books burning in the inferno, and suddenly remembered – it was behind the books that she had hidden away her legal papers, the land deeds, the titles to the estates. The lawyer will have copies, she told herself. On the island, a lone peacock opened its sparse tail and danced determinedly for her. The others were nowhere to be seen. She watched it until it walked away, its tail brushing the ground.

She moved towards the generator room. It was falling to pieces, but Kupu suddenly crept out of it barefoot and dressed in rags.

'Ama,' he gasped, and rushed to fall at her feet. Poor man, he must be living off the land now, she thought, and took off her chain to give it to him. But he shook his head violently. 'What for, Ama? The forest and sea will feed me and be my grave too.'

She looked towards the house. 'What happened?'

'It was horrible, just horrible, but there was nothing any of us could do.' His lips trembled. 'It began after the Japanese soldiers stole away the silver bowls from beneath the floor of the temple. After that "it" came upon us from the East and the West. "It" came in the guise of Communist insurgents with side-arms, rifles, grenades, and carbines. They held us at bay and set fire to the house. The wooden floors burned easily, and in the incredible heat the glass panes began to explode. We were driven further and further back until in the end, we were standing in the sea, while one by one the great iron casings collapsed. The noise was deafening and flames leaped hundreds of feet into the air. I'm surprised you couldn't see it from the town. When the burning tree in the middle of the house finally crashed into the flames, I cried. I knew I would never again see anything else more heart-wrenching.'

Watching him, Parvathi suddenly noticed that his tic was gone. It must have been a manifestation, a way of warding off the unendurable. Now that he was returned to the land, he was glorious again.

'I must go and see the temple,' she said.

'Ama,' he said sorrowfully, 'I'm afraid I have bad news. The day after they killed the snake, the temple was bombed by the British. They must have mistaken it for a Japanese station. But come with me anyway, and see what is left.'

She looked at the devastation in silence and in silence he led her out of the jungle back to the edge of the house, where he bade her goodbye. She watched him walking through the shimmering, waving, long grasses, head bent like a tiger, and a great sadness descended upon her. She would never see him again; she felt that in her heart. She would bequeath that square of sacred land to him. He was the rightful owner of it. She was walking away when she heard him call her name and turned around. He was standing at the edge of the forest.

She cupped her hands to her mouth. 'What it is?'

For a moment he did not answer and she thought the wind had snatched her voice away. But then the same wind brought his reply as if he stood beside her and said, 'I've loved you from the first moment I saw you. And that day in the forest, I slept not for three nights that it was not my right to touch you.'

Her hands fell to her sides. They stared at each other from their distance. So far away she could not even make out his features.

'I just wanted you to know,' he called, and turned away.

'Wait!' she shouted, but he had already stepped through the dark green wall and become part of the jungle once more. She waited a while longer, even though she knew he would not come back.

She picked her way through the wreckage, past the black tree stump, onwards to the west wing. The north wall of the ballroom was gutted and wind blew through it. Her appearance startled a pale iguana that scuttled away. She went up the staircase. Under her feet it creaked, unstable and dangerous. She stopped, closed her eyes, tasted tinned salmon and heard the haunting call of a *shamishen*. A mouth was running kisses down her spine. *Kiss me one more time. Don't slip away so quickly. Everything without you is agony*. She opened her eyes. He must vacate his throne, this God of Sensuality, and return her heart to health.

In the distance the fishermen were coming in; little faraway figures. Their women were waiting, their fires already lit. Hardworking, blessed people. She stood there for hours while they cooked their fish, ate, packed their things and left. The sun was setting and the house began to fill with hostile shadows. All the people who had been murdered in the basement while she made love upstairs rose up pointing and unforgiving. She became frightened. She knew she would never again be able to live there. The wind whistled eerily through the shattered glass. Some small animal wept. She ran blindly.

The driver was sitting on a stone by the car. He had eaten some fish; the bones were by his feet. He stood when he saw her, but she held her hand up and he resumed his seat. She walked to the beach. Her husband had left without her. She was standing at the water's edge, one hand shading her eyes, looking out to the horizon when she heard the sound of a Jeep. She turned, her heart leaping. Why, he had come back for her, the owner of a ruined palace.

He was holding a long flat box in his hand, and was dressed in the way he had been when she had first seen him. Formal, proud, a General. He stood still watching her, her sari fluttering around her, the way a kimono never would. And she knew he was committing her to memory. Because of course he had not come to take her away or stay. This was goodbye.

She took a step forward and he began walking towards her, one arm swinging loosely beside his body, but his steps were slow and tired. He was prolonging the moment.

She stopped. She was suddenly too exhausted to make the journey. Let him come when he would. So many lonely nights waited with her. A cold wind blew from the sea, and she hugged herself. He took off his cap and stood before her. She gazed up into that destroyed face. The war, the war, he had lost more than the war.

'You found the heart to leave me?' But she didn't say it.

'They told me you would be here,' he said. His jaw was clenched.

Her mouth dropped at the corners; but he understood it to be a smile. 'Will you be all right?' she asked.

He shrugged. 'Will you?'

'Yes, I think so.'

But when she saw how uselessly he was looking down at her she pushed her face desperately into his chest. She felt the metal in his uniform digging into her cheek. He smelled different too. Musk – fear. For the uncertain future. For the change. For the loss of face. A fate worse than death. In his dreams he had taken his hand and the dagger under the trailing sleeve into his own body. This was defeat and yet, this new way of thinking said, it was braver still to face another day, and the punishment that was coming. And when he opened his mouth to speak, it was not about desperation or loss, but hope. 'I'll come back for you, Sakura. I promise. Will you wait for me?'

'I will wait at the shop until the day you come,' she promised, though Kasu Marimuthu's words were ringing in her ears. '*Sell the shop. It will ruin you.*'

He smiled wanly. 'And I will. My word is good.'

She smiled. 'So is mine.'

'If for any reason we lose contact and are unable to reach each other, remember that on the day this country gains its independence from the British, I will meet you at the main railway station in Kuala Lumpur, let's say noon on the platform where the trains depart for Kuantan.'

'I'll be there,' she said.

'Will you wear blue or white?'

'White with a blue border.'

'I will dream of it.'

'The star-crossed lovers.' She smiled ironically. 'We are missing only the bamboo bridge.'

'I must go now.'

'Yes, you must go.' Soft; almost inaudible. *Go, your ancestors are watching.*

Instead of kissing her, he put her away from him, turned smartly, energetically, his back ramrod straight, as if executing a military command, and marched away from her. Ridiculous man. How could he march away from a lover? And yet she did not complain or cry out. She understood. The hero's fall had been too swift. She thought of all the things they did not say to each other. Generations of silence and holding back was so imbued into his every cell that he could not show emotion, and certainly not this kind of ferocious, tearing pain. Even she could see they were inappropriate on a lonely windswept beach.

The driver held open the door; he got in and shut it. The driver went around the other side and started the ignition. Her feet ... oh, but oh, how they longed to run after him! He turned a frozen face towards her. The Jeep's engine came to life. His hand reached out. Instantly her body responded, started forward. His mouth opened to issue a tragic sound, her name perhaps, but the wind made off with it, and the vehicle bore him off.

She stood a long time, squinting into the distance.

Inside the box she found an umbrella. An umbrella? The gust of wind sailed the discarded box and lid onto the waves. She opened out the umbrella and holding it away from her, studied its pattern. Cherry blossoms. She held it over her head. He was not coming back, not just yet. But one day. He had promised, and he was a man who kept his word.

She peeped out from behind the umbrella and saw some old newspapers half-buried in the sand. Dusting the sand off them, she used them to wrap up her gift. Even now there was the danger that someone would see and say, 'So: it was you.'

Her hand went towards two envelopes tucked into her blouse. One was from Samuel West, but the infatuation with Europe was truly over. She tore that into small pieces, which the wind bore away even before they touched the ground. The other was from home. Whatever it was, it wouldn't be good news. Dully, she beheld her brother's untidy scrawl on the cheap blue envelope. Later, she thought, and put it back into her blouse.

Then she went to the swing and lunged into the sky, every backward tug at the ropes taking her higher and higher while around her the shadows grew longer and longer.

True love knows how to wait.

Rubini

He stared at the girl swaying towards him. Her hair was cropped close to her head, but she had decorated it with a surfeit of combs and cheap jewelled ornaments. And it is true that a frock is a frock is a frock, that is, until a twelve-year-old girl in her mother's high-heels gets in it, and holds it up with a couple of safety pins, then it becomes the slipping, sliding cloth of Jezebel herself. In her beautiful face her mouth stood out pouting and scarlet.

That there should have been more censorship and control in her dress and manner was plain to see from the stares she was attracting, but the youth understood; the war was over, the Japs were gone, and she was luxuriating in the femininity she had been denied for four long years.

As she neared, her eyes flicked down his person briefly, contemptuously, and finding nothing worthy of interest, slid away to resume their focus on some wonderful point ahead. When she had passed him by, chewing gum like an American, he turned and gazed longingly at her retreating hips. Her disdain, he knew, was real. Nevertheless, she had *looked* at him. She had actually looked at *him*. Her eyes had lain upon his person. And that was enough, for the youth was impossibly smitten with her, had been from the first time he saw her, a child in school, tumbling down from the top of a human pyramid on Sports Day. He was a senior then. As he watched her fall, it was as if someone had called from the outer reaches of his vision, *'Colour, lights, music.'*

And though he made it his business to listen to gossip about her family, and followed her from a distance, it was always without hope; always she had remained out of his reach, the great Kasu

Marimuthu's daughter. But that was before the war. The war had changed things and now, one could say, the girl was almost within his grasp. He should go and see the beautiful, reclusive widow, once known as Rolls Royce Mami and now simply called Kadai (Shop) Mami. He had heard that she had not cut her hair since the day her husband died and it was floor length. Once or twice he had glimpsed her at the upstairs window. One day, perhaps not that day or the day after, but one day he would sit before her. To ask for the girl's hand. Until then he would wait. His love was not transient, amorphous or passing.

True love knew how to wait.

Somewhere along the street a lone Gurkha soldier had appreciated her defiance and started clapping. Another pair of hands soon joined his. The girl-woman flushed, smiled and tilted her chin that bit higher. Others followed. More burst further on, until the entire street was clapping.

Parvathi stood from her chair and went to the window to see what the commotion was about. Ah, Rubini. She smiled sadly. Life was changing day by day. She had not yet told her daughter that all the title deeds to the numerous tracts of land her father owned were lost in the fire, and the copies held by her father's solicitor were who knows where. The man was dead, beheaded, and all his records carted away when the Japanese found a radio in his office. Since she was clueless as to where all the lands were, it was impossible to locate them, especially the ones overseas. It seemed almost impossible that such a thing could happen – that she owned land to which she could not lay claim, because she did not know where they were.

Another solicitor she contacted agreed that such was the case and added that much land lay unclaimed in this way. He predicted that when enough time had lapsed, the Government would reclaim it all. He could only urge her to try harder to remember where her husband's properties were. Parvathi did not need to try. She had never known. The only one she knew of was the rubber estate in Malacca that her husband had told her about, and that only because he wanted them to shelter there if ever there was trouble in Adari. Her husband had never taken her into his confidence in financial or business matters. To him she had always remained the uneducated peasant girl.

Parvathi went back to her chair and reread her eldest brother's letter. She was not – and the word was underlined twice – to sell the shop. He was coming to help her run it. She understood what 'help' entailed and knew she should have written to tell him that her husband had left strict instructions for her to sell the shop. But what then, of her promise to Hattori. Never mind. Let him come. Let him take. What would it matter? He was family and she had more than she or her children needed.

When Parvathi announced that her brother was coming to take charge of the shop Maya said, 'Who can tell how much water the frog in the well will drink?'

But Kuberan immediately demanded an increase in his pocket money to compensate for the loss of privacy and space by having another bed put in his room. Her brother arrived older and sterner about the mouth. 'Running a shop is man's work,' he said. 'You should stay upstairs and take care of the children.'

Her brother disapproved of Maya, called her a 'cracko' in Malay costume, and wanted Parvathi to get rid of her.

'She is family,' Parvathi said, so resolutely that he dropped the subject. But poor Apu was quickly relieved from his duties for being 'incompetent'. Thus her brother took over completely, while Parvathi was banished upstairs not to be seen or heard, exactly as she had been in her father's backyard.

She woke up every morning, bathed, dressed and said her prayers. Except for when she went downstairs for her meals she hardly left those four rooms, not even to meet the Black Umbrella Club members. Mostly, she sat and daydreamed of the past, Kalichan lying against the sun-warmed garden wall, Kupu walking away in the long grass, and always Hattori San standing immobile on the balcony staring at the moonlit ocean. When the children came home from school they told their stories and she listened, smiled and nodded at the appropriate places, and sometimes she even made comments. But they were growing away from her, especially Kuberan, and there was nothing she could do about it. So time passed outside the window of that little flat, hardly touching her life.

1953

Parvathi stood at the window and remembered the first days after Hattori had left when she had lain on her narrow bed, bereft and without any thought but loss, afraid even to fall asleep, fearful that Rubini would, like that one time, shake her awake with questions she didn't want to answer. 'Who is Hattori? Why are you calling for him?'

'An old friend of your father's,' she had answered immediately, even dazed and half-asleep. And that unsuspected, instinctive cunning made her heart ache.

Until the morning Maya came to sit on her bed.

'Love is a splendorous thing,' she said. 'We come again and again to taste its glory, and too often we forget that we are just passing through. Nothing can last for ever. Tragedies will come to knock on all our doors, but the successful remember it is only a guest. Even jagged glass will not cut if you don't travel right to its edge. Love, any love, no matter how long it lasts, is a gift. What if I said I can make your pain disappear, but in exchange, you must be willing to give up all your memories of him?'

Parvathi had sat up slowly, frowning. 'There is no moment I want undone. All of it is precious. I can give up nothing.' And she rose from her bed, and they went down to the kitchen where they separated a sack of hibiscus flowers from their stems and mixed them with honey and lime juice.

'Ama!' the boy who helped in the shop called up the stairs.

She turned away from the window. 'Yes, Krishna?'

'The school Headmaster is downstairs. He wants to see you.'

Parvathi frowned. 'Show him up,' she said.

'Yes, Ama,' he said. She adjusted her sari, switched on the landing light and waited. The Headmaster negotiated the steep wooden stairs cautiously. When he reached the top she greeted him politely.

'Come in and have a seat,' she invited, gesturing towards the long sofa.

He leaned back and looked around the sparse accommodation. 'How are you? It has been a long time since we last met. It is no secret that I was a great admirer of your husband, which makes this so much harder.' He paused and looked uncomfortable. 'I'm afraid I have come about your son. He was always a handful, but we have tried to discipline him as best we could without troubling you. Even that time when he left excrement in the cleaner's cupboard and scratched filthy words on his desk top.'

Parvathi's eyes opened wide. 'Kuberan? Are you sure?'

'He confessed to it.'

'He confessed to it?'

'Yes, after his friends told on him, of course.' There was a brief, horrid silence while the man gathered his thoughts. 'But unfortunately I am here today because this time he has gone too far. One of his schoolmates has accused him of trying to rape her.'

'What?' Her voice sounded hoarse. It was a good thing she was sitting for she felt dizzy, as if she might faint.

'I have no choice but to expel him. He is an exceptionally intelligent boy, of course, and despite his complete disregard for his studies his grades have always been first-rate. There are other schools that might take him on, or you can have him privately tutored. I can let you have the names of some excellent teachers.'

Parvathi's breath came out in a gasp. 'Wait one moment!' she cried. 'I just need to know what happened. Exactly what did he do?'

Kuberan's Headmaster squirmed awkwardly. 'He apparently dragged her behind the canteen. If not for the noodle seller who came to the girl's rescue, he would have done the deed. He had already torn off her under-things and bitten ... her ... chest. There were also scratches . . .'

Parvathi felt herself flush. 'I see,' she said, but she did not, she could not. Kuberan on top of a girl, biting and scratching. She looked up. 'And when did this happen?'

'Yesterday afternoon.'

She thought of her son at dinner the night before, his behaviour in no way altered. Pressing her lips together for composure, she rose to her feet. 'I want to thank you sincerely for all you have done. I appreciate your coming here. My husband always said, "He's a fine man, that Thuraisingam." '

The Headmaster stood regretfully. Truly, how such a fine set of parents could have spawned a boy like him, he would never know. 'Coming from your late husband, that is a great compliment. I also want you to know that this matter has been and will be, treated with utmost discretion on my part. Goodbye, Mrs Marimuthu.'

She did not extend her hand in a handshake or accompany him to the top of the stairs, but stood hugging herself, so shocked that her mind had gone blank. As soon as his footsteps died away she heard her brother's leather sandals, two sizes too big for him, slap up the stairs. She closed her eyes desperately. Oh! not now, not when she was so low, so exposed! She took a deep breath and sank back into the chair behind her.

Her brother put his head in the door. 'What did the Headmaster want?'

'He came to tell me that he has to expel Kuberan.'

'What?' Her brother came fully into the room. His eyes were round. 'Why?'

'There was some trouble with a girl.'

'What sort of trouble? Did he get her pregnant?'

'No, no, it didn't get that far.'

'So what's the problem then?'

She covered her throat with her hand and wiped her lower face. He was still staring at her curiously and she remembered the comment that Maya had made the first moment she laid eyes on him, 'I know his type,' she said. ' "I'll bring back gold," he has told his wife.'

'Look,' Parvathi said distractedly. 'I . . . I'm a bit tired now. Can we talk later please?'

'Where is that boy now?'

'I don't know. Shall we talk later? Please.'

'As you wish,' he said huffily, and walked off towards his room. She dropped her face into her hands. Maya was out and she must have sat there for ages. Eventually she went to stand by the window.

She didn't know what offended her sensibilities more, the heinousness of the crime itself or the unendurable nonchalance Kuberan had displayed afterwards. She tried to find extenuating circumstances for him. What if it was not rape? What if it was youthful passion carried too far? What if it was all a mistake? But in the end it was his chilling lack of conscience that bothered her. Dully, she watched the man selling pickled fruit on skewers outside the cinema. She wondered at his life, whether he was happy, whether he was fulfilled. He must have sons and daughters and a wife at home.

She heard a sound behind her. Kuberan was leaning casually against the doorway.

'I suppose you're wanting to talk to me,' he said, pushing himself upright, and sauntering into the room.

'Yes,' she said slowly, and turned more fully to confront him. The evening light fell on him, and she saw that there would never be room for remorse on that spoiled handsome face. It was wrong and vile, and if he was older it was something that would have earned him time in some filthy prison, but she found even then that she could not aim an angry word at him. Instead, she looked at him with pity. She did not know what the future held for him, but she was afraid it would not be as rosy as she had imagined. She had cherished such high hopes for him.

'What would your father say if he was alive?'

'He could hardly be too critical, seeing that he sired an illegitimate child himself.'

'How can you even begin to compare yourself with him? You tried to *rape* a girl.'

He dropped onto the settee opposite her with a long-suffering sigh. 'As it happens,' he drawled, 'she was very willing. What do you and that self-righteous fool imagine she was doing at the back of the tuck shop with her blouse off when we were so rudely interrupted? And to be perfectly frank she gave every indication of enjoying it just as much as me, well, at least until the last bit when she wanted to stop and I didn't. I'm afraid I couldn't quite appreciate her modesty at that stage of the game. But never mind . . .'

'Never mind? You're getting kicked out of school, Kuberan!'

'No loss that, surely? Schools are for breeding reliable employees and I don't intend to be one. And anyway, I thought the Head's home-tutoring idea a rather sound one. After which I could read law in England.'

'Read law in England? What madness is this? We can't afford that. Not now, anyway.'

'We could, if we used the sixty thousand pounds in Coutts.'

She had a flashback of the three of them, Rubini, Kuberan and herself trooping into the study to huddle before the lawyer. Kuberan was still in shorts then, not even five. It seemed a lifetime ago. She remembered his eyes, so enormous, so innocent as he stared gravely at the lawyer reading out what seemed to her complicated legal jargon that made up Kasu Marimuthu's will. It had never occurred to her that her son had not only understood but had found use for the information.

'Is it a deal?'

Parvathi looked at her son. 'And during this period of home tutoring, can I trust you to *behave*?'

He laughed easily. 'Well, that's a new word for it.'

She looked at him and wondered at the instinct in her son that pushed him to pour scorn on, and find the fatal flaw in, absolutely everything. Was it just to see how far he could go?

'All right, yes, I will . . . *behave*.'

'You know you will have to obtain the kind of grades necessary to enter a British university?'

'Could have done without you saying that, but . . . yes.'

'Don't let me down again.'

'You won't regret this, Mother,' he said, and tumbling forward like a huge, clumsy puppy, hugged her. She was so startled by the spontaneous show of affection that for a second her hands stayed limp by the sides of her body. Then they went around him, noting how his body had grown, become harder, leaner, longer, different from what she remembered. Her beautiful boy had become an unrecognisable stranger.

He pulled away and walked to the door.

'In any case, you have to admit that spending money on educating me must be a better move than letting my lying, cheating uncle steal what is left of our inheritance,' he threw casually over his shoulder as he exited.

She went back to her position by the window. She could tell from the queue outside that a Tamil movie was about to start at the cinema. Time had become meaningless to her but she deduced that it must either be the seventh or the twenty-first of the month, when the labourers got paid and they screened Tamil films. How eager they all seemed, milling through the open doors. Once this hour used to fill her with magic and excitement too. Now it meant an empty bed, listening to her brother snoring next door. Her son was right, of course, her brother was a blatant liar, claiming no profit ever since he sacked Apu for being incompetent and took over himself.

'It is the times,' he would shrug. 'These are bad times. No one has any money to spend.' The store was hardly breaking even, but every month he sent money – she did not make it her business to find out how much – to his wife and children. He was, in fact, building a brand new family home with bricks and mortar.

The time came when he stood before her to say that he was returning to his family, but not to worry, it had been decided that her second brother would come down to take care of her interests. She nodded her agreement. What was money to her, after all?

Kuberan was as good as his word, he behaved impeccably, studied hard with the tutor his mother had engaged and passed the necessary exams with flying colours. He was to leave with Kundi

Mami's son, who had also been accepted by the same institution he had applied to.

'I'll drop you a postcard when I get there,' Kuberan called cheerfully from the taxi.

The Keys to Heaven

With Kuberan's first letter from Oxford, he sent a packet of Jaffa cakes. She savoured them slowly, saving the middle bit of orange jelly till last, letting that melt on her tongue.

When Kundi Mami came to visit she offered them to her.

'Oh these,' her guest said. 'Yes, my son says they are very cheap to buy in England. You can always tell the good types, because they come in tins. Like the chocolates he sent me. Quality Street.'

Parvathi's eyes dropped. So what if they were cheap. She liked them. It was the thought that counted.

'I've taken a vow to walk barefoot to the temple every Friday until my son passes his exams,' Kundi Mami went on importantly.

'Oh,' Parvathi said, and held the plate of Jaffa cakes up to her guest again. The woman helped herself to two.

'I see you still have that Indian servant of yours with you, then?'

'Maya's more of a companion.'

Kundi Mami frowned. 'Wasn't she once working for you as a servant?'

'No, not exactly. Actually, she's a healer and quite famous too. Every afternoon there is a queue of people at the back gate waiting to see her.'

'What? You let her use your home like that! All those diseased people coming to your house . . . What a cheek that woman has, to do that to you. You are too naïve, my dear. Just as you wouldn't put a broom in your showcase, these low-class Indians too have to be kept in their proper place. They are no good as anything but servants, and even then they have to be watched very carefully or they will laze about and steal.'

Parvathi stood abruptly. 'It was so nice of you to drop by, but I've just remembered that I promised to go to a friend's house.'

Kundi Mami stared at her, open-mouthed with astonishment, and then she lifted her posterior, that the years seemed to have made more imposing still, off her host's chair. Trembling with humiliation and rage she stalked to the door. She knew Parvathi had no prior appointment. Everyone knew that she never left the shop house any more.

Parvathi went downstairs into the kitchen. The radio was on and Maya was kneading chapatti dough. She searched Maya's face to gauge if she had heard anything, but the woman only smiled blandly and asked, 'Has your guest already gone?'

'Yes.' Parvathi looked around the spotless kitchen. 'I've decided that from now on we are going to cook together.'

Maya stilled her pressing and pulling, and looked at her employer fully. 'I like being your servant. It is my pleasure to serve you. It hurts some people's pride to admit it, but we are all here to serve. From the meanest servant to the most illustrious king, at one level or another, we are all serving someone. Please don't change anything between us because of what that lady said.'

'You heard, then.'

'It was impossible not to.'

'I'm so sorry. She's just like that, mean about the mouth. Please don't feel bad.'

'Why should I? Women like her are a gift: they hold in their hands the keys to heaven. Although at first glance it may seem they are our enemies, in reality, they have undertaken to provide us with valuable opportunities to be gentle and patient. To act with love. They do this at great cost to themselves – all the tears I cry she will wipe from her own eyes. It is the law of the universe that as you stretch your hand to give to another, you give to yourself. If today she happens to look askance at me, tomorrow, the day after, the following year, or a decade later, when even she has forgotten she once did the same, she will endure an equally disparaging sideways glance.'

'But I get so angry when anyone condescends to you.'

'I once worked in a doll factory. First they make the soft cloth body and then they sew in the delicate porcelain feet and hands. The hair goes on after the faces have been painted and attached. Afterwards they clothe it, and it is ready. If you think about it, we're the same. Step by step we are being refined. All of us are at different stages of perfection. Are you better than your friend because she has not yet her hair and you do? Don't ever despise or judge anyone. The condition of being human is hard, but here's the really nice bit – no one ever falls by the wayside. All will make it to perfection. God doesn't love me any better than he does you or her. We are all his children.'

Maya went back to kneading and after a while Parvathi said, 'What are you thinking about now?'

Maya smiled broadly. 'Actually, I was wondering what you would like to have with your chapatti tonight. Lentils or deep fried potatoes curried with those tinned peas.

'Potato with tinned peas, I think.'

'I agree,' Maya said, and they smiled at each other, and in their smile was a deathless love that was already centuries old.

Out in the front, Parvathi's second brother was sitting at the till gazing out into the street. He had already taken much more than the other had dared, but he wanted still more. He was aware he was running the shop into the ground, but he didn't care. As a representative of his father and in order to put the shop back into order he would insist that Parvathi sell the rubber plantation in Malacca.

At first Parvathi was reluctant. 'It belongs to the children,' she said.

Then her father wrote to her, ordering her to sell it.

She sold it.

'Why would you let them finish all that Papa left for us?' Rubini asked resentfully

Parvathi shook her head. 'I'm sorry,' she said, 'but I cannot disobey my father.'

It was a week before her second brother was due to go home and her third brother due to arrive, when she heard through the grapevine that her son had married a white woman. Shocked, for he had never mentioned it, she wrote to ask him. He replied on a postcard.

Your source is giving out old news, he wrote. *The wife's gone and good riddance, I say.*

She went to look for Maya, who was stirring something in a black cauldron.

'Ah, there you are,' she said to Parvathi. 'You can help. Bring me those herbs. It looked like we might have a hot day today so I thought I'd prepare these for drying later.'

Parvathi dropped the herbs in handfuls into the boiling milk. 'It's true, Maya. He got married without telling me.'

'Hmmm . . .' said Maya, but her eyes were endless wells of compassion.

Kupu

Kupu stood motionless, listening to the jungle that had become deathly quiet. Suddenly, seven large spheres of light flickered into the sky: bright orange balls with luminous circumferences. And yet, he found he could see through them as if they were coloured glass and look directly into their centres. They were moving at a stately, unhurried speed, but fluidly, like large fish do in water. When they got closer he found he had the sensation that not only were they coming towards him, but that they were also aware of him.

In the trees yonder he heard first his name being called, and then the unlikely sound of children's voices. Without conscious thought, and as if guided by some old memory stored within his cells, he fell to his knees, and in an ancient gesture of learning and submission, covered his mouth with his hand.

The spheres responded simultaneously; they stilled. For a while there was neither movement nor sound from man nor sphere. Then he blinked and all the spheres spontaneously turned off, and then on again. He laughed, certain they were displaying a sense of humour. They held still for a few minutes more and then began to move away, slowly, regally.

He wanted them back, but all of a sudden he felt exhausted to the point of collapse. He lay back and before him appeared tall, elongated figures, some winged, a few with two bands of light coming out of the backs of their necks, but all full of iridescent, glowing colours. They seemed to be neither male nor female. In turn, they spoke to him, beautifully, but without words. Full of awe he listened to their sacred commands. Sometimes their words were given to him as pure white balls of light that hovered over the crown of his head, before pouring down his body, penetrating his skin, entering his flesh, his blood, his bones; blessing, instructing, changing him for ever.

By the time they left, it was already light, and the jungle was full of sounds again. Kupu sat up slowly. His heart was beating erratically, but he felt no fear. They had asked him to restore the silver bowls and rebuild the temple over them. He frowned. Their purpose was obscure to him. Perhaps they had not told him, or perhaps they had, and he had simply forgotten. He looked around him. The world was exactly as it had been before the spheres of light had come to him, and he could only remember the celestial beings as one does a marvellous dream, but as he looked at the piles of rubble, he was startled to realise that he knew exactly where each and every stone had to be placed to rebuild the temple. It had to be constructed to new specifications, since the old ways could no longer be understood by humans; not while they were awake, anyway. And in the place of the communicating stone a deity that the human mind could identify with had to be installed. In his mind the image of the deity stood crystal clear.

From a small leather pouch tied to his waist, he extracted the pearl. Putting its butter-coloured body in the palm of his left hand, he stroked it and thought again of she who had given him such a treasure. Instantly, that time he had spied on her dancing under the glittering chandeliers with the Japanese General came back. He had been afraid of being discovered, but he had gone as close to the French doors as he dared, and stared mesmerised as, totally absorbed in each other, they circled the vast ballroom.

Usually, he relished living off the land, using only his skill and instinct to provide for himself in his lonely solitude, but the memory of her with the other made him feel as if he had taken a wrong turn. He had never understood why he did not respond to her that time in the jungle when every cell in his body had bade him to, but he had stood immobile, his expression hidden, and allowed her to slip out of his grasp. Now, he felt the need to call out to her, to actually hear his own voice say her name.

His whisper faded to nothing. A tear escaped and rolled down his face. He dashed it away roughly and squared his shoulders. When his cows were unruly he gave them cottonseed oil. Should he administer some to himself? What was this sense of despair and defeat that poisoned his mind? So what if there would be no more new adventures with her, only old ones revisited, and so many times that they changed and grew, with new dialogues and imagined moments of affection and passion.

He would not uproot whatever part of her that remained, of course not, but he must prune those restless roots or they would surely strangle him. Ultimately, they were only echoes. All fake. A great trick. Now he understood that life meant sacrifice, not fulfilment. Self-abandonment was the only way.

A small monkey twittered by his feet. He picked it up. 'Haimo,' he said, in the language he had invented living alone in the jungle. The monkey clambered onto his shoulder and chattered amiably. Kupu stood undecided. He must go to the city, as much as he dreaded the thought of leaving his beautiful jungle. He had not left it for years now. Almost, he had forgotten how to navigate the cars, the noise, the people, but there was work to be done, God's work. He blew on the monkey's face and it scampered off up a tree. The two hand-fed, golden-necked roosters sleeping in the tree woke up and began to crow. In an old trunk he found a torn shirt that he slung on his back, and over his loincloth he pulled on a pair of trousers. They felt strange. 'Haimo,' he said again, and went into the city.

In exchange for the pearl drop, he commissioned the silver bowls. In two weeks they were ready. Always he had had the quick keen eye that came from being in the jungle and observing before he was observed. Now it gave him the instinct to know exactly where to position the gleaming bowls. Then he returned to the jungle to a spot by the stream where the dream beings had told him to dig. There he found clay and scooping it up with his bare hands, began to make his god.

He worked for hours. When night came he lit a lamp and worked steadily on. Neither tiredness nor aches came to obstruct or hinder him. Even when his hands became numb and raw he did not stop. They moved of their own accord, tirelessly, without hesitation or doubt. As his creation grew taller he stood on a stone and carried on with his labour until it towered over him.

He stepped off the stone, and with his spine and arms aching, backed away from his work. There was still paint to be applied. He knew where the fruit, leaf, sap, and insects that needed to be hunted and crushed to make the colours were, but he would hunt for those later.

When he was far enough away and could see his creation in all its lamplit splendour he fell to his knees and gazed at his deity with awe. He was no artist, but glowing radiantly and rising taller than any idol he had seen was the exact vision the angels had revealed to him. There was a slithering sound in the bushes nearby; he paid it no attention. Clasping his hands together, he bent his head and began to pray fervently at the miracle before him.

Bala

Curiously, Parvathi eyed the youth seated in front of her. Bala. Plain, dark and poor, but he sat before her as a hopeful suitor for Rubini's hand. Why such a one as he would ever imagine he might be of any interest to Rubini was what made her sit and listen, though she knew rejection was imminent. He explained that he was in love with her daughter. So deeply that he would have her even without her considerable dowry. He planned to provide for her on his teacher's salary.

'I think,' Parvathi interrupted gently, 'my daughter is not interested in getting married just yet.'

But this dampened the young man's spirit not at all. Instead, he smiled kindly at her as if he was dealing with a child or someone without all her wits about her. 'I am willing to wait.'

For a moment Parvathi was silent. Despite Rubini's well-known reputation as a thoroughly spoiled, demanding madam, rumours of her beauty and the large dowry left by her father had spread far and wide, and proposals continued to pour forth from all over Malaysia. Doctors, lawyers, accountants, businessmen. But true to form she had rejected them all: too short, dark, fat, bad skin, ugly, bald, stupid.

'Well,' Parvathi said, 'perhaps you should also know that to date, my daughter has already turned down thirty-two men.'

Behind his glasses, all remained calm. 'All things come to he who waits,' the suitor remarked sagely.

Parvathi sighed. 'Of course, you may wait as long as you wish, but I must warn you all the same that my daughter has her heart set on marrying a doctor.'

'Mother,' he said gently, 'I have said what I came to say. If ever at any time, for any reason at all, she changes her mind, will you remember me?'

She wondered if he was a little mad. No, just bookish, probably a bore too. 'All right,' she said, just to get rid of him.

He went. But every month, he sent flowers and chocolates for Rubini, which she, of course, completely ignored. Once Parvathi asked her about him and Rubini lifted her chin proudly and in her snootiest voice denounced him an idiot. 'I despise him,' she said. 'As if I would ever marry someone like *him*. The cheek to even ask!'

And all the while proposals came and as quickly went, but just when Parvathi was beginning to despair, a doctor appeared: tall, handsome, fair, and with it all, lashes so long and sooty that they seemed to rest on his cheeks when he looked down, which was often. In fact, he hardly spoke during the time he was in their sitting room, but he seemed to Parvathi, to be a good, well-brought-up boy. He was still doing his internship in Johor, but since he would be finished before the wedding, it was decided that the couple should move to Kuala Lumpur and live in the house Kasu Marimuthu had left for Rubini.

It became impractical, and a cause for talk, if Parvathi, a widow alone, remained in Kuantan. She sold the shop and used the money to buy a three-bedroom terrace house in Kuala Lumpur on the next road to Rubini's beautiful custom-built two-storey house. The new owners of the shop had promised to send her mail on, but Parvathi experienced such a sense of despair as she closed the door of the flat for the last time, that she found it impossible to answer a question the taxi driver directed at her.

However, by the time she walked through the folding doors of her new home her body, at least, was calm and resigned. It was not a bad house. There was the living room in the front, and in the middle, an air-well to let in the light; a good place for Maya to dry the ingredients for her medicines. A corridor beside it led off to its three bedrooms. She took the one closest to the sitting room and Maya the one closest to the kitchen. The women settled in quickly and began preparations for the big wedding. The most auspicious time was calculated: 15th February at 2 a.m. Eight hundred people were invited to witness Kasu Marimuthu's daughter get married.

The Wedding

A thing of great beauty and expense, the bridal sari had been crafted especially and then hand-carried from India. Months of preparation came together in a great hall full of people. In a small room at the back, Rubini sat surrounded by the usual clutch of women fussing over her attire. It was 1.30 a.m when Parvathi walked in and asked everyone to leave for a minute. Rubini looked up into her stepmother's eyes and something inside her shrank back in fear.

The handsome nice boy was a spineless coward who had finally, one hour before his wedding, decided to confess that he was already married, secretly, to a Malay woman. He had a Moslem name and a baby boy. Rubini put her head down and remained so for a long moment. When she emerged, she was a different person. Pushing aside a curl from her pale face she asked in a flat, listless voice, 'That flowers and chocolate boy, he lives around here now, doesn't he?'

'Yes,' Parvathi said with a frown. 'I think he shares a house in Brickfields with a few other bachelors. Why do you ask?'

'Send word to him that if he will still have me, he can take the place of my bridegroom.'

'What? You despise the man. You don't even know his name.'

Rubini fingered a bead on her costume. 'What *is* his name?'

'His name is Bala, but this . . . is unnecessary. We will find you someone else. You are young and beautiful. There will be many others.'

Rubini raised her eyes. They were large and dead. She shook her head slowly, implacably. The loose curl bounced against the curve of her cheek. 'I will marry him or no one else,' she said softly. In silence they stared at each other. Then Parvathi turned away and went downstairs.

'Is this the right thing to do?' she asked Maya.

'We must respect the lessons she has chosen to learn in this incarnation.'

The friend she had sent to call upon Bala with Rubini's offer came back with him. With shining eyes Bala rushed to humbly prostrate himself at Parvathi's feet.

She touched his shoulder gently. 'It is not I you have to thank. I would not have chosen you for my daughter, but I will always be grateful to you for coming to her rescue. Come, let us see if we can find you a costume from my son's wardrobe that will fit you.'

'No need,' Bala said. 'I've had it ready for the last ten years.'

'Oh,' Parvathi said sadly, and moved away.

Alone, Bala placed the cream and gold headgear on his head. Meticulously, he wiped his spectacles before placing them back on the bridge of his nose. Then he looked up at his reflection in the mirror and could not help the victorious laugh that burst forth. Immersed in his own good luck and happiness, he had not heard anyone enter, and jumped when he saw another face suddenly appear in the mirror.

Whirling around, he came face to face with a large woman. He knew her to be the family's servant, but when he looked into her eyes, that corny phrase, time stopped, actually happened. He then did what all men do when they find themselves in the presence of a power greater than themselves; he bowed to it while some part of him tried desperately to figure out its source so he could make it his.

She grinned suddenly, her teeth and gums stained red, and his breath came out in a rush of embarrassment. He was mistaken, she was only a servant, after all. But then she opened her mouth and said something so beautiful that he would live the rest of his life by it.

'Son, the path of marriage is full of thorns and can only be walked on naked feet, but every time a spine embeds itself in your flesh, rejoice; for it would have hurt her tender foot more. Then one day, you'll look ahead and see that the thorns are no more and the road runs straight into a rainbow.'

Robbed of words, he stared at her.

'Be good to her.'

He nodded.

'Well then, go,' Maya smiled, 'your great dream awaits.'

Bala grinned.

As soon as Bala went to take his place beside Rubini's brother on the marriage dais, a murmur went up in the crowd. In the confusion that followed, some of the guests invited by the bridegroom's side stood up and began to leave. Bala did not care. He stared ahead proudly. No one could take the magic of the day away from him.

'Ah, the flowers and chocolate boy triumphs,' Kuberan drawled at his side. 'Isn't it amazing that this many people would actually kick themselves out of bed to see my sister get married? Bet three times more would have turned up if they had known they would get to see Kasu Marimuthu's daughter brought so low.'

Bala was so taken aback by the sardonic amusement Kuberan took in his sister's shame that he turned and stared at him. Kuberan did not return the look but said cheerfully, 'No need to fret about it, old boy, she'll get over it. I'm with Nietzsche on this one – all vows of eternal love are exercises in self-deception.'

Now Bala understood why hatred of this boy had been so universal in both teachers and students alike at his old school. He remembered the time his former Head had said, 'That boy's a rascal beyond discipline. The only difference attending school makes to him is he has his mid-morning break in the canteen instead of his mother's dining table.'

'While I am a great proponent of philosophy as a substitute for religion, Nietzsche, I believe, should be quoted only with the greatest caution,' Bala said stiffly. 'His wisdom was sustained on saltwater and bitter earth.'

'Enter the blushing bride,' Kuberan sneered. Bala swung his face towards the entrance of the hall, and instantly forgot all about Kuberan and his malicious, hurtful words. He stared awestruck at his bride. No one had ever seen her more beautiful or more glorious. Her eyes remained demurely downcast until she arrived at the marriage dais when she raised them to him. There was nothing shy or flirtatious in those dead depths, however, and he felt his palms go cold and clammy.

She took the place vacated by her brother, and Bala caught a whiff of her perfume. It smelled expensive. It made him think, and he couldn't think why, as he had never been there, of Paris. He placed his eyes on her hennaed hands and fingers as they lay limp in her lap until it was time for him to tie the *thali* around her neck.

Once more he was disconcerted by her still eyes boring expressionlessly into his. His hands shook and he dropped one end of the chain. The curious eyes of the matronly woman standing behind them met his nervous ones. He smiled shakily at her. Dipping her hand into the back of the bride's blouse, she found the end and placed it into his hand. Thankfully, he managed to screw the *thali* without further incident. Rubini turned her eyes away listlessly as rice rained upon them.

After that, everything blurred into relatives, friends and well-wishers. He could hardly remember any of it. And then the newly married pair were driven to their new home in Bangsar. He wandered through rooms decorated in a Western style and thought of the bare room he shared with another teacher.

Eventually, he found himself tapping softly on the door of the master bedroom, waiting and then entering although there had been no encouragement to go within. His bride was sitting on the edge of a decorated bed. She had changed into a soft nightdress that seemed to be entirely made of little lace flowers. She stared mutely up at him. For a moment he stared back, at a loss. This was not the girl he knew. That girl was fire and passion; this one was ice and stone. Nevertheless, he went to her.

'Are you all right?'

The ice maiden nodded.

'Are you tired?'

She shook her head.

'Would you like some fruit or a cake?' he suggested moving towards a laden tray.

Another stony shake.

'Are you sure you're all right?'

A nod.

His eyes dropped to the curve of her breasts under the lace. She watched the movement passively. He moved and switched off the bedside light. The room was plunged into deep shadows. Only momentarily. Light flooded back into the corners. He looked into her eyes. She returned the look expressionlessly.

'All right,' he said calmly, but the hands that he employed to lightly push her backwards were clumsy and shaking. Her unresisting body fell backwards.

He had to lift her a little off the bed to undress her and found the unfamiliar clasp of her bra a long fumble. It was almost a surprise when her breasts tumbled out. Distracted by the way they bounced, he stopped to stare. Then he slipped his fingers into the waistband of her white knickers, ah, lace – but lovingly chosen for another man. He tugged, heard a tearing noise, and knew a mean satisfaction with the destruction. They fell limp by the wayside.

She was naked.

For a few minutes he had to stop to marvel at the loveliness he saw in the light of the bedside lamp. Then he reached for her knees, and as they had in his dreams, they fell apart easily, without the least resistance. He did not want to look into the eyes that he knew were open and watching, but of their own accord his eyes flicked up and he caught her watching him calmly, worse still, impersonally. Nervously, he attempted to mount her, but for what seemed an age he was defeated by even the simple task of finding an opening he could enter. This was not at all how he had imagined it. Worse he was beginning to lose his erection. Putting his hands on either side of her and closing his eyes, he saw her again walking down the street dressed to bite and claw. Proud, aware of her own sexuality, and unalarmed by it.

With his eyes firmly shut, Bala had sex with Rubini's inert, unresponsive, beautiful body.

When it was finished he pulled out of her and, still without meeting her eyes, vaulted to the bottom of the bed where he sat with his forehead in his hands. In attaining his great dream, he had shattered it. His humiliation, he felt, was complete, the disappointment unbearable. He could never look at her again. All that unrequited love of years had flown away in minutes. It was true – expectation should be defined as a disappointment about to happen.

No one could have lived up to the illusion he had nourished through so many years of lonely yearning.

He rubbed his eyes tiredly. The fault was his, in agreeing to be a stand-in. But what to do with her staring accusing eyes now? She was in love with another man and she would punish him always for not being the other. He felt his heart harden in his chest. How could she love such a coward? He had thought more of her. He shifted his body slightly and her quiet foot came into his vision. He glanced more fully its way. It looked so soft and fair that his heart melted once more and he reached out and took it in his hand. He squeezed it gently and brought it up to his nose. Yes, it was as redolent as the rest of her was. He was still besotted by her. He brushed its softness against his cheek.

He ran his other hand up the silky calf. The muscles underneath neither tensed nor reacted in any way. He sighed. There was no way out. But he did not want out. He lowered the leg and gently laid it on the mattress. Then he rose and went around to the side of the bed. She did not move; only her eyes – dry, uninvolved, unaffected by what he had done to her body – turned up to follow him. Sitting down beside her, he scooped her limp body into his arms. Holding her face close to his chest so his mouth was in her fragrant hair, he said, 'For so many years I believed that I would have done anything for this night with you, but now I know that in fact, I would do anything *not* to have had it. I'm so sorry. I can't undo what has been done, but this much I promise you: I'll never touch you again unless you ask me to.'

At first he thought there had been no reaction to his words or to his slow rhythmic rocking of her motionless body. Then he felt his chest become wet. The wetness trickling down, spreading, becoming a hot dampness between their joined flesh. She cried without sound or movement. He held her for a long time, even after her body had exhausted itself and sagged against him in sleep. His hands began to ache, but every time he thought of laying her down he remembered that this was almost certainly the last time, and he held on until day began to break through the slits in the curtain.

Finally, reluctantly, he laid her down, and stood looking at her, open, vulnerable, bruised and heartbreakingly beautiful. His heart swelled in his chest until he could hardly bear it. He must not fail her. He would, he must, return her to the awe-inspiring creature that had once caused an entire street to burst into spontaneous applause. He bent down and kissed her hair lingeringly. She did not stir. He placed little butterfly kisses on her eyelids, her forehead, and very, very gently on her slightly parted lips. Still she moved not. He straightened. He had trodden on his first thorn, and it was bearable.

'Sleep well, Mrs Bala,' he said, and switching off the light, left. He dressed quickly in another room. His last-minute role as bridegroom meant that he had not been able to book any leave and he had to go to work. Downstairs, next to the telephone, he left a short message and, in the event of an emergency, the school's phone number. It was still not fully light when he opened the front door and found the cleaning lady sitting on the steps, waiting to be let in. Unwilling to shatter the morning quiet he pushed his motorbike out to the road before he started the engine. He could not subject his wife to the indignity of hanging on to the back seat of a motorbike. He had some savings. He would buy a car.

With the brisk morning air in his face, he did what he had not done since he was a teenager. He raised both arms high over his head so the cold wind rushed into his entire length, and laughed with the great joy of being alive. What a wonderful, magical thing was life.

*   *   *

Bala was halfway through the second-last lesson of the day when the office boy came to tell him that there was an urgent phone call for him. With a rapidly beating heart he hurried to the Headmaster's office. The Headmaster turned around at Bala's approach, but without greeting him Bala snatched up the heavy black receiver, and was so relieved to hear his wife's voice that it took a while before he realised that the emergency consisted of a spoiled lunch and a suggestion that he should eat out.

'Don't worry, I will eat it even if it is a complete disaster,' he said, sagging against the desk. 'Yes, I'm very sure,' he insisted, and returned the receiver to the cradle.

'Everything all right?' the Headmaster asked with a sly grin.

'Fine, fine,' he answered distractedly.

She served him the food and stood watching.

Smiling at her, he put her offering into his mouth, chewed it, then looked up at her with a surprised expression. 'It's not a disaster at all. It's actually *very* good.'

She frowned at him. 'Are you serious? It doesn't matter if you don't like it. I won't be offended. It's only my first attempt.'

'No, no, it's the absolute truth. I love it,' he enthused, and eagerly wolfed down the appalling concoction of undercooked rice, chicken pieces in watery brown swill, a mushy vegetable that he could not identify for certain, but thought might have been cabbage, and runny yoghurt.

When his plate was clean he patted his stomach and went upstairs to rest for a bit, and Rubini popped down the road to her stepmother's house.

'What is there to eat?' she asked, lifting the lids of food containers on the table and peering inside.

'Did you not eat with your husband?'

'Well, I tried to cook today. Rice, chicken curry, and that aubergine thing Maya does. And I didn't think it turned out too well, but Bala genuinely seemed to enjoy it.' As she was spooning food on to a plate she missed the look Parvathi and Maya exchanged.

'Oh, by the way, I've decided to take up voluntary work in a children's home. It's appalling how those poor children have to live. There is one that I really feel sorry for. She's just a baby, but no one will adopt her because there's something wrong with her foot. I can't imagine how anyone could give a child away, let alone such an adorable one as her.'

'Why don't you adopt her?'

Rubini shrank back with the suggestion. 'Oh, no, no, that would be too much responsibility.'

Maya spoke into the silence. 'Since you'll be busy during the day, I will cook a little extra for you and Bala too.'

'No, it's only for a few hours a day. I think I can manage. Besides, Bala really loves my cooking. This is delicious, Maya.'

Sri Nagawati

News came that Kupu had passed away, and with it a letter for Parvathi. She looked at the grubby, unaddressed envelope, touched the fingermarks on it and wondered if they were his. She did not open it immediately, but laid it on her altar, and all day long as she went about her business, felt a vague pleasure thinking of it, waiting for her. It was as if he himself, full of sweet goodwill, awaited her. Finally, when everyone was asleep she took her sorrow in her hand.

The letter was a page from an exercise book. He must have used a sharpened twig to write. She studied the muddy ink. Not ink, she realised as she looked closer, but blood. An animal's? His? It took her a long time to make out the words – the writing was that of a child, a thick, spidery scrawl, difficult to decipher, and the spelling was appalling – but how amazing that the man could actually write. She had never guessed. But then, she had only seen a sixth of him, if that. There was so much more.

Parvathi,

My Goddess is calling. I am utterly spent, but I wanted you to know that while I lie here alternately burning and shivering I long only for the sound of your voice. To hear it one last time before I leave. I wonder, is it still like the first rays of sunlight that filter through the leaves? Be sure to visit my temple quickly, for it is not built to last. It will be a relief to let the fever win this time.

Kupu

'What does he mean by saying his temple is not built to last?'
'I don't know,' said Maya thoughtfully, 'but I do know that he

was a highly evolved soul on an important mission, and if he says it is not meant to last, then it will not.'

'Why would anyone build a temporary temple?'

'It will either have served its purpose by then, or by its very destruction bring about vital change.'

Parvathi wanted to take the trip with Maya, but Rubini was decisive – they were not capable of making such a trip on their own. 'Do the two of you even know the way there?'

Maya smiled humbly. 'No, you are right. You had better take us. We are two old women now.'

So the three made the trip back to Batu Tujuh. It was noon as the steel-grey sea came into view. Parvathi closed her eyes and for a moment had the impression that she was in Kasu Marimuthu's Rolls, driving up to Adari for the first time, and when she opened her eyes she would see a marvellous jewel glittering in the sun.

'Oh wow! Look!' Rubini cried, and Parvathi opened her eyes.

A gleaming eleven-storey hotel.

Rubini left the car with the parking valet and they passed through the swishing glass doors and entered a faceless place of polished chrome and marble.

In their room they found air-conditioning, twin beds, and a folding metal cot, which Maya claimed for herself. Parvathi went out on to the balcony. Everything had changed, even the beach. Land had been reclaimed from the sea to form a U-shaped, blue-green lagoon surrounded by palm trees. There was no one on the beach, but the swimming pools below had children splashing about and foreigners sunning themselves on deckchairs. She looked further out to sea and suddenly she was back in time. How often she had stood right here staring out to sea, waiting, always waiting for the great love to come. And then one day it had.

Looking through a bunch of glossy brochures laid out in the shape of a fan, Parvathi found Kupu's temple. Underneath was a brief description of him as a modern-day Tarzan who, by divine intervention in the form of seven glowing balls of light, rebuilt an ancient temple destroyed during the war.

The jungle was much receded and there were signs directing visitors to the temple. A high brick wall enclosed it, so it was a shock to walk through its gates. To think that Kupu the honey collector and cowherd could have constructed such a fine edifice. And what could he have meant by saying it would not last? It looked exceptionally solid, the stones so beautifully fitted together into their new shape that it was impossible to imagine they had been part of a different structure before.

Parvathi climbed the low steps and walked through an open space towards an inner vestibule and there found his god. A six-foot rearing cobra sitting on its coiled body, and framed inside its open hood a human face.

' "Sri Nagawati",' Rubini read aloud the inscription at the top of the entrance to the Snake Goddess's antechamber, before wandering off towards the ancient tree where the Siamang family had once lived. But there were no more Siamangs now. At the bottom of the tree lay many votive offerings of milk and eggs and dolls, from people praying for fertility.

Parvathi frowned at the goddess. There was something very familiar about her face, and then it struck her: that was *her* face, the same long neck, widely spaced eyes, even down to the blue stone nose stud. Shocked, she turned to look at Maya and saw that the likeness had not escaped her.

'Has Kupu fooled everyone with a false goddess?' she asked.

'Hush, child,' Maya chided, and looked meaningfully in Rubini's direction. She made a small beckoning motion with her arm and Parvathi followed her to one of the many pillars that had been built with the white stones from the original tower. She plucked a strand of hair from her scalp and proved that the stones were so precisely fitted together that her hair could not enter the crack. She tried again in another place. And another. With the same results. She turned to Parvathi. 'Do you really imagine that Kupu could have accomplished *this* on his own?' she asked.

Parvathi shook her head slowly.

'Exactly. Everything he saw and experienced happened, but remember, the marvellous must co-exist with the ordinary. It is the way of all manmade religions. As divinity passes through human consciousness some of it gets stained by earthly memories, customs, beliefs, and the deepest desires of its founders so that it becomes half-myth and half-truth. A desert religion's heaven will speak of trees, cool shade, and the delicious sound of running water. A heaven founded by a prince who gave it all up to be a beggar will naturally be entirely encrusted with precious gems. A race of dark people will come upon a blue-skinned god, and a white people will find theirs in a blue-eyed god. It is this taint of personal egoism that makes all religions divisive in nature, but the essence is still the same. Again and again, every religion says: *I am God, I exist. Here is yet another of My faces.* She's beautiful, isn't she? Kupu simply recognised God in his beloved. I've told you before, haven't I? You are not God's little slave. You *are* God.'

Parvathi looked again at the goddess and remembered Kupu in the swirling mist, a civet cat on his shoulder licking the salt off his fingers.

'I have to go into the jungle to look for a certain plant that I hope has not disappeared like so much else. See you later in the room,' Maya said.

Parvathi nodded and Maya moved away.

A thin middle-aged man, the caretaker of the place, came towards her.

'You look very familiar. I'm sure we've met before, though I can't remember where,' he said with a frown. 'You're not from around here, are you?'

'No, we're from KL. We are just down for the weekend. I used to know Kupu a long time ago.'

At that, the man fell to the ground and touched his forehead to her feet. Greatly embarrassed, Parvathi urged him to stand.

He stood and wiped the tears from his eyes. 'He was such a great man that I am always honoured to meet anyone who knew him. You must have known him as a young man. What was he like?' he asked eagerly.

'Gentle, good, honest, and able to communicate with any creature he came across.'

The man nodded approvingly at the fine words he found on her lips.

'What are those?' she asked, pointing to a wall full of all manner of things.

'They are offerings people make when their prayers are answered. She is extraordinarily powerful, this goddess, and every day this temple becomes more and more famous, and more and more people arrive from all over Malaya to ask favours. Once even a Muslim lady came because she was barren. Those gold earrings the goddess is wearing were given on the first birthday of her child. And that large chain, that is from a Chinese man who asked for a lottery number and struck second prize.'

'Will you tell me about the temple and something about Kupu?'

'Well, you know of course that except for the surrounding wall that was erected by the hotel, he built all this with his bare hands in seven days, not stopping to eat or rest.'

'But why would such a grand hotel bother to build this wall, advertise this temple in its brochure, or lead its guests here with a paved lighted path? It is hardly a tourist attraction.'

'In the beginning the hotel owner, a Chinaman, was furious that he could not buy Kupu out even though he had increased the price by ten times the original offer. I think they were planning to make a golf course and this place was right in the middle. The locals didn't dare do anything to the temple so I think he brought in workers from Johor. They started cutting down the trees. Kupu warned them not to cut that one,' he said, pointing to the Siamangs' old home, 'where he said a holy spirit lived. But they came in the night, while he had gone to bathe in the stream. However, with the first hit of the axe, blood started pouring out of the tree and the workmen fled screaming. The next day the businessman himself came to meet Kupu. Kupu told him that his hotel would be very prosperous if he did not disturb the temple. You know how the Chinese are, promise them a profit and they'll do anything. The man immediately built this surrounding wall as a gesture of support and remorse. Business, I believe, is very good.'

The Unbeliever's Explanation

'Right,' said Bala briskly, 'let's start with the easiest, Kupu's torch-waving figures. As Maya and you had already established, the entire area was criss-crossed with energy lines, and a well-known phenomenon of several lines meeting at one point is the capturing of images of a person or persons, objects, or events, as a hologram which automatically repeats. In this case, the ritual gathering of the original builders or users of the tower temple.

'The other explanation is as simple as a visual hallucinatory experience. Apparently these places of geomagnetic anomalies emit radio frequencies, or microwave energies that penetrate into deep brain space and interact with the brain's nerve cells causing powerful hallucinatory images. Hearing one's name called is a common sub-clinical effect of electrical surges in the brain. Both music and sound, especially a constant rhythmic noise, like the trickle of water in a cave, or a repeated sound echoing in a hollow place, have that ability. Remember, Kupu had been listening to the wind in the wind-shafts. Did you not yourself hear that same sound during a windstorm?'

Parvathi nodded slowly.

'Good. Now for the matter of Kupu seeing his body asleep on the stone bed. That is called the "ecsomatic" state of mind, or in simple language, an out-of-body experience, regularly practised by monks and shamans but which can sometimes occur accidentally to ordinary people like you and me, just before falling asleep, or upon first awakening. In Kupu's case it was a most likely possibility, since he spent a great deal of time in that high magnetic field where strong eddy currents would have constantly stimulated his parietal lobe.

'Next, the seven glowing balls of light that appeared to him. Such lights are actually a natural earth occurrence. They have been observed in the Americas, parts of England and Scotland, and China. Even when these apparitions seem to show an "awareness", or appear to "interact" with human beings, they are still only earth energy spirals or blind springs caused by the release of seismic stress and electromagnetic conditions.

'A little bit harder, but still explainable, are the tall angels. There are universal cycles that give energy and life to all organisms on earth: the breath of every living thing, the beating of a heart, the tides, the waves of light and sound. Everything, down to the smallest particle, is a repeating cycle. This cycle is a constant and we are all part of this resonance. Our planet too has its own harmonics, actually the F-sharp chord on the scales. There are special places on earth where it is more abundant than others. Although it exists in frequencies that are well below the range of human hearing, our ancestors were aware of them and their effect, and accordingly built all their megalithic monuments, pyramids, prayer sites and pilgrimage shrines upon these places. Through meditation, fasting, isolation, pain, drums and the use of mind-altering drugs, man can train his mind to a heightened state similar to that of the earth's, thereby bringing that person closer to accessing whatever he or she believes to be God.

'The effect of this is the sensation of "illumination", making that person believe that he is in contact with God or divine beings. And at this point, the special ability of man from the time he is born to recognise a face in a paper cut-out comes into play. This ability to see representations of himself means he can be in the sand, water, rocks, smoke … even the clouds. Since he knows it is not man, therefore he deduces it must be God. And there is a name for this phenomenon. It is called anthropomorphism. In Kupu's case he attributed human characteristics to a snake and called it his "Goddess". It has been happening for centuries, ritualising the magnificent fable into a believable religion.'

'But—' began Parvathi in protest.

Bala raised a silencing hand, 'Let me finish first. With regard to the stones that fitted so well together that not even a strand of Maya's hair would pass between. Did you yourself not say that Kupu was the greatest imitator alive, and that his powers of observation were second to none? Since he was the main person who excavated the site and knew the place intimately, I suggest you consider the reasonable possibility that he simply rearranged the stones back into their old shape.'

Parvathi wanted to say that the temple had been rebuilt to a completely new design, but Bala was in full stride and she did not want to interrupt his grand words.

'I am sure that if you and Maya had tested out the entire building with her strand of hair you would have found many places where it went through with plenty of space to spare. As for accomplishing the task in seven days, women have been known to lift automobiles many times their body weight when their children were trapped underneath. Feats of superhuman strength and endurance are available to humans when they are in an altered state of consciousness or are convinced of the rightness of their actions.'

Bala stopped not even to draw breath.

'Right then: the bleeding tree. It's certainly not the first; there are numerous accounts of them. I think if people studied them less hysterically, they would find the phenomenon might very well be as simple as tree sap. Brown sap in lamplight at night has not only the colour, but also the consistency of blood.

'Finally, let's tackle your own experience at the ancient site. All evidence points to a fault in the earth's crust in that spot. Both old and active fault-lines can produce fissures in the rock strata that can then cause trapped earth gases such as hydrogen sulphide, ethylene and methane, to travel up. These gases cause breathlessness, disorientation, hallucinations, they affect emotions, slow or increase heartbeats, cause tingling in the hands and feet, sudden exhaustion, voracious hunger, the onset of menstrual bleeds, panic attacks, relief from pain, and time loss. These effects the Ancient Greeks called *atmos entheos* or "to be possessed by

God". The most famous, of course, being the Oracle at the Temple of Delphi. All right, I'm done. What was it you wanted to say just now?'

Parvathi opened her mouth and shut it again. Sometimes the best answer was silence.

Independence

31ˢᵗ August 1957

At the newly built stadium the proudest moment in the history of the nation was taking place: the Union Jack had been lowered and the Malayan flag, with its moon, star and stripes, was being raised for the very first time. Tunku Abdul Rahman, Malaya's first Prime Minister, raised his hand and seven times proclaimed, '*Merdeka!*' Independence.

No one took any notice of Parvathi, on foot, in her white sari with a blue border, and half-hidden under a black umbrella. Certainly, no one noting her easy, steady pace could have guessed how nervous she was, how clammy the hand that gripped the umbrella. Some of the celebratory parades must have been over, because people began pouring into the streets, waving flags, laughing loudly. They seemed drunk with excitement and jubilation. It was a great day.

It was nearly noon when she entered the cool interior of the railway station. How many times had she been here before this, playing this scene again and again in her mind. The platform they had agreed to meet on was empty, save for a man sitting with his back to her. He was resting his forehead in his palm. Something about the gesture . . . She began to walk towards him, hesitantly at first, then faster and faster. Then she came to a halt.

The man, she realised, was far too young. She should be looking for someone older. It came to her, with absolute clarity: *she would never see him again.* Even though he had never written, she had found excuses for him and had refused to consider the possibility that he would forget his promise. Was she really only one of the many abandoned women of that time?

There was a wooden bench close to where she was standing and she sank weakly down on it.

Announcements were made of train destinations, platforms and times while she stared blankly at a patch of sky. Fluffy clouds came into her patch and floated out again. Slowly, she became aware of being watched. Intensely. And turned, unafraid. A porcelain doll, perfect in every way, was balanced on wooden clogs and looking at her. She recognised her instantly: Hattori's wife. They stared at each other.

Parvathi stood and the woman came forward on delicate steps. Parvathi wiped the sweat gathering on her forehead. She felt large and clumsy beside the cool figurine. Surely, she must be wondering what madness had possessed her husband to couple with such a creature. Then the horrible realisation. If she was here, then . . .

'Please sit,' his wife invited in a tinkling voice. Of course she would speak like that.

Parvathi fell back heavily, and the woman perched beside her. For a while neither spoke.

Then: 'He became sick in the camp that they sent him to. They only let him come home two months before the end. Before he died, he asked me for a last favour. He had lost your address and had been unable to contact you. He asked me to make this meeting.'

Thou in me and me in thee. And now *death in thee?* Parvathi turned her head to look at the powdered face.

'Why did he want you to come?' Her voice was strained.

'To give you this.' The woman held out an oblong box, and at the sight of it, Parvathi's heart started to thump painfully in her chest. So it was coming back to her again. The gift exchanged hands without their skins touching.

'He said to tell you that you were wrong. He did not steal it. It cost him three months' salary to buy it.'

Parvathi couldn't help herself. Right there, in front of that rigidly held, beautiful woman, she began to cry. The woman did not try to comfort her. Instead she sat very still, a hard, cold presence, an adversary after all this time. Still, Parvathi could hardly blame her. She bore it well, but it must be an intolerable indignity, sitting beside her husband's 'comfort woman'. Why had the doll come? Perhaps, for this. To watch the pain she could cause the other.

'At first, I wanted to throw it away. I hated him for what he had done, but I couldn't turn away from it. And the longer it stayed in the cupboard, the more it haunted me. I wanted to see you, the woman who had made him look like that. Now that I know, I can go back in peace.' With those words she stood and left, her wooden shoes making a dull, lonely sound.

Outside, waves of heat came off the tarmac and hit Parvathi in the face. She walked blindly until a man drinking cheap whisky directly from a bottle at a bus stop caught her attention. People were standing a little apart from him and looking at him with disgust, but he seemed not to care. She wondered why he needed to drink at noon. Perhaps he had suffered a blow. As she had. She watched his flushed glistening face and thought of Hattori, and of all the things they did not say to each other.

Then, as now, she wished he had not been so complicated, that generations of silence had not made it impossible for him to show emotion or vulnerability. Only when it became completely unfeasible for him to hold them back, he turned to the bottle. Even love was that for him. Something that had to slip past the iron doors of his soul when he was inebriated.

The man's drifting unfocused eyes crossed with hers. There was pain there. He called out to her, something garbled, and she looked away and quickened her pace.

When she reached Bangsar she walked into a pub. It was dim. There was only one person inside, an old Indian man sitting in a corner reading a newspaper. The barman, a Chinese boy with spiky hair, looked enquiringly at her. He assumed she had entered to ask for directions. What would a woman like her want in a pub?

She ordered a whisky.

He served her without changing expression. She looked at the single shot he had poured with the help of a measure. In her mind she saw a less yellow, creamier hand pour without measure, with generosity, and suddenly she felt old and lost. He is gone, she thought. That moment is gone for ever.

'Some more, please,' she murmured.

The boy didn't blink an eye. Without the help of his measuring thimble he filled up her glass. She looked into the black eyes of that spiky-haired boy who could not have possibly known of her pain, and smiled gratefully. They had nothing in common, but that afternoon while his boss was not watching he proved what Maya had once said: *'We are all connected. Whenever you see a tragedy that has happened to another, take it that it has happened to you. For we are all cells of the same body. Know that not a single cell in your body can die without the express permission of the entire body.'*

That afternoon, the boy was part of the healthy body looking at a dying cell. Although he had given permission, some part of him suffered at the destruction.

The house was deserted when she arrived home. She went into her room, closed the door and leaned her forehead against it for a moment. In front of the mirror she put on the necklace. It was dented in one place from its impact with the wall. With her fingers gripping the edge of the dresser so hard her knuckles showed white, she wept silently.

Thousands of miles away, her son awakened on a stranger's bed. Except for an ornate Venetian mirror over the fireplace it was a sparsely furnished room. Sunlight streamed in through the high windows and fell on the wooden floor. His head throbbed, but that was to be expected. What was worrying was the sharp pain coming from the middle of his body. Something, he knew, was very wrong with him. Even his skin was turning grey. He needed to stop drinking or he would die like his father.

He got out of bed carefully, not wanting to wake the woman, and dressed quickly. He had intended to walk to the door, but found himself going towards the gilded mirror, pulled as if by some mysterious force. For years now he had not looked at himself, not really, and now he was almost afraid of what he would see. He stared into the speckled glass and blinked. That fleshy, debauched man with his desperate eyes, telling of bad money troubles, loan shark deals gone bad, that embezzler of company funds, surely that was not him.

A criminal.

An ugly cry rose unplanned from the depths of him, and reaching for the iron poker hanging next to the fireplace, he swung it violently at the glass. The woman was so rudely shaken out of her sleep that she bolted upright and looked around in terror. When she saw what he had done she leaped out of the bed and flew at him, her eyes red and furious and her mouth screaming abuse. She was soon upon him.

Without thinking, he raised the poker and brought it down hard on her head. She dropped into a sitting position, stayed that way for a few seconds, and then collapsed sideways. There was no blood at all. He watched her crumpled, naked body with mild surprise. Her brown eyes were still open. How easily it had come to him. The only other time was with the chick in the nest and that was only because he knew his father was watching.

He looked at himself in the fragmented mirror. A murderer. Calmly, he redid a button on his shirt that had come undone, and left. He saw no one in the hallway, or the cobbled, private mews outside. He walked for a long time until he came upon the Odeon Cinema, and suddenly he remembered the cinema opposite their provision shop. He sat on its steps and, holding his hurting stomach, felt the tears begin to roll down his face. The party was over. There was only one option left.

The Prodigal Son Returns

1967

'You know he is coming back here to die, don't you, Da?' Maya asked quietly.

'Why won't you cure him?'

'I can hold the disease at bay for a while, but cancer is energy. It is alive and conscious. If you had the "eyes" to see it, you would see a grey shroud that completely covers the person while it draws his energy out. It comes to people who, at one time or other, reject life at some fundamental level. And it will always come back unless that person learns to embrace life fully and return to the state of spirit, pure joy. Joy, I must add, is not happiness. Happiness is dependent on factors outside oneself. Joy comes from within for no reason.'

Then Bala's car was driving in through the open gates of the house and Parvathi went to the door to watch her son, changed beyond recognition, helped out of the car as if he was an old man. When she saw him lean, exhausted, against the side of the car, she ran to her room and brought out her husband's old silver cane. Kuberan took it from her and shook his head in wonder. 'You kept it all these years.'

She did not trust herself to speak.

He made to straighten, coughed, fell back to the side of the car, and then righted himself again. Leaning on the cane, he grinned. 'And a perfect fit too,' he said, and she was struck suddenly by pain. It was him. This was her son, after all. Only trapped inside this wasted stranger.

He made it slowly to the grille gates and hit the cane softly against its thin curlicued patterns. The noise startled her. He turned to look at her. 'Takes you back, doesn't it?'

She nodded. It was so long ago. Kasu Marimuthu moving around, his cane knocking on the metal bar at the back of the wheelchair.

That night Kuberan slept in the room by the air well, but the next day he was admitted into hospital.

A nurse came and introduced herself as Mary.

'A Christian,' Kuberan said.

'Yes,' she agreed cheerfully.

'Haven't you heard yet, your God died on a cross?' Kuberan mocked.

For a moment she seemed shocked. Then she stiffened her back and looked at him coldly. 'I am a born again Christian. We do not pray to the figure on the cross. Our night nurse, Sister Madeleine, is a Catholic. Speak to her about it, if it pleases you.'

'I certainly shall,' Kuberan promised, and the nurse left without a smile.

'Why do you have to annoy them?' Parvathi asked. 'They are here to help you.'

'It's good for their soul,' he said carelessly, and ignoring Parvathi, looked moodily out of the window.

At lunchtime Rubini popped her head around Kuberan's curtain.

'Hello,' she said. 'Can I come in?'

'Might as well.'

'I've brought you something.' From her handbag she produced a lead soldier in a crimson frock and a Busby hat, hoisting a sabre.

'Good God, where did you find him?' Kuberan asked, accepting the toy and feeling its familiar weight in the palm of his hand.

'In your old room, when we were moving out of there. I knew it was your favourite. Papa brought him back from a trip to the States. He's straight from the store window of Fifth Avenue, isn't he? I remember how Papa used to watch while you set them up in rows for the great battle, Knights of Agincourt against the dashing Hussars.'

Kuberan set the toy on the low bedside cupboard. 'He loved you better though. In fact, I was always jealous of you. Might even have hated you.'

'I know you did, but you had both your real parents.'

'You don't understand. It's not a biological thing. I adored Papa. I loved him more than I've ever loved anyone else.' He paused. 'Well, with the exception of one other person. Her, I love even more than I love myself.'

Rubini's eyebrows shot up. 'Who is that?'

He looked at her consideringly before twisting over and from the drawer of the bedside cupboard extracting his wallet. Its side pocket yielded a photograph which he passed to her. She gasped, looked up at him and said, 'Where is—'

But he raised his right hand and said, 'Don't say anything. Let's never talk about her.'

She looked at the picture again and this time touched it lightly with her index finger. When she gave it back to him, he tossed it carelessly into the drawer, and a strained silence ensued. An old man two beds away coughed long and hard, and in the corridor children laughed and played. Kuberan turned his head to watch a neglected widow stare forlornly out of the window.

'Remember when you were five and Papa bought you a brand new Jaguar for your birthday?' Rubini said.

'Yes, I remember,' he said. 'What happened to it?'

'The Japanese requisitioned it.'

'Of course. I'll never forget that first day though, when those brutes burst in. If that General had not come when he did . . .'

'It's funny, but I wasn't scared that day. Maybe I was too innocent to comprehend the full horror of what they had in mind, or maybe it was Maya. I caught her eye and she smiled, and I knew then that nothing could or would go wrong.'

'Ugly bastard though, wasn't he? Did you ever find out what he said to Ama? For a moment she looked as if someone had punched her in the gut.'

Rubini shrugged. 'I never asked her.' And then curiously, 'Do you really think he was that ugly?'

'Absolutely. Why, didn't you?'

'No. I dreamed of him once. We were all at a tea party back in Adari. Dad was standing with a glass of whisky at his usual place by the stage when the General took my hand and said to Dad, "Have you met my daughter?" And then I woke up.'

'You always were a weird one. What do you think happened to him?'

'I don't know, but I hope he's well, wherever he is,' she said softly, a faraway expression in her eyes.

'What a sterling bit of irony though, to get a Jaguar for a birthday present at five and end up in a third-class hospital ward at thirty-five.'

Rubini's lips tightened. 'You shouldn't say that. Your mother sold her house to pay for your debts and medical bills in England, Kuberan. She really has nothing left.'

'Nevertheless, it's still ironic, isn't it? Never mind, enough about me. What about you? Are you happy?'

'Yes, I suppose I am.'

'How could you be? You married a man who reads Flaubert.'

Rubini giggled. 'Stop, or I'll have to defend him.'

'Surely he's indefensible.'

Rubini stopped giggling.

'I say, Rubes,' Kuberan said, shaking his head in wonder. 'Don't tell me you're in love with the man.'

'Don't be so silly. You know the circumstances of my marriage.'

'That I do.' He sighed heavily and rolled his eyes up to the ceiling. 'Hell, I'm so bored.'

'Have I outstayed my welcome? Shall I go?'

'It's not you. You were always too quick to run and hide.'

After she left, Kuberan closed his eyes and brought back to mind that time when he had walked into a nightclub in London. Blue and white spotlights in the ceilings, fingermarks on the mirrored walls, and a bar with a blonde in a silver dress . . . and his favourite: bare legs. Look at him, swaggering up to her. What style. What class. And her pretending to ignore him. Honestly, she stood no chance.

'Oh, *those* legs,' he says wickedly.

She giggles (silly thing) and looks sideways at him. 'Bet you'd like to know where they end, wouldn't ya?' The accent's no good (he knows that), somewhere rough and ready, but he has never been into accents, not as a rule, anyway.

'I'll say.'

'Get us a drink, then.'

'What's in the glass?'

'Vodka and orange juice. Double.'

'Oh, Baby!'

Kuberan holds a hand up to the barman, and in his head hears that famous line, '*Give me women, wine, and snuff, until I cry out, "hold, enough!"*' Sure, for you on Resurrection Day; for me not even then, mate, he thinks. And later in the back of his dark green open-top . . .

A rattling sound came from above, annoying, interrupting . . . But he had not cried out 'hold, enough!' Reluctantly he opened his eyes. A large nurse was standing by the bed holding a transparent plastic cup with his medication in it. She looked at him impassively. That holier-than-thou attitude annoyed him. He wanted to shock, even to disgust.

'You know Sister,' he said conversationally, 'I *really* miss those white bitches. Especially the ones that used to bite the pillow while I was fucking them.' Sister Madeleine did not alter her expression, and he sighed and held out a despairing hand. She tipped the little pills into his palm and watched with dislike as he swallowed them down.

In Parvathi's kitchen, Maya faced a woman who had been told by the doctors that she must have her spleen removed. 'The spleen distributes *prana*, life force, to the whole body. If you let them take it out, your immunity will be compromised and you will become susceptible to many diseases. I have a much better plan for your spleen . . .'

Fear

Kuberan returned from hospital three weeks later looking no better. Maya was not in the next day, so Parvathi made breakfast and waited for her son to awaken. But by mid-morning there was still neither sound nor movement from his room. At first she hovered uncertainly in the corridor by the windows of his bedroom. Then when she could bear it no longer she peeped through one of the half-drawn curtains into the dim recesses of his room. She could make out the lower portion of his legs. She called out to him. The legs stirred not in the slightest.

She rapped on his door and tried the door handle, but it was bolted from inside. She rattled the handle, banged hard on his door and called loudly, but when she looked through the gap, he still had not moved. Rushing for the telephone in her panic, she nearly tripped over the edge of the hall carpet. Her hands trembled so badly she could barely dial her daughter's number.

Bala answered. 'I'm sure it's nothing,' he said sensibly, 'but I'll come over right away.'

She went back to her son's door and called to him, but her voice sounded fearful and weak even to her own ears. Restlessly, she paced the corridor. If only Maya was here.

'Oh God, oh God,' she muttered, and while the fear clawed at her chest, she went out to the front gate to see if Bala was coming. When she spotted his figure running down the street she nearly cried with relief.

'Quick, quick!' she called. 'I think he might be unconscious.'

Bala hollered and shouted outside Kuberan's room, but everything remained dim and still inside.

'Stand back,' he told Parvathi, and put his shoulder to the door. It was a cheap door and it crashed open at his first lunge, the momentum causing him to fly headlong into the room and land on his back on Kuberan's bed. He turned his head and saw Kuberan's body shaking helplessly. He was so convulsed with laughter that he had doubled up. He had been pretending to be dead! Bala scrambled to his feet and stood watching his brother-in-law incredulously.

When Kuberan could finally bring himself to stop, Bala said quietly, 'Your hero Nietzsche observed that when a man roars with laughter, he surpasses all the beasts by his vulgarity. I didn't agree with him then, for it seemed clear to me that the opposite was true. When a man laughs, he rises *above* all other animals in his humanness. But looking at you now, I can see what he meant.'

'Oh, for pity's sake,' Kuberan said, wiping his eyes and swinging his legs off the bed. 'Isn't that horse a bit too high for you? I only wanted to see how everyone would react after my death. Aren't you people even a little curious to know?' he asked, his hands holding on to the edge of the mattress on either side of him.

Completely ignoring him, Bala walked over to Parvathi, who had not moved or spoken. He smiled gently at her. 'A powerless unfortunate will come to use that one last power he still possesses, the power of causing pain. And that will be his amusement. I won't tell Rubini about this. We'll come later this evening to see you. Are you all right?' She nodded and he kissed her forehead and left.

Parvathi continued to look at her son, 'Would you have played this joke if Maya had been here?' she asked.

'No,' he confessed.

'Why not?'

'Because I know what she will do when I die.'

Parvathi stared at her son and he looked back at her unsmiling.

'She will do what she did for Papa. She will sit on the floor and stare into nothing until she leaves this world and enters the world of the dead, and there she will guide me with the words, "You are confused and afraid, but there is nothing to fear. Go to the light. Light be your home. Light be you. You be light." '

Kuberan fell back on the bed and stared at the ceiling, and Parvathi understood for the first time that he had not come home to spend his last days with her, but Maya. The mocking façade was only a front. He was just a scared boy.

As she had done so many times when he was little, she moved towards his bed, and he turned his head to gaze at her beseechingly, asking what of her, she did not know, but she knelt by the bed and tenderly touched his limp arm. With a jerky movement of pure desperation he fell upon her consoling hand and sobbed like a lost child.

'I once heard Kamala saying that when bad people are about to die they will start seeing black cats. I have seen three this week alone.'

'That's ridiculous. This whole area is overrun with stray cats and most of them are black. I think I might have seen five in the last two days. Anyway, Kamala had some strange ideas. When I first arrived in this country, she tried to convince me that strawberries grew on trees.'

The ghost of a smile flittered across Kuberan's face. 'Did she really? Good for her.'

That night, Kuberan lay in bed with his lamp extinguished and watched the light under the door of his mother's room. Even after darkness had fallen under her door he lay quietly and waited another ten minutes. Then he stood slowly so his bed did not creak and tiptoed into the kitchen, where Maya sat alone on the floor bottling medicine. She looked up when he came in, and nodded in silent acknowledgement.

He pulled out a chair and sat on it, but it felt wrong to be higher than her, so he went over to the fridge and sat on the floor with his back against it. He stretched his thin legs out in front of him and then respectfully shifted them so that they did not point towards her.

'How are you feeling today?' she asked, glancing up briefly from her task.

'Today, good.'

'I am happy to hear that.'

'Maya?'

'Yes.'

'Why me?'

'Ask yourself. You are the creator of everything you have in your life.'

'Not true. I never asked for this.'

'It is a cosmic law that something can only be known when it looks at its own reflection. Therefore we are always creating reflections for ourselves. The people in our lives and our diseases serve us in this way. Our limited perception means we deem sickness and injury as bad, but in fact, they are simply reflections of our perceptions of ourselves. For example, if one felt unsupported, he might develop brittle bone disease; feeling unloved will bring heart ailments; lack of self-esteem might manifest as unsightly skin diseases. Sickness is knowledge of yourself, and a time of great spiritual growth. Think, child, what's eating you up?'

'Nothing,' Kuberan replied quickly. 'I'm not at all sorry for any of the things I have done, but since we're talking it'd be interesting to know your opinion of what sort of punishment awaits me.'

She placed a cap on a bottle and screwed it tightly. 'There is no punishment awaiting you. No one sent you here, a planet in the middle of nowhere. We are all sparks of pure light that chose to gain density, not only to *experience* but also to transcend the third dimension, and to realise that one is not only one's thoughts, emotions and body, but pure consciousness: all-knowing, deathless, limitless. It is only then that the wheel of rebirth will stop. And because you are the architect of your own awakening, you will choose to return to the same situation, again and again until you mend your ways.'

Kuberan's eyebrows shot up. 'That's it! I come back to more or less the same sort of life as this one, and if I still don't manage to improve, I simply keep on getting more and more chances.'

'Is it the thought of coming back as the favoured son of a rich man that pleases you? Remember, your situation might be the same but your circumstances could be completely different. If, for example, one of the lessons your soul had undertaken to learn in this lifetime was to resist the temptation of easy money, you could come back once again entrusted with a great deal of money, but if you steal it, this time you would get caught and suffer brutally in a prison. You see, with every repeat, the consequences for not learning get worse and worse.'

Kuberan stared moodily at the sink.

'Perhaps,' Maya said mildly, 'it might be easier for you if you think of time spent on earth as a sacred and humbling act of love. Of taking on the limiting restrictions of physical form to learn to transmute the negative conditions of man – lack, pain, anger, greed, hate and confusion – into love. We are here with a mission to fulfil, the biggest of which is to love ourselves, not in a narcissistic way, but compassionately, unconditionally.'

'It is possible my soul is irredeemably covered in dust and sin,' he said sadly. It was a long time since he dreamed of the sightless staring brown eyes. He had got away with murder.

'Don't feel especially guilty. First of all the idea that one gets away with anything is an illusion. The law is fair. Every action has a consequence. If not in this lifetime then in the next we must all pay for our sins. Besides the shadow is in us all. I believe even Jesus had to spend forty days alone in the desert facing His demons, did He not?' She looked up to Kuberan, who nodded in confirmation. 'There is no doubt you have transgressed, and while explanations and excuses are unnecessary, atonement is essential.'

'How does one atone?'

'There are a thousand ways to kiss the ground. There is even a special entrance to heaven hidden in the soles of a mother's feet. Make good the hurt you have inflicted there.'

'Oh no,' he groaned, leaning his head back against the fridge. 'Not that.'

'On this earth a mother's love is the closest you can have to divinity. Let me tell you a story about the nature of this love. Once in India there lived a mother who had a very great love for her son, even though he was a loathed criminal. One day, for a dare, for a small amount of gold, he killed her and cut out her heart. But as he carried it over the threshold, he tripped and nearly fell. Luckily, he managed to hold on to the door lintel, but the blind heart he clutched in his hand had felt only the awful lurch and cried out, "My beloved son, you're not hurt, are you?" '

Kuberan gave Maya a cynical smile. 'I believe there is also a story about another paragon of virtue who loved her son so well that she did not discipline him, even when she knew he had turned bad. When he was caught and sentenced to be hanged, his last request was for an audience with her. When she came to him he bade her come closer so he could whisper his last words directly into her ear. Crying and sobbing she moved closer and he bit her ear clean off, saying, "If only you had loved me enough to discipline me, I would not be at the gallows now." '

Maya chuckled. 'Child, your words have always flown on wings, and when they didn't, they were good enough to make salted fish swim again. When you were younger I could call you unripened, but now you are just a fool. God always places at least one wise soul in the vicinity of a young one. That person is their doorway into a better life. Only a fool would refuse their counsel to the last. True, your mother could have been more severe, but she always brought you up to know right from wrong.'

'What can I say? Only that she loved me so well, she became another one of life's annoyances.'

'The mother's heart is melting with love and the son's is hard as stone. You think the emotions of ordinary people are petty and beneath you. From where I sit, you are completely indistinguishable from those you seek distance from; even now when it is nearly time to return and give account, you will, like most of humanity, postpone to the next time an effort as simple as humility.'

For a while there was silence. And then Kuberan said, without the least sarcasm in his voice, 'What's God like?'

'Have you ever loved – really loved – someone so much that you actually felt you loved that person more than yourself?'

He thought again of that heart whose love was innocent, and a look of pain crossed his eyes. It was true what he had read that even the most cold-blooded assassin could break down and cry with love for a dying pet. This innocent heart was his raw wound. 'Yes, yes, I have,' he whispered.

'Then you have already known God. God is not a force from above, but an ally of which you are a part. Whenever you act from love, you don't become godlike, you become God. Stop being so frightened. Even if the table does not agree that the carpenter is his maker, the carpenter will always consider the table his sweet creation. You are only going home, where you will realise your true magnificence, how vast, eternal, and powerful you really are, and how small you had to make yourself to fit into this human body. Hold on to the knowledge that you have come from goodness, strength and infinite beauty, and as surely as I sit here, you will return to that again.'

Maya carried on bottling her medicine silently, and after a while Kuberan stood up. At the door he paused and turned back. 'When I die, will you light the orange lamp and pray for me?'

'Child,' she said, 'there will be no orange light for you, but remember it is not I who decides where you go. We go to the places that match our earthly vibration at the moment of our departure. If you leave in darkness and confusion, you will stay in darkness and confusion.'

He found his eyes full of tears, and turned away blindly. He had died a long time ago. He knew that now.

He was put in the last bed of the ward.

Two days later Parvathi found him clutching his father's cane so tightly his knuckles showed white. 'Did Maya not come?' he asked tensely, his breathing shallow.

She covered his cold, waxy hands with her own and prayed, 'God, take Your child back. I give thanks for the time I have had with him. He was a good son and I loved him well. Keep him safe until we meet again. He is afraid of the dark. Switch on a light if there be darkness where You take him. Let him be light. Light be him.' And as she prayed, the resistance went and she saw his face relax and a soft glow come into it.

There was a shout of laughter from the nurses gathered around the duty counter, some private joke. And she remembered how the cows had cried when he was born and now when he was dying, there was the sound of laughing. Suddenly he smiled, and she recalled Maya saying the sense of hearing is the last to go and without all the other senses, the hearing becomes so acute that you can hear a long way off. Kuberan was sharing in the nurses' joke. The smile disappeared slowly, his eyelids drooping until they were half-closed. Peaceful now. She did not try to check if there was still breath in the boy. And she did not call the nurses. One would appear eventually.

What she did was sit on the chair beside his bed and simply look at him in his deep slumber. *If God sends children then takes them back again when He wishes why do you weep over it?* Did he ever belong to her? Was that wasted body even her son?

Soon a nurse happened along.

'Hello, Auntie. Is he sleeping?' she asked cheerfully.

'Yes,' Parvathi said.

The nurse looked at her motionless patient and threw a quick backward glance at the woman sitting very still on the chair, but Parvathi looked back at her without the least expression. Swiftly the nurse pulled the curtains surrounding the bed, the curtain rings rushing on metal. Professionally, she took a wrist between her fingers. 'I'm sorry, Auntie, but your son has passed away.'

Parvathi nodded, and the nurse pulled the sheet over his calm head. And that was that.

Outside the hospital entrance she stopped. The sun was the colour of ghee. A great flock of pigeons flew up and over her head. She looked up at their flapping wings, grey, black, brown and white, and thought they looked rather festive. She stepped out on to the road and a car screeched to a halt. Her heart jolted. She turned to see a red-faced Chinese man. He shouted rudely, '*Loo mau mati kah.*' Market Malay for, 'Do you want to die?'

When she arrived home she avoided Maya at her afternoon clinic, slipping instead into her son's dim bedroom. Sitting on his bed she went through his things. There was so little he had collected during his lifetime. No books, a few clothes, a plastic cigarette lighter, a comb, shaving things, odds and ends and a wallet. She stared at the old wallet. Flattened to the shape of his body, it brought the whole of him to her. Cautiously, she reached out, first touching, then stroking it. She picked it up and held it against the bare skin of her midriff. Eventually, she opened it.

There was a picture in it: Kuberan, already some dissipation about his chin and mouth, but still terribly handsome, was carrying a dark-haired little girl, perhaps four or five.

There was nothing of him in the girl, so white, bold and foreign, and yet Parvathi knew without a doubt that this was her granddaughter. She turned the photograph over, but it was blank. Nor had he left any clues amongst the rest of his things.

Still, she was so fascinated by the discovery that her son had left the evidence, he could so easily have destroyed it, of his secret life for her to find (whereas she herself had already buried in the ground all material that was connected to her furtive past), that she did not feel hurt by his decision to exclude her from the joyful knowledge of a granddaughter. He must have known how it would warm her heart to learn about the child. There was little chance she would ever know the girl, but somewhere in the world her bloodline lived on. And because of this she forgave him his last treachery.

Her son-in-law said, 'Mami, your own son is dead but don't worry that there will be no one to light your funeral pyre. I will send you to your God myself.'

When her daughter came to lightly touch her shoulder, she said, 'You know Rubini, once I too could bring forth no children; until Maya filled my body with her medicinal herbs and made it fertile. Wouldn't you like her to help you too?'

Rubini's pretty cheeks turned crimson. 'No, no, everything will be fine on its own,' she said, looking away quickly.

13th May 1969

Bala rushed into the women's house, a bulging sack slung on his back. 'The fighting has started,' he panted, dropping his load on the floor. 'The Malays are hacking the Chinese to death in the streets of Kampung Baru. Many have been killed and more are expected to. Shops and houses are burning and the Riot Squad and the military—' He stopped suddenly and asked, 'Where's Maya?'

For a few seconds Parvathi was too stunned to answer, and then recovering herself, said, 'She's out at the back.'

'Thank God. I was afraid she might be out somewhere looking for shoots or roots. Rubini is home safe, but I just came to drop this off.' He jerked his head towards the sack. 'Food provisions. Who knows how long this rioting and killing will go on.'

'How did all this happen so suddenly?' Parvathi asked.

'No one knows for sure yet. I'll try to find out more tomorrow. For now stay indoors and don't open the door to anyone,' he cautioned before he left.

By 8 p.m. that same day, the curfew had been extended to the whole state of Selangor, but Bala, dressed from head to toe in black, broke it every night to dart down the street, using parked cars and bushes as cover, to give the women unreported incidents he had heard on the grapevine. Awful stories of machine guns being opened into crowds of ordinary citizens, bodies floating in the rivers, children being killed, and the morgues so full of bodies that the newly arrived had to be put into plastic bags and hung from ceiling hooks.

On 15th May the King proclaimed a State of National Emergency. Parliament was suspended and the army sent out in full force. Parvathi and Maya hunched indoors in front of the radio and heard the Prime Minister blame the riots on Communist terrorists.

Two days on and the nights were still glowing with burning homes and vehicles, when Bala came in to report that the trouble had, in fact, nothing to do with Communist activity, but the election results. The ruling Malay party had lost too much to the opposition. This was their way of fighting back.

'All over Malaya, Malay youths are wearing white armbands to signify their alliance with death and carrying sharpened bamboo spears to demonstrate their intention to annihilate the Chinese, or anyone else for that matter who tries to take their political power.'

'No,' said Maya. 'There is something strange about all this. The gentle Malays are being depicted as an uncontrollable lot, but the real law-abiding Malay detests hooliganism. True, he can run amok out of passion, but this careful organisation of bands of thugs with armbands acting simultaneously in different parts of the country is more likely to be political intrigue. Hidden hands are at work. The Malay population is being used by the ruling party to restore their dominant political position and at the same time oust the Tunku from power.' She paused. 'Look for whoever ends up with all the power at the end of this, and you will know that he is responsible for this massacre.'

When the curfew was lifted for two hours during the day to allow people to go about their business, Bala brought new food supplies and the odd anecdote, like how a chicken escaping from a basket in Central Market had caused panic and a stampede, or news that the leaders were still blaming the Communists even though almost all the dead were Chinese.

Then Bala came to say that Maya was right – it was a coup. The Deputy PM, Razak, had used Emergency Rule not only to establish himself as the undisputed leader, but also to formalise Malay rule.

'It looks like we're really done for. Now they can use their two-thirds majority to amend the Constitution at will to implement discriminatory racist policies that will suppress non-Malays and promote Malay dominance,' Bala said.

But Maya only smiled and said, 'There is nothing wrong with Malay rule. After all, they were here before the Chinese and the Indians.'

'Actually, the aborigines were here first,' Bala reminded her sulkily.

'Son, where in the world do indigenous people wearing sarongs of bark become masters of their own land? Though they are much connected to the earth, they haven't the slightest desire to rule it. Be thankful that it is the Malay who are the master race in this country, not the Chinese. It is a question of tolerance. The Malay man views dark skin without contempt; he calls it "*hitam manis*", sweet black, an endearment almost. The Chinese, who revere whiteness, see brown skin and say "*hak sek*" black. And in this colour he finds dirt, darkness, lowliness.'

But the very next day, Bala arrived, looking visibly upset. He had heard the rumour that some Indians had been paid to carry out the despicable act of throwing excrement into a mosque. 'How can these Indians be stupid enough to do the dirty work of the Chinese, no doubt for a bit of cheap alcohol?' he raged. 'Have they no pride? Can they not see that they have disgraced not just themselves, but the entire community? This is not even our fight, but now all the Indians in this country will suffer the consequences of their shameful act. Idiots. Bloody idiots.'

'Yes,' said Maya, 'today is a black day for all Indians, for more than ever now, it seems the Indian is a despicable creature. Indeed, he was without political power or wealth, and now, he even lacks pride. But remember that he came to this pass because he was told time and time again that he was not good enough, until he came to believe it. It is the reason why he will remain a barber while the Chinaman sets up as a hairdresser and earns ten times more. And if he does not take up scissors, he will content himself with the menial work of road sweeping, toilet attending, or grass cutting. Decades will pass this way. Even the elected leader chosen to represent and protect Indian rights will oppress and steal from the poorest of them. In rubber estates there will be communities of ignored, marginalised Indians living in squalor like rats, denied even the most basic of rights.

'The plight of the Indian will be such that to be born an Indian in this country will be equivalent to being born ashamed and full of self-hatred. Everyone will look down upon him: dark, dirty, uneducated, poor; a beggar. Believing his disgrace, he will consider the other races his superior and will always prefer to serve them before he does his own.

'I know throwing excrement in a place of worship is inexcusable and vile. And you are right to stand here full of wrath for the shame it has brought you, but wait a while and the day will come that this same Indian will learn that the colour of his skin alone cannot make him lowly, and all those who have told him so in word, deed or action are wrong. That same day he will learn to temper his passionate nature, (for the Indian man takes spices into his body directly from his mother's milk) and instead he will use it with intelligence and cunning to raise himself up once more. At heart the Indian is a fighter.'

But Parvathi kept her eyes lowered so no one would suspect that she remained unconvinced. She had of course believed Ponambalam Mama when he said that the Indian was once worthy of admiration but she couldn't see how he could possibly rise again from the depths he had fallen to.

The Shining One

Parvathi pounded the betel-leaf ingredients in a mortar, meticulously wrapped them in a betel leaf, put it into Maya's mouth and watched her chewing slowly.

'When my soul issues its call for me to return, you mustn't cry,' she said suddenly.

'I'll try my best,' Parvathi answered, tenderly stroking the iron-grey head on her lap.

'No, you have to promise you won't.' Maya's eyes were pools of the clearest water.

'All right, I promise.'

It grew dark and the light from the television became blue. 'I had better go and light the lamp for the altar,' Parvathi said, putting a pillow under Maya's feet and pulling a blanket over her body. With the lamp lit she went into the kitchen to make scrambled eggs. When the butter was bubbling she poured in the beaten eggs.

Then she warmed some milk in a pan. Outside, it began to rain. She thought of the coconut trees on the beach blowing so wildly. Everything always happened during the rainy season. In the living room the news came on. She poured the milk carefully into a mug and put it on a tray with the eggs.

Her hearing had always been sharp, but that day she heard the brass lamp falling like a thunderclap. She hurried to her bedroom. Maya was prostrate on the floor facing the altar, her hands stretched out over her head. She could have been praying, if not for the oil from the overturned lamp quickly spreading through her clothes. Kneeling beside her, Parvathi shifted one of her massive arms, and Maya's face sagged towards the floor. Gently, very gently supporting the inert face with one hand she returned Maya back to her original position.

But when she tried to move Maya's leg, she found her weight impossible to shift. She brought paper towels and managed to soak up most of the oil. Then she went out to the sitting room. The grille gate was already locked so she pulled shut the sliding wooden doors and bolted them. Switching off the lights she went to the linen cupboard, where she found blankets, and spread them out beside Maya to make a bed for herself. She touched the dead woman's fingers stained with the ink from indica leaves, and shook her head. 'So soon you went,' she whispered, and snuggled up to her greatest ally for the last time. 'See, I did not cry. I'll sleep a bit for now. Bala will arrange everything in the morning. He's good like that.'

When the funeral was over Bala came to her and said, 'Mami, you can't live here on your own. It's not safe and it makes Rubini nervous. You know how she is about you. Anyway, we've talked it over and after the thirty-one days of prayers are over we want you to come and live with us. After all, we have four empty bedrooms.' He smiled. 'Besides which, it would be a real pleasure to have you with us.'

She looked into his kind eyes. Her son-in-law was like a rock; unshakable in strength, patience and determination. Gratitude flowed through her, warm, comforting. She knew exactly what she could do for him. She could move into their house and cook for him. He had been pretending to love his wife's inedible food for twenty years now. It was time she told her daughter the truth and this poor man had proper meals for a change.

'I think I'd like to move into that storeroom you have downstairs, and if I could, I'd like to bring Maya's sleeping bench with me.'

'*The storeroom?*'

'I really don't think I could manage all those stairs every day Bala,' she said.

'No, absolutely not. What a ridiculous idea! You can certainly have Maya's bench, but I won't allow you to move into our storeroom.'

Thirty-one days later she went to live in Bala and Rubini's storeroom. It accommodated Maya's bench-bed perfectly. Now that she had seen Maya go so easily, she no longer feared death.

Without Maya

During the day while Rubini was at the orphanage Parvathi cooked, and when Bala returned from giving tuition classes at lunchtime, they ate together. He seemed to look forward to this hour with her. Theirs was an easy relationship, unlike the minefield of his marriage. Over the months, Parvathi had noticed that they never touched, though it was perfectly clear that Bala was deeply in love with his wife and she cared for him far more than she was prepared to admit. When she was home there was always a fine tension in the air, the strain of unresolved feelings. If only Rubini would let her guard down, then poor Bala would not have to become a shadow, moving noiselessly about the house.

But during lunch he was a library of information, some amusing, some so obscure she wondered how and where he had gleaned it, and some so important that she was surprised more people didn't know it. After their long companionable lunches Bala went back to his tuition classes and she began preparing tea, which she then had with her daughter. A silent brisk affair in comparison. But not uncomfortable. Afterwards, Rubini disappeared upstairs to work. She liked to bring home what she called projects – plans she had for the orphans. Parvathi would potter around the garden for a bit before beginning to prepare their simple family dinner. This, they ate mostly in silence. If they spoke at all, it was briefly, about day-to-day matters, and never touching on anything of importance. Sometimes Bala switched on the TV and complete silence descended upon the little group. Afterwards, Rubini washed up and Parvathi left the husband and wife alone for the night and retired to her quarters.

The storeroom was very small and quite bare, but she liked it like that. It had about its dusky silence something eternal and unchanging. Like the weatherbeaten faces of fishermen the world over. Time seemed to make no difference. The light from the streetlamp shone in through the high window falling directly on her snake statue, making him gleam with protective benevolence. Parvathi sat on her bed and remembered as a young woman how impatient she had been of her time alone at the window, watching the comings and goings at the cinema. Now that her body was no longer new, her hair all white, and her sexual instinct refined away, she had learnt to relish the solitude and the emptiness of her life. In the end, the bars that hold the prisoner become precious to him.

Each night, she returned to those dying hours eagerly. Alone, in that still, shadowy silence she had only to close her eyes and a rich unrecoverable world came flooding back. Her mother combing her hair. Maya calling to her. Kupu in the soft morning light surrounded by colourful birds. Standing on the balcony dreading the first light of day, Hattori. And these ghostly figures didn't just turn to smile at her, no, they moved, sometimes ran towards her, their faces lit as if by lamplight. When they got close enough she captured and held them all fiercely in her thin bony arms, where she intended to keep them always, next to her heart. And so she thought to spend the rest of her days in her secret twilight world, forgetting that once when she had asked Maya, 'But if everyone comes with a purpose, what is mine? I have done nothing. On my last minutes on this earth, what can I be proud of?'

And Maya had replied, 'Da, the day will come when you will inspire someone to do something for the Indians of this country. For it is a very long process, giving pride back to a broken people.'

Thirty-Five Years Later

Hindraf

Kuala Lumpur, December 2007

'A new girl has been brought in, one of them mongol kids,' the cook at the orphanage was saying as Rubini walked through the door. 'Never ceases to surprise me the depths of cruelty people are capable of. After the poor thing's mother died four years ago her uncle kept her chained to a post like a dog to claim money from her grandmother, but the old woman died last week and he abandoned the kid here this morning. Poor little thing, I think he hit her so hard once, she's deaf in her right ear.'

Rubini walked along the narrow corridor where the children's schoolbags and shoes were kept. Outside Mother Moses's office she saw the girl, a creature, no more, squatting on the floor although there were empty chairs behind her. Her hair was a tangled mess and her dress was filthy. She had sores on her arms and legs. Her head swung around warily at the sound of footsteps, but when she saw Rubini, her dark eyes grew large and astonished and then a huge clueless grin broke on the round, dirty face.

'Grandmother!' she shouted joyfully.

And Rubini thought, Oh, my heart. What will I do with you? She squatted beside her. The girl smelled bad. Suddenly this poor sod, who had been shackled to a post for four years, flung her thin arms up around Rubini's neck, and asked, 'Have you come to take me home?'

Rubini disentangled herself and shook her head slowly. The child gazed at her blankly so Rubini drew her bad ear close to her mouth and whispered, 'I can't, you see. I always lose the things I love, and I know even now that I could never bear to lose such a one as you.'

But the child moved away from her mouth, clueless as ever. Without warning she grinned, opened her palm, and showed a dead bee in it. Rubini felt the onslaught of incomprehensible emotion, so strong it shocked her. She pushed herself up and walked quickly down the dark corridor into the sunlit porch. Out of the gate and down the road at a brisk pace.

The child would be too difficult to take care of. *'No she wouldn't,'* said a voice in her head. But the extra work; it would be unfair on her stepmother. And the little voice jeered, *'Why should it? Obviously you'd take care of her when you're at home and bring her with you to work.'* It would disrupt Bala's peace and quiet. *'Liar, liar, you know he'll love her to bits. He adores children.'*

Rubini came to an abrupt halt. 'No,' she said, so decisively, that the voice knew better than to argue. She turned around and went back to the orphanage.

Bala came into the kitchen while Parvathi was at the sink draining the excess water from a pot of cooked rice.

'Do you need help with that?' he asked, moving towards her, but she shook her head and half-twisting, saw that he was so excited by something he could hardly contain himself. She put the hot container down and, with her back against the draining board, said, 'What's going on?'

He sank into the nearest chair distractedly. 'Remember a long time ago during the May 13th riots when Maya said the Indians in this country will rise up again to make good?'

Parvathi nodded.

'Well, though I didn't say anything then, I was sceptical, very sceptical, but you know what? I think she was right.'

'Oh,' Parvathi said, coming to sit beside him.

'At first, I didn't connect the different events that have been taking place with what she said. An organisation called Hindraf filed a class action on behalf of Malaysian Indians at the Royal Courts of Justice in London to *sue* the British Government for four trillion US dollars, that's one million for every Malaysian

Indian, for bringing Indians as indentured labourers into Malaya, exploiting them, and thereafter, when Independence was granted, failing to protect their rights in the Federal Constitution.

'They planned to present the Queen of England with a petition requesting her to appoint a Queen's Counsel to argue their case. To submit their petition to the British High Commission they planned an enormous peaceful rally, but the police refused to grant them a permit. Despite threats from the Government in all the newspapers, more than twenty thousand Indians from all over Malaysia turned up. They carried a picture of Mahatma Gandhi to show the non-violent nature of their demonstration, but five thousand riot police threw tear gas and fired chemical-laced water cannons at them. Many were arrested and the Prime Minister himself personally signed the detention letters to imprison the leaders but I have decided to join their cause.'

When Rubini came home that evening she listened with rapt attention while Bala quickly repeated everything he had told Parvathi earlier, but when she heard that he wanted to join the movement and march with them, she said, 'You can't be serious, surely?'

'Why not? When Maya said all those things about Indians and their self-hatred I always thought, Yes how can it not be the case, for I have seen the way the other races sometimes look at the Indians. But I have tried to distance myself by saying, "I'm not really an Indian, I'm a Ceylonese." But she was right, go back far enough and you find hiding inside yourself a lowly Indian. You see, I too *do* think the Chinese are better than us. I've always admired their discipline, their industry, their single-mindedness, their ability to defer pleasure in the pursuit of their goals, and though I hate to admit it – the whiteness of their skin. Being born in a country where the sun is fierce means you are caught up in the race for that rarity – whiteness.

'But last Thursday, I was driving down Abdullah Street and I saw an Indian girl at the edge of her front garden plucking flowers for her prayer altar. In one hand she was holding a metal tray, and in the other an umbrella, no doubt to keep from getting darker, so I could only see her hands and legs. She was not one of those people with a lot of different shades on their body. She was simply, evenly brown, and honestly, the smoothest brown I've ever seen. And suddenly, I discovered that inside the poisoned chalice is blessed wine. For the first time ever, I thought My God, brown is so beautiful.'

Bala leaned forward passionately. 'You're really fair and I've always loved that about you, and of course, I wouldn't change a single thing about you, but I know now that I was wrong. Dark skin can be the most beautiful thing. For it tells of a heart that has suffered prejudice and in the process become soft and compassionate. It tells of a person who has yet to call her own skin beautiful, someone who has to be taught when presented with a choice to willingly choose brown, because it is no less than any other colour. Imagine being the person to show her that. Imagine her face when she finds out.

'You see, I realise now that it is not the fault of other races that we fall, but our own inferior mentality. They are just mirrors of what we secretly feel about ourselves. A mother thinks she is improving her child when she tells him, "Look at the Chinese, look how successful they are. Be like them." She doesn't realise what her child hears is: "You are not that. Pretend to be that because you are not good enough as you are."

'But as Maya said, the Indian would one day wake up. And that day is here. Indians came out in force knowing they could be arrested, injured, or killed.

'The Government have been stirring up racial hatred on purpose in their divide and rule policy, but during the demonstration the hurt and injured ran to the houses nearby. It was a Malay neighbourhood, but they all helped. The Malays are not our enemies. We can do this if we stand together.'

But Rubini covered her mouth and turned away.

'Don't turn away from me, Rubini. I'm not doing this just for the downtrodden Indians, but for myself too. I need to be a part of this change. Remember when Maya said that *everybody* comes to this earth with a specific purpose to fulfil during their lifetime, a purpose that only they are equipped to do in their own special way. This is why I came. All my life I've been preparing for this – to teach the rest of us to think like this. I'll be doing it for the children at the orphanage too. For their future. Don't you want something different for them?'

Rubini pressed her eyes tightly shut and did not answer.

'No, you cannot understand, can you? You don't know what self-hatred is all about. You've always been fair and beautiful. Everywhere you went, men looked admiringly at you and women were surreptitiously studying your clothes, bags and shoes. You may look more Eurasian than Indian, Rubini, but these people are your people.'

'Hang on a minute,' Rubini interrupted hotly. 'I'm not ashamed of my roots, but haven't you just told us, the Government is tear-gassing and shooting chemical-laced water cannons at protesters. And if they don't die in these clashes then they get thrown in jail under trumped up terrorist charges. Don't you care that something bad might happen to you? What if something does? What then?'

Bala shook his head with disappointment. 'Rubini, you are my day, my night, my right and my wrong. See, as I stand here that you are everything to me and have always been, but can't you at least try to understand that I have to do this? I am only a man, but if I can change the lot of my people I am willing to give up my life for it. It is a worthy cause. You see,' he said sadly, 'they need me. You don't.'

Rubini stood so abruptly, her chair toppled over. Her face was pale. She opened her mouth but no words would come out. In fact, she seemed almost to be gasping for breath. When finally the words did come, they were a harsh unfamiliar screech.

'You think only you have any idea of self-hatred. You think I am exempt. Open the drawers of my dressing-table and you will find them full of skin-bleaching creams. All and I mean *all*, Indians are obsessed by shades. Even the most minute differences are noted and made to count. And it is a merciless exercise; it cuts, because there will always be someone fairer than you, but we do it anyway, and regularly, because this blade has two sides. We wait to cut down those who are darker then us so we can feel better again. And we pretend to forget that, to the other races, we will always be black.'

Parvathi remembered the time she had stood before a picture of Lord Krishna and cried, 'You are dark and everyone loves you. I am dark but even my husband despises me. Why oh why couldn't I have been born fair?'

But Bala was so taken aback he could only stare at his wild-eyed wife. Without warning, tears began to roll down her tense cheeks. But his beloved didn't cry. Not even at funerals. He blinked. She was his heart. He could not bear tears from her.

'It's all right,' he whispered softly. 'Don't cry, please don't cry. I won't join them or attend their rallies.'

With his words her face crumpled. 'I'm so sorry to ask this of you, but I just couldn't bear it if . . .' But unable to finish her sentence, she stood miserable and lost in the middle of the room. Bala made a move towards her, to hold and console her, but she flinched and rushed up the stairs. He heard her lock herself in the bathroom and turn on the taps. Slowly, like the old man he was, he went into the back garden. Parvathi was on the swing. He went and sat beside her and stared ahead of him blankly. She put her hand gently on his arm.

'You know how she is.'

He nodded. He did not trust himself to speak.

'You can still help the movement. I'm sure they need financial support or administrative skills in their offices. With the kind of knowledge you have, I'm certain you will be a far greater help behind a desk.'

He nodded again. For a long time neither spoke, and then he said, 'There is another reason I want to join this movement. You know I don't believe in bleeding trees and suchlike, but I do believe that our religion is our right. I wanted to join the movement to expose the unofficial temple destruction policy of our Government.' He paused for such a long moment and Parvathi turned to look at him. 'Kupu's temple was bulldozed yesterday,' he blurted out suddenly.

'What? How can they! That land was legally mine and *I* bequeathed it to Kupu. They didn't have the right.'

'They said it was unlawfully acquired. Apparently the papers were not completely in order.'

'The original deeds were burned in the fire but I took care of that years ago.'

'Yes, but there is some confusion as to whether it actually fell into the boundaries of Kasu Marimuthu's land.'

'I know for a fact it did. My husband was nobody's fool. If he said it was part of his land, then it was.'

'Anyway, they justify their actions by arguing that as soon as it was established that there was a find of national importance on the property, the proper authorities should have been alerted. But that is just an excuse. This is not the first. Thousands of temples have been defaced, mysteriously burned down, or destroyed using flimsy excuses. A 120-year-old temple was demolished to make way for a police building. And seventeen years on, the site is still vacant. Another was forcibly destroyed and relocated next to a sewage plant. The level of disrespect is intolerable.'

Parvathi took her hand off Bala's arm. 'Maya once said that for a people to be healthy they need their myths and their traditions. They need to know that in their blood runs the intelligence and strength of their forefathers. And this birthright gives them the platform from which they launch themselves into the world. Both the Chinese and Indians can boast of a long and illustrious past, with ancestors who have come upon great inventions, founded new religions and conquered foreign lands. The Malays do not have this. The only way the Malay can feel superior to the other races is to view them as Godless creatures.

'There is much of Hinduism in the Malay culture. One look at a Malay traditional wedding will show just how much Indian influence has been absorbed into their traditions and customs. Difficult to change a culture, much easier to destroy every ancient temple that suggests this infidel past. To them such destruction is not wrong: didn't the Prophet command it as the duty of every good Muslim to crush to powder every idol that stood in his path?'

Bala looked thoughtful. 'You know me, I'm not into temples and religion, but I've been aware for a long time that the authorities had started rewriting history in the school textbooks, and emptying out the national museum of "non-heritage artefacts", but when they brought down Kupu's temple it touched me in a way nothing else before has.'

'Yes. Maya said that the destruction of Kupu's temple would bring about great change. Kupu always knew his temple would not last, he was not meant to start a new religion – his purpose was deeper, you see. Maybe the felling of his temple is supposed to inspire the Indian psyche into the realisation that their culture and ways are worthy of preservation. Perhaps instead of envying the other races, we will finally learn to appreciate and admire our own significance. We have been taught to hate the colour of our skin, but we have much of value, much. This will be the beginning.'

When it grew dark Bala stood and held his hand out to his mother-in-law. She put hers into it and together they made for the darkening house.

The End

Parvathi was looking up to the blue sky through the small window of her room when Rubini knocked softly and entered. Stiffly, as if she was wooden with moving parts, she walked up to the bed and looked down upon the figure curled around the water bottle. It had been a very cold night. She should have given the old woman an extra blanket. Too late now. She did not touch the figure or cry, but stood very straight and tall by the bed. And from her position by the window Parvathi marvelled once more at her daughter, at how she could be all at once magnificent and dignified, even in grief.

After a while she went to Parvathi's hiding-place, the one the old woman imagined no one knew about, and brought out the wrapped package. Placing it on the bed she began to undress her stepmother. Carefully, lovingly, she straightened out the cooling body. Bones, she was nothing but bones. Tears, oh! hers, fell upon the dead woman and in the guise of wiping away those drops, she stroked the pitifully thin body, her hand lingering on the only part that time could not wither. And Parvathi heard her first husband's voice say, 'Show me your heels.'

At the foot of the bench her daughter untied the strings of the package. Gently, so gently, as if it was fragile tissue, she lifted out her stepmother's kimono. And Parvathi took great comfort that, of all people, it should be her stepdaughter who knew her secret. Rubini did not do a good job of dressing the dead. The kimono, someone should have told her, needs the firm hand of a matron or a man. But even she knew the *obi* was beyond her, and did not attempt to tie it. Instead, she folded it and laid it on her stepmother's stomach. It did not look bad, arranged so. And then she laid her head on the dead woman's chest and for the first time in her life called Parvathi, 'Mother'.

'Oh, Ama,' she wept again and again, as if by so doing, she could make up for all the years she had nearly said it, but did not from sheer bloody-mindedness. Parvathi wanted to comfort her, but she had no body with which to speak or touch, so she hovered by the window uncertainly, until a voice so dear and familiar said, 'Direct the loving thought to her temples.' So that is what she did. 'I love you,' she said, and Rubini suddenly sat up and looked around the room. Then she touched her heart and the corners of her lips lifted slightly.

There was a bright light shining somewhere to the left of Parvathi, but Rubini could not see it, and she turned her gaze back to her dead stepmother's face. Parvathi looked into the blinding light. And there he was. Hattori. Saying nothing, smiling. He had come back for her. It was only a dream. But what a wonderful dream it had all been.

As she began to move towards him she could see the others waiting further back and she knew that Maya had been right all along. *Of bliss these beings are born, in bliss they are sustained, and to bliss they are returned.* Nothing was ever lost. Not husbands or sons or lovers. You take them all with you. Only love exists beyond death. Now she knew. Love alone is the reason everything is created and everything exists.

Bala walked into the room and with a great sob Rubini launched herself into his arms. He embraced her tightly.

'I love you,' she sobbed. 'I've loved you for years. I just didn't know how to say it. And I'm sorry we never made love after that first night. I was just so afraid of losing again, of getting hurt.'

Astonished Bala kissed her hair. English roses. 'Don't be sorry,' he said. 'What I had from you was more than enough for me.'

She pulled away from him and gazed anxiously up into his dear, lined face. 'And I'm really sorry we never had any children, but if you wouldn't mind I'd like to bring home a little girl. Her name is Leela. Her uncle kept her tied to a post for four years.'

Bala grinned. 'This home could definitely do with a Leela in it.'

'Thank you, my love. And I won't stand in your way any more.

Go ahead and make the world a better place. In fact, I might even join you,' she said, and smiled tearfully at him.

He pulled her close to him. He had removed the last thorn from his foot. The road ahead ran straight and unimaginably beautiful.

Parvathi turned and looked at the cassette player. For a moment she was confused. She could not remember talking into the tapes, but she must have, since every cassette had been taken out of its plastic covering and used. Then she understood: they had all gathered in Adari for a reason, Maya was the healer, Kupu was the prophet and she was the scribe, the keeper of records. And she had not failed in her task. She had done it, and done it well. She smiled.

The white light was becoming brighter. In the luminous air Parvathi saw that the double helix shape that her son-in-law called DNA, was in fact, serpent energy. The basis of all life. So religion was a hard science, after all. What a surprise? She saw through the secrets. There was no such thing as junk DNA. She wished she could tell him about that rich and wonderful awareness that lived inside DNA, of the millions and millions of years of memories residing in each and every tiny atom. That was the reason why the same protein that existed in a bean could, with a change in code sequence, become human – and love, hate, pray, sin, destroy, create, laugh, feel joy, sorrow, anger, envy, pleasure, despair, and fight for right. Everything: disease, threat, and instincts were preserved for ever. Fate was not a cruel, merciless thing. And humans were not frail beings, after all.

We are beings of light. We gush forth into lives where we are temporarily blinded to our own light, not knowing that we'll meet ourselves coming back, before going out again and again, each time unimaginably jubilant. For our light is immense and beautiful.

Full of bliss Parvathi moved towards the beings of light that awaited her.

Ouroborus
Every end is but a new beginning

Glossary

Abhishekam – Hindu holy bath for sacred idols

Ama – mother, madam

Apa – Father

Apam – a flat sweet cake made of rice flour

Kasu – money

Arathi – the ritual in which lighted camphor is turned clockwise in front of a deity or a person

Asura – demon

Bhagavad Gita – Song of God; sacred Hindu scripture: part of the epic *Mahabharatha*

Dei – a rude way of addressing a boy or man

Dhobi – men in the profession of laundering clothes

Dhoti – white cloth that is slung around the neck and shoulders of a man

Devas – celestial demigods

Fakir – religious mendicant

Hantu – ghost/devil

Jambu – a local fruit

Kajal – eye liner

Karma – The law of cause and effect. Also the effect of a person's actions in previous births

Kempetai – Japanese secret police

Kolumbu – curry

Ladhu – colourful sweet balls made of fried lentil flour and syrup

Lidi – a broom made from the spines of coconut leaves

Mama – uncle

Mami – married lady, aunty, or respectful term for older woman

Muram – a flat, usually round, woven tray used by women to separate rice grains from stones and husks

Muruku – fried rice flour snack

Panchangam – almanac

Pandals – temporary halls and other structures suitably decorated

Pottu – the dot worn on the forehead

Pulliar – another name for Ganesha, the Elephant God

Rishi – a highly realised soul who has renounced the material world

Rongeng – a jaunty Malay dance popular at fairs where professional women dancers sit on a stage and wait for men to partner them

Sambar – dhal based thick soup

Santhanam – sandalwood paste

Sivarathri – the night considered sacred for the worship of Lord Shiva

Swaha – I offer this oblation to you; let my light be in union with your light

Tantra – one of the sciences of worship as ordained in the *Vedas*

Thali – sacred pendant worn on a cord around the neck by women symbolising their married status

Thulasi – a sacred plant of the basil family

Toddy – fermented coconut water

Vadai – a round flattish dhal cake

Vahana – celestial vehicle

Varuval – curry but so thick it is pastelike

Veshti – a piece of material tied sarong-like around the waist by men

Vibuthi – sacred ash

Vipala – a measurement of time

Yagna – sacrificial offering in fire

Yemen – the harbinger of Death